THE LAST TIME
I WAS ME

Books by Cathy Lamb

JULIA'S CHOCOLATES

THE LAST TIME I WAS ME

And in the Anthology
COMFORT AND JOY
"Suzanna's Stockings"

Published by Kensington Publishing Corporation

THE LAST TIME
I WAS ME

CATHY LAMB

KENSINGTON BOOKS
http://www.kensingtonbooks.com

KENSINGTON BOOKS are published by

Kensington Publishing Corp.
850 Third Avenue
New York, NY 10022

All Kensington titles, imprints and distributed lines are available at special quantity discounts for bulk purchases for sales promotion, premi-
ums, fund-raising, educational or institutional use.

Special book excerpts or customized printings can also be created to fit
specific needs. For details, write or phone the office of the Kensington
Special Sales Manager: Kensington Publishing Corp., 850 Third Avenue,
New York, NY 10022. Attn. Special Sales Department. Phone: 1-800-221-
2647.

ISBN-13: 978-0-7582-1463-8
ISBN-10: 0-7582-1463-4

First Kensington Trade Paperback Printing: May 2008
10   9   8   7   6   5   4

Printed in the United States of America

For my mother-in-law, Doris Mae (Lindsay) Lamb
1925–2002
and to her son, Bradford Howard Lamb,
with love and laughter

CHAPTER 1

Women can look so innocent.

And a few of them might be. Innocent, I mean.

Most aren't.

Most have secrets. Pretty big ones, if I do say so myself.

They silently nurture raging passions they've smothered for years because life has insisted they do so. They hide who they truly are because they're in a box and no one in their families would feel comfortable if they broke out of that box like a rose on speed. They think non-innocent thoughts like: Should I castrate my husband? Should I leave my family and pesky in-laws, head for Tahiti, and have a fling with a lifeguard while downing daiquiris?

Women can smile and be gracious and kind. And most women usually are. Gracious and kind, I mean.

But to assume that a woman, any woman, is *completely* innocent is to be completely naïve.

For example, take my recent not-so-innocent nervous breakdown.

The breakdown happened to occur in front of eight-hundred-thirty-four advertising execs and their minions. All of whom think they are imminently cool and vitally necessary to the earth's continual spinning around the sun.

As the creative director for a stratospherically successful advertising firm in Chicago I suppose you could say I went out in a big way.

My mother had died two months before.

I had also found out that my longtime live-in boyfriend had not one current girlfriend on the side, but a small harem. This had prompted me to retaliate against him in a colorful and creative manner using, among other things, a hot-glue gun. The police were called, handcuffs were snapped, charges were filed, and now I had to be in court in a few months to fight assault charges.

Plus, Jared Nunley, the boyfriend, who will heretofore be known as Slick Dick, was suing me for every nickel I had.

Me, an ex-soloist in my church choir, who sold the most cookies three years in a row in Girl Scouts, had charges filed against her for assault.

The truly bad thing about it was that my ex had no lasting damage done to his body.

I had worked days and nights for a week for this particular presentation and Jessica, my insanely competitive twenty-three-year-old intern, kept implying that I was creaky-old and out of touch, with one of those saccharine sweet smiles you want to rip off people's faces. I suddenly felt this insidious crack in my body breaking me open right up at the podium.

It was a small crack starting in my small toe on my left foot. The crack raced by my ankle like a miniature rocket. The crack said, "Cancer has killed your mother. You are alone." The crack wound up my thigh. "You have nothing," the crack mocked me. "Your fun little town house doesn't count. Neither does your sports car. Neither do all your little trips. To say nothing of that silly shoe collection of yours." The crack zipped up between my legs and another crack joined it right in the heart of my femaleness.

"You have worked incessantly for almost twelve years, with hardly a break. You have traveled to keep persnickety, picky clients happy all over the world who would only be satisfied if you brought them Pluto. You have handled other creative people, most in their twenties, who are crazed and edgy and who insist on riding their motorcycles through the building for inspiration, wear no shoes, drink beer for breakfast, and don't wash.

"Jared cheated on you," the crack whispered. "You slept with him, and only him, for two years. God knows how many women he slept with during that time. You paid for all the groceries, including that vile sushi he loved, cat food for his mangy overgrown rat, his various electronic toys, and his nose-hair razor. He took off with the stereo equipment, your mountain bike, and nineteen-hundred dollars in cash. You had to fake every single orgasm with Jared. You miss that mountain bike."

The crack arrowed straight for my heart. "And you still miss Johnny and Ally." The crack splintered into a million pieces and each crack burned its way across every pulsing artery and spindly vein in my body until I was one throbbing mass of aching pain.

The crack wound its slippery way up to my mouth. "That drinking problem of yours that started two weeks after that night has got to go. It's out of control. You're out of control. It is going to kill you."

So the tears started. Right up at the podium with eight-hundred-thirty-four shallow schmucks looking on. I felt a surge of laughter bubbling and it rolled right out of my mouth—loud, rollicking laughter, who knows why.

Now, anyone who is relatively smart like me—not that I have always been smart in my life but I do know I'm relatively smart—would have hightailed it off that stage. But I didn't.

I stood there and laughed and cried, my body quaking with pain.

The schmucks' mouths were hanging open in shock. Slack and loose.

I decided to make a speech.

An odd speech, a little speech, definitely a speech.

I spoke my little mind. All that I had been thinking about during my years in advertising came right out of my perfectly lipsticked lips as I stood in my perfectly fashionable blue suit and blue high heels with the tiny gold chains in my perfectly way-too-thin body, and my perfectly sparkling jewelry that Jared supposedly "gave" me, but I ended up paying his credit cards off even though he had a trust fund from his daddy.

I talked about what a shallow profession we were all in, announcing, "Our profession is utterly ridiculous! Our days and lives are dedicated to packaging and selling products to the American public who really, truly don't need or want what we're selling. Every minute of our existence is wrapped up in lies and deceit! Wrapped up in crap! We could all die tomorrow and we'd have to face God and tell him we wrapped our lives up in crap. How's that going to go over?"

I talked about a recent potato chip campaign that took eight people working almost round the clock for months to complete. "Potato chips! And Americans are already way too fat!" I boomed. "Way toooooo fat!"

I talked about the endless discussions that occur in the halls of advertising about how to market a new car that, if bought, would slap the average person into deep debt for years on end. "And what about the panty and bra ads where overgrown women with impossibly large *bowling ball* breasts strut around on high heels? Do we think that most women can wear any of that lingerie without looking utterly ridiculous? Who thinks cottage cheese thighs are sexy? Who thinks saggy boobs can be made to look better with red satin?

"And frankly," I bellowed, "who even cares about having a perfect body except the shallow schmucks sitting right here? Yes, *you people! You shallow schmucks!*"

I decided to yell that part at them. "Don't we have better things to do with our time on this planet than to worry about how we look? No wonder we're all so miserable."

I talked about the complete self-absorption I had seen in people in advertising. "All we do is think about ourselves, our next ad, our next success, our next promotion. We are the most boring people on the planet!" I decided to pound the podium while I cackled like an overgrown witch. "That's not the worst of it! We're not good people. We're not! Our profession means nothing *to anyone*. We make people's lives worse, not better. We tell them in print and on TV that if they don't have these products, they are useless people, that they're not keeping up, they're not cool, they're ugly and poor and bottom-dwelling failures. And folks, guess what? It's all a bunch of shit!"

I suppose hysteria makes one acutely aware of life. As does death. Death is a great equalizer. It brings your own life into pinpoint focus. I decided to speak of that pinpoint focus. "When I die, what do I have to be proud of? That I designed a campaign that sent Tender Tampons skyrocketing? That Baucom's vaginal cream is now used by more women than ever before for irritation? That overly sugared cereals for children that surely rot their teeth are being sold at a record pace? All that so a few thick-headed asshole white men with limp dicks at the top can become even richer? It's pointless."

I looked around the room. I dare say everyone looked mighty stunned. Schmucks look even uglier when they're stunned.

"*We're pointless*," I said, taking a deep breath. "We're pointless. There is more to life than this." I cried a bit. For my mother, for my useless self, for those pesky assault charges, and for the blazing realization that I had done nothing worthwhile in my entire life. Almost forty I am, and I had done nothing. *Nothing*.

Well, I had assaulted and humiliated my ex, but I didn't think that counted. That made me laugh and snicker again. I sobered up quick. "There is more to life than figuring out how to persuade women to buy a certain brand of yeast infection medicine that resembles small white bullets. There *has* to be more."

I thought of my mother, with that doctor straddling her as he forced a tube down her throat so that she could die more peacefully, of all the other doctors and nurses who had tried so desperately hard to help. I wanted to bang my head against the podium. Hard.

Now *they* had become Someone Useful. They had tried to save my mother's life. I had only tried to convince some exhausted mommy in suburbia to buy some unhealthy cavity-causing crud for her child's breakfast.

"There has to be more to life than Tender Tampons." I said this so quietly I could barely hear it myself, yet at the same time the words seemed to echo right off the walls of that room like thunder.

And then I left. I walked off that stage in my blue heels with the tiny gold chains, right out the door to my car, a low, red, expensive, humming machine.

I sold it on the way home without a second glance back, bought a big hulkin' Bronco and a storage trailer to haul behind it and pocketed the cash. On my cell I called my friend, Joyce Herber, a real estate agent, and told her to sell my town house. I called a man named Isaac Porter who owned an estate business and told him to sell my stuff. It was modern and sleek and I hated it. I called my lawyer and my mother's special friend, Roy Sass, and he told me to stay in touch because of my little problem with the police. He also reminded me I needed to enroll in a court-ordered anger management course to show that I was getting help for my poor behavior.

When I got home, I piled everything I wanted into the back of the Bronco and the trailer in boxes, including my silly shoe collection and my photograph books filled with pictures of my mom and Roy and my brother Charlie and his family that I had spent hours putting together.

I wrapped up my grandmother's teacup collection, my mother's china, and a set of tiles with a fruit bowl painted on them. I grabbed a violin I'd hidden way back in my closet that made tears burn down my cheeks like a mini-fountain, a gold necklace with a dolphin that my father gave me two weeks before he died of a heart attack when I was twelve and, at midnight, with that moon as bright as the blazes, I left Chicago.

I stopped by my mother's grave and dropped tears all over her gravestone, the night dark and silky but not creepy there in the cemetery, then drove from Chicago, Illinois, toward Oregon wearing my dolphin necklace. Charlie lives in Portland, Oregon.

Me and my insanity drove off. Together. As one. I shook my brain, my nervous breakdown making me nervous.

I wondered if there were anger management classes in Portland?

But who cares, I yelled out loud. "Who cares?" Life was currently quite sucky so I yelled, "Sucky! Sucky!" In fact, I might give up on it altogether and drive my ole engine-grinding, muffler-roaring, growling Bronco straight to the west coast and make a permanent dive right into the ocean. Headfirst.

CHAPTER 2

Although my grief for my mother covered me like the wings of a thousand black crows for the initial six days of my journey, by the seventh day I felt those wings lifting me up for the first time since her death. I talked to her in the car, pretending she was sitting right by me. We had stimulating conversations and we laughed a lot. She had cheered my speech to the advertising schmucks and revealed that she thought my retaliation against Slick Dick was justified.

I stopped in the small town of Weltana because I liked the trees and it was raining when I arrived.

I love rain.

I rolled my growling Bronco to a stop off the side of the highway in front of a little yellow building with green trim. It was called The Opera Man's Café. The walls inside were made of logs. A fire burned in the brick fireplace and a chef with a white braid flipped pancakes two feet up into the air and sung along at full throttle with Bocelli on CD. Little white lights twinkled from the open rafters over long wood tables.

When my pancakes arrived I smothered them in maple syrup and butter, the way I liked them; the way I have not eaten them in twelve years because that would have driven me into a downward emotional spiral into hell.

During those years I craved pancakes so much I would some-times dream of them in the approximately four hours of sleep I snatched each night when my caffeine fix and whacked-out stress level would soften to a dull roar in my head or when I passed out from one too many drinks.

I dreamed about those pancakes and hot syrup far more than I dreamed of sex.

Come to think of it, I rarely dreamed about sex.

Which tells you something about me.

So I poured the syrup on until it formed little lakes and started in on my pancakes in that cozy café under the fir trees in the foothills of Mount Hood made by a cozy chef with a white braid.

But if I had been able to see the future, I would have trembled in my knee-high black boots that day and headed for Kosovo or Mongolia.

But how was I to know that a naked run along a river, a raucous bar fight, a self-painting ritual to decrease my self-anger, and a court trial that exploded into a media circus, would follow?

How was I to know that I would finally be forced to do battle with my deep and abiding obsession with liquor?

Oh, and one more wee little tidbit: How was I to know that the woman in the café who looked like she'd stepped off an Italian Renaissance painting, who spoke at great length with the cook about germs and germ-killing, would decide that a certain man had polluted our earth long enough and would execute the Elimination Plan, and that the other woman in there would help hide his body?

That "other" woman?

That would be me.

How was I to know that?

Had I known, I would have choked on my pancakes.

And that would have been a shame because I love pancakes.

"Welcome to Weltana, young lady," the chef said to me as he rang up my bill, his braid over his right shoulder. "Are you stay-ing around town or passing through?"

I'd put him at about seventy. He reminded me of a white crane—but he was the most attractive white crane I'd ever seen. His name was Donovan and I later found out he used to be an opera singer in New York.

"I'm not sure," I told him. "I'm not too far from the ocean, am I?"

He shook his head, handed me my change. "No, ma'am. You're about three hours from it. Did you want to see the ocean?"

Did I want to see the ocean? I sure did. Up close. Intimately knowing my own grave site would be helpful. "Yes."

"Well, by gum, if you take the highway outside of town toward the city you can bypass Portland and head straight on out by driving west. The sunsets are spectacular."

I could use a spectacular sunset. I couldn't even remember the last time I'd seen one. I had been too busy working my way into burnout and convincing myself that my faster-than-lightning life was dandy. That takes a lot of time, you know. Lying to yourself.

" 'Course we have spectacular sunsets here, too. Take a drive straight up the mountain. You know, a sunset is God's last painting of the day. It's his last gift to all of us before he gives us the gift of a sunrise."

I nodded. A last gift. I had given my ex a last gift and Slick Dick had called the police. It had been a particularly prodigious, poignant, and profound present to the prick that his psyche would probably be hard-pressed to forget. (I have always liked alliteration. Goes back to a favorite English teacher in eighth grade named Mrs. Gaddinni. In times of stress it comes in handy.)

"Are you on vacation?"

Vacation. "Well, I wouldn't call it a vacation." I needed a scotch on the rocks.

"Ahhh." Those blue eyes looked hard at me. Like I was worth something. "So, makin' a change in your life?"

Got me. "Yes, you could say that."

"Changes are good sometimes. Changes keep our hearts pumpin'."

"Sure does." Sure as heck they do. Sometimes a change allows us to disappear, too. Disappearing for good appealed greatly to me.

"So you're looking?"

"Looking?"

"For a place to stay, a place to settle down for a while."

Hmmm. He was a smart one. He was peering at me closely and I knew he was paying more attention to what I wasn't saying. "I guess you could say I am."

"Gee whizzers. I've got the perfect place for you." He looked longingly at the Italian Renaissance woman for several seconds before he said, his voice gentle, "Rosvita, this is . . ." he paused.

"Jeanne Stewart," I said.

"Jeanne Stewart. Jeanne, this is Rosvita DiLorenzo." I shook hands with the Italian Renaissance woman. Her black hair, shot through with angel-wing white hair, was wrapped in a loose bun with a red flower tucked in the back. She wore no makeup. She had one of those curving figures and was wearing a sparkling red shawl, red jeans, and cowboy boots. She wore white gloves.

I was later to admire her work with a .45.

"Nice to meet you."

I murmured some pleasantries. I can be polite when pushed.

"Rosvita has the finest bed-and-breakfast in town, Ms. Stewart. Rosvita, this young lady is looking to settle down for a while, although she wants to see the Pacific Ocean."

I looked at the chef. He reminded me of banana bread and cinnamon.

I had not decided to settle here. Not at all. But I had to admit that I liked the tiny main street of town. I liked all the trees and Mount Hood towering behind me. I liked the pancakes and this chef who was pleasant and sung opera so well I shivered. Not a bad start.

"I have a room if you're interested in staying in town," Rosvita said, her gaze intense "It overlooks the river, breakfast is included, and there are no germs there. I clean with disinfectants, two types, and bleach. I vacuum each day after dusting. Food is fresh and the refrigerator is completely cleaned out and scrubbed down twice a week. With bleach."

I nodded.

"All food is cooked to a pulp to kill any and all bacteria. So you don't need to fret that you'll get salmonella poisoning. Salmonella poisoning is caused by gram-negative bacilli. Salmonella is a virulent member of the *Enterobacteriaceae* family. A family you don't want to belong to, Ms. Stewart. Symptoms are fever, stomach pain, and diarrhea, although constipation can also occur."

I nodded again. Valuable stuff.

"I make sure that the bathtubs are cleaned spotless. Inside a tub that other people have used can lurk many germs and diseases, and I am utterly aware of it. In fact, I've even heard that in a hot tub there's a possibility—however slim—of contracting herpes. You do know what herpes is? Herpes is caused by *Herpesvirus hominis* which is an infectious agent, not unlike a secret agent, and it does horrible viral damage. Symptoms are—"

"Rosvita, please." The chef held up both hands. "Let us not talk about herpes in a place that sells pancakes and bacon. It's bad for the digestive system." I could tell he found her immensely entertaining, despite the herpes talk.

Rosvita put her hands on her red jean-clad hips. Closed her mouth. "My brother is a famous criminal defense attorney and he will tell you that there are many businesses that have been sued for enormous amounts of money because of diseases they have inadvertently passed on to the customer—"

I jumped when Donovan burst into an opera song, his voice diving and soaring. When Rosvita stopped talking, Donovan stopped singing. "My dear Rosvita, why don't you show Ms. Stewart your place?"

She looked me up and down. "Come along."

As we left, Donovan stared with mopey eyes at Rosvita, threw his arms out wide and burst into another opera song about unrequited love.

* * *

Rosvita's house was not far off the main street. It was painted light blue with white trim. Flowers tumbled from boxes at each window. The yard was huge with a rolling expanse of grass, a few old fir trees, and a gated garden that was high on flowers. She guided me to the backyard and down some steps to the river. The river water was pure and rippling, trees towering on either side, the sunlight dancing off each crest.

We stood in silence for a moment as I breathed. I still needed a scotch, but the quiet rush of the river was de-sizzling my overheated mind.

Rosvita abruptly sat down and crossed her legs into a yoga position.

What the heck. I sat, crossed my legs, palmed my hands. We breathed in and out together and, after about a half hour, we headed back to the bed-and-breakfast. The parlor was lush and cheerful, stuffed full of comfy furniture, about six different lamps with funky lamp shades, several plants, and a ton of books. On closer inspection, I noted that all the books had something to do with diseases.

Current diseases.

Past diseases.

Jungle diseases.

Diseases during wars and famine.

Diseases pioneers suffered from on the Oregon Trail.

I paid her before I had even seen my room.

"It's a super place for me to indulge in my nervous breakdown," I told Rosvita.

She didn't blink an eye as she took off her gloves and placed them neatly in a white box lined with lace. "I'm pleased to hear it. You go ahead and do your flipping out and I'll make sure that it stays quiet around here for you and your nervous breakdown. And clean. It's clean here."

"Thank you, Rosvita. But so that you are fully informed—my nerves are in tatters; my psyche has been ground to pieces in a mental garbage disposal; and my emotions have been through a meat slicer. I cry easily, although I have made serious efforts not to cry for the last twelve years. I am prone to embarrassing outbursts. I have recently made rash and wild decisions, but have yet to regret any of them. I have found that I have a vindictive and vengeful side and am pleased to welcome it into the fold of my other personality characteristics. I am simply," I told her, "not altogether."

There was silence for a moment as we pondered this.

"Well," said Rosvita. "If you can gather up your tattered nerves, your shredded garbage-disposal psyche, and your meat-sliced emotions, I can take you upstairs to your room, where you can further your nervous breakdown." She spun on her cowboy boot heels and headed up the stairs. She reminded me of Tuscany and flamenco dancers and cotton balls. I followed her.

If there is a room in heaven that is light blue and pristine white, it would look like this room. The bed had a spread that was fluffy and white with a white lace canopy fluttering in the breeze overhead and at least eight blue and white pillows. There was also two white wicker nightstands, each topped with a lamp with a frilly blue-flowered shade, and a white wicker desk and dresser. Charming.

French doors opened to a deck which overlooked the Salmon River. I could hear the river gurgling and burbling, the fir trees making their wind-whistling noise. I thanked her and she left, patting my arm gently. "Nervous breakdowns are challenging mental diseases," she said. "Call me if you need me."

I grabbed a bottle of scotch out of my suitcase and had a few drinks. To christen my bed of blue heaven, I decided to pull a pillow over my head and cry.

And cry.

And cry some more.

And this is what I learned on that bed of blue heaven: When you live your life trying never to cry, when the tears finally bust through, they make a real wet mess.

I put the scotch on the nightstand. I was gonna need it.

CHAPTER 3

For the next several days, I strolled along the river and told it my problems while drinking the very best wine I could find at the local store. It was made in the Willamette Valley vineyards. When I could walk no farther, I stumbled to a rock, sat down with my wine, stuck my feet in the water, and cried until I felt my guts were about ready to spring forth.

When I could manage to stand without bursting into another round of tears, I toddled my way back to my bed of blue heaven room. That became my routine: Walk. Drink. Cry. Pass out.

When I woke up on the fifth day, I called Roy. It was 3:00 in the afternoon. I decided to have a scotch. He reminded me of my court date. I agreed to show up.

He told me how much money Ex-Asshole wanted.

"That is a lot of money," I mused, swirling the ice in my glass. "But I have to say it was worth it."

My lawyer, Roy Sass, laughed. "I'm sure it was, honey."

After my townhome and furniture were sold and the money added to my savings, I knew I would have an impressive chunk of money. As a workaholic who made a large salary, and a naturally frugal person, except for buying mammoth amounts of shoes, money was one thing I had. But I sure as heck wasn't going to hand over a darn dime to Slick Dick despite that small assault.

"Lemme tell you something, Roy," I said, trying to rein in the sudden but not unexpected fury that surged through my voice like burning brandy. "I. Will. Not. Give. A. Dime. To Slick Dick. Ever. I would sooner set up a trust fund for female beetles battling sexist cultures in the backwoods of Alabama than give any to him. I'll try again for another analogy: I would rather give my money away quarter by quarter to support the ongoing search for ghosts. One more example: I would rather rip all of my money into tiny shreds and eat it."

I could hear Roy chuckling. He has a short ponytail, a weathered face, and kind eyes that harden up to something scary when he's in court. He is at least six foot six with shoulders like an overgrown ox. He's been a massively successful lawyer for four decades. In his spare time, he runs a dog rescue operation on his farm. People bring him strays or he rescues them from the pound and finds them new homes. He is partial to beagles, mutts, golden retrievers, black labs—and did I mention mutts?

"Roy, did you get my check for twenty thousand?"

"I did, honey."

"Good."

There was a silence. "You didn't cash it, did you?"

"Of course not, honey."

I rolled my eyes. "This is business, Roy. I want to pay you."

"It is never business with you, honey, it never was, it never will be. I'm doing this for you for free because I love you, and every moment of every bit of work I do for you I'll be thinking of your mom. I couldn't help her, but I can help her daughter and damned if I won't do everything to make this right."

"Roy, I—" I can't hear the word "mom" without getting choked up.

Losing my mother was like losing light. And warmth. And joy. I put a pillow over my face.

"Don't 'Roy' me, sweetie. This is final. Now, what do you want me to do to Jared?"

I pulled my wet face from the pillow. "I want you to make his balls rot."

"I'll see what I can do, dear," he said. "You know, your mother would enjoy knowing his balls were rotting."

Yes, she would.

She hated the man.

"We meet Thursday nights from six to nine. You are to be on time. You are to control your anger and temper. You are to come ready to spill your guts and prepared to hear what your co-anger management classmates tell you. You are to take responsibility for the problems that got you here in the first place. You are not to whine or feel sorry for yourself, because I have no pity for you and neither does anyone else. I don't give a shit if you had a lousy childhood and that's why you're angry or you have a rabid ex-husband or psycho-freak wife. I don't give another shit if you're mad at the system, the police, the judge, the exterminator, your dentist, or the local pet shop owner."

"I'm not mad at the pet shop owner," I told Emmaline Hall-wyler, my new anger management counselor with a voice like a drill sergeant. "Not at all. I will have to admit to some lingering, simmering anger with my dentist, though. Every time I see him, he tells me I have bad gums. Bad gums!"

She ignored that part. "You are to dance when I say dance and to fly when I say fly. You are to sing when I say sing and to scream when I say scream. You are to create when I say to create. You are to be, above all, honest with yourself and with others. No prayers, no religious talk allowed here, no telling other people that they have to accept Jesus Christ as their Lord and Savior or they're going to hell."

"It is highly unlikely that I would suggest that anyone was going to hell. Even if there's a wait line into hell, I can assure you I will be shuttled to a place quite near the front. Do you have a religion problem in anger management class?"

I could feel her animosity surging over the wire. "I had a man who proclaimed himself to be a religious person in my last session. I let him preach to everyone in the room about God and forgiveness and hell for exactly forty-seven seconds and then I informed the others that he was here because he had beat up his three previous wives and all three had restraining orders against him. That shut him up damn quick. There's nowhere in the Bible, I reminded the sanctimonious prick, that says you can beat the shit out of your wife—so cut it with the religion."

Her voice rose and fell like a drill sergeant preacher.

"He muttered something about only the Lord being able to change him. I told him the Lord helps those who help themselves, and that currently the Lord was undoubtedly wondering exactly which fiery compartment in hell he should be assigned to for beating to shreds three of God's children. I asked him if he thought the Lord approved of the way his fist managed to bust open his third wife's jaw?"

"Ahh. A real charmer."

"He said he didn't think that God was happy about that, but that we all sinned and that Jesus died on the cross for our sins, so his sins are covered and he's forgiven. I told him that his sins are covered in the blood of his ex-wives and that he was going to go straight back to jail and to hell which is where God puts all wife-beaters, if he couldn't get a grip on his God-given fists."

"What did he do?"

"What they all do," she said. "I stared at him until he squirmed like a worm. The other people in the class tore into him like you might tear into a lobster tail and he cried until he slobbered. I told him to shape up, quit being such a religious hypocrite, admit that he was a wife-beater, and fix himself. I tell people how it is, Ms. Stewart. They don't like it, they shouldn't have been shits and landed in my class. After that I told him to sing."

"Did he sing?"

"It took some prompting, but yes, he did. It was awful. Sounded like a dying rat. So, Jeanne, I have your record. Lemme take a look at it, though. Haven't read it. Hang on a sec."

I waited. I knew what was coming.

There it was.

A chuckle.

A snort.

A giggle.

A quickly inhaled breath.

The phone became muffled and I knew Emmaline Hallwyler had put her hand over it so I couldn't hear her, but I knew what she was doing.

Laughing. She was laughing.

Emmaline Hallwyler eventually got back on the line with a little hiccup. "Seems like you had a little incident with an ex-boyfriend." I heard that muffled sound again. She sounded like a hyperventilating chicken. She coughed. "Also looks like this is your first offense. Is that right?"

"Yes, it is my first recorded offense, although if I had the opportunity I might try to commit another offense against Slick Dick."

I heard her snort. "Ran out of time?"

"Yes. The police arrived at my door. The police kept laughing as they read me my rights."

There was the hyperventilating chicken again. "Those damn police." The chicken harnessed her laughter with a cough. "Now, back to the requirements—don't be a second late and don't be pathetic and we'll get along fine."

"Right. I will endeavor not to be pathetic." I wondered if I could bring my knitting? Rosvita had decided that I needed something to do with my hands that was germ-free so she was teaching me how to knit each evening. But perhaps knitting would make me look pathetic?

"So, your screening interview will be this Friday at noon. Do not be late."

"My screening interview?" What, she had to evaluate me to see if I'm angry enough to be included in the class? Perhaps I should bring something to throw while I was there to display my anger? Like Slick Dick's head?

"Yes. Your screening interview. You and I can get to know each other and I can decide whether or not I like you."

Whether or not she liked me? Now that's a tricky one. Most people do like me, I think, if they weren't scared of me. I do think that. Except for my twenty-three-year-old ladder-climbing assistant who wanted my job, but that was nothing personal and I can't blame her for it. "Why would you care if you liked me or not? I'm a client. I'm not coming to be your best friend."

"Well, hell's bells," she snapped. "Can you hear me crying onto my files? Sniffling into my hankie? For God's sake, I don't need a best friend. I have one already, the same one I've had since fifth grade. Her name's Sheri and she's got big teeth and laughs all the time. No, I need to know if I like you enough to fix your problems for you."

"Gee whiz. Lemme see," I said. "I have a true abundance of problems: I have no job. I'm so skinny my bones rattle. I have assault charges filed against me. Slick Dick has also filed a civil suit against me for a horrendous sum of money. He will probably win, leaving me bankrupt. I'm currently, even at this very moment, having a nervous breakdown. With a criminal record, it will be difficult for me to become employed again. Would you like me to repeat what I told eight-hundred-thirty-four people in a meeting in the near past about vaginal cream and sugary cereals? That's going to be a real problem in terms of being employed in advertising again. And, dear me, I don't want to forget to mention that my mother also died recently. I miss her more than I would miss my own heart. Did I mention Slick Dick took my mountain bike? If you could solve even one of my problems, that would be super. I had no idea psychologists could do so much for people these days. None."

There was a silence. "I thought I told you not to be pathetic," she said.

"I'm not pathetic." Yes I was, I told myself. Pathetic and mean and extremely stupid.

"You are. PA.THET.IC. Be here Friday at noon. We'll test your likability factor."

She hung up without saying good-bye. I stared at the phone awhile then told her that she was a supercilious, superior slug who was probably super-fat, much like a hippo pregnant with triplets, and hung up.

CHAPTER 4

Several days later, on my daily multihour crying/drinking walk, I decided to go to see what Rosvita kept referring to at our knitting sessions as the Hell of All Germs of Hell. In other words, the migrant camp. I crossed back toward town, then took a gravel road, which gave way to a dirt road, planted fields.

Miles and miles of planted fields.

My eyes were caught by a row of sheds starting at about ten feet from the road. They looked like they were slouching. I mean it. They were slouching sheds. Each building sagged like it couldn't possibly stand up straight. The roofs were made of metal. There were two windows in the front of each shed, but they were lopsided, one or two were broken. The doors barely hung on a hinge.

I stared at those doors, all hanging on one hinge. They were like my mind, I thought, my mind was currently unhinged. Still there, still clinging, but with a big gust of wind . . . well, whoosh, anything could happen.

As I got closer the smell of raw sewage settled over me like a giant rotting toilet. I yanked my t-shirt up over my mouth and nose. Yuck. I assumed that the farmer had used an extrapotent fertilizer on his property.

That's when I saw the dot.

A tiny little jumping dot. The dot was red.

As I got closer and closer to the red dot, a blue dot with black hair joined it. They ran about in circles, tackling each other.

Children.

In front of the slouching sheds with the tin roofs, almost unhinged doors, and broken windows.

I strode closer to the children so I could tell them not to go into the sheds because they didn't look safe. I also wanted to inquire where their parents were. This was a huge field; it didn't seem right that children this young should be out and about by themselves.

When I was twenty yards away, a woman appeared at the door of one of the sheds. She wore a blue shirt and jeans. I blinked. She spoke to the children and the children ran to her and grabbed something out of her hand.

She saw me and froze. I froze.

The truth hit me, ugly and rotten and suffocating.

People lived in those sheds.

This was the situation that enraged Rosvita.

People lived in those sheds.

The only person who should live there is Slick Dick. I felt a wave of bitterness rain down on me like a human-size tsunami.

The woman stood staring at me. I pitied her—who wouldn't?—but I smashed that smack down. She would not appreciate having to deal with my white-woman pity. I waved my hand.

Reluctantly, it seemed, as if an invisible string were yanking her hand up, she waved back.

I glanced at the fields again, the dilapidated sheds, the huge white house about a half mile away, up on a little hill.

Appalling.

Sickening.

People lived in those sheds.

I jogged past the sheds, past the debris on the ground, past the smell that wrapped itself around me like a viper choking on bile. I jogged back through the fields to the path. I found the river again and continued jogging, the water rustling and bubbling and gurgling, the trees overhead swaying and blowing.

The river offered me no peace the rest of that day.

None.

With every step I took away from the Hell of All Germs of Hell I became more angry. Soon I was livid and knew I would not be surprised if my head blew off with flames of fire.

You see, though I am currently demented and stumbling through life in a wretched manner, I know something valuable: The reason I am in the position I am is because of luck, pure and simple.

People get so snotty about their stations in life, the money they have, the homes, the toys, but what it mostly boils down to is luck. I was lucky to be born in America and not in a war zone in Somalia or Afghanistan. I was lucky to have loving parents not strung out on drugs. I was lucky to have a father who worked hard and provided for his family even after he died. I was lucky to have a mother who insisted I drag my rear through college. I might also mention that I have had plenty of food, water, electricity, and plumbing in my life.

I was not lucky in other parts of my life, but the ability to make a living, to make money, and to have opportunities was all luck.

And this situation was an example of zero luck.

I was furious because the whole situation was personal.

Way too personal. I couldn't even go there yet. Couldn't even begin to think of her there. Couldn't think of the abject deprivation she suffered.

People lived in those sheds.

I stopped by the liquor store and bought the highest quality scotch they had. Yummy.

I took it down to the river with me that night and drank myself into oblivion. I awoke to Rosvita prodding me awake. At first I thought she was a mini-robot using a power drill against my forehead to smash a thousand aching brain cells to smithereens.

"Get up, honey," Rosvita said. She wore a lacy, green silk robe that billowed behind her and her white gloves. "Your body is awash with alcoholic poisons, your liver struggling, your kidneys squeezing, your blood drenched with drunkenness. You, my dear, are a skinny alcoholic germ and you must come inside this instant."

I nodded, closed my eyes, fell back against the wet grass.

She prodded again.

"Go away, Rosvita. I'm going to sleep here tonight. I'll still pay you, of course."

"I will not allow you to soak up even earth's natural germs here on this grass. Come now, dear."

"Nope."

"Yes, dear." I felt that power drill against my forehead.

"Nope, nope."

"Please. Jeanne. I care."

It was those two words that did it: "I care."

Sheesh. These country people and their caring would be the death of me.

I hauled myself up, leaned against Rosvita and wobbled into my blue heaven of a bed.

Two hours later I spent six hours leaning against the white porcelain throne. I threw up, I am sure, my struggling liver, my squeezing kidneys, and my blood awash with alcohol.

I felt like human vomit.

Why must I be such a drunk?

I slept my drunkenness off for most of the next day and when I awoke, Rosvita made me breakfast. Breakfast at 4:00 in the afternoon can be particularly tasty. I also downed about a keg of coffee, then went to town to buy a gift for Rosvita.

Knowing what her taste in art was like, I stopped by three galleries. Each of the shop owners looked so hopeful, I bought three different paintings—one from each. I brought one downstairs to Rosvita that evening. It was a painting of a pristinely clean country kitchen, a gust of wind blowing the red-checked curtains, a little girl eating a chocolate ice cream cone on a stool, the floor gleaming, the counters cleared.

She loved it so much she danced around the room with it, declaring that the artist clearly knew the importance of a clean and sterile kitchen. She hugged me. Danced again with a wriggle and a wiggle.

I went up to my room and out to my deck to examine the stars.

A dull ache still filled my head and I felt like congealed oatmeal, but I was still breathing, at least.

I knew I had to get a hold of my drinking, before it killed me.

Dying still held vast appeal for me, but last night was not good, not good at all. One should not hug toilets for long periods.

I thought of the trigger to my drinking binge: That putrid migrant camp.

When the woman at the shed raised her hand to wave at me, I saw my late grandma in the doorway. My funny, laughing, loving grandma.

Rosa Sanchez had been born in Mexico. She and her parents lived and worked as migrant workers on various farms in the United States. They stayed for the growing season, then moved on. She had told me about working ten hours a day in a field as a young child, her head getting so hot she thought her hair would burn off. She told me about staying in barns and sleeping next to farm animals on some rich landowner's property. She told me about being cold and hungry and scared and tired. She told me about the white farmer who attacked her mother. When her father fought back in her defense, he lost the job. They almost starved that summer. She told me about never learning to read or write until she married my grandpa and he taught her.

It was a hideous way to live.

And there she was, in my mind's eye, in the doorway of that pathetic shed.

My grandpa, a white American, with pure Norwegian roots,

met my grandmother when her family worked on his family's farm.

"She was my soul mate, Jeanne," Grandpa told me. "I knew it when I saw her because my heart damn near jumped out of my chest. I told her she almost killed me that day."

My grandpa was nineteen when they met. She was eighteen. They married two years later.

He shook his big head, his white hair cropped close to his head. "The only way I could get her to stop talking some days was to kiss that woman. We always ended up in bed after that. Couldn't help ourselves. Passion and love crosses cultures and language barriers, dear girl, don't forget that, and your grandma and me were soul mates whose souls talked to each other even though our languages didn't. But, dear God, she was a talker. Constantly talking, talking, talking."

My grandparents' black-haired daughter, my mother, married my father, a white American with British roots and blond hair. I grew up speaking Spanish to my grandma and to my mother, although my grandma spoke English, too. She said she loved this country, she was an American woman now, and she wanted to be able to talk to her neighbors, but she talked Spanish to me so I would never forget where my family was from, *what they came from*.

And even though my grandpa said Grandma talked all the time, my grandpa decided he couldn't live without all that talk. One week after my grandma died, after he'd given her a beautiful funeral, he laid down under the giant cherry tree on their land, right where he said they'd made every one of their four children, closed his eyes and died.

After sixty years of marriage, he was done without his wife. He had been in perfect health until that point, too. The doctors said he'd had a heart attack.

How silly. He died of a broken and lonely heart and he willed it upon himself.

As I thought of my grandpa's love of my grandma and I

thought of my grandma bent over double picking strawberries for hours on end as a child and of her poor mother being attacked by some sick landowner who thought her mother was his property, I made a vow to myself: I would get those people out of those sheds.

I swore it.

CHAPTER 5

Anger management class is located in Portland, so I had to drive about fifty minutes west to get there. I go from towering fir trees, homes scattered along a river, and a main street that moves about as fast as melted taffy, to a city filled with rushing people, darting cars, skyscrapers, and a bunch of preposterously high and mind-numbingly scary bridges spanning the Willamette River.

I cried my way into the city, because I felt like it, shoulders shaking, sounding quite like a dying warthog. How I am relishing my nervous breakdown!

I slowed way down when I went over a bridge. The car behind me honked and the driver flipped me the finger, but I ignored him, eyes straight ahead, not looking down, down, down into that river below filled with who knew what kind of eight-headed human-eater or monster shark. (I do not like heights or bridges.)

By the time I reached the Diamond District my face was red and blotchy and pale, my lipstick smeared. My mascara had trickled across my face and it looked as if dead ants had been buried in shallow graves across my cheekbones. I am a multicolored freak, I told myself, looking in the car mirror, a multicolored freak.

I cleaned up as best as a crybaby can, running my fingers

through my gold curls and adjusting my clothes. I was wearing jeans, a purple, lace-lined camisole, a lavender-colored silk blouse, some cool gold hoop earrings, and about three inches of bracelets. I also wore black heels with a strip of lavender on the toe that exactly matched the camisole. They are completely cool.

Anger management class was located in a building that used to be a warehouse. In fact, this whole area of town, dubbed the Diamond District, used to be an industrial wasteland, according to Rosvita. Lots of rundown factories, warehouses, old stuff. But the location was too cool—close to the river, to downtown, to shopping and work—to stay that way.

So one by one the factories were either bulldozed or converted and glass-walled buildings shot up. But the Diamond District had not yet been perfected, which probably lent to its appeal. Streets weren't always paved right, tired factory buildings butted up to new, sleek structures, and there was a bit of a rough edge to it. I found parking near the address, crossed one street with potholes the size of Denver, and dodged a huge dump truck and an earth-mover.

I looked at the address in my hand again. The anger management woman had told me that when I could smell beer, I was there. I could smell the beer. In fact, as I circled the building, I knew I was looking at, and smelling, a brewery.

The temptation was almost too much for me. Beer and me have a long and golden and messy history and to slug one down right at that moment, or three or four, had vast appeal. I had heard that Oregon was home to a bunch of brothers who knew their beer, and I was anxious to taste the products of those bros.

Two things held me back: One, I had been told to be prompt or else. Two, I was driving home. I have often been drunk in the last twelve years of my life, but I have never, ever driven after drinking.

It's like my other rule: I have been a bit slutty at different times in my life, and the sex left me colder and lonelier and more withered inside than I was before, but I don't mess with anyone else's man.

Those are about the only two hard and fast rules I have, but they've worked for me thus far.

I circled the building, trying to banish the thought of pouring gold beer down my throat, and looked for the double doors. Finally, I saw them. Painted green with a gold sign to the left that said, EMMALINE HALLWYLER, COUNSELOR.

The entry was dark when I stepped in, but I saw stairs to my right and started to climb. The building, by my deductions, was probably one hundred plus years old with dust the same age, and dark as a caveman's cave.

I reached one landing and saw another gold sign that said EMMALINE HALLWYLER, COUNSELOR, and pointed up. This led to a hallway painted bright white. The white paint was thick, like frosted icing. At the end of the hallway, there were black and white photographs on both sides. All featured close-ups of people in the throes of one acute emotion or another: Joy. Surprise. Grief. Despair. Exhaustion. Depression. Panic. There must have been thirty pictures, all framed in black.

The sign above the photographs said, PHOTOS TAKEN BY EMMALINE HALLWYLER. Super. She could photograph me when I was screaming, my face puffed like a red marshmallow, my mouth twisted like a red snake. I glanced at my watch. It was exactly 12:00.

I was prompt. I looked like hell, but I was prompt and had not succumbed to golden beer, and guzzling.

I turned one more corner and faced about twenty stairs.

When I reached the top of the stairs, I had to blink. Light shone from all corners of the huge room from a multitude of windows. The floor and the walls were bright white, too. In one corner of the room, there were five red boxing bags suspended from the ceiling.

In another corner, there looked to be a craft area. It was filled with glue and ribbons and tape and Styrofoam and wood. Scraps of metal, cardboard, egg cartons, and piles of stuff that looked like it came straight from the dump.

In the third corner there was a number of huge pillows. A large sign above the pillows labeled it as the SCREAMING CORNER.

In the fourth corner was a piano, a set of drums, guitars, and other musical instruments. I saw a violin. My heart squeezed real tight over that violin.

In the middle of the room were seven beanbags. They looked like a rainbow—purple, blue, green, yellow, orange, red. In the center of the beanbags was a bigger-sized black beanbag and in the center of the black beanbag sat a woman.

Now, I was expecting Emmaline Hallwyler to be about as wide as the Amazon jungle, with perhaps a black panther curling behind her and a venomous snake wrapped around her neck.

There was no black panther, no venomous snake, and Emmaline Hallwyler was positively tiny. I could tell because when I looked in her direction she stood up.

She was dressed all in white. White pants, white blouse, white high heels. It would have looked ridiculous on anyone else. Me, I would have looked like a gawky, temperamental angel who had had her wings taken away for punishment for some lousy offense.

Emmaline, with her brown bob of hair and huge brown eyes and finely cut features, looked positively elegant. I would later learn that under the fragile elegance was a she-demon quite capable of knocking heads together and ripping people down to the size of pesky mice.

"Do not move." She said this with great authority.

I hate when people order me about, but I obeyed. This class was court-ordered, after all, and with a good report maybe I could keep from getting too screwed with the judge.

I didn't move.

She stared at me. I stared back. When you are used to working with male, egotistical advertising pricks who believe the earth was made for the pleasure of them and their dicks and everyone else is squash vermin, you get in the habit of not being intimidated.

"I can feel your anger," she told me, her voice ringing off the walls.

"Gee, what are you, psychic or something?"

"Stuff it, Jeanne. Your hostility is like burning hot rocks."

"Gee again. That's why I'm here. Anger and hostility. Can I move now?"

"No."

I waited. Perhaps she was taking time to feel my hostilic anger.

"You're barely hanging on."

"No shit."

"No, there is no shit," she snapped. "None at all. You're a repressed chick. You've dug yourself into a psychological cave by not allowing your emotions out. It's all your fault."

I paused at that one. *My fault?*

"Your pain and anguish have shaken you like an internal earthquake and you've grabbed hold of your loss in a deathlike grip. Fury is the emotion that comes out when people are scared. You let your problems run your life by packing them away in your anger. They stay because you won't examine them and throw them out. When the problems grew and grew to unimaginable heights, like a mountain range, you hid from them, convincing yourself you could handle life, no problemo. But you hit a crisis valley and you were shoved right off a cliff and your life exploded."

Well, she certainly boiled things down quickly, didn't she? And in such geographical terms, too! "You're a genius," I told her. "Brilliant. May I come in now? That purple beanbag is looking pretty good to me."

I started to walk toward her.

"Stop."

I stopped. Sighed. This was a bad day.

"Hit," she said.

"I'm sorry?"

"Hit."

"Should I hit you?" I asked. "How hard?"

She glared and pointed at the punching bags hanging from the ceiling like giant bloodred splotches.

"Hit the bags until your anger is gone."

I dropped my purse on the ground.

"That would take days. No, it would take months. No, it would take years. Will I be charged by the hour? And, if you go home to go to bed while I'm still hitting, do I still get charged?"

She crossed her arms across her chest. "Start. Hit. Now."

I shrugged. I would pretend it was Slick Dick's face. I really missed my mountain bike.

"Stop."

I eyed the she-demon. "Whatever could it be now?"

"Take off your shoes. Shoes carry bad energy with them. All of our anger and frustration rolls right down our bodies to our feet and our feet expel that impotence and blackness like an upside-down volcano into our shoes. Leave the shoes, leave the lava and flying rocks of your past behind."

I glanced down at my black and lavender heels.

I have a tragic relationship with my vast shoe collection, this I know. My shoe obsession started after I lost Johnny and Ally. Before that, Johnny and I had worn tennis shoes, hiking boots, or flip-flops, spending as little as possible because we were broke college students. Those shoes were, and always will be in my mind, the best.

But when I started a new job at an advertising agency about six months after they died, still believing that the pain of my overwhelming grief could stop my heart from beating at any second, I bought a pair of new black heels. The heels distracted me when I got stressed, so I bought a pair of red heels, next a taupe pair, and soon I got daring and slightly hysterical and bought four-inch-high pink heels with little red daisies on the sides.

The heels distracted me when I thought of Johnny and Ally. I know that sounds bizarrely shallow, but I had nothing to hold onto. I would think, "I want to die I want to die I want to die," and I'd peek down at my bright red or striped or polka-dot heels and I'd start thinking of which pair of shoes I wanted to be buried in and for some reason, that shook me out of my severe and pervasive depression a bit.

At least enough to go on living through the next hour or until I could get to a mall and distract myself again.

"Take off the volcanoes of anger, Jeanne," Emmaline ordered. "Get away from the hot lava flow of frustration."

I swallowed hard and started feeling hot and very insecure at the same time, but I flicked off the heels. I stood flat-footed and felt more and more vulnerable by the second, a whole bunch of emotions I didn't want to have to deal with running into my head at breakneck speed.

I did nothing in front of the red blob, for long minutes, but the blob morphed into everything I was mad about. I whacked that thing and darn near broke my wrist.

"Don't be a wimp." I had not realized Emmaline was right in back of me. "Hit it again."

I hit it again.

"Again."

This was not too bad. I hit it again and again, like a boxer, using both hands.

"Use your feet," Emmaline ordered.

I kicked it with my feet.

"Kick the negatives out of your soul," she insisted. "Kick those soul-crushing negatives from your kidneys and liver and pancreas and prostate, and let it flow from your feet."

I stopped at that. "I don't have a prostate."

"Whatever," she boomed. "Kick the prostate you don't have outside of your body."

I focused on the bag again, then kicked the negatives out of the prostate that I didn't have.

"Use your butt."

I was sweating now but feeling better. I dropped my purple silk blouse to the floor, and charged backward into the bag. It swung back and almost knocked me over. I hit it again, it swung back and into me, back and forth we went. It became my red-blob enemy.

"With your elbows," Emmaline called out, her voice strident now. "Again with your fists." I swung and swung. Sweat dripped off my forehead. This went on for way too long. Hit, hit, hit. Sweat.

"Stop."

I sank to the floor, panting. I wondered if she had decided if she liked me or not. I decided I didn't care. Slick Dick's face had been beaten to a mangy pulp and that's all I cared about.

"Come to the center of the room, the center of peace."

I struggled to my feet, followed obediently behind her, much like a wussy dog.

"Sit in the purple beanbag." I was too wiped out to argue. I sat.

She settled in the black one.

"Let's get rid of the black mold over your heart," she said, her eyes narrowing. "It's destroying you."

Mold over my heart. A sumptuous thought. I needed a beer. I needed many beers. Maybe after this little session I would drop into the brewery and drink straight from a keg lying on my back.

She reached out and ran a finger across my forehead and studied my sweat. For fun, I ran a finger across my forehead and studied my sweat, too. Clear. I was somewhat surprised. I half expected it to be black. Maybe with a little mold.

Emmaline studied my sweat on her tiny little finger as if it might hold the answer to eliminating menopause. She held it up to the beams of light glancing through the windows, then held it about five inches from her eyes. Next she smelled it.

"I bet that smells yummy," I told her.

"No, not at all," she said, her voice accusing. "It smells like fear."

"Fear?"

"Yes. Fear. Truckloads of it. So, let's start with that. What are you fearful of?" She wiped my sweat on her pant leg, and fixed those sharp, brown eyes on mine like lasers.

"I'm not afraid of anything," I told her. I sat up straighter in my beanbag, glad that the rest of my sweat was drying. I am a firm believer that sweat washes away all the bacteria infesting our bodies—the germy yuck that runs through our veins (Rosvita would be proud of my antigerm inner rhetoric), although I would rather not be wearing a silk shirt when punching a bag.

No, I wasn't afraid of anything, but it's not what you think. I wasn't afraid of anything because I didn't care anymore. Not at all. I was done. I wasn't sure I cared to live anymore. The analytical part of me knew it was a dangerous place to be.

"Yes, you are." She whacked the side of the beanbag. "Fear is lacing your life. It's behind all of your problems. It's behind your anger. And your impotence."

At the word impotence, I thought of Slick Dick's little dickie. He obviously had enough kick in his dick to get it up for his girl-friends—as well as for me. I had heard from my doctor. I had insisted on being tested for every STD under the sun. All tests were negative and I was healthy. Good news, but it did not diminish my need to jab needles into his butt.

"You're getting angry," Emmaline told me, spreading her arms out wide. "I'm going to catch your anger for you."

"Spread your arms out wider, Emmaline. I've got a heck of a lot more anger than that. Here it comes, one roll of fury after another," I said, noting the bitter, mean tone. "Perhaps I'll send you that tad bit of anger I felt when I realized that my career was pointless." There was that word again. Pointless. I'm pointless.

"Send it over," she instructed, arms waving.

"Or maybe you would like the anger I felt when I realized that I have hooked up with one loser after another. Let's see, there was Devon who talked incessantly about himself and only needed a board with eyes painted on it and inflatable boobs to be happy. There was Carl who wanted sex and nothing else, and when I tried to talk to him about anything he pulled a pillow over his head—and for some reason I felt compelled to stay in that relationship for six months. There was Andy who was in love with his mother and wanted me to mother him and left when I wouldn't fold his socks a certain way."

I tilted my head at her. "You get the picture."

"No, I don't," Emmaline said. "There's more. So much more. Tell me."

"No. No, that's it." I crossed my arms. No more.

"Yes. You're raging. I want you to heal. Tell me."

"I'm healed."

"You're not, Jeanne. You're raw. You're hurting." She leaned toward me, took both my hands. She lowered her voice. "I'm here to help you. I want your anger. I want you to get rid of it. Keep talking, Jeanne."

I thought about it. Why the heck not. "I'm so angry. I hate myself."

"I know that. Kick that hate out, don't be pathetic, don't be weak. Kick the burning anger out."

I don't know why but I felt the tears form in my eyes again. "Okay, well if you can take real burning anger I think I'll send you the anger from my mother's death. She was my only friend and now I don't have any friends besides my brother who I rarely see because I can't stand to look in the eyes of his children. Perhaps I'll send you the fury I felt watching cancer eat her alive. Why couldn't the cancer have landed in the body of a criminal or a creep? Why her? And why do so many people I know who do nothing but pollute the earth with their venom and hate and perversity get to live and she doesn't?"

"Keep it coming, Jeanne. All of it. There's more, I can feel it."

I tried to pull my hands away, but she wouldn't let me.

Oh, yeah, there was more and I felt that anger ripping through me like a chain saw, noisy and relentless.

"Well," I tried to sound nonchalant but my voice caught on a sob. "There was Johnny Stewart. We met when I was in graduate school and he was in medical school. We were twenty-five." I started to shake. Surely I was over this, almost twelve years later?

"I'm feeling your fear again, Jeanne. This is the worst of it. Your negatives are radiating. Don't be a wuss here. *Get it out.*"

"Johnny always liked to sing." I wiped tears off my face because my cracking heart was making me cry. "We would sing together all the time. He played the guitar; I played the violin. We decided we were going to get married and live in the country and have five kids and a farm." I wrenched my hands away from Emmaline's, then got up and slammed both hands into the punching bag, not bothering to wipe my tears. "He was going to be a doctor and I was going to raise the kids. We would go camping in the summer and I would volunteer in their classrooms and take care of the cows and chickens and horses. We would go to church on Sundays and have a bunch of friends. Did I mention the five children? We had even picked out names we liked."

"Hit it out, Jeanne. Rip it out and let's deal with it. Be strong enough to deal with it." She flapped again. "Speak of it. Get it out in the open, out of your heart."

"It's never leaving my heart," I told her, pummeling my hands into the bag. My body shook again, like a leaf would shake if you grabbed it by its stem and held it up in a tropical windstorm.

"Tell me."

"Well, there was the little matter of my being pregnant. When I was twenty-five, during my last year of graduate school." I smiled. My smile wobbled. Salty tears flowed into my mouth. "We planned on getting married after we graduated and having kids. But he was so happy that I was pregnant and I was so happy and we both cried. He always put his head on my stomach and talked to the baby.

"Before the ultrasound told us we were having a girl, Johnny would tell the baby he loved her, that her mother loved her. He would talk to the other side of my stomach and tell the baby that he loved *him*, that his mother loved *him*."

I shuddered, smacked both fists into the bag.

"We would name it Grayson if the baby was a boy, after my father, and Ally, after my mother, if the baby was a girl."

I felt ill. I hadn't even spoken about this in twelve years. I had only talked about it with my mother who rocked me back and forth, in and out of my hysterics. I felt like it was yesterday and felt the full force of my grief. I could still smell it.

"Tell me, Jeanne."

"No, I can't."

"You can, I'm listening. Let it out."

Let it out? Let it out so it could eat me alive once again? So it could drive me to my knees? How fun. This counselor knew how to make a client have a good time. "Two weeks after I found out I was pregnant we got married in the church chapel with his family and mine and about fifty friends and professors from school. I wore my mother's white lace wedding dress and the veil that she wore and her mother before her and her mother before her. And flip-flops. No heels for me. We were so happy together. We always had pancakes on Saturday mornings and Wednesday nights for dinner."

I remembered those evenings. We were students. We were broke and we bought pancake mix in bulk. We'd smother the pancakes in syrup and butter and eat naked by our fireplace and laugh. Afterward, Johnny would play his guitar, I'd play my violin. Naked.

"Months later a drunk driver decided that it would be best if he sped down the highway and crashed his car into ours head on."

I heard Emmaline make a strangled sound in her throat. She wrapped her arms around me. "I'll take the anger, Jeanne," she yelled. "Give it to me! Give it to me!"

"Johnny lost his head." When I said this, I heard my own tone. So nonchalant, so casual, so dismissive of the horror, and yet I saw it as if it were yesterday, as if I were up in a tree watching a shameful tragedy unfold. "I tried to help him, but I couldn't move. My legs were broken in six different places. My stomach felt like it had exploded. Ally died. She died. Our baby died."

I tried to pull away from Emmaline, but she wouldn't let me. I finally leaned against her, my body shaking like that leaf, the leaf breaking off, piece by piece, ripped and shredded by that windstorm.

"The drunk got out of his car and managed to call an ambulance before he passed out."

I could feel the cool of that night around me. Feel the heat of my blood. Of Ally's blood and mine mixed together, outside of my body not inside where it was supposed to be. I was six months pregnant. I saw Johnny's headless body in the dark and then everything slipped into oblivion. It was like my mind shut down and I closed my eyes and I shut down and out.

I woke up alive and without Ally in my stomach in the cold sterility of the hospital. I woke up knowing Johnny was long gone. I woke up screaming and had to be sedated. I remember the nurses and my mother holding me, hugging me, loving me in Spanish and in English as I screamed.

Emmaline rocked me, my hands at my side. I thought I would throw up. My eyes moved to the craft corner. Could I not have simply made a craft today? Could I not have simply headed straight to the screaming corner? Could I not have simply died that night?

"Like we planned, she was named Ally after my mother with the middle name of Johnna after Johnny." My voice cracked and the windstorm met with a tornado and the tornado swept that leaf away and soon that tiny little fragile leaf broke apart piece by piece. Emmaline rocked me back and forth, back and forth as I dropped to the floor and slipped into what would politely be called hysteria. "That's why I stopped playing my violin. That's why I didn't eat pancakes for twelve years. I couldn't. There were no more pancakes in my life. No more music. None. That was the last time I was me."

My dry, hacking sobs came up from my soul, ragged and razor sharp. "I miss Johnny. I miss Ally Johnna. God, I miss them. I miss them, I miss them, God, I miss them."

Before I left Emmaline's, I slipped into her shower. It was tiny but perfectly clean. First I burned my skin and face with steamy hot water, then I cooled off in freezing cold water. I dried, dressed, cleaned up after myself (I like things tidy) and left the bathroom.

Emmaline was waiting for me. She held up her hands above her head. "Put your fingertips to mine."

I did so.

"I sense no more anger in you right now, Jeanne, not right now. You must kick the crap out of your anger, your pain. It's controlled you for too long."

I bent my head again, and glared at the floor between us.

She put both hands on my stomach, massaged it gently. "You will have more babies, Jeanne, you will."

She bent onto her heels and wrapped her hands around my knees. "You will heal."

Frankly, I would be grateful if my healing involved leaving this building and being smashed by a bunch of suicidal pigeons. Dying by suicidal pigeons is not an idle wish. Would I *ask* the pigeons to dive-bomb me into oblivion? Maybe not, but if they did, I would be okay with that. And that's a sorry place to be.

"I can't do it." No, I could not do it. "I can't even begin to heal because I would have to think about it. And I can't. I can't go through it again."

"You can," she told me. She wrapped her fingers around mine, hugged me close and rocked me back and forth, back and forth. "You can. You can. You will."

I slipped my feet into my heels, left her office, pulled my chin up and, like a drunk homing pigeon, found my way straight to the brewery. To hell with my good intentions of not getting blitzed.

The memories Emmaline had stirred up were raw and crashing down on my head, one after the other. Each horrific moment.

The doctors and nurses had told me at length that I had not sustained any permanent injuries and would be able to have children again, that my bones would heal, the scars would fade. Their earnest reassurances and worried looks meant nothing to me, their voices coming at me as if from disembodied floating heads.

When I still had my legs in slings, dried blood on my face, and an empty, lonely womb, I decided that I would never fall in love with any man again—so in my throbbing, damaged, completely mentally unsound mind, that precluded children. Of course, the screaming would begin again and those same doctors and nurses with the worried looks would sprint over and give me a shot that would put me back to sleep for a little while and out of my misery.

Johnny and I rarely drank alcohol. But two weeks after they died, at my mother's house, I reached for a glass of wine. Then two. It was the first night I'd slept more than a few hours without waking up screaming, the flashbacks intense, vivid, and terrifying. That was the start of my downward slide. I started drinking more, drinking harder.

My drinking fairly soon got out of my control. My mother and Roy and Charlie all stepped in to help me, but I didn't want their help. I wanted their love, but not their help. Alcohol fuzzed over my life, and that's what I really wanted—the fuzziness. I did not want clarity, did not want to work through the past, did not want any more mind-screaming agony.

I wanted the fuzz. And I wanted not to think. So I got a job at an ad agency and I worked. All the time. I was a wunderkind. An unsmiling wunderkind that could somehow put together television ads that brought tears to people's eyes, laughter to their hearts, and tubloads of money to my bosses.

Two years after the accident my legs and pelvic area didn't hurt much anymore, probably because I was young and continued running (almost obsessively, I ran) and physical therapy, but my heart felt like it was being pinched by a vise, so I kept drinking.

In fact, I thought to myself in a sudden flash of predrunken clarity, believing I would never let myself fall in love again, hence no pregnancies, might explain the motivation behind my long list of bad men: Choose dickless men, don't fall in love, use all protections and hence, no pregnancies and no heartbreak.

I headed to the brewery around the corner from Emmaline's. A young man with a goatee, a big grin, and a hooped earring in his eyebrow helped me pick out a six-pack and a little scotch. He made reservations for me at a nearby bed-and-breakfast when I asked for recommendations. "My mom and dad always stay there when they want to get away from us kids," he told me, dialing. "Can't blame 'em. There are nine of us."

Well, wasn't that what I needed to hear at that moment? I hated his mother instantly. Nine kids.

Nine.

She had nine and I had nothing.

Gall.

I drove my car up to the bed-and-breakfast, greeted the two friendly male proprietors, one short and one tall, and entered my room. I had a view of Mount Hood. I vaguely thought of calling Rosvita and telling her where I was, but decided I would do it after my beer.

I drank one beer in the soaking tub in my room and a little scotch. I had another beer out on my deck in the dark and a wee bit of scotch. I had one more beer while I watched a movie and a tad more scotch. One more after I sat out on my deck again and cried into my scotch. I passed out in bed, visions of Johnny's smile and my darling, dead baby dancing through my head.

My mother was there, too. She smiled at me.

CHAPTER 6

I woke to a splitting headache and a pounding on my door. I had slept naked so was feeling quite nude.

I said something unintelligible to the door, which sounded like, "I don't want any tomatoes."

"Jeanne?" A person, perhaps of the male species, called through the door.

I tried to speak but during the night someone must have snuck in and stuffed cotton balls mixed with turpentine in my mouth, so I grunted. The grunt sounded like a boar in heat.

"Jeanne? Are you all right?" Another male species' voice.

I grunted again, boarlike.

"Jeanne? Please let us check on you."

I shoved the hair out of my eyes, swung my legs over the edge of the bed and felt instantly irritated because floors should not shake when one stands on them and this one did. "Stupid floor," I muttered.

"What?" the male species' voices said as one.

I wrestled with my jeans, slipped my purple camisole over my head and stumbled across the swaying floor to the door. I would not stay here in this swaying-floored hotel again, I vowed. The two men I had met the night before, the owners, looked at me with great sympathy when I opened the door. The short one said something to the tall one. I thought I heard the word "blood." The tall one nodded, then left.

"Perry will be right back," Short One said. "May I suggest that you sit down?"

He may. I trudged back across the swaying floor and tumbled to the bed, holding my head with both hands. "The floor moves and shakes. It's too noisy in here," I told him. It came out like "Da foor moo an shake. Ith u neezy inair."

He didn't say anything, but sat down on the bed beside me. Now, in any other circumstance I would have been alarmed by a man I didn't know sitting on the side of a bed with me. But I knew that Short One and Tall One were gay so I didn't much worry.

"Yes," he said, his voice low and soothing. "It is very noisy. We're trying to get the volume of the noise down right now."

"And it's too hot." Came out: "Anithtu ot."

I felt Short One move and knew he was looking at the open patio doors. I could hear the rain.

"Yes, it is very, very hot in here. Steaming. We're working on that, too."

"Will you turn the cool up?" I asked. Came out: "Illuturnda-coolup?"

"Yes, we'll turn the cool up."

"Good." I laid back on the bed. I felt him lift my feet. He covered me with a blanket. I decided to go back to sleep. "I'll pay you for another night." Came out: "Allpath u pour nother wight."

I heard someone enter the room. Must have been the tall one. Short One and Tall One pulled me up against the headboard. I smelled tomato juice.

Yummy. I love tomato juice. It's the only thing I'll drink when I'm flying on airplanes.

"Have a nonalcoholic Bloody Mary," Short One said. "Then we'll let you go back to sleep."

I complied. One of them held me up; the other held the drink to my mouth. I drank the whole thing.

"Super," I told them. "It's quieter now that's it's not so hot. Thank you." ("Ith kwiter now ot tho ot. Thk u.")

"You're welcome," Short One said. "We've turned up the cool and we've turned down the noise."

"Yes," Tall One said. "More to your liking. Now let's lay back down and relax since the heat is cool now and the noise is gone."

I felt them lower me back to the bed. They straightened the blanket.

"Why did you wake me up?" I asked ("Ididjawakeeeup?")

"We wanted to make sure you were still with the program," Tall One said. "It's important to us that none of our guests slip from this world to the next while still on the premises."

Good idea "Slkjweoiure," I said.

Even in my hungover state I could see their looks of pity.

I hate pity, but was too hungover to get feisty. Plus, they had brought me a (virgin) Bloody Mary.

The door clicked shut when they left.

I decided to sleep again. This time I hoped I wouldn't hear the sound of my own screams in my nightmares.

I dreamed of my mother. Her face. Her smiling face. She came to me in my dream. I love you, Mom, I told her.

"Quit drinking," she yelled back at me. "I've told you once, I've told you twice, *quit drinking*."

When I woke up the second time I had to pee so bad I could feel it slipping out in hot dribbles. I envisioned my bladder swollen up to the size of a small pig. I waddled to the bathroom, legs crossed tight, barely made it to the toilet, did my business, relaxed on the white throne with my poor head nestled in my hands, then stood up with not too much balance and looked at my face.

I looked like death.

Skeletal, pale, and gaunt. The light outside the window told me it was time for dinner. My stomach told me I had to eat or die.

I contemplated my choices and decided that death by starvation was not on my list of things to do today. I showered, washed my hair and body with this fabulous smelling lemon-and-vanilla scented soap and shampoo, feeling my drunkenness rinsing away under the blast of the steamy hot water. I dried my hair, being careful with my aching head, and got dressed. I realized when I looked into a mirror that my clothes were rumpled and tired-looking, so I located the room's iron and ironed away. I must say I was presentable when I was done.

I made the bed (I mentioned I like things tidy?) and opened the window to get rid of the stale, rotting body smell in the air. I grabbed my purse, shoved my feet into my fabulous shoes, and headed downstairs, my stomach roiling.

Short One and Tall One were in the living room when I headed down, drinking coffee. They both stood, smiling when I entered.

They were so cute, so eager to please, and so seemingly concerned with me, I couldn't help but smile back.

"Coffee?" they asked.

I accepted, and pulled out my wallet and paid them for the second night. "Thank you," I told them. "Sorry about my little drunken bout."

"No problem," Short One said cheerily, taking the money. "We're delighted you didn't vomit on the floor."

"Or break things," Tall One added.

"Me, too. Vomiting is repulsive," I told them, sipping my coffee. Darn, that was good. I added a liberal dose of cream and not more than four tablespoons of sugar. "I never break things. Broken things make a mess. I like things tidy."

"You also know how to drink coffee," Short One said.

"I do indeed. No reason to skimp on cream and sugar, none at all."

Tall One eyed me. He had brown eyes the size of chocolate kisses and huge shoulders. He was the kind of person you felt like hugging. "I think you need more cream in your life."

"You're definitely too thin," said Short One.

I added more cream. I knew I was too thin. I didn't particularly like how I looked. Fact was, I haven't liked how I looked since Johnny and Ally died. When I was in love with Johnny I had curves. Hips, boobs, thighs. I weighed at least twenty pounds more than I do now. Johnny loved it. I felt healthy. After he died, I couldn't eat.

Come to think of it, I haven't been able to eat well since. Basically I live off of white wine, mochas, bananas (good mood-stabilizer), red wine, donuts, beer, cheese (goes good with wine), and bread.

Some days, I hardly eat. I wake up feeling ill.

Yes, I know I'm too thin. I look like a stick. Women have hated me in the past for this, but I will tell you this: I would far rather be plump than stick thin.

"Yep. I am too thin. I look like a bag of bones. I can almost hear myself rattling around. So, gentlemen, in honor of my latest binge, I think I'll take myself out to dinner. If you could point me in the direction of a decent restaurant?"

Short One clapped his hands together. Tall One nodded. Both were instantly eager. "We were going out to eat. Would you like to join us? Our treat."

"I'd love to go to dinner with you. You are not treating. I am. Don't argue. I owe you one. Let's go. I'm starving." We went to a place called Jack's. Fabulous clams in this buttery, garlicky sauce. Fabulous steak. Fabulous Caesar salad. I had only two drinks.

Tall One and Short One invited me to a club after dinner. The thought of going to a bar where men would scam on me as if I was a succulent and easy piece of salted meat held little appeal. They insisted on escorting me back to the bed-and-breakfast.

I semiboiled myself in a hot bubble bath, cried on my patio while sitting in a tight little ball, then tucked myself into bed.

Talking to the counselor had loosened too many mind-numbing memories. That night I dreamed of my baby. But she was joined by four other children. In the background there was a farm and a family of lambs.

I slept better.

*   *   *

"Okay, call Bob Davis, he's the governor's chief of staff, he's at the number I gave you, so I can quit worrying, and make an appointment to meet Jay Kendall, our current governor, who is also going to be our next governor," Charlie said, his voice anxious. "Jay's going on vacation in a couple of weeks and I want you in Portland before to meet him. He needs a new communications director, our other one decided she wanted to study kickboxing full-time, whatever that means, and you're it. Do it right away and call me when you've done it so I can quit worrying. This is a shoo-in. You're a shoo-in. It's one phone call. That's it. One call."

I kicked the water in the Salmon River with my feet, careful not to let my cell phone take a nosedive.

I did not miss the note of desperation in the voice of my older brother, Charlie. Charlie, the dear man, is insanely kind and smart and almost always worried sick about me. He is married with four children. His wife, Deidre, does not work outside her home and never intends to. My brother is smart enough to know that a woman with four children has more than enough to do at home. I have seen a photo of their white, rambling home in Portland and it made my throat close up because you know by looking at it that a happy, rambunctious, and chaos-plagued family dwells there.

I was wearing jeans but had decided to wade into the river up to my thighs anyhow. I glanced at the sun. It was about 4:00 in the afternoon on a Wednesday, or was it a Thursday? No, it was Wednesday. Thursday. Wednesday. Anyhow, I had been on the river since 7:22 that morning and had decided to end my day immersed in it.

"Jeanne?"

"Yes." I bent to examine some neat rocks in the river.

"You'll call and make an appointment? I really want you to do this. It's an opportunity you can't miss. Can't miss."

"Of course." I flicked a few of the rocks over. A little fish swam by.

He sighed. "I don't like the way you said, 'Of course.' You're humoring me so we can get off this subject and you can get back to your nervous breakdown."

I sang, "I will call," in English, French, Spanish, Pig Latin.

"Okay, okay. I got it. Please. Now listen, Jeanne, listen up, I'm worried about you."

"I know, darlin', but I'm fine. Perfectly fine. Needed a bit of a change of scenery, that's all." Was that a frog?

"That's not all—"

"I know it." It was a frog! A tiny frog, right by the bank. Should I catch it? "And, I know you know what happened and I don't want to talk about it." My brother knew everything. From a young age he was reading all about politics and politicians. He can tell you, in great detail, all the ins and outs of all of the presidential elections for the last one hundred years. His favorite presidential campaign, however, was Abraham Lincoln's.

Anyhow, he earned a scholarship to a fancy liberal college in Oregon, hooked up with a bunch of people there, graduated, got involved in politics, and was currently running the reelection campaign for Oregon's governor. Along the way he had met about a zillion people. As one of his best friends is also a high mucky-muck in advertising in Chicago, it is not surprising that he had heard of my latest episode. Hopefully, he had not heard about the assault charges.

"Look here, Jeanne Beanie," he sighed, using my childhood nickname. I could see him rubbing with two fingers that one lock of blondish hair that always fell over his forehead. Women were crazy about him, but he was so in love with Deidre that a person of the female sort could dance in front of him naked with a purple parasol and pink high heels and he probably wouldn't notice.

"You're a whiz kid. A whiz woman. Clear, articulate, funny, damn smart. People listen to you instead of tuning out like they do with everyone else. You know how to sell people stuff. You know how to lead, how to organize, research, market, create, how to get things done."

Yes, and after many a day hard at work at the salt mines getting things done, I usually got quietly smashed out of my mind in the privacy of my own home.

"So, Jeanne, listen. I need you here in Portland. Right now. Why did you stop in Weltana anyhow?"

"Because I liked the pancakes." That was the truth. Look at that! The little frog jumped to another rock. I tried to inch closer. The river lapped around my legs.

"*Because you liked the pancakes?*" I knew my brother's hand was now rubbing that little space on the nose between the eyes. I could see him glaring out his office window in some high-rise in Portland.

"They're delicious. Unbelievable. Can you drive out here and have some with me?"

"No, Jeanne, *no*." He raised his voice. I knew he was back to curling that curl. "No, not now."

I strolled down the middle of the river. I watched a small wave crash into another, blend, crash again. There went the hoppy little frog. I followed.

I decided to tell Charlie the startling truth so he would get off my tail, God love the man. "I don't want to work right now, Charlie."

He swore very quietly, but I heard it. "Don't swear," I said, with quite a prim note in my voice.

"Jeanne, do it for me. You're making me anxious. I feel anxious about you."

I almost laughed. My big brother needed me employed so he could stop worrying about me and he specifically wanted me near him to make sure I didn't drive my Bronco into the Pacific. "None of the other people Jay's got in his office are the remotest bit as competent as you are, plus you'd be awesome—awesome— with the media. You speak like you know what you're speaking about."

"Charlie, political campaigns are nightmares. I'd rather poke my buttocks with sharp needles while cartwheeling."

"Plus, *plus* you've always been interested in politics—local, state, even on a national level, you're a walking, talking political history book. You have a mind like a trap, a good trap, not a bad trap. Come on, Jeanne—"

"I know nothing about Oregon politics. Nothing. I don't even know what the gubernatorial candidates look like. I don't know, or care about, this 'Jay' you're talking about."

"He's a phenomenal man. He's honest. He knows his stuff, Jeanne, honestly knows it. He's innovative. He's decisive. The polls have us in a dead heat against a closed-minded conservative state senator. Please, Jeanne, the pay's good and I would consider it a personal favor."

"I don't owe you a single favor," I told him.

We both laughed.

I owed him a thousand and one personal favors, and we both knew it. He had saved my life on many occasions. I watched the frog leap again. What a leaper!

"All right, Charlie, I'll do it. I'll make an appointment with this guy."

He sighed with relief. "Good. When?"

"Soon."

"How soon is soon?"

"Soon, darlin'. How's Deidre?" The river kicked up a notch. Little baby waves splashed around my legs.

Asking about Deidre took Charlie's mind off our conversation. "She's doing great."

Deidre is athletic-looking. She wears no makeup because she doesn't need it and tells me that she makes their four kids play outside a lot because, "God made their skin dirt-proof so even if they roll in a puddle I know they'll clean up good." She does not allow video games. She hardly allows TV. She is super kind, well read and educated, and can talk about any topic under the sun. Beneath her cheer and good humor, she is a flaming liberal, a true and ardent believer in women's rights.

I am sure that everyone she comes in contact with loves her.

And I cannot recall a time that I have ever been friendly to Deidre.

In fact, I have been snappish and often rude and dismissive of her stay-at-home mom's life, the fact that she doesn't work—isn't she bored? Does she feel bad about not developing herself to her full potential? How can she be fulfilled? Is she, like, screaming to get out of her narrow and dull domestic life?

The truth of it is that I am crazily, greenly jealous of Deidre.

She has everything I want.

A husband. Many children. Lots of pets.

I thought I was going to be Deidre. I wanted to be Deidre. That dream was obliterated.

"She's always wished that the two of you were closer."

"I know, but I'm too cranky." And currently mentally unstable. And a drunk, and a raving lunatic who appears normal from the outside. But who wants to state the truth about one's mental health aloud?

"The kids would like to see you, too," Charlie said, his voice so quiet. "You haven't seen them in years. You've never even met the younger three."

"I know." Their first child is right about the same age as my daughter, Ally Johnna, would have been. Her name is Jeanne Marie (named after me). Charlie and Deidre always send me pictures of my nieces and nephews and I have scrapbooked every single one of those pictures. I love those children even though I have very rarely seen them. I send fabulous presents at their birthdays and Christmas, after consulting with Charlie about what they want. It is too bad they have such an off-her-rocker aunt who can hardly stand to look at them in real life without feeling like a sword is sticking perpendicularly through her heart, but I do adore them from afar.

"I'll come see them, Charlie, I will."

"You will?"

I almost cried at the hopeful note in Charlie's voice.

"When? How about this weekend?"

"I can't this weekend."

"Why not this weekend?"

"I have plans."

"What plans?"

"Fun plans. Thrilling plans." Plans to watch this frog leap from one rock to another. I decided not to voice that.

"Jeanne, I know it's hard for you, but the kids need an aunt. Deidre has no siblings, they need you—"

"I don't want to talk about that, Charlie." I snapped the words out like the rat-a-tat-tat of a machine gun, and regretted it. "I'm sorry. I will come and see the kids. I want to, I do." I thought about it. Maybe I did. Maybe I could handle it.

I closed my eyes, waited for that tight vise on my heart to loosen.

"And you'll call Bob Davis right away? He'll set you up with an appointment with Jay. This'll all go quick, you'll be interviewed, offered the job, and we'll get you moved to Portland. This is all settled. No problems."

"No problems." But there were problems, pesky problems. I didn't want to work, didn't want to write, didn't want to help some egotistical whack-jerk lying politician get reelected.

Charlie reeled off a phone number twice, told me he loved me, I told him the same thing, and we said our good-byes and I love yous again. I watched the water swirl around my ankles. I love the colors in water. In very clean rivers, it looks clear, but the water is actually made up of different colors, clear colors, but colors all the same, and beneath the surface is a whole other life.

I bent my knees and submerged myself completely in the river, except for my cell phone. I closed my eyes, life blocked out, the current gently pushing me this way and that. When I couldn't hold my breath another second, I stood up again. Dripping wet, I got out and headed toward Rosvita's, picking up the almost empty wine bottle I'd left on the grass.

I thought about Charlie's call. I didn't want to work, but life is filled with all of these jolly, money-sucking surprises, isn't it?

For example, I didn't know at that wet moment that I was going to buy a decrepit, sagging home in desperate and sad need of immediate and extensive repairs in the next weeks. That was a money-sucker.

I did know that dealing with Slick Dick was going to be another herculean money-sucker.

I went to Rosvita's back porch, stripped naked, then climbed up the stairs to my room. There were no other guests, and Rosvita was out visiting a friend in Portland who was a bacteriologist.

As soon as I was dry and dressed I headed to The Opera Man's Café to get myself pancakes, as I did at least five times a week. Call it therapy. Call it coming to terms with my pancake past. I couldn't get enough.

For the first time in years I actually felt like I was making a few friends. The people in The Opera Man's Café smiled at me when I brought my sorry self in, waved me over, talked to me in a normal tone about normal stuff as if I was a normal person. I often ate with them and their good cheer always warmed me as much as the coffee.

Bring on the syrup.

CHAPTER 7

"He should die," Rosvita declared several evenings later, as we drank cognac in front of her fire. "Dan Fakue, owner of the infested, teaming, steaming migrant camps, should die." She thudded her mug of cognac down on a little wood table next to her. Rosvita believes that cognac should be drunk from a mug, no need to shortchange yourself.

"There are so many germs doing their germy thing there. For sure there is *Cryptosporidiosis*. That is a disease caused by itty-bitty microscopic parasites, crawling and twisting in the intestines. *The intestines.* It can be spread through feces. *Feces!*"

Yuck. What a vision.

Rosvita counted off on her fingers all other diseases she thought one might acquire in a migrant camp. I settled deeper into my cushy red chair, put my feet up on a leather footrest, and had a nice long drinkie. We had flipped off all the lights so we could "rest our eyes."

"Plus, there are children living there, *children*." She shoved both fists up in the air. She did not wear gloves in her own home because she believed not a single germ lived or flourished there. "And I know something very creepy and illegal is going on there, *very creepy*, but I can't get the women to tell me anything. I speak a little Spanish, but not much."

I nodded. Rosvita was correct. She spoke *a little* Spanish, but not much. She had no idea, however, how absolutely awful her accent was with the little Spanish that she knew. I could barely understand her Spanish myself and I knew it backward and forward. I could see why a conversation with Rosvita would be a might challenging.

"I can smell it," she said.

"You can smell something creepy or illegal? That's not too surprising, Rosvita. It should be illegal to live in squalor. What's the creepy part?" I tilted my cognac up to my lips again.

"I don't know," she muttered, twining her fingers, her black hair shining in the firelight. She was wearing a kimono. Red and black with a dragon on it. "I don't know, but I know that pissant Dan and something's up. He's hiding something. I'll bet he has paraphilia. That's someone who has strange sexual desires and behaviors. He's a dirty, germ-filled devil."

I nodded. "He's definitely the devil." We both settled back in silence in our chairs.

I had seen Dan Fakue at the grocery store the other day. He was built like an old tank with fat, thickened shoulders, a bulging stomach, and the meanest face I'd ever seen. It looked like a combination of slug, bulldog, and vomit. He gave me a Boob-Waist-Butt Look (BWBL) and smirked at me as if he thought a flaming passion would overwhelm me because of his physical analysis and I would be sure to hoppity-hop-hop into bed with him, legs spread, ankles grooving in the air.

I stopped, staring at him from the top of his head to his toes, stopping at his nipples, his stomach, and his penis area. I gave him the once-over again—and laughed. Nice and loud.

He bunched up his fists like he was going to slug me. I was holding two gallons of milk, which I held up like I might heave them at his gnarly face. We stared at each other for a while until this weird light came into his eyes and I knew he was a demented man who liked to dominate feisty women and he would find it pleasurable to "tame" me, so to speak.

"Forget it," I said aloud. "I don't date men who force their employees to live in miniscule sewage-infested pits of hell."

Dan the Migrant Devil, as I'd instantly dubbed him, looked surprised that I spoke, then recovered himself. "I didn't ask you for no date, lady."

"I know. I was giving you the chance never to waste your breath in future."

He looked furious again. I do love my smart mouth.

"Do you want to go to hell?" I asked.

"When we die, we die, woman. There ain't no hell and there ain't no heaven."

I nodded. "You're so very wrong. I hope you like heat. Scratch that. I hope you like feeling as if your body is boiling. Scratch that. I hope you like catching on fire because you are going to hell when you die for the appalling way that you're treating your workers."

"Hey, fancy pants, I don't give a flying fu—"

"Please don't swear," I told him.

He gave me a look of disgust, his face red, a vein throbbing in his neck like a pulsing snake. "Stay out of my business."

"No." I swung the milk gallons back and forth.

"What?"

"I said, no. No no no. I won't stay out of your business as long as you're abusing people."

He laughed. It was a mean, sticky, black and gooey laugh that made my skin crawl. "All right. Go for it. Try to shut me down. Happened before, it'll happen again, and I'll win. But it'll be fun to see more of you. A lot more." He gave me the slimy, gooey look. Up and down (BWBL).

When he was done, I did the same. I cocked my head, got down on my haunches, set down the milk, and stared right, straight at his groin. I laughed. I laughed and laughed. Laughed at his groin. Laughed until I cried. (Tears come easily to me now, I might have mentioned.) "Is that it? *Is that it?*" I held up two fingers three inches apart.

"It's more than you've ever seen!" His face was splotchy red, making his yellow teeth look all the yellower. "I ain't had any complaints in that department."

Wasn't he a funny man! "You're a funny man, Dan, so funny." I held my fingers up again. Three inches. "How could you not have a complaint?"

He huffed and swore.

"Please don't swear!" I cackled, still staring, straight at that midregion.

He took two steps toward me, which for some insane reason made me laugh even harder, and swore again.

"Please don't swear!"

"Stupid bitch."

I admonished him once more for his foul language and he spun on his fat foot and left the store, after bellowing "Cunttttt!"

Several older ladies with white hair were staring at me when I stood up.

I muffled my chuckles. This was not good. I imagined what they were thinking: New gal in town. On haunches. In grocery store. Staring, laughing hysterically at Dan's dick.

Again, not good.

But, the above-mentioned situation proves that most of the time you shouldn't try to guess what people are thinking about you.

One of them hobbled toward me, hand outstretched, smile beaming. "I don't believe we've met, dear," she said. "My name is Linda. These two crazy gals are my cohorts, Louise and Margie."

After the introductions, the three women ogled me through these huge, matching glasses. The frames were either purple or blue or green. Louise leaned heavily on her cane, struggled down onto her haunches, and cocked her head, exactly as I had done to Dan when I was looking at his crotch. "Is that it? *Is that it?*" she asked, her voice cackling with age. She held her fingers up about two inches apart. "Is that it?"

Linda and Margie both sputtered, and the three of them, together, I kid you not, flung back their heads at the same time and laughed like hyena triplets.

Margie scooted her walker closer to me, peered at her friends through narrowed eyes and said, "Do you like heat? I hope you like feeling as if your body is *boiling*!" She said the word "boiling" deep and gravelly, for emphasis.

"I don't date men who force their employees to live in miniscule sewage-infested pits of hell!" Linda cackled.

"Please don't swear!" Margie announced. "Please don't swear, dammit!"

"You're a funny man," Louise announced, shaking her finger. "A funny man!"

The women found themselves terribly amusing and their laughter tunneled through that store. Dear me, but they thought they were funny.

When they settled down, Linda wiped her eyes and said, "He's trouble, Fancy Pants, you watch out." Louise told me he was as dangerous as a rattlesnake. She hissed for emphasis. Margie said that she wished he would fall into a hole and land in hell, that everyone did, and wasn't it disgusting how he treated the migrant workers? Shameful, horrible, we all agreed before the ladies ambled out, telling me to come to tea and vodka next Wednesday.

Why, golly gee, why do I court trouble? I asked myself as I left. But the answer came quick: I will not keep my mouth shut about sick and horrible things like vermin-filled sheds.

Rosvita and I had both made complaints with the state and the county about Dan the Migrant Devil. They all knew exactly who he was and all about the problems.

Clearly nothing would get done.

I knew that I would have to do something about dissolving that migrant camp. I didn't know what, but I would.

Little did I know that the problem would be taken right out of my hands.

*   *   *

The next morning Rosvita and I went to breakfast at The Opera Man's Café. Donovan was singing a song of joy, his voice booming off the log walls. When he caught sight of Rosvita, who was wearing a trio of white flowers in her black hair and a purple lace dress, he hustled on over. As soon as we were seated, menus in hand, coffee before us, he burst into song about a man in love with a woman who did not know that he existed. He sang it in Italian and English. With great gusto. He about blew my ears out.

Rosvita hummed along with him while she glanced at the menu, her white-gloved hands tapping the table. I marveled at Donovan's incredible voice; Rosvita hardly seemed to notice. When he was done, everyone in the restaurant clapped. Rosvita asked for a mushroom and cheese omelet. "Cook those eggs until they are almost as hard as rocks," she told him. "Hard as rocks."

Donovan was our waiter, as usual, though he rarely waited on anyone else, I was told, except for Oregon's governor, when the man was at his vacation home here in Weltana. Donovan thought the governor was a "real man, not a pansy. He says what he thinks, he does what he wants to do, and when he gets vacation time, he goes fishing."

As I watched Rosvita and Donovan, I was surprised to feel a bit of a smile tugging at my ole mouth.

A wee smile. In that café with a brick fireplace, twinkling white lights, long wood tables, an ex-opera singer, and a germ fanatic.

A wee, tiny smile, but it was there.

That surprised me.

Each time I ventured into the river for my daily multihour crying/drinking walk, I noticed a two-story white house across the way from Rosvita's. The paint was cracking and chipped like dead skin; the floorboards of the front and back decks rotted through and sagging; and the siding was falling off strip by strip like a house stripper. The house looked like it was sagging into itself as a deflating silicon fake boob might. It looked like it felt done for.

I related to that house like no one's business simply because it looked like me. Only it was a house, I am a person and, I assumed, it did not have half the shoe collection that I had.

A few days later, on the way back from my crying/drinking walk along the river, with a bottle of wine, I stopped and stared. No one lived in the house, Rosvita had told me. The old man and his wife who had lived there died six months apart years ago and there were no relatives. A Realtor had tried to sell it for a while, but no one was interested. The sign lay flat on the grass.

I gingerly tiptoed up the sinking front steps and tried to open the door. At first, it wouldn't budge. I pushed against it and it crashed to the floor. Dust and dirt billowed up in great clouds.

While I waited for the dust to clear, I took another gulp of wine straight out of the bottle. It was only 2:00 in the afternoon, so I was restraining myself.

I stepped on the door and invited myself in. The largish living room was to my left, the dining room to my right. Stairs climbed to the second story. It was dark and dreary inside, like an oversize cave, and the floor creaked beneath trodden-down green carpet. I smelled the expected must and mold.

The floor in the little hallway to the kitchen wobbled and I wondered if it would give out under my weight. The mice scrambled to hide, thoroughly put out, I'm sure, that a human had invaded their home. The kitchen cabinets, dark brown like poop, hung at odd angles and the laminate counters were chewed up and stained.

The kitchen opened up to a large family room and eating nook, but it had only one window over the sink and a cracked sliding glass door.

I decided to do some miniremodeling and pulled at the blinds. They came unhinged and crashed to the floor. Sunlight flooded in, making even that damp and dark room seem a thousand times more cheerful. I pulled the blinds off the sliding glass door, opened it, and let in clean mountain air. I could almost feel the house exhaling around me with relief.

I peered out at the river sparkling beyond the trees. The house had a great view, at least. I heard birds chirping, leaves rustling in the breeze and, right beneath my feet, the sound of an animal moving. I guessed it was a possum or a raccoon. I also heard a munching sound in the wall near me. I guessed it was termites. A spider crawled over my shoe. I guessed there were probably millions of them here.

I took another swig of wine, and studied the ceiling. It had a multitude of water stains. The wood paneling over the walls, also the color of poop, was peeling off, and the carpet was alternately wet, crunchy, or almost nonexistent. The putrid diseases Rosvita could find!

There was one bathroom. The tub was filled with mouse shit. The shower curtain was covered in yuck and, again, the ceiling was stained. The faucets on the sink were rusted through.

Feeling adventurous, I climbed the stairs up to the second floor, stepping carefully, much like a tightrope walker.

Upstairs, all the windows were covered with dark blinds. I yanked those blinds off again and the sun did its work. The landing was quite large, more like an upstairs loft, and there were three bedrooms. The mattresses were still in all of the rooms and smelled like urine, so I figured a few homeless people had been here in the past. There was also a collection of sick and tired furniture, including a rocking chair. Outside of the master bedroom, there was a small deck. I did not dare step on that deck. Falling through the air is not my idea of fun.

In the distance, about 100 yards beyond the house, I could see a smaller white structure nestled in a few pine trees. It was one level, but it looked like it might have a basement. I figured it had been used as a guest house.

I poked around again downstairs. The whole house smelled like a nursing home for old people without the disinfectant. I knew the stains on the ceiling indicated terrible water problems.

The roof reminded me of the caved in part of a diaphragm. A rat scurried across the floor as my eyes located a pile of ants in another corner.

The house that looked like me was in ruins. It should be bulldozed.

Demolished and hauled away.

I loved it.

I ran back to Rosvita's with my wine and called the Realtor.

I asked the price.

He told me.

I laughed, choked a bit on my wine, offered him half that.

He refused.

I laughed again, as if he had told a smashingly good joke. "If you can get someone to pay that price for that mouse-infested, urine-stained, mold-growing dump, I will eat my left arm off while wearing fake vampire teeth, buddy. Have a nice day." I put the receiver down and waited.

The phone rang two minutes later and he agreed to the price.

I thanked him for his time.

When we were done with our little chat, I went back to my new house and listened to the music of the river, the high notes and low notes and all the notes in between.

CHAPTER 8

In my anger management class there are four other people besides me and Emmaline Hallwyler, the woman dressed in white, who yells and tells people not to be pathetic.

There is Bradon King who is African-American, about six-feet-six inches tall, bald, and a man who favored pink, lavender, or sky blue dress shirts. When you look that macho you can wear any darn color you want, you know. After talking to him for several minutes at the beginning of the first class, where I found out he plays the piano because his grandmother insisted he do so for two hours every day so he stayed out of trouble, I could not for a minute think that he would have the slightest bit of a temper, let alone hurt anyone. He is forty-five years old, has been married to the same woman for twenty-five years, and they have five children.

Bradon was there because he is rather unhappy with the way the city's school system treats minorities, particularly African-American students, and at a recent school board meeting he felt compelled to stand on top of the table, where the all-white school board sat glaring at an almost all African-American audience, and refused to get down. He informed the board that they obviously didn't care about black kids, didn't care about their futures, didn't care that they weren't getting a decent education, didn't care, didn't care, didn't care. He smashed two chairs. He smashed the chairs to show what would happen to black kids' future if they weren't educated.

"Their futures are smashed. Splintered. Broken. Gone. Their futures are gone. We need to educate these kids!" he yelled to the raucous, supportive cheers of everyone in the room, except the all white board.

The police were called. Bradon refused to apologize for not apologizing when he yelled that the people on the school board were a bunch of lazy-ass, racist, rich, white people, living in their own tight little boxes, and completely out of touch with the troubles that minority kids face every single day. The paper wrote about it—ya-dee-da-deeah and wham. Bradon King, owner of a very successful local construction company, King Construction, landed in anger management class.

"Every year more black kids drop out of school. Every year no one cares. I think the schools are glad to see 'em go. But what happens to them? They're teenagers, Jeanne," he told me. "Kids. And their future is, at that moment, zero. Why doesn't anyone care? Because the kids are black? You can damn well bet that if a bunch of rich, white sixteen-year-old girls all started dropping out of school and selling drugs on the corner that people would be screaming their heads off and demanding change. And change would happen. So are black kids dispensable? Is that what they're saying? If not, why aren't the schools doing something?"

"The answer eludes me," I said.

"Me, too. That's why I threw chairs," he sighed, making his green beanbag look tiny. I could tell by that sigh he was very tired of this fight. "I threw chairs for black kids."

Then there was Soman Fujiwara. Soman Fujiwara was from somewhere in the Pacific Islands and has worked as an electrician for almost fifteen years. He has a ton of beautiful black braids that drop to his shoulders, kissable lips, and black eyes. He sang for us as a way of "introducing his past and present." It was a lovely, melodious song, even though it was in a language I didn't understand. It filled my mind with images of color-infused sunsets, the smell of cooked ahi, and the taste of mango and pineapple.

When he was done Soman told us it was a song of suffering and death.

Before I could even think for a minute that he was a psychopathic killer and that we were all soon going to be mowed down by an AK-47 he had hidden near his groin, he said, "I'm glad to be here." He patted the side of his yellow beanbag. "I do have a temper. But I have rules to my temper."

I nodded. I had rules to my warped, selfish behavior, too.

"I don't ever show my temper around women. My dad taught me that. He thinks it's disrespectful and so do I. My mama always tells him what to do and he does it. He told me it makes life easier for him. I never hit a woman in my life, no way. None of the men in the Fujiwara family have ever hit a woman and none of them have ever divorced. Ever." He slammed one giant fist into his open palm, then slipped a glance toward Becky, a woman who looked like she wanted to disappear into her beanbag. "But I'm not married. Never been married. But I would like to get married. Someday. I mean, not tonight, but someday. If I meet, you know, a woman, who wants to get married." Another glance went sliding to Becky. "Someday. Like, you know, to me."

I swear I could see a hint of a blush. He flicked his braids over his shoulders, cleared his throat. "I also don't hit when there are any children around. Children cry when they see that type of shit and man, they get their feelings hurt so easily and they get scared. Can't do that. I got nieces and nephews and they love their Uncle Soman." He scratched his chin and looked contemplative. "But I don't seem to have a problem with sluggin' men when they piss me off. My fists get like this." He showed us his clenched fists. "And I go boom, boom, boom, and they're down. Down and mushed."

I could relate again. Only I preferred using peanut oil.

"That's why I'm here. I got a sluggin' problem."

Soman sat next to Drake Windham. Drake was a white guy around the age of forty. He wore an expensive suit and a tie. He was about six feet tall and looked slimy in the way that men look when they are dishonest and value money above all else and think women are toys and believe that the more gals they sleep with the longer their dick gets. I am sure that there are women out there who would say Drake was gorgeous with his slicked-back black hair and his not-quite shaven jaw and big lips and big shoulders, but all I saw was this—gonorrhea.

His face looked like a lemon to me. A lemon who didn't like lemons. He had a snotty, snobby expression as though he thought he was a simply sensational, stylish, and super-fabulous slice of mankind (pretty good alliteration, although not perfect). When he held my hand he did the ole BWBL (Boob-Waist-Butt Look) with his limpid eyes half closed, as though he was trying to be sexy wexy.

He had smirked at me when we first met, his hand limp and wet and reminding me of a used condom. I refrained from saying that.

He leaned close and whispered, his breath smelling like dead garlic mixed with manure: "Looks like we're the only normal ones here, sweetheart. Goddammit, getta load of this lot of losers. We've got jungle men and a drug addict and a counselor who is so New Wave I want to hand her some drugs and leave, goddammit. What a joke. Drink afterward?"

I removed my hand from his wet condom. "Unlikely," I said.

First he looked shocked, his eyebrows bursting toward his slick hairline. "Married?" He glanced down at my hand.

Sheesh. Men always think this. If you won't go out with them the only *possible* reason is that you are married. "No."

"Ah, got it." He winked at me, did the BWBL again. "Dating a married man? Don't worry, honey, your secret's safe with me."

Now, how he jumped to that sick conclusion was beyond me, so don't ask.

"I like married women the best." He rolled his tongue around in his left cheek like a human weasel. "They don't want anyone to know what's going on, they don't press you for commitment, and all they want is to have sex and go home to their kids and vans."

This puzzled me. Married women wanted to have sex with Mr. Gonorrhea? "This puzzles me. Do you actually mean to tell me that there are married women out there who wish to have sexual intercourse with you?" (No need to be crass here.)

I heard a gurgle of shock erupt from his throat.

"Do they come back after the first time?"

He gurgled again, composed himself and winked at me. BWBL. "Smart-ass. I like that in a woman."

"Fab!" I said, not smiling. "So fab!"

"I like feisty women. I like when women pretend they're not interested when they are. And I like the chase. God, I like the chase. Women love it when I'm chasin'."

"Women chase you?" I leaned forward, conspiratorially. "Really?"

"Shit, yes, I've got women after me." But he flushed red, the color creeping from his creepy neck to his creepy hairline.

"So, to be clear. When you say women are 'after you,' you mean in the sense that they want to have sexual intercourse with you? They do this willingly?"

He flushed redder, but he was royally pissed off, too. "Yeah, they do, I already said that. What's wrong with you? You can't hear or something? I got a ton of hot women after me for that."

"You're flushing redder," I said. "Is redder a word, do you think?"

"Hey, whatever your name is, I've forgotten it already. I made more money in a week than anybody else here does in a year so get off my case."

Now, how he jumped to this conclusion was beyond me, so don't ask.

"You're kidding me!" I rearranged my facial features so I would look appropriately awed. "You have actually viewed all of our tax returns? Is that legal? Well, rats! It's that Internet again. So much information! I'll have to tell everyone here that you're the richest so we can be impressed together!"

"Hell, all I'm saying is I'm looking around here and I know I've got more money than anyone and I'm stuck with this bunch of lower rung losers."

I opened my eyes real wide. "So you're making a ton of money, more than anybody else here, more than us losers. So much you can probably *buy* a bunch of women. A harem." I snapped my fingers together three times. "In fact, is that why those women are after you? I bet that's it!" I put my hands on my hips and cocked my head at him, as if the mystery had been solved. "Hookers should not count as 'hot women after you.' That's stretching things a bit, don't you think?"

"No . . ." He was totally flustered. "I mean, yes, I mean, no! I got money—"

"Yes, I've heard that. You have money to buy women." I gave him a BWBL, although he had no boobs.

"I don't have to buy my women—" He was a'flustered.

"Poor hookers," I whispered sadly. "Poor hookers."

"I don't buy hookers!" This he shouted in frustration. Everyone in the loft stared at him and there was quite a silence.

"Well, that's jolly good to hear!" I announced. "Women should never be bought!"

"Shove off, Jeanne." He glared at me, all red, all fidgety.

"Shove off?" I tilted my head at him. "I don't think I can 'shove off.' I assaulted my boyfriend and my attorney says I have to be here so it makes me look repentant in court. What did you do?"

"This," Emmaline announced as she floated toward us, arms outstretched, white silk outfit floating behind her, "this is Drake Windham. He's in anger management class because he has a history of beating up women."

I stared at him, pretending to be aghast. "Do you beat up the poor hookers before or after you pay them to have sexual intercourse? Or do you beat up all the wives with the minivans who are panting after you?"

Soman had to step in between us at that point and a little shoving and pushing went on as Drake said bad words to me. When Drake said to Soman, "Hey, Jungle Man, get the fuck away from me," Bradon had to intervene when Soman shoved him up against the wall, his huge hand plastering Drake's neck to the wall like a strangled rooster.

Soman said, his barrel voice ringing through that room like thunder, "Only sissies beat up women, you hear that, you stupid wimp white boy? Only weak, scared, sick sissies attack women, you fuck. And only men who can't get laid go after hookers who are only hooking 'cause they got no choice in the matter, you gay asshole."

(I did not ask Soman not to swear. It would have been inappropriate.)

Bradon and Emmaline got Soman to calm down. Drake looked like he was about ready to pee his pretty pants. He huffed and puffed against that wall, and when his rooster neck was released he squirreled around with his tie and ran his hand through his pretty hair while whining, "Don't touch me again and I don't . . . I don't . . . I don't *buy* women!"

Emmaline stepped forward. "I will have no lying in this class, Drake! None! I will not spare you! You have two arrests for soliciting prostitution! Two!" She held up the pointer fingers of both hands. "Disgusting, appalling, horrible! We will be discussing at length that particular perversion and your continual assaults on women!"

Bradon and Soman looked disgusted, both shaking their heads.

"Sick, man," said Soman. "You fuckin' sick."

"*Hookers*," Bradon said. "How can you take advantage of women like that? How can you debase someone by participating in that act? How can you disrespect a human enough to pay them to do something that they actually abhor doing? How can you live with yourself after you've committed such a repulsive, criminal act? The poor hookers."

I laughed. Couldn't help it. Bradon had echoed my words exactly. "I said the same thing," I told Bradon.

Drake stared up at Bradon's chin, who was still towering over him. "Back off. I know all about your kind of gangs and you don't scare me." His voice quivered and he leaned hard against the wall as if his spine was made of goo.

For a moment Bradon stared straight down at him, all six-feet-six disgusted inches of him. "For your information, I am not in a gang and neither is Soman. I have been married to my wife for twenty-five years and I can tell you she would not approve of my involvement in any sort of gang. Furthermore, we do not allow our children to run around in gangs either, unless it is called the Philharmonic Gang of Portland, in which both of my older boys play their instruments, or the Galaxy Gang, which is a science exploration group that meets weekly after school. All of my children have participated in that program because of their interest in space, aeroneutronics, thermal dynamics, and the engineering involved with the building of the space shuttles."

Bradon put both his palms, flat down, on either side of Drake's head and leaned in close, his dark face inches away from Drake's. "Now you listen close, you white priss. You and I are not going to get along unless you can control that ugly temper of yours, you got that? If you take a swing at anyone in here, or if you are rude or display unsightly behavior again, I will personally shove your head through the wall with one hand, do you get that, you hooker-buying, woman-beating loser?"

Drake seemed to get that. He nodded weakly.

"Good. Now go sit in the orange beanbag and do not speak, so we can all pretend you are not here." Drake nodded, swallowed hard, and pushed his pretty hair back again. He sat in the orange beanbag with his spine of goo.

And finally there was Becky Norwick. She looked like a blond shadow or, to describe her better, like string cheese and depression mixed up together. She sat in the blue beanbag.

"I'm Becky."

I wanted to say, "Hi, Becky" like I hear they do in AA meetings, but this was not AA; this was anger management. This was AM, so I didn't. At that moment I vaguely thought I should get my butt into AA, too.

Becky said, "I've got an anger problem because I've got a drug problem. I started doing drugs because I was angry about how I looked. I wanted to be thinner."

I studied her, her blue beanbag almost engulfing her tiny body. She sure got herself the "thinner" wish.

"The drugs destroyed my life which made me more angry. So I took more drugs and got angrier when I couldn't get more. I started doing things . . ." She broke off and her voice cracked. She wrapped her arms around herself. "I did things I can't get out of my mind, can't believe that I did." Soman reached over and patted her shoulder.

"Hey, girl, we all done things we regret. It's okay. Gotta forgive yourself. Get it out of your head, you know?"

"That's the problem." Becky looked up and dried her tears. "It's stuck in my head like an arrow right through my forehead. I went into treatment last year, got out, screwed up, and went back into treatment for a long time, and now I'm scared I'll screw up again. It's like the drugs are calling my name. I can hear them."

We waited in silence for Becky to continue.

"I started in all this when I was a teenager. My brothers and my parents tried to help me, but I ran away. I ran away from all these funny, loving people with my drug dealer. I was seventeen. I lost my family." She ran her hands through scraggly blond hair, then over her pale, makeupless face. "Seven years ago I lost my family."

We waited for her to say more, her face twisting in misery.

"For what? For a drug dealer, then another drug dealer. Instead of sleeping in a house with a pink room, I've slept in slimy hotels and doorways and parks and cars. Instead of riding my horse in the afternoon, I've spent my afternoons trying to buy drugs. Instead of celebrating birthdays with cake and candles, I count the needle scars on my arms. I'm angry. Angry at myself. Angry at how stupid I am. My anger always leaps up at me, it seems. It's always leaping." Tears funneled down her cheeks. "I cry and cry. Then I cry more."

For some reason all of us strangers seemed content with the silence as we contemplated Becky's leaping anger.

I felt for the poor woman. I did.

It was time for me. I was in the purple beanbag. "I'm Jeanne Stewart. I'm here because I took revenge on my cheating boyfriend. His name is Slick Dick." That was a little extra information they didn't need, but I felt compelled to throw it on in. "The police have seen fit to file assault charges against me for a small incident against Slick Dick and now he is also suing me for all my money plus any money I make in this lifetime and in heaven, if I make it there, which is doubtful." I thrummed my fingers against the beanbag. "I'm here because I'm trying to make myself look better in front of the judge, but my true wish is that I had done more damage to Slick Dick."

Becky, Soman, and Bradon nodded their heads. Drake glared.

"Some people need to be damaged," I said. I raised my eyebrows at Drake when I said that.

Becky, Soman, and Bradon nodded their heads again. "Damn straight," said Soman.

"Although I don't condone or indulge in violence," Bradon said, adding, "well, usually I don't. But the people who are so damn comfortable in their cushy privileged lives that they can't reach out and change one iota to accommodate or help someone different than themselves are infuriating."

I snuck a peep at Drake. His pretty face had this stricken look on it.

Emmaline sat in silence.

"I have a lot of anger." I said this quite matter-of-factly. "Some days I think I live for it."

I was done. There was silence again.

Becky spoke. Her voice was rough and yet soft, too. Like rocks and cotton candy mixed. "Me, too. Sometimes I think the only thing alive in me is my anger."

"Yeah, I'm plain pissed off sometimes," said Soman. "Plain pissed off."

"I think anger is in my genetic muscles," Bradon said. He smiled. The man had a beaming smile that reached those dark soft eyes.

"You want to see anger in muscles, man?" Soman asked. He stood up and flexed, making grunting sounds, his braids dropping over his muscles. He did a front flex, a back flex, arms up, arms curved down. He hummed the same song he sang at the beginning of class. We were all quite impressed with his muscles, everyone except Drake who looked rather pale. Like glue.

Emmaline's voice cut across the loft like a dull razor on a chalkboard. "Pathetic. All of you. You are not grasping the goal of anger management class. This is not a joke. It is not a laugh. Your anger is eating your insides and you all sit there and laugh. Stand up before I throw something!"

We didn't move.

"I said stand up, you miserable, anger-ridden people. Stand!"

We stood.

"Close your furious eyes and channel your anger."

We tried to channel. I closed my eyes. I channeled my anger toward Slick Dick and hoped that he would get hit by a piano dropping from a high-rise.

"Unbelievable." I flicked open one eye. Emmaline had her hands on her hips. "You're not trying to fix yourselves, not trying to get rid of all this stupid, useless, unproductive anger. I can tell. You're indulging yourselves. You're not thinking of peace, you're thinking of everything that pisses you off. You're making lists. You're thinking of ways to get revenge."

Soman coughed.

Bradon sighed.

Becky said, "My thoughts are stuck."

"Stop. Now. Keep your eyes shut, you ridiculous people."

I didn't feel ridiculous. A flying piano was possible, but I didn't feel that was the time to bring it up. I wanted a good grade out of anger management class or a sticker or something.

"Hit!" Emmaline suddenly roared, arms outstretched. All of our eyes popped open. I jumped, so did Becky.

"I said hit! Hit! Hit!" Emmaline screeched, flapping her arms.

Knowing that Bradon wouldn't hit me because he is a gentleman and knowing, too, that Soman wouldn't hit me because none of the men in his family hit their women, I was not alarmed. Drake shrank into his beanbag. He did not want to get pummeled. Out of the corner of my eye I looked at Becky. Emmaline's yelling had made her go pale. Was I supposed to hit Becky? Hitting Becky was terribly unappealing.

"The bags!" Emmaline bellowed. "Hit the punching bags! Hard! Release the anger forever! Come on you downtrodden, seething people! Hit!"

The five of us downtrodden, seething people faced those bags and started punching. Soman and Bradon sent theirs flying, but Becky didn't do too bad, either, for being a skinny gal. Drake punched his carefully, as though he didn't want to mess up his nails.

I beat mine senseless.

After about thirty-five minutes our fearless leader told us sweating people to head to the craft table that instant.

"The violence is temporarily out of you people, now let's replace it with art," she said, throwing little pink towels at all of us so we could wipe our sweaty anger away. Soman and me and Bradon were soaked. Drake had removed his tie and jacket. I knew Becky had cried while she'd hit her bag.

"Art your anger," Emmaline ordered.

None of us except for Drake seemed to have a problem with arting our anger. All he could think to draw was the two policemen who had arrested him. "I'm going to sue their asses off. They will never work in this town again. I know everybody. Every. Body. *Everybody who's somebody* and these two will be lucky if they can get a job in a tiny town in Idaho when I'm done with them."

"Shut up," Soman said, standing up again. "Shut the fuck up."

Bradon stood up, too. Without a word, Soman grabbed one side of Drake, Bradon the other. They picked him straight out of his chair and dropped him back into his orange beanbag.

"Hey, you touch me again, and I'll sue your asses off," Drake quivered. "I got a bunch of lawyers in my back pocket. When I say jump, they'll jump, when I say—"

"For God's sake," Emmaline screamed. "Shut up! Really! None of us want to hear any more out of your farting mouth, Drake!"

Drake's farting mouth fell open in shock. I guess no one had ever referred to his mouth as a "farting mouth." Soman and Bradon picked up his beanbag and flipped him over on his stomach. He said, "Ooofff," when he landed, his legs spraddled out.

Soman brandished a very large piece of metal in Drake's direction when it appeared that Drake might speak again, then settled back into his seat at the art table when he didn't. He made a six-foot-tall tower using metal and rope. I must say it was quite stunning. Somehow he blended all the rust colors and the ragged edges and the silver shine to form this modern-looking piece of art, like something you would see in the middle of a city park.

"His name's Oscar," he said when Emmaline told him to tell the class about his art piece. "Like Oscar the Grouch. Oscar's sick to shit of his anger, man. His anger is eating him alive and it's gonna keep eating him until he's got no guts left and his flesh is green. Plus his anger makes his knuckles hurt when he bashes someone's face and he's tired of that, too."

Bradon grabbed watercolor paints, dipped a brush in water, and sat doing nothing. Finally he painted a scene of a rundown school. In front of the school was a young African-American boy. In his arms he held another African-American boy. It was clear that the boy was sick. On the ground there were two syringes, beer bottles, and a bong. A wooden cross lay at his feet. The boy was looking straight up at the sky, as if asking God why he hadn't helped. "It's the hopelessness I see in so many black boys' eyes," Bradon told us. "Hopelessness. Emptiness. Detachment."

Becky traced her hands with colored pencils over and over on the same piece of white butcher paper. The hands arched like a rainbow. She decorated all of the hands with sequins, beads, and glitter.

When it was a gleaming, bright, beautiful design, she poured black paint over the whole thing, covering every inch of the design. "The hands reflect how I was before the drugs; the paint is how I am now. Not very original, but there it is."

I couldn't figure out what to do. Art my anger? I grabbed a huge piece of light green paper. I told Emmaline to trace me on it. I used different colored markers to write down on every inch of my body what I was pissed off about. I wrote down Slick Dick's name on my vagina. I wrote my mother's name, Ally Mackey, and my father's name, Grayson Mackey, and my grand-parents' names, Henri and Rosa (Sanchez) Monihan, across my heart. Across my whole body I wrote Johnny's name and the name of our baby girl, Ally Stewart. I wrote a ton of words all over the paper, too, in various sizes. Lost. Alone. Lonely. Dead. I kept writing and writing and writing.

When I looked up, Emmaline, Bradon, Becky, and Soman were all gathered around, watching me.

"Damn," said Bradon, awe in his voice. "You are one angry woman."

Becky patted me rhythmically on the back, sniffling and murmuring, "Everything will work out, everything will work out." I decided that I should take Becky to lunch one day. I liked her. Soman covered my hand with his, his braids mixed with my gold curls. "Give me some of that anger, Jeanne. I'll put it in my fist and the next time I smash someone I'll transfer all your anger to him and that's a promise."

I sat back on my rear. "Thank you, Soman, that's a good idea. 'Cause I swear if I don't get rid of this anger I'm going to end up looking like your Oscar."

The anger management class did not end well that evening.

After the art lesson, we sat in a circle in our beanbags: Me in purple, Bradon in green, Soman in yellow, Becky in blue, Drake in orange.

Drake opened his mouth and started farting again. "You people . . ." He shook his head as if we were all pathetic. "Hey, I'm sorry for earlier, but I don't even belong here. I clearly don't fit in."

"That'd be the damn truth," Soman said. "You're like a boil."

"There does appear to be some differences," Bradon added.

"Do you all know *who I am*? Do you have any clue? Well," he scoffed. "Of course, you don't. We don't travel in the same social circles, do we?"

I rolled my eyes. "No, I make it a habit not to hang out with men who buy hookers. In fact, I am rarely trolling the streets to buy sex, so we would not have rubbed elbows, or any other body part."

"That's fucking *it*. I'm calling my lawyers—do you get that, Jeanne? That's lawyers, in the plural—"

"Gall. Do you get caught so often with your hookers that you need a whole phalanx of attorneys? I love that word! Phalanx." I snuck a glance at Soman. He grinned and flipped his braids. "It's so phallic, phalanx is."

"You're defaming my character, you loose-mouthed, stuck-up—"

"That will be all!" Bradon roared, leaping to his feet. Soman was right beside him, bright smile gone.

"You will not be mean or rude to women!" Soman shouted.

"Dammit! We already told ya this in the beginning of the class! Ya don't get it? Ya slow or something?"

"Sit! Sit!" Emmaline flapped, her white arms making motions like a seagull. "Sit!"

Soman and Bradon sat, but only after Bradon leaned way down, eye to eye with Drake and said, "Never, *never*, in my presence, be rude to a lady."

"Hey!" Drake said, but his voice was a tad more conciliatory. "I'm trying to point out who I am. I own a company. Okay? You get that? I'm a CEO of a company. Ever heard of D.W. Financial Services? I started D.W. That's me. I'm D.W.—Drake Windham. Built it from scratch two years ago. I employ seven hundred people and control two billion dollars in assets, you got that? Not million, billion. We're growing each day by millions, nationally, internationally—"

"Sounds like a house of cards," Bradon said, yawning. "Any company that grows that fast is growing too fast. Not enough capital behind it. Not enough 'real' money, as I would say. You got debt? You owe somebody a bunch of dough that you don't really have? You paying one debt with other loans? How fast could you really get money out of that company or is the money in thin air?"

Drake started to squirm and twitch and his face flushed itchy red again.

"Your face is red again," I said helpfully. "It looks itchy."

Drake shot invisible spears at me with his eyes. Pow! Pow! "Debt grows a company, don't you know that?"

"Massive debt will sink a company and it'll bring down all the other companies that it's attached to. When that happens, it hurts lots of innocent people in the process. They lose money, jobs, retirement, the whole nine-yards, all because companies have no capital behind them, only debt," said Bradon.

"What are you, King Morality?"

"No. I am Bradon King."

"But you can call him King Bradon, if you want, I should think," I said.

"Stop! Stop!" Emmaline yelled. "Drake, no one gives a monkey's testicles who you think you are. You're here because you beat up on women, because you're a turd with an anger problem, because you won't take responsibility for what a prick you are, and the court insisted that you come here. Now again, shut up! *Shut your farting mouth!*"

CHAPTER 9

It was early in the morning three days after anger management class and I was in no mood to move my body. I'd had three drinks at The Opera Man's Café the other night and Donovan insisted on driving me home. I had planned on making my own drunken way home on foot whilst singing to the stars.

"We're gonna get you all cleaned up here, Jeanne, don't you worry," Donovan had said, as we took a shortcut home along the river. "With all these trees, the river, the deer, and other wildlife, why, how could you not get cleaned up? Nature will give you the power you need."

When we arrived at Rosvita's, they both helped me to bed. "We gotta get this one straightened out," he whispered to her before they both left. "She's a good girl, but she needs help."

When my cell phone rang I fumbled around the white wicker nightstand with one hand, settling back hard onto my pillows on my bed of blue heaven. I grunted a greeting. Like this, "Grrrrm-mmxxx."

"You haven't called Bob Davis yet."

My brother's voice had that pinched tone to it, as if his throat was being wrapped tight by a rope. I knew it was Saturday, and I pictured him at home, at least one of his four well-loved children on his lap. In the background I could hear the other little sweethearts alternately fighting and running around, the birds, the dog, Deidre's voice, and a video game.

"I have called him in my mind," I quipped.

"In your what?" He made a groaning sound way in his throat. "Okay, now you need to quit calling him in your mind and call him for real."

Call him for real. What was real? Was life real? Was I real? Was my depression real or some evil, dark force that had come to live within me, sneaking into my bone marrow in the dead of night? Was my Bronco real and would I really drive it into the Pacific?

"Look, honey, I know you've been through a rough time."

"I'm fine, Charlie. Everything's going fine." I laughed a little. Crazy people laugh inappropriately, I reminded myself. Please stop.

He sighed. "It's not fine. That might work with other people, but it won't with me. I'm worried about you. Why don't you come and see us? You can arrange for an interview in town with Bob and come by for dinner."

"No, I don't think so." I eyed the box filled with photograph books of his children by the dresser, the pictures entered chronologically and decorated with all kinds of colors and shapes and sayings.

"Please, Jeanne, you can't hole up like this, you can't shut down on life, can't disappear."

The brittle laugh popped out again.

"Okay, Charlie, I'll call Bob."

"When?" His question came back ricochet quick.

"I'll call him soon."

"You said that last time."

"But this time I mean it."

He groaned again.

My brittle laugh danced on the edges of his sigh like a sharp steak knife. "I love you, Charlie."

"Call him. I'm worried."

"Soon."

* * *

On Monday, when the sun was making a peek over the river, golden and new, I went out for a run. The water crested like whipped cream. I cried as I ran, letting my tears mix with my sweat. I ran for about an hour, sometimes slow, sometimes fast, trying to outrace my thoughts and my grief for my mother.

Grief is a fast runner, though, so I really had to run.

When I got back to Rosvita's, my feet felt like they were stuck on burning coals, so I kicked off my running shoes and stuck them in the river. My legs, which had both been smashed in the accident, ached a little, so I sat in the river and let the water massage them. They felt better in about fifteen minutes.

When the sun was fully awake I headed toward the mailbox and grabbed the newspaper for Rosvita, water streaming off my butt.

It was an "alternative" newspaper and a photograph on the front page caught my eye. I cackled. I'll be double-darned if it wasn't the mouth-farting idiot from anger management class, Drake Windham!

It appeared that Mr. Windham had crashed his car through the glass windows of a mortuary about 2:00 in the morning. Luckily, there were only dead bodies around at that time of the evening so no one except the corpses were startled by a flying car. When the police found him, he was vomiting in the street, said one of the officers. "The smell of liquor was strong and the open bottles in the car are indicative that alcohol may have been a factor."

The most juicy part of the article mentioned that the married Mr. Windham who, the paper noted had been convicted of assaulting his wife recently, had been drinking and driving with a young woman who was a well-known and well-loved hooker in the city working for an expensive call girl outfit.

The article detailed the comments of the young woman in the car who stated that she was going to call a lawyer first thing in the morning because Mr. Windham had paid her for (sexual acts that were not printed in this newspaper), and it was not her idea of fun to go crashing through the front doors of a mortuary. Her left arm hurt, she noted, *and* her toes, her big toe especially.

"I mean, that's really disrespectful to be popping in on the dead. I had no idea he was going to do that," she said. "One second he has his hand down my shirt telling me I was huge, huge, huge and the next we were flying through glass and he was screaming, 'Oh my God! I'm gonna die! I'm gonna die!' I'm going to sue him for emotional distress and nonpayment. I lost a whole night's work. You can sue for that, can't you? Don't you think I should be compensated?"

It took awhile before I could stop laughing.

I had not forgotten about the migrant camp. My memory was alive and sickened. It had grown claws and fangs and had sunk itself right into my tender skin like a tick the size of a vampire.

I suppose it was the flaming liberal in me that didn't think people should have to live in sheds. I had called one phone number after another in the state department to complain about the situation in the camps. After cutting through bureaucracy as thick as a river of mucus, I finally reached the right place to lodge my complaints again.

The helpful lady there explained to me that the owner, Dan Fakue, had been charged on numerous occasions for neglectful conditions at his camp and had been fined.

"Fined? That's it? He didn't have to go to jail for eight years or, worse, live with the farmers?"

"He had to pay money as a punishment."

"It obviously didn't punish him enough to make him change."

"No, the fine isn't very hiiiiihhhhigh." She dragged the word out, like a stretchy Gumby doll.

I asked her the amount. When she told me, I rolled my eyes. If it were possible, they would have rolled right out of my head and into China. All this monster had to do was figure out how much it would cost to fix up his place vs. pay the annual fine and he had a no-brainer. It was cheaper to pay the fine, by far, than fix the dump up.

"Did you hear me rolling my eyes?" I asked the lady.

She sighed. "I did. I know you're frustrated. I'm sorry I can't do anything else."

I asked to speak to her supervisor and, I dare say, she was happy to hand me off. I spoke to *his* supervisor too and got stonewalled again. The Migrant Devil had paid his fine and that was that, although the man I talked to, who sounded like a snail might if a snail could speak, assured me that they would be returning soon to the Migrant Devil's farm.

I am not sure how, in a democratic society, we can justify letting people live like this—people who are doing the work the average Joe Blow American wouldn't do for an hour without calling his lawyer to report physically abusive conditions, and demanding ten years wages and punitive damages in the millions.

But, there it is.

So, I started thinking about what I could do to help the families. I didn't want it to look like charity. They had their pride. And yet, in those conditions, with children by their sides, would they be willing to set aside pride and take what was given?

Would my grandma's mother have done so for her kids?

From my cushy bed in my room of blue heaven I looked out at the river for an answer.

After a few moments, the river told me what to do.

The next morning, with the birds tootling and the river churning, I pulled on my jeans, sweatshirt, and pink tennis shoes and headed to the local bakery. The bakery is in a dollhouse-size red house fit for a gnome on Main Street. The owner, Zelda Robinson, who is not a day over eighty, I don't think, but over six feet tall, insisted on chatting with me for thirty minutes before she took my order. We were the best of friends by the time we were done.

Her white head bobbed while she packed the pies. "Will you

be needing more next week?" She peered up at me through these thick-lensed eyeglasses. She had perfect teeth.

It is amazing how good dentures look. I should get some myself.

"I'm not sure yet," I said. I watched her pack two apple pies, two marionberry, two chocolate cream, and two pumpkin. I had never seen pies that looked this good.

"Dear, I make the best pies in Weltana." Her voice sounded like crackling fall leaves, but steel still ran through each syllable. "Everyone knows that. I make blueberry pies, lemon meringue pies, pecan pies, apple pies, apricot pies, peach pies, pear pies, meat pies with carrots and celery, and Zelda's shepherd pies. My crusts are light and tasty. I use butter, lots of butter. Some young people have tried to eliminate butter from their diets so they'll be skinny. What they need to do is eliminate eating themselves silly, not eliminate the butter. I tell them, they don't listen."

I ordered eight pies.

I wanted to take a fork and start eating one of those pies with the friendly butter right now. "I'll take a slice of chocolate cream pie, please."

It was 8:00 in the morning, but Zelda didn't blink. "Okay, dear, and I'll bring you out some coffee and cream. On the house."

She finished packing the pies, I paid her in cash, and I settled in by a tiny table fit for a gnome by the window and took a bite of my chocolate cream pie.

Unbelievable.

No. It was past unbelievable. The chocolate was cool from the fridge and as silky as chocolate silk. The crust was made of crushed chocolate cookies.

It is not every day that one gets a taste of gastrointestinal heaven, so I decided to take advantage of it. Next I bought a slice of pumpkin pie (for the vegetable, of course) and one of meringue (for the eggs, of course). I drank four cups of coffee with cream.

Maybe the pies would add some boob to my chest and some butt to my butt bones.

Zelda hugged me before I left, staggering out with my eight pies. "Come back anytime, dear, anytime. I make the best pies in Weltana."

I would. I did.

I set the pies by each doorway in the migrant camp, along with two bulging sacks of groceries per shed. I had included breads, chicken, cookies, milk, eggs, vegetables, canned chili and soups, peanut butter and jelly, chips, and fruit. I saw the curtains move in most of the little sheds, but no one came out.

Good, I thought. That's the way I liked it, too.

I waved to my grandma up in heaven.

"The town house is sold; all of your stuff is sold," Joyce Herber, my real estate agent, told me by phone about a week later. "The people who bought it paid cash and, since you didn't owe anything on it, the bank will be sending you a whopping check pretty soon here. I'll send you a check from the estate sale, too, where you made seventeen thousand dollars. Sign the faxed papers and we're good to go."

"I like being good to go," I told her. "I like to be good to stop, too."

She paused. I heard the silence loud and clear. "How are you, Jeanne? You haven't gone totally bonkers have you?"

I leaned back against my bed of blue heaven at Rosvita's. "I'm fine."

"No, come on, Jeanne, be real. How are you?" I heard that tone.

"Okay, Joyce, I'll give you the scoop. I found a new house. It's infested by mice and termites and at least one raccoon. The stairs wobble and will probably give way. The roof is caving in; the bathrooms are miniature sewage swamps; and the floors rock and roll because of water damage."

She laughed.

"I'm not kidding."

She stopped laughing.

"You bought this house?"

"Yes."

"Have you already signed the papers?"

"Yep."

More silence then: "Have you utterly and completely lost it, Jeanne?" she whispered.

"I think I have. And that's not the worst of it. I'm going streaking along the river."

"Streaking?" Joyce's voice sounded like a train whistle. "As in *naked* streaking?"

"Yep. Naked streaking."

"I don't understand."

"I don't either. But I'm doing it."

"You're going to run naked along a river?" Toot-toot! "Alone?"

"That would be correct. Running. Naked. Along a river. Alone."

"Why? Why? This is mad, stupid, dangerous. Naked running? Why?"

"Because I'm chasing away my anger. Nakedlike."

I would have to blame my naked run along the river on one of my weekly anger management classes.

"Your assignment for this session," Emmaline said to all of us from her black beanbag, "is to do something you've never done before. Something daring, but not illegal. Something fun, but not dangerously wild. Something you've always wanted to do or experience. Something fresh that takes your breath away."

Soman and Becky and Bradon and I had sunk into our beanbags after arting our anger. Soman had painted a six-foot-tall grinning pink ostrich on yellow butcher paper. " 'Cause I'm a friendly dude but sometimes my big fat head's in the ground."

Becky had made a collage out of sticks then painted it black.

"I am trying to get rid of all the black in my memories." She smashed it with a hammer.

Bradon had used black charcoal pencils to draw an Alice-in-Wonderland-type clock, curving and off-centered. "Time's wasting. Time is wasting for the kids in my neighborhood." He wiped a tear from his eye, and laid his forehead on the table.

I made crosses out of clay. A few medium-sized, one giant, several small ones. "For my mother," I said. Emmaline told me she'd fire them. I went to the screaming corner for a few minutes and held a pillow over my head.

When we were arted out, Emmaline ordered us to the beanbags.

Soman sat in the yellow bag; Becky in blue; Bradon in green; Me in purple. Drake Windham had been rejected from anger management class because he was in jail for assaulting two guards after his mortuary incident. Apparently he head-butted them both when he woke up from his drunken stupor in jail and informed them he was going to "sue their butts."

Emmaline did not look pleased. "The purpose of this exercise is for you all to begin reinventing yourselves, making yourself new and different." She slapped both her arms against her beanbag, taking long seconds to pierce all of us with her snappy eyes. "You need to create better paths for yourselves, better avenues, better streets, better alleys, better cul-de-sacs. By breaking out of your negative anger molds, you'll be able to think without the usual smoldering anger that leads to your own personal demolition."

"So I can go back to doing drugs, but I need to do a different type of drug?" Becky asked.

"No!" Emmaline shouted. Becky jumped. I wished Emmaline wouldn't shout; it made Becky so nervous. "Doing drugs would fall into the illegal category, for God's sake, Becky, think! Think! You need to quit being so damn weak. So willing to take the easy way out of life. You've made some ruinous mistakes, ruinous! Your biggest one was not being strong enough to pull your

own sorry, skinny ass out of the fire. You kept going back to the
drugs, and there's no excuse for that, none! Find a backbone and
stick it behind your ribs. Quit sulking and wallowing in your
sulking. Suck it up. Deal. Quit being pathetic."

Becky cowered like she wanted to disappear into her beanbag.
Goodness. I was going to have to say something about this
yelling to Emmaline.

Emmaline spread her arms wide. "We have four new lives
right now, four new lives blooming, four new lives emerging
from degradation and despair, four new souls escaping from the
anger that has encapsulated them for years. You're starting a
new life, a new way of being, a new way of thinking. New, new,
new."

She burst from her beanbag and pointed at Soman.

"Now, Soman, we're starting with you tonight because you appear to be the most dangerous of the group."

"Me? Man, I'm not dangerous."

"Do not deny what I'm telling you!" Emmaline thundered.
"I've seen your record. Bar fights. Fighting on the street. This
will stop! You're an uncontrolled machine with fists. So. What are
you going to do that's fresh and new to get you off your path of
mayhem and human demolition?"

"Man, I dunno. I'm gonna go to work. I'm gonna go out with
the guys and I'm gonna go home. That's about it. I'm gonna try
not to smash anyone's face."

Emmaline was on him in a flash, tilting his huge head up, not
so gently. His braids poured down his back. "Idiocy!" she
screeched. "Self-failure! Lack of motivation! You must reach into
yourself and find the tranquility within you and build on that.
The tranquility will kill your violent nature, your natural inclina-
tions to smash people. Reach inside your violent-self. Surely you
have a gentle hobby, something you like to do that is soft and
safe? Tell me instantly: What is that hobby?"

Soman looked away, to the side, up to the ceiling, anywhere
but in Emmaline's flame-bursting eyes.

"Soman!" Emmaline tilted his head, again, none too gently.

He uttered something. It was muffled.

"What was that?" Emmaline asked. "Speak! Never silence yourself when you're on a new pathway to change! Silencing your peaceful innards will smother your fight for a peaceful life! You must cling to the peacefulness within you and belt it out, feel it, live it."

He said it again. More muffling.

"Speak up; don't be a wuss, Soman! Be a stud on the outside and the inside! Say what you think, believe in what you say, take action on your actions, come on, Soman!"

"I like to dress like a woman."

There was a deep and pervasive silence as we all stopped breathing.

Emmaline dropped her hands from his face, and clapped. She was delighted with this progress.

"I ain't gay or nothin'. I dress like a woman at home now and then. I got this pretty yellow dress and yellow heels. A pink dress with flowers. And I got a nice, soft purple dress. Some beaded necklaces."

"Bring it out, Soman! Bring it out!" Emmaline chortled, clapping her hands together, her wee feet pounding the floor.

Soman groaned. "My Nonni, that's my momma's mom, died when I was six. She lived with us and taught me how to sing and how to fight. My dad said I started dressin' like a woman after she took off for heaven. He caught me in her closet all the time puttin' on her dresses, trying on her shoes, her jewelry . . . I loved my Nonni and I missed her."

"So you hide this part of yourself, your peaceful inner being?" Emmaline asked.

"Hell, yeah, I do. I'm sharing it with these guys 'cause we're all off our rockers, ya know, so I feel like I fit in."

I did not take offense at the "off our rockers" comment.

"On your new path, your new life, you need to take yourself public," Emmaline said.

"What?" Soman shrieked. I kid you not. Huge Soman shrilly shrieked.

"Take it public. One day, go out in your pretty little yellow dress and the beads. Explore the city. Feel yourself in your new environment, your new outfit. When you stroll down the street, tell yourself you're taking a new street away from your street of anger. When you see an alley, tell yourself to leave the anger in the alley. When you come to a freeway, picture yourself as one with the speed. Speed away from your anger. Be you, Soman."

His giant head was shaking back and forth, back and forth. "No way. Bein' a woman ain't me, Emmaline. That's you. And this here Jeanne, and Becky. Y'all are women. Not me."

"Find the man in you, Soman, and do it." Emmaline fisted her hands. "That's your task. Find the man in you and take your pretty-self out and about town as a woman. Don't forget your hat."

"I don't got no hat," Soman said, protested. He protesteth weakly. "I got a wig."

The silence was, again, all encompassing. Thunderous.

"Good. Be a woman, Soman, be a woman." Next Emmaline fixed those bright eyes of hers on poor Becky. I hoped she wouldn't yell at her. "Okay, Becky. What do you like to do besides drugs?"

"Hey!" Soman said. "That ain't called for."

"I call the truth," Emmaline snapped. "*I call the truth.* If you and everyone else don't want to acknowledge the truth, you all will never escape the pits of your despair and self-pity. Acknowledge the truth, change it, and you won't land your sorry asses in anger management again. So what is it, Becky? What do you like to do? Or what did you like to do before you chose drugs, which then dragged you through muck and mire?"

Becky fidgeted. I wondered if she weighed as much as the beanbag. "I like to sing."

"To sing? Like la-la-la?" asked Emmaline. "That's not bad, Becky, not bad. Do you sing only to yourself?"

"Of course." She seemed petrified at the thought of singing for others.

"Your task, your way to yank yourself away from your past hellacious life, your problems and troubles that *you and only you caused yourself*, will be to go to a bar and sing karaoke." Emmaline mimed singing into a mike. "We even have instruments here you can practice on if you need to." She nodded to the corner.

"Oh, God, no," Becky said. The skin of her face metamorphosized into a putrid shade of green right before our eyes.

"Oh, God, yes," Emmaline insisted. "You will go and sing at a karaoke bar and that will open up a whole new avenue of life to you."

"Oh, God, no," Becky said again.

"Don't argue; do it, Becky. And invite the rest of us. We'll all come."

We would?

"Oh, God, no," Becky whispered.

"How many times do I have to tell you 'Oh, God, yes'?" Emmaline yelled, arms out wide like a falcon. Becky jumped. "Say yes to a change, Becky; it's about time! Say yes to being responsible for yourself. Say yes to a real life, not the life of a drug-addled meek, weak freak. You. Will. Sing."

Harsh, I thought, so harsh.

"I was thinking I could find a new life by singing here."

"Here? Well, that's nothing! Nothing! You must sing in a karaoke bar so you can sing your way to serenity, la-la-la your way to lasting love, hmm-hmmm-hmmm your way to a clean life. You must dare with your singing and dare to have a new life. You do know that your drug addiction is completely your fault, don't you? *Completely.* You were weak and stupid, you wanted a high. It was all about *you.* You destroyed yourself and almost destroyed a family that loved you. When I think about what your addiction did to your parents' emotional and mental health I want to squish you! Squish you!"

"I want to squish myself," Becky said.

"Good. Now change, Becky. You're young. There's time. And,

if you don't change, you will die. Got it? You change or you die. Too simple."

Emmaline whipped her head over to Bradon as though she hadn't just tossed Becky into an emotional-wreckish wasteland. "And you, Bradon? How will you chart your new life, a life filled with tranquility and no anger?"

Bradon was silent for a while. He stared off into the distance, crossed one ankle over a knee and said, "I think I'll plant roses with my wife." We were puzzled by this gardening tidbit. Bradon is huge. When he's not smiling he looks fierce, like he could smash two heads together with his pinkies. Roses and Bradon don't jive real well.

"She's been wanting me to garden with her for years, but I have never found the time."

"You mean you have never *made* the time," Emmaline pounced. "We talked about this when you came in for your screening interview. Tell everyone what you told me."

It did not appear that Brandon wanted to tell everyone what he told her.

"Do it, Bradon, or I will."

Bradon ran his hands over his face and looked suddenly, insidiously, terribly miserable. "My anger has torn me and my wife apart, according to her. She told me that weeks ago after my chair-throwing incident. She can't stand living with someone who is always angry, even though she believes what I'm trying to do for African-American kids is the right thing to do. She said to me, 'I can't live angry anymore.' I asked her what she meant and she shrugged her shoulders." He wiped tears away from his eyes with both giant hands. "But I didn't need for her to tell me what she meant. I knew what she meant. She's leaving me unless I get rid of my anger. She's had it. She has had it." He wiped away more tears.

"So, Bradon," Emmaline said, working herself up to another tither. "You've blown it. Big-time. You need to assassinate your anger and repair your marriage. Gardening is a hobby that your wife loves. She's probably loved it your whole twenty-five-year marriage, am I right?"

Bradon nodded. He hung his big bald head.

"But you've rarely made time for what she wants, for what she wants to do *with you*, have you? It's been about your time, your schedule, what you want to do with your life. Your crusade for black kids. *You*. While she's been holding the marriage and the family together, you're going about your life *for you*. And all she wanted was for you to get your ass out to the garden now and again and plant roses with her. *And you couldn't do it?* Everything else in your life was more important than making your wife happy? For your entire twenty-five-year marriage?"

Bradon's head hung so low I thought it might fall off.

"I have a client right now who last Sunday was poised on the Marquam Bridge, ready to take a high-dive into the water. The police plucked him off the ledge. Do you know why? Because his wife had left him. Do you know why she'd left him? Because she didn't think he cared about her. Why? Because he rarely talked to her, never wanted to do anything with her; in fact, he hardly knew her. And he didn't know he hardly knew her. He worked all the time, jetted in and out on business trips, and when he was home, he kept working. He thought everything was fine in the marriage, that they were happy because he made a lot of money. How the hell could he think that? Because he was happy, *ergo* she must be happy. It never occurred to him that she might be lonely and hating him and hating her life. It never occurred to him that she had a whole other life outside the marriage. And now, she *is* happy. She has a boyfriend who talks to her, listens to her, and treats her like she's of value. Do you want to be like my bridge-jumper, Bradon?"

Bradon's huge shoulders started to shake. "No, I don't."

All was silent for a minute as Bradon got himself together. "My wife is the reason I breathe. She's the reason I live. She always has been."

"She's the reason you live, but you haven't been willing to change your life one iota to please that woman? For God's sake, Bradon, for God's sake!" Emmaline yelled, her control snapping again. "Have you asked yourself if you're the reason that *she* lives? Have you asked yourself if you're the reason *she* breathes? Of course you haven't. Have you asked her if she's still in love *with you*? And if she says yes, do you really think she's telling you the truth?"

Now Bradon pulled his knees halfway up to his chest like a baby in the womb.

"Look at me!"

Bradon's miserable bald head snapped up.

"You're happy with how things are. Your wife handles the house and the kids and the garden. She handles the relatives and in-laws, many of whom she probably can't stand. She brings Christmas to your house every year—not Santa—your *wife* brings Christmas. And she works as a nurse full-time. She takes care of *you and everybody else*. Well, now you're going to spend the next twenty-five years making life about *her*, making *her* happy. Making yourself the reason that she breathes. Do you have that, Bradon? Your life is not going to be about YOU."

"I get it, Emmaline, I get it," Bradon whispered.

"Do you, you selfish man?"

"Yes, I do. I cannot lose my wife. I. Can. Not. Lose her."

Emmaline reached out and put her tiny hands on Bradon's enormous shoulders. "You're going to plant roses and more roses and more roses until she begs you to stop. You're going to plant them when she tells you to, exactly where she tells you to. You're going to take her on rose garden tours and to rose contests. You're going to take some of those millions of dollars you have and take her to England so she can see all those English gardens and have tea and crumpets. And you're going to be damn happy while you're doing it and remember why you're doing it—for her. Completely for her."

"I'll plant the roses." He wiped another tear off his face with a huge hand. There is something so touching about a manly man crying over his wife, I'm telling you.

"Getting your fingers into the dirt will connect you to the basics of the earth which will connect you to peace and you won't burst out with these inappropriate, chair-smashing, table-toppling incidences that land you in the newspaper." She glared at him. "Much more important than that, you will reconnect with your wife."

A couple of Bradon's tears splotched on his purple shirt. "Don't screw this up, Bradon. It sounds like you have one more chance with your wife. One more chance. Be a man and fix this."

Without any warning, she stood up and whipped her long ostrichlike neck and tiny head around to me, piercing me with a mean hawklike stare. "And you, Jeanne? What are you going to do that will help you smash your anger to smithereens?"

I didn't know. I felt like I was at the art area again watching all these people create something out of nothing. I couldn't think. Couldn't possibly figure out something new and daring that I could do. I'm boring. I've been in the corporate world for so long I don't know how to think or feel anymore, so I simply said the first thing that came to my mind.

"I'm going to get naked."

Emmaline nodded. "Good. And what will come after your nakedness?"

"I'm going to go on a run," I added.

Emmaline raised her fists in victory.

"I'm going to run beside the river on my naked run."

Emmaline flapped her arms.

"I'm going to run beside the river on my naked run in the dark."

Emmaline shouted, "We have an anger breakthrough!"

"I'm going to run naked so I can be one with dirt and one with water and one with trees. I'm going to take my anger and I'm going to stomp it into the ground until it can't breathe. Until it has collapsed and shriveled up and died. I'm going to greet the moon and salute the stars and keep on truckin'. Naked."

Becky clapped.

Bradon choked out, "You go, girl."

Soman laughed so hard he snorted. Twice. "You be naked, you be cool, you run and run and run."

"Thinking of those germs makes me feel like I have gangrene and leprosy and a rectal bacterial infection all at once," Rosvita muttered, grabbing a frying pan and a colander from her kitchen cabinets.

Rosvita said this in all seriousness, so I did not laugh, although I did think that a leprosy outbreak here under the pine trees was somewhat unlikely.

I took a bite of an apple and stared at the moon through the windows. They sure had a large moon out here in Oregon. The night was clear, although we'd been drenched thirty minutes ago. I was learning that was typical Oregon weather. I was told you could see snow, hail, wind, and sun, all in one day in Oregon.

Rosvita tossed the colander on the counter, banged the frying pan on the stove, and began slicing onions and carrots and celery at bionic speed. "I want to dump bleach over the top of each of those sheds, bulldoze them, burn the whole wasteful rubble, and bury it deep, deep down into the earth." She threw a steak onto a cutting board. "One day I saw Dan in town and I ran back to my car and grabbed my bleach and water mixture in the spray bottle."

"You carry bleach and water in a spray bottle in your car?"

Rosvita looked at me as if I'd suddenly grown a snake head. "Of course I carry a bleach and water mixture in a bottle in my car! What good, clean citizen wouldn't?" Her face collapsed. "This isn't happening, this can't be true," she whispered. "You don't?"

Rosvita would be so disappointed in me, but I couldn't lie, either.

"No." I said this more quietly than a mouse's hiccup.

She closed her eyes and stared at the ceiling. "I will give you one tomorrow. No. I will give you two. So you will not run out. You always need germ-busters around you. Always."

"What did you do when you saw Dan?"

She looked at me with feigned patience. I did not take offense.

"I already told you."

"You did?"

"Yes!"

"I forgot." I went over our conversation. I could swear she hadn't said what she'd done with that bottle. "Tell me again."

She lifted the knife from the steak and brandished it between her and I. "I went back to my car and grabbed my water and bleach bottle, and I ran back to Dan and I sprayed him!"

I choked on my apple. Coughed. Struggled to breathe. Coughed again. Rosvita whacked me on the back. The apple popped out.

"Rosvita, back up," I gasped. "*You what?*"

"I sprayed him! Right on the back of the neck. And when he turned around, I sprayed his goodies!"

"You sprayed his goodies? He was naked?" I coughed again, wheezed.

She looked disgusted. "No, he wasn't naked! We were in town! You're not allowed to be naked in town! He was wearing clothes, but I know he was infested by germs! *Infested.*"

"What did he do after getting sprayed?"

She chopped through the steak rapidly. "He yelled at me, screamed! It rattled my eardrums. Four men had to come running out of the grocery store to make him stop! It was Hamilton Nelsen, Yiang Chan, Byron Peeks, and Austin Cho. All of them came running before Fakue attacked me, but I kept spraying!"

"You mean, Dan was screaming at you and you didn't stop spraying your bleach and water mixture?"

"I couldn't!" she defended herself, knife pointed in the air.

"Spittle from one's mouth carries numerous bacterial colonies. Numerous! Every time he uttered a word, I had to spray to defend myself and my cleanliness!"

I envisioned that delicacy. Dan yelling; Rosvita spraying. Dan yelling again; Rosvita spraying again. Dan completely losing his temper; Rosvita spraying and spraying. I put the apple down.

"So these four guys dragged him off?"

"They did indeed. And to thank them I made each of them my special Rosvita's Special Stew and homemade rolls and wine. Their wives were so grateful when they saw me. Byron and his wife have four kids and she's pregnant again. She grabbed the wine bottle a little too quick though, I thought," Rosvita mused.

"But what happened to Dan?"

"He blew smoke for a while, but those four boys held him tight while I got into my car. Paul Nguyen, that's the police chief, and his deputy came over that night at dinnertime and we all sat around the table and had seafood parmesan over angel hair pasta, garlic bread, Caesar salad, and chocolates. That was when you were at your "I'm-So-Angry" class. On the way out the door Paul told me to refrain from spraying Dan with bleach and water."

"So that was it?"

"Mostly. Dan huffed and puffed, saying he was going to sue me, but Paul told him he should be careful, seeing that he houses people in rat traps with germs the size of Wisconsin and, if he were him, he would shut his own trap. I was so proud when I heard Paul use the words 'germs the size of Wisconsin.' That tells me he is fully grasping the concept of rampant germs and has been listening to me ever since we were in kindergarten together and learned how important it is to floss."

"So that was it?"

"Yes. All done. Dan shut his trap tight, like Paul told him to do. And when he saw me in town again and I ran to get my bleach and water bottle, he got in his big ole expensive pickup and drove away. What a pussy."

"What a pussy," I echoed.

"I wish the migrant camp was as clean as . . . as . . . The Opera Man's Café!" she declared in victory. "Now, Donovan's a man who understands the importance of cleanliness." She shook her head in admiration. "That is one clean man," she muttered. "But I will put an end to this. I will put an end to Dan and his germs."

I nodded and bit into my apple again. I did not know on that moon-filled night that Rosvita would make good on her threat. I also didn't know that she would bring me into her whole totally cracked up scenario.

But she did.

And that made me an accomplice.

CHAPTER 10

I was hesitant to run naked.

It is not something I can say is in my comfort zone.

It is not something I've done before.

Still.

I had told Emmaline and the others at anger management class that I would do so.

Now, the first thought racing out of your mind might be that being a naked woman outside your home isn't safe. You might also say that a naked woman running alone alongside a river isn't safe. You might further say that a naked woman running alone by a river, at night, is asking for trouble.

You are right.

But, you see, I had agreed to do it to take me off my path of anger. As life did not seem especially precious to me, I was feeling a little reckless.

So I had pancakes for dinner at the café with a bunch of chatty, cheery townspeople who somehow soothed my soul, and listened to Donovan sing his favorite three opera songs, dedicating them to his "secret love." Afterward I promised to come to a retirement party for Bill Brayson on Friday night and a bowling tournament on Sunday.

(I tried to ignore the warm gush in my body at these invitations. I was very rarely invited to do anything in Chicago except to get more work done, find more clients, and deal with artsy creative types who insisted on doing yoga in the hallways, brought their giant dogs to work, or hummed when they got nervous.)

I did not share with my newfound friends my further plans for my evening. Around 10:00 that night I pulled on sweatpants and my sweatshirt and headed to a private place along the river. Here, I could still see the trail, but there were no homes.

The rays of the full moon slanted through the trees. It smelled like pine and river water and wood and I sucked in a deep breath.

I took off all my clothes and put them in a small backpack. I retied my tennis shoes. (I do not consider wearing tennis shoes as breaking the rules.) I knew I should feel embarrassed standing there naked by the rushing river, but I didn't. In one avenue of my mind I realized I'd lost my marbles.

I don't have huge boobs, so it didn't bother me that I would be bopping along without a bra. I looked up at the star-studded sky again, catching a glimpse of the full moon. It was clearly a wild night for werewolves and weird women on wacky quests of self-awareness.

Overhead an owl hooted and somewhere on the other side of the river another owl hooted back.

I shifted my backpack and started into a slow jog. From having run this trail on numerous occasions, I knew that it went a long ways, and I had a pretty good idea when to head back around.

I figured I'd run about thirty minutes out, thirty minutes back in.

That should satisfy Emmaline and the rest of the angry group. My legs jumped into their usual pace.

As I ran I tried to block out everything but the cool, velvet air, the whispering trees, and the rush of the river. Soon I was sweating, but I kept running.

I peeked at the moon and the Big Dipper through the tree branches as I ran and ran. I knew I had run for more than thirty minutes, but I kept going, my breath coming out in pants, my heartbeat even and steady, the sweat pouring from my pores.

I thought of all the lousy men I'd dated and I thought of Slick Dick and his stupid lawsuit. I made myself sprint.

I slowed down as I thought of my "pointless" speech at the convention, and how I'd worked so many years of my life away for, let's see, *nothing*. I sprinted again.

I thought of Johnny and Ally and slowed down, glancing at the night sky to say hello to them.

I thought of my sweet mother, and the cancer that ate away at her body, and I blinked the tears out of my eyes but didn't bother to wipe them off as they mixed with my sweat.

I ran and ran.

And ran.

I careened around a curve on the path at a sprint and ran straight into a towering, steel-hard, barricade.

The steel-hard barricade made a sound like this—"Oooof."

Next, it stumbled and I stumbled over it. We were pressed together tight. It landed first and I landed on top of it, spread-eagled, bone smashed against bone.

Did I mention that I am a woman, running alone, at night, naked, by a river?

All of my air rushed right out of my lungs and I gasped and struggled to find that elusive oxygen.

The steel-hard barricade grasped my shoulders, shoved me to my back, and rolled on top of me.

I realized that the steel barricade was a man and panic roared through my body, every nerve end blitzing with fear, blood rushing through my body like an indoor waterfall. My brain screamed at me to hit and run, hit and run.

So I did.

It was too dark to see the steel barricade's head so I couldn't see what he looked like, but I assumed he was a rapist and had a very long and sharp sword or other weapon in his back pocket, and I would soon meet my untimely demise.

But not without a fight.

I brought one hand up, remembered to bunch it into a fist, and let it fly. It connected with his face.

He said, "Goddammit." His voice was gravelly and rough and close to my ear.

I brought my other arm up to slug him again, but he caught it deftly, grabbed my other wrist, and I was trapped like a spider on a pin.

I raised up a knee and connected. Everything in me screamed to fight, fight, fight!

"Ah, shit," the steel-hard barricade said. He threw a jean-clad leg over mine.

"Shit yourself, asshole," I said as I struggled to bring my captured wrists toward my mouth so I could bite him. (I did not reprimand myself for swearing at that moment.)

He saw what I was trying to do and shoved both my wrists above my head and caught them together with one hand.

I was so afraid I thought I was going to pee. I kept fighting against him, wriggling and twisting and lifting my head and trying to bite him on the neck. I brought my knee up again, but he flattened me back down.

His weight pressed me down into the dirt and breathing became difficult.

"Let go of me!"

"Let go of you?" he asked with that gravelly voice. I could see the outline of his face. He had this impossibly square jaw and his cheekbones were sharply angled.

"Yes, let go of me! Right now!"

I felt his breath float over me. It smelled good. Like mint and the woods and wine.

Super. A rapist with good-smelling breath.

I struggled again, past panic, and thick into terror.

"Stop it!" he snapped.

Shocked, I stopped for a second. His voice had that authoritative edge to it.

"Stop it? I'll stop when you take your grimy hands off of me!"

"And I'll let go of your hands as soon as you agree not to bite, hit, or scratch me."

The moonlight outlined his head. His hair wasn't short, but it wasn't long, either. His cheeks had felt rough, like he hadn't shaved in a couple of days. Ordinarily, I might find that sexy.

"I won't, I won't. Just let me up." I tried not to sound out of my flippin' mind with fright.

He hesitated. "How do I know you won't attack me again?"

"I won't attack you if you back off. Get off! *Get off!*"

I watched his eyes wander over me, from my eyes to my mouth to my neck to my shoulders, to my breasts which were halfway squished by his huge chest. He was wearing a jean shirt, warmed by his body heat.

Why did I ever leave my slice of blue heaven? I asked myself.

What in God's name ever propelled me out the door, at night, and why the hell did I run naked?

Couldn't I have chosen an easier task for anger management class? Maybe gone to a pottery or yoga class or something?

I watched him carefully, panic doing the rumba through my body, my mouth dry, my heart hammering.

He lifted his body up a little, for a millisecond, and he looked down.

I quivered. Now he knew, if he didn't before, that I was completely in the raw. His heavy body covered mine again real quick.

I could hardly see his eyes, but I knew they were definitely looking right at mine. I saw the corners of his mouth twitch a little.

"You're naked," he said. He tried to smother the laughter in his voice.

My chest was heaving and I could hardly breathe, but I didn't want to show my free-ranging fear. "How sharp of you to notice." I did not try to keep the sarcasm out of my voice. "Incredibly observant."

"Why are you naked?" He said it with the same tone one might use if one said, "Why is the sky blue?"

I was a little too strung out to lie. "I'm naked because I told my anger management counselor and the other people in my class that I would run naked along the river."

I had enough moonlight to see him blink a couple of times.

"Your anger management counselor?"

"Yes." My legs started quivering. Terror will do that to a person, you know. I hoped I wouldn't pee.

There was silence between him and me and I heard those owls again.

"Why do you have an anger management counselor?" Super, again. A *curious* rapist.

"Gee, maybe it's because I'm angry?" I tried to struggle away but it was no use. It felt like a human tractor was crushing me into the ground.

"You're squishing me," I told him.

He elbowed himself up.

"Better?" he asked

Joy! A polite ax murderer.

"Yes, thank you." *Yes, thank you?* My teeth were beginning to chatter with fear and I ground them together.

Something warm dropped on my face again and he briefly lifted his hand and wiped it off my face.

"Sorry. Looks like I'm bleeding on you."

Blood. The thought of it made me feel weak. Will I bleed a lot after he's through with me? My heart skipped one hundred and eighty-seven beats.

"You have a good punch," he said.

"Thank you." *Thank you?*

"So let's get back to my question."

"Let me go and I'll answer your question." I could hardly breathe.

"I asked why you were running naked and you said you were doing it for your anger management class and you're in counseling because you're angry. How does running naked fit into all this?"

I took a quivering breath. *Surely this conversation wasn't really happening?* "We were supposed to do something daring, something different, something to take us off of our usual path of anger."

"Did everyone choose to run naked?" I felt his chest shaking a bit.

It took me a second but I got it: My rapist was laughing. He was trying to hide it, but he was not doing a very good job. A laughing attacker. I smelled aftershave.

Everything in that class was supposed to stay confidential, but I had a feeling that Bradon, Soman, Emmaline, and Becky would understand my predicament. "No, not naked. Bradon is going to plant roses with his wife to save his marriage; Soman is going to dress like a woman and shop around town to get in touch with his inner woman; and Becky is going to sing in a bar because she's ruined her life thus far."

I saw him blink again. "So no other nude runners. Only you."

"That's right. Only me."

I realized my mistake instantly. I should have told him they were all behind me. "My husband is behind me. He'll be here any second."

I felt him fiddling with my left hand.

"You're not wearing a ring."

"A ring?"

"Yes. A wedding ring. I don't think you're married. Besides, what kind of husband lets his wife run by herself along a river, at night, alone, naked?"

Now I'm getting a little ticked. "What kind of husband *lets* his wife? You sexist creep. I can do whatever I damn well please, but he's gonna kick your butt when he gets here."

I saw the corners of his mouth twitch again. "Nice try."

I was furious. "What? You don't think anyone would want to marry me? I'm not the marrying type? Too overbearing? Too opinionated? Too angry? That's what you think, right?" I was near tears. Still frightened shitless, but also near tears. I hate men, I do. All they want is some fluffy, brainless, big-boobed floozy who will pander to their engorged, fragile egos. Vomitous pricks.

My attacker didn't say anything for a long minute while I got myself under control. "I didn't say, nor did I think, that you were unmarriageable. You're not wearing a ring and you're not a very good liar."

I swallowed hard. The owls were hooting all over the forest, their hoots echoing off one tree, then another.

"Why did you have to go to anger management counseling?"

"Why? *Because I'm angry.* Did you think I went because I'm filled with serenity?" Men are so stupid.

"What are you angry about?"

"Right now I'm angry that you're squashing me and I can barely breathe. Would you get off?"

He shifted a bit so there was not much weight on me anymore, but not enough so I could pull a Houdini and wriggle free. "Tell me why you're angry."

I closed my eyes. Humor him, I told myself. When his guard was down, wham his balls with your knee and whack them into putty.

"No." I bit my tongue. Why must I be argumentative with my attacker? Surely the police would not advise this? My boobs were still somewhat flattened by him, but my body had warmed up miraculously under his, even though my legs were still shaking and trembling and quivering.

"Please?"

I looked into his eyes, then I looked at his mouth, which was smiling. He had a lot of white teeth, I noted.

"Why should I?"

"Because I want to know."

"You want me to tell a man who has tackled me to the ground and refuses to get off of me why I'm angry?" *Men.*

"A, I didn't tackle you. My house is right up this hill. I was standing by the river when I heard running feet. Next thing I know, you come flying at me and I'm on the ground with a woman on top of me. Which brings me to B: I'm only holding you against your will for a few moments until I can ascertain that you will not attack me again. Try me. Tell me why you're angry."

What the heck. "All right, you creep, I'll tell you." I looked right into his eyes. "I'm angry because cancer careened into my life and killed my mother, bit by bit. I'm angry because Slick Dick cheated on me and took my mountain bike and I liked that bike. I'm angry because I don't have a husband and five kids and a house out in the country with a bunch of cats and chickens because a drunk driver decided I shouldn't have those things. I'm angry because I'm useless and my job has been useless and I have no plan for being less useless and I'm thirty-seven and haven't done whack that's good with my life. In fact, I've worked almost every minute of my life and it has metamorphosized me into a nonperson. I'm angry because I've been semidead for the last twelve years and I'm sick of living and think that it would be a good idea if I drove my new-old Bronco into the Pacific. I've never even seen the Pacific Ocean. But I can't do that for a while because I've committed to playing poker and to a garden tour, and I don't even like to garden. I'm angry because I haven't been able to get rid of my anger. There. That's a little bit about my anger. Now will you get your huge body off of me so I can breathe again?"

For long seconds, he didn't move, but his eyes stared straight into mine. His lips were not twitching with laughter and there were no chuckling sounds.

"It sounds like you have a right to be angry."

I did not expect that out of a man. I especially didn't expect it out of my attacker. I opened my mouth to speak but no words arrived.

He took a deep breath. "I'm sorry about your mother. I'm sorry that Slick Dick took your mountain bike and cheated on you. I'm not sorry he took off because he didn't deserve you. I'm mostly sorry that a drunk driver took away your dream of a husband and five kids and cats and chickens. Don't drive your new-old Bronco into the Pacific until you've driven up and down Oregon's coast. It's beautiful and once you're there, life will look better. I'm sorry you've had so much in your life happen to cause you to be this angry."

When he was done, a huge sigh from the heart of my soul escaped my body, a sigh so deep and long I felt it was a breath I had been holding for years. Maybe for twelve years.

I closed my eyes.

Finally, somebody had apologized.

Someone was sorry.

The tears came, hot and heavy. Liquid emotion. They blurred my vision, but that didn't matter because in the darkness I couldn't see him very well anyhow. I blinked my eyes and they rolled down my cheeks.

"Hey," he said. His voice had lost the gravelly sound and was now all honey.

"Hey, yourself," I snapped. "I can cry if I want to. Most women would if they had a stranger straddling them when all they wanted to do was run naked by the river for anger management class!"

I knew how stupid I sounded, but hysteria was lurking right off my left shoulder and I was going to indulge it shortly and start screaming.

All of a sudden, the cool mountain air whisked over my entire naked body. My wrists were free; my shaking legs didn't have a tractor's worth of weight on them; and my boobs weren't squished under the man of steel.

He sat by me, his elbows draped over his knees. "There ya go," he said.

I struggled up, pulled up my knees to my chest, and put one arm over my boobs. With my other hand, I swiped at the tears on my cheeks.

"Maybe you should let yourself cry for a while," he said.

I laughed. The laughter sounded crooked and jagged. Like a crazy woman's. "I do cry. I've cried more in the last month than I have in twelve years. I've raised the water level of that river with my tears." I glanced at the man's face again. His hair looked to be dark brown with some gray streaks through it. He had serious eyes, with lines fanning out from the corners. By the way he was sitting, I figured he was pretty tall. Definitely much taller than me.

I wiped at my tears again. "I'm leaving."

"All right. How about if I drive you back home?"

"God, no."

"Why?"

"Because I'm not getting into a car with a stranger."

He chuckled. "You'll run naked by a river, get tackled by a man who lets you go, but you won't get in his car." He paused, looked at the river, then back at me. "But now that I think about it, that's probably a good decision. I'll run back with you. Any chance you have clothes in that backpack?"

"You're running back with me?" Lovely. My own naked-run escort.

"Yes."

"Why?"

"So you don't get attacked."

"I'm not going to get attacked!"

That mouth twitched again.

The man obviously had a difficult time suppressing his amusement. "Get dressed."

"No."

"No?" I noticed that jaw again. Very square. I could tell he was used to telling people what to do.

"You want to run naked with me behind you all the way back?" Twitch.

"I'm forgoing my naked run and you do not need to run back with me."

"There's no point arguing."

He stood up. Yep. He was very tall and had the shoulders of a minijet. "You're right." I was surprised by my own timidity. "I'll get dressed. Turn around, please."

I saw him smile. "I think I've seen it all."

"You find me very amusing, don't you?"

His smile disappeared. "I don't find you amusing at all. I don't find your situation amusing at all, actually. I find it tragic. I find it sad. However, you are the most honest person I've met in a long time. The most truthful and real. I appreciate you for it."

I wet my lips. At least my mouth didn't feel as dry as dead leaves anymore. "Really?"

"Yes, really."

"But you think I'm insane to do this."

"Yes. Slightly. But in an insane way, it makes sense. Now get dressed before you freeze. We've got a run ahead of us and it's getting late." He turned his back, crossed his arms.

"You're right," I said. "It is late." But for some strange reason, I didn't feel tired. I ignored that little fluttering in my chest, dug my clothes out of my backpack, and dressed while keeping an eye on his back.

"Ready to run?" he asked.

"Yes. Definitely ready to run." His eyes took me in from head to foot. I saw that twitch of his mouth again. He insisted on holding the now empty backpack.

We ran.

The owls hooted.

The river rushed by.

The moon followed us.

I felt something new. Something better. Something soft.

Peace.

Later that night, I indulged in a long, hot, lavender-scented bubble bath, then ate two pieces of chocolate cream pie from Zelda's bakery. I climbed into bed with a book, but couldn't concentrate so I switched out the light.

I should have thought about the stupidity of my own actions that night. Should have thought about what could have happened had I literally run into the wrong person in my birthday suit.

Instead, I thought about running back to Rosvita's bed-and-breakfast, the stranger by my side, taller than me by at least six inches. I had been reluctant to show him where I was staying, but I realized that was ridiculous.

If the man was a danger to me, he would have taken advantage of the situation right there. Besides, when I told him he had run with me far enough, that we were almost on the edges of town, and I didn't need him to run with me any farther, he refused. "I'm running you to your door. Don't bother arguing about that, either."

And so he did.

The porch light was on so I was able to study this fine male specimen. He had light-colored blue eyes. His hair was brown and thick with gray streaks running through it. He had good teeth. In fact, he looked like a man's man, a bit too angular, a bit too harsh, lines engraved around his eyes from the sun, and not a pretty bone in his body. I cocked my head. Yep. Lots of testosterone in there. I like testosterone.

I swallowed hard. What's the etiquette in this situation? I could see Emily Post: After running naked along a river and knocking over a strange man, make sure that you sincerely thank him for his time and efforts while politely shaking his hand. Send a note of appreciation in the mail the next day expressing your gratitude.

I stuck out my hand. (My manners are often hidden, but they're there.) He grasped it. My hand disappeared in the enormity of his. "Thank you," I said.

He nodded, didn't let go.

We locked eyes for long, long seconds, as if we'd known each other for a few light-years and could do that.

"It was nice meeting you," he said.

"It was nice meeting you, too."

"Remember what I said about the Pacific."

I nodded.

He took a step closer to me, our clasped hands the only thing between us. Did I mention that hard jaw of his? "Do you live here?"

"I'm currently visiting. I left Chicago last month. As I'm sure you've realized, I'm not quite all together yet. I haven't made any final decisions about living arrangements; my living arrangements being the least of my worries at the present time."

He studied the river rushing behind Rosvita's house as though thinking, then those eyes were back to me. "I have a home here, but I work in town and have to be there for the next couple of weeks. When I get back, I'd like to take you to the Pacific Ocean for the day. It's beautiful."

I shook my head, pushed the hair out of my eyes. How weird. I went from thinking I was going to get attacked to being asked out on a date. "I don't date," I told him, even though he was tempting. "I'm too unhinged for that." Plus, I was a little nasty to my last boyfriend. "As you can tell."

I caught my breath. My almost-attacker sure looked good.

"We won't call it a date. We'll call it a Beach Exploration Day so you can determine if you still want to drive your Bronco into the waves."

I grinned and he grinned back. Great teeth, I thought, great teeth!

"I'll come by," he said. Gravel and honey.

"I might agree to see you."

"In two weeks."

I nodded, told my heart to slow way, way down and told my nether regions to cool off.

I watched him run back into the quiet night. He reminded me of musk and fir trees and Valentine's Day and kahlua and cream mixed.

In the silky darkness of my bedroom, with the French doors opened wide, and the babbling noise of the river providing a watery melody, I snuggled into the blue heaven of my bed.

I couldn't stop smiling.

That surprised me.

CHAPTER 11

"This week, Jeanne," my brother said to me. "You have to call Bob Davis *this week* to make an appointment. He'll talk to you by phone and Jay Kendall will interview you for the campaign and, hopefully, you'll have yourself a job."

"I'll call him." I love Charlie. He's a kick-in-the-butt brother. Everybody knows that he's brilliant and moral and strong and kind and gives out the best advice on the planet. If you don't follow it, you're a fool.

Meet the fool.

"How about dinner over here on Friday night?" he asked, his voice eager. "We're only about an hour from Weltana, you know. We'd love it. We painted the house last summer, I built a trellis for roses . . ." Charlie went on and on.

I thought about it this time. I thought about perfect Deidre and all the kids. Something in me craved the peace and joy and chaos of their family life. Something else in me felt like screaming when I thought, for the most fleeting of moments, about standing in that kitchen with the kids, dogs, all the cats, and the birds squawking about.

"No, but thank you. Tell Deidre and the kids I love them." And I do. Love them. I love them dearly. But, again, the screaming won out over the desire to see them in real life. Their oldest is the same age as my daughter would have been—I believe I've mentioned that?

I heard the disappointment in his voice, but he doesn't get on me about it. "Call Bob."

"I'll call Bob," I told him.

"Right away. Right after this call. You're making my anxiety problems worse, Jeanne."

"Right away." I nodded even though he couldn't see it. "Right after this call."

He told me he loved me, I said the same, and closed my cell phone.

I let my mind travel to Naked Run Man over a couple of glasses of white wine that night. White wine and Naked Run Man went well together.

I only had two glasses.

I woke up in the morning and felt normal. No hangover. No fuzziness. No anger.

Better.

The next week at anger management class we met and "communicated with no turbulence" to each other how our week had gone. "No turbulence" means we must keep our anger in check like normal people. No screaming, bad language, or throwing of any items or nearby people.

Before we started we were allowed to go to the screaming corner, pick a pillow, and scream into it to get out our screams. We did so. The talking came next.

Bradon had trouble with the union so he worked a ton of hours and his wife was mad at him. "Which is the worst, the very worst. When my wife doesn't like me, I don't like me, either. Plus I had to sleep on the couch one night. I hate sleeping on the couch. I swear, that woman bought the least comfortable couch in the universe so that when I'm stuck on it, I'd suffer. It's built for an elf." He sighed. "She's damn smart."

Emmaline said, "And you're damn stupid. You didn't work with your wife in the garden, did you?"

"Emmaline, I was hardly home, I was working—"

"Did you read a rose magazine with her? Did you even buy her a bouquet of roses?" Bradon's hands trembled while he held his big head. "Idiot. You are an idiot, Bradon. Your work and your anger, *your lack of correct priorities*, is strangling your wife and you and your marriage like a serpent around a squirrel. It's gonna squish you because you're not making a decision *not* to let it squish you."

Soman had not dressed like a woman that week, as assigned, but neither had he got in a fight, as also assigned. Becky said her week was fine, perfectly fine. As she was pale and exhausted and appeared to be shriveling up into nothing, I knew she was doing the ole "everything's fine" routine that many of us perform.

I swear, some people's lives can be falling apart and they'll still declare, "Everything's fine, fine," while others are living extraordinarily fortunate lives but they still whine and complain endlessly 'til you want to hang yourself with your own silk scarf so you don't have to listen to their rambling drivel anymore.

I said my week was fine. "I did not assault anyone nor was I arrested. I didn't make any inappropriate speeches. I did not make any abrupt moves, like shoving my head through a meat grinder. I also endeavored not to be pathetic," I told everyone. I did not mention Naked Run Man.

Bradon gave me a thumbs-up. Soman sang a few notes. "It's a hummingbird's song of triumph," he said. Becky patted my knee. I noticed her arm and shirt were dirty. Poor Becky.

Next, Emmaline led us in a number of gymnastic activities where we cartwheeled, somersaulted, and jumped around like grasshoppers on drugs.

In the dark.

No kidding. Emmaline flicked off the lights. "The darkness is to help bring you to a time of flexibility and strength, resilience and determination and daring," she told us. "Also to remind you that you have been in the dark but you need to search for the light, no matter how small."

She affixed these little wraparound white lights to our ankles and wrists and we became regular Nadia Comanecis. "Skip!" she'd yell. Or, "Somersault! Bradon, you look like an old, constipated white guy! Bring some rhythm into your arches. There! Cartwheel everyone, cartwheel! Do it like Becky. See? She's graceful. Soman, do you have a stick up your butt? Loosen up. Jeanne, you remind me of stomach acid the way you're bopping all around. Jump, like a real woman, jump!"

Emmaline is so inspiring.

After our lighted calisthenics, we collapsed into our colored beanbags, panting.

"Soman, tell us what you're going to do that's new and enriching and appealing to set your mind on a course of forgiveness and gentleness, casting aside your usual route of anger," Emmaline said, her little lights flashing on her tiny ankles.

"Hmmm," said Soman. "Maybe I'll smash someone's face with my left hand instead of my right." He slammed his left fist into his right, his lights glowing in the dark.

Our laughter got us all in trouble and Emmaline sent all of us to the punching bags.

"Hit. Hit. Hit! Punch away your anger." Emmaline flapped her arms up and down, screaming into all of our ears.

We hit, our lights arching and streaking through the darkness. When any of us stopped punching, Emmaline came straight up to our faces and yelled for us to keep hitting. "This is not optional! Hit until you can hit no longer!"

When she gave us a break, we all crumpled to the floor. Becky was on all fours. I was bent over double. Soman and Bradon leaned on the wall, groaning.

"You four are the most emotionally treacherous angry people I've ever met," Emmaline said, her voice angry and—might I say it?—incredulous. "You don't want to give up your anger, do you?"

There was silence for a moment.

"Not me," Bradon coughed out, sweat dripping to the floor. "Somebody has got to be mad enough to make changes in the school system, and I aim to make that change."

"I'm tryin' to get rid of my anger, but it likes me. Won't give me up. It's got me in a headlock," Soman panted, flicking his braids back. "But I'll keep tryin', Emmaline."

Emmaline looked at Becky. Becky shook her head, beads of sweat dropping down her tired face. "Anger's better than spending time thinking your life is a total loss, and it's better than despair. Despair is bleak. When you feel nothing, that's when you're dead. With anger at least you're still fighting. I'll take my anger."

"Jeanne?"

"I sure as heck am not giving up my anger. *I like her*," I panted, gathering my sweaty body up inch by inch and hitting the punching bag again. I felt like I was going to throw up. "I'm not giving up my anger 'til Slick Dick's balls are fried. *Fried*."

"I'm mortified! Mortified! All of you!" Emmaline's voice echoed off those pure white walls like ricocheting bullets. "Hit. Hit. HIT! Hit harder! Hiiiiitttttt!"

When I got back to Rosvita's that night, Roy had left me a message about my upcoming legal issues, court dates and depositions and fun stuff like that. He ended the conversation with, "I sure miss your mom, honey. I know you do, too." Then he laughed. "She would love what I'm going to do to Jared. I think she might even had taken a day off teaching to see the trial! Now wouldn't that have been something!"

Unless my mother's head was slung over the toilet because of stomach flu, she went to work, so I got Roy's point.

My mother had hated Slick Dick on sight and refused to offer him dessert the one time we went to her house for dinner. That was a sure sign from my mother. If she didn't like you, you didn't get dessert when you came to dinner. When there was no dessert offered to Slick Dick, Roy rolled his eyes. My mother glared at Slick Dick. And I suggested we get back to the city.

My mother could be difficult sometimes, her mother's temper working its way down the gene pool.

When I didn't come and visit her enough, she would send me the clothes she'd worn out to her garden, tell me to wash them, and bring them home to her *that weekend*.

She would also send me crosses. Small crosses if she thought I was doing fairly well in my life, a large cross if she thought I was really screwing up. After the dinner with Slick Dick I received a very large package on my front door. My mother had the local carpenter make me a six-foot by four-foot cross.

If she was mad at Charlie and me when we were kids she would bang her cupboards while she was cooking. When she was irritated with me for burying myself in my work, dating the wrong man, not dealing with my drinking, or she thought I was too thin, she would call my answering machine and all I would hear is banging cupboards. Bang, bang, bang.

I often wouldn't see her for weeks at a time because of my work and travel, but we talked on the phone almost every day. When I did see her she always had our day planned: She had me volunteering at her school, antique-shopping, exploring ethnic restaurants, volunteering at her school, touring a garden, cooking her favorite Mexican recipes, volunteering at her school, traveling to another town so we could get another "flavor" out of life and meet more "flavorful" people. She also made me participate in local paintball competitions and had me volunteer at her school.

We spoke Spanish during these visits so she could impress upon me the things she wanted me to change in my life. I believe I mentioned these issues above: Working too much, dating bad men, too much drinking, too thin.

And the next time I spoke to her I would get the same lecture.

Lecturing came easy to her. As a devoted English teacher she loved her students and would, at times, take on the school board for more funding for books, cultural field trips, visiting authors, etc. Her lectures were legendary. As she was enormously popular, she was able to rally the troops—students, their parents, and other teachers—to get what she wanted. It got so bad that when my mother made a request of the school board, they started nodding yes so they wouldn't have to endure all the mobbed meetings, the letter campaigns, the articles in the newspaper detailing what a stodgy, tightfisted board the school had, and those legendary lectures that were printed, in full, in the newspaper.

Still, at her funeral, the entire board—past and present—attended.

My mother laughed all the time, danced all the time, and Lived with a capital L.

What I wouldn't do to hear those cupboard doors slamming on my answering machine.

I can see my sagging, dilapidated house from my deck at Rosvita's bed-and-breakfast. Today I had my first contractor coming to the house to give it a once-over.

The house looked like it had been beaten and spit out, but I am somewhat confident that I can change that.

Later, I am to laugh at my own naïve optimism, but that morning, sipping my decaf coffee and munching on a cinnamon roll, everything seemed a little better.

It had been about eight days since the naked run and ever since my body had felt slightly on fire.

I wondered about my Naked Run Man. I wondered if he had four ex-wives and drug dealers after him. I wondered if he had a girlfriend already. I wondered if he laughed like that, so rumbly and earthy, all the time. I wondered if his gravel and honey voice would haunt me forever in a good way. I did not wonder if he meant it when he said he was sorry I was so angry and that my anger was warranted. I knew he had meant that.

I spent a lot of time wondering about him which surprised me. What surprised me more was how warm and fuzzy I felt every time I thought of him. I am not a wuss but this was definitely wusslike behavior.

I wondered if he were the type of man who said, "I love you" a lot to the woman in his life or if he simply showed her.

I had a feeling he was a "shower" which meant he would get laid a lot.

Men don't get that.

The getting laid thing.

They think that the words "I love you" are hot foreplay.

Those words are nice to hear if you think the person truly loves you and you trust him and the relationship and your future and you know that the sex you're going to have is healthy and right and he'll be there in the morning and the next morning after that, and the morning you're passing a kidney stone or grieving over your dead mother, and the morning they cart you away to a nursing home when you're ninety-five and he's there, packed up, and ready to go with you so you don't have to be alone.

I've had several men tell me they love me over the years, but I haven't believed any of them, because I knew they weren't being honest. I have never been in love with any of them, so I never told any of them that I loved them, except Johnny.

He was the only man I ever said, "I love you" to. He said it to me all the time, too. Even made up several songs on his guitar about his love. I would love him back with a song on my violin. Johnny was the only one I ever made love to that I trusted. The only one who I knew would be there for me the next morning and the morning after, kidney stones or not.

But you can always tell if a man is truly and deeply in love with a woman by his actions.

For example, if a man spent hours hand-cleaning the oven because he knew it was a mess and he knew his wife hated doing the job and he hated it, too, but he did it anyhow, I would know that that man was absolutely crazy about his wife.

Or, if a man went with his wife to visit an elderly relative in a nursing home once a week or if he built her a picnic table so she could watercolor outside, I would know there was bucketfuls of love there.

You see, the words *I Love You* are only words. Three of them strung together. Easy to say. No problemo. Men who are cheating on their wives or beating them senseless routinely use them. Men who are mean or sarcastic or lazy in their relationships use them, too.

Love, as I see it, is a series of actions. If I ever got remarried—impossible—but if I ever did and my husband never said the words "I love you," but he showed me every day that he did, I would click my heels every morning and be eternally grateful for my good fortune.

Are there men like that?

I thought of Naked Run Man.

"Lady, you would be better off to bulldoze the bitch right over and start again," the contractor said as he looked around my home. His name was Gordon, his body was a lump of clay, and he looked like he'd slept outside for the last eight years. He had lines down his face like railroad tracks and a giant red nose.

"Yep, she's a bitch," he sighed, and lit a cigarette. I pictured black clouds of poison filling my lungs as they cried for relief. I am all for indulging people's destructive habits, but I cannot stand the smell of cigarette smoke. I am rabid about it, I will admit.

"Gordon, A—do not smoke in my house and, B—my house is not a bitch." How dare he call my house a bitch? I heard the mice running and skipping about in the walls. I noticed a giant crack in the plaster above the front door. I took a glance at the kitchen cabinets, one of which had come loose when Gordon opened the door.

But still, my house was not a bitch.

He looked at me, let his ferrett eyes wander down my hair to my waist and hips and back up again. I had not missed his constant assessment of my body during the house tour. "Yeah, baby, but I could be persuaded to give you a real good deal on this work here on the bitch if I'm happy. You know what I mean?"

I knew what he meant. The "bitch" did not mind when I ripped off one of her dangling wallboards and swung it in the general direction of Gordon's head.

I swung again and it connected with his shoulder. He tried to hit back, but I took another swing. The cigarette dropped out of his mouth and he started swearing.

"Get out of the bitch's house," I told him, my voice low. I brandished the board again, then swung one more time, my always bubbling anger coming forth with a vicious vengeance. Emmaline wouldn't like this display.

Gordon's eyes flew open in shock and he waddled his lumpy body out, but not before I spanked him with the wallboard.

When I was sure he was gone, I apologized to my house. "There's nothing wrong with being a bitch," I reassured her. "Nothing at all. I would rather be a bitch than a wimpy woman any day of the week." I patted the countertop and felt something wet. I smelled it. It smelled like pee. Animal pee, I thought, unless someone who stood on two legs was taking the time to stand on my counters and pee on them. "Bitches rule," I told my house. "*We rule.* I should know."

The next morning I met with another contractor. He had gray curly hair and a wild expression on his face, as if he had been chased by a herd of zebras.

"It's beautiful," he told me, his voice high-pitched and sort of whiny. "Beautiful." He sat on the floor and laid down flat, his arms and legs spread-eagled. "I want her."

"You want her?"

"Give her to me, give her to me," he sighed, trembling a little. "I want her freshness, her softness. I want her to come to me."

I helped him up. I was sorry that he had been chased by a herd of zebras, but I had a house to repair.

I waved good-bye and told him I'd get in contact later.

* * *

Another two days went by and I heard nothing from Naked Run Man. Perhaps that's best, I thought. Dreaming, fantasizing, obsessing even, about a man, is almost always better than the reality of being involved with one.

Still. I indulged myself. I found my mental meanderings and wanderings quite entertaining.

I screened another three applicants to remodel my home. One wanted all of the money up-front. He revealed that Vegas was his favorite place and whenever he had a dime to his name, it was the first place he went. Another wouldn't discuss with me what he thought should be done to my house in order to remodel it. He flicked his hands in the air when I asked him questions. "Don't worry, little lady, don't worry your pretty little head."

I told him I wouldn't worry my pretty little head at all. Goodbye.

One admitted to a short prison stay. "The mashed potatoes were the best, but when they took away Sandwich Friday I 'bout blew my brains out. I had to go to isolation to cool off. Took me a week." He blew air out of his mouth. It ruffled his bangs. "Isolation's the way to go when you need to chill."

It would be hypocritical for me to be against people who have been guests of the state prison system because of my pesky assault charges, but I decided to steer clear when he told me that he had a violent temper and not to tick him off. He said all this so pleasantly it made the hairs on the back on my neck do a warning dance of danger.

I vowed to keep searching. My house deserved it. She was going to be given the best house makeover I could find.

"Last time, Jeanne," Charlie said, with great exasperation. I heard the kids yelling and playing and laughing. His oldest would be the same age as Ally, had she lived. Did I already tell you that? "Call Bob. He says he's holding the position, but he can't do it much longer."

"Why?"

"Why what?"

"Why is Bob holding the position?"

"Because of you, Jeanne! I told him all about you. Come on, Jeanne Beanie."

I told him I'd call and tried to change the subject. He told me he knew I was trying to change the subject. We talked about the job for a second more and I changed the subject again and he repeated his first objection. I heard the littlest one crying in the background and I thought, thank heavens, and we had to say our I love yous and hang up.

I looked across the grass between the bed-and-breakfast and my house. The front and back porches were sliding off and the deck off my master bedroom was at a slant. The roof was sinking. Two windows were broken out.

But still I felt victorious. I had bought the house outright, so I had no mortgage. If I was invited to be a guest in a jail for the tiny assault on Slick Dick I figured I could write a check out for the property taxes and utilities until I was released from my state-sponsored mandatory vacation.

But even with a tidy profit from my old home, all the repairs were going to make my bank account look dicey.

I studied the house again.

She was old. Tired. She had been neglected and abandoned. She was lost and alone. She needed a makeover and a new life and a new spirit and new color.

She *needed*.

But then, by God, I knew she would blossom. Like a woman freed from a lousy man. Like a rose on speed.

I wanted that house.

So exactly how bad do I want that home? I asked myself.

Bad.

Real bad.

I snuggled under the covers of my bed of blue heaven and called Bob, chief of staff to the governor. I have been told that I have a nice phone voice. I have also been told that I'm a good chatterer.

Bob and I had a nice long chat. It did not take me long to find out Bob is sixty and has a lovely wife of forty years, whom he eloped with because her father thought he was one step short of a two-headed convict. They have six children and fourteen grandchildren. We found that we both like Italian calzone and Mexico for the margaritas. He thought he could spit a watermelon seed farther than me. I told him I could hula-hoop all day if I wanted. He doubted that. Bob told me, in confidence, that he wanted to retire soon so he could travel with his wife and their goal was to attend every single grandchild's birthday party. I told him I thought that was a swell idea. Damn all these people with all these grandchildren, was what I was thinking deep inside.

I neglected to tell him about my assault charges, but I had a feeling that he'd understand; I did.

We were the best of friends by the time we were done.

We set up a time for an interview with the governor.

"Jay is a great guy," he told me, "but he can be intimidating. He's eight hundred steps ahead of everyone else, has a brilliant and agile mind, and does not mince words with his staff or anyone else. He can be blunt, and brusque. On the other hand, you will not find a more honest, sincere, compassionate man, and he knows what he's doing. Take a deep breath, give him short answers, and don't let him run you over like a steamroller."

I agreed not to be rolled.

I had enjoyed the retirement party, the bowling event, and a tea party with Linda, Margie, and Louise, although all four of us had a bit too much vodka and ended up singing, "She'll be coming 'round the mountain!" in rounds.

My social calendar in Weltana continues to heat up. I'll tell you that.

Whooeee.

*   *   *

The Oregon state capitol in Salem is the expected, sprawling white building surrounded by manicured lawns and gardens. There are marble sculptures on both sides of the entrance and a steep incline of stairs. One sculpture depicts a covered wagon and pioneers, the other Sacajawea (my kind of gal) leading Lewis and Clark. I noticed that the men are on horses and she is on foot, poor woman.

On top of the dome of the capitol is a golden pioneer, to celebrate those brave, but probably slightly nutty pioneers who endured starvation, disease, bone-grinding exhaustion, and other dangers like drowning, freezing in snow, storms, cholera, gunshot wounds, and the deaths of one's children, parents, and themselves, just to get to Oregon.

Inside the rotunda, on the floor, is a humongous Oregon state seal in bronze. Quite pretty. When you drop your head back and look straight up from the seal, you can see the capitol dome, which is intricately painted and has thirty-three stars, since Oregon is the thirty-third state, and proud of it. It makes me dizzy even to think of painting something like that.

There are also four truly stunning murals wrapped around the rotunda depicting historical Oregon events. To the left and right are stairs leading up to the Senate and House chambers. The governor's office is between them. It has a smallish-sized reception room, a public office where the governor puffs out his chest and makes announcements or signs bills, and there is his/her private office.

The whole place echoes. Echoes in history, echoes in the click-click of women's heels and cell phones, echoes with groups of men and women stuffed into suits arguing and debating, and with the voices of tired teachers directing their students.

I was sitting in the reception room, waiting for the governor to finish up a meeting before our meeting. I didn't mind the wait. The secretaries chatted, people came and went, including two groups of schoolchildren, one with a child who was wearing a space suit and carrying his helmet. Some people wore suits. Others wore jeans. One person had a fishing pole and was carryng a small cooler. I don't know why. The secretaries waved him into the inner sanctum.

I had enough time to compliment myself on my outfit. I was wearing these new pinkish heels with a gold buckle. I wore a light beige linen suit, a white lacy silk shirt, and several long necklaces with these funky pinkish glass stones.

I do love shoes.

I wondered what I should wear to court back in Chicago. The black slingbacks with the leather toe? The green faux alligator heels? The black leather knee-high boots? None of my shoes felt exactly right. Now that was troubling.

"Ms. Stewart?" A secretary with a cute face, wearing a red dress and these fabulous red and purple polka-dot shoes, came over to me. "You can come on in now. The governor will be with you in a second."

I thanked her and followed her down a short hallway to the governor's "real" office. I complimented her on her shoes; she did the same to me, which somehow launched us into a conversation about premenopausal hot flashes (she has them), herbal treatments (her sister recommends them), and whether we feel more comfortable with masseuses who are men or women (women—who wants a man rubbing your fat?).

By the time she went back to the front office we were bosom buddies, and I was thankful that I had a better idea of how to handle vaginal dryness during menopause.

I took time to look around the governor's official office.

It was medium-sized, overlooked the park, and had many flags from various armed forces deployed overseas pinned to the walls. It was not ostentatious or flashy, which is so Oregon.

Two fishing poles, crossed at the top, were hung on the walls, as were photographs and paintings of Oregon's rivers, the beach, and the mountains. The desk was massive, something that will be around for generations after I and this present governor are rotting away in the earth, our skeletons hollow and brittle.

I found a chair, then crossed and recrossed my legs while tugging at my waistband. I had lost weight since arriving in Oregon. It did not feel good. I was too skinny to begin with, now I was even thinner. I wondered if I already looked like that rotting skeleton.

I re-recrossed my legs and wondered again what in tarnation I was doing there. I remembered my home. *My very own home.* My home by a rushing river. My home with decks. My *charming home* even though she was also home to rats, mice, insects, and other beasts and would cost a gazillion dollars to fix.

I heard footsteps in the hallway and a deep, gravelly voice that sounded eerily familiar. I stood and eavesdropped as the voice gave out directions and instructions, his words at a premium, his tone authoritative. There was no doubt that the governor was coming this way.

I envisioned a short man. Someone I would tower over in my heels. Someone balding. I regretted not reading the papers since arriving in Oregon or at least looking the governor up on the Internet. That was stupid. Why didn't I do that?

But I knew why. I didn't want to work.

Here's a tidbit of info I have learned during my nervous breakdown: If you have worked your buttocks off for years and you suddenly find yourself in the position of being able to work for yourself or at home, or maybe not even working at all (by choice), it is almost unbearably impossible to put yourself back in the position of working those hideous hours again with strange, mind-boggling people you would not normally want to hang out with unless forced to by a gun. You feel like the life is going to be sucked out of you an inch at a time. Through your nose. And the sad reality is: You are right.

That's why I didn't look the governor up.

The voice stopped, the footsteps didn't.

The governor entered his office.

I drew a quick breath as my knees got a gooey feeling like pancake batter and my nerves started to shriek and my feet got a definite urge to hop, skip, and jump the heck out of there. Through the window if need be.

Because there, standing in front of me, was Naked Run Man.

CHAPTER 12

"Good Lord." I slammed my mouth shut as soon as I realized I had spoken. The words came out way, *way* too loud, as if someone was at a religious rally calling to *the* Lord through a megaphone.

Naked Run Man came to a dead stop and stared at me. His eyes flared a bit and his facial expression froze, but there was no other reaction.

I, however, stopped breathing. All of my blood took a nosedive to my feet. I couldn't speak. I couldn't move. I couldn't think. I couldn't react.

I was going to die.

For shocked, nerve-shattering seconds we stared at each other and I felt more naked and exposed than I did when we were rolling on the hard ground, the moonlight slivering onto my raw butt.

For those of you women who have never run naked along a river and literally run into a tall, rough-looking man, and nearly all your free thoughts are monopolized by that manly vision for almost two weeks, and you meet your Naked Run Man in the governor's office, and you find out that he is the governor of the state of Oregon, I can tell you that it is an experience that is, well, *unnerving*.

Especially when he is intimidating in a formal blue suit and white shirt and red tie and he is even taller and broader than you remember and one corner of his mouth is tilted up and his eyes are steely blue and they are staring right at you and he puts both hands in his pockets and kind of rocks back on his heels and his eyes run over you from head to toe and he smiles a bit and the lines around his eyes crinkle. . . . Well, I can tell you it puts you in the rather awkward position of wondering exactly what it would be like to make love to this man on his big governor's desk next to the official state of Oregon seal and you snap your mind back to reality darn quick because you feel faint and the pancake batter in your knees is spreading to your ankles.

So as Naked Run Man/Governor Jay Kendall was silent I said something relevant and important. Something that reflected my massive intellect.

"Good Lord!" Once again, the words were way too loud.

The governor stopped rocking back on his heels, shut the door to his office, then took a few steps toward me, *real slow*, his light blue eyes never leaving mine. I took a step back when he got about two feet away. He took a step closer and I took a step back, but my knees hit a chair and I was stuck.

Stuck like a rat.

A rat with pinkish-colored heels with gold buckles.

The governor took one more step closer and I reminded myself to breathe or perish. He was so close I saw the darker blue flecks in his eyes and the lines around his mouth and those streaks of gray in his hair that I wanted to touch. His eyes looked like they were laughing and they were soft, so soft. So very soft.

"Ms. Stewart."

"*Gooooood Lord.*" This time the words came out sounding like a squealing weasel.

"No, I am not the Lord," he said and I heard the laugh in his voice. "Only the governor."

I exhaled and wished the blood would come back to my brain.

Thinking is so much easier when your brain cells aren't gasping for blood.

"Would you like to sit down?"

I nodded, swallowed hard, and dropped myself into the chair before I fainted.

Instead of walking around to his side of the desk, he pulled another chair out and sat down. Too close. Terribly too close.

I crossed my right knee over my left because both legs were shaking. I had run into this man bare—bobbing boobs and all. I uncrossed my leg, sat up straight, and looked anywhere but in his laughing blue eyes. Those soft blue eyes I mentioned previously.

For long seconds there was a dead silence in that governor's office.

I breathed in, breathed out, tried to think of something to say. I thought of something that would, again, reflect my wide-ranging intellect, "You didn't come by," I said. Next, I wanted to remove my own tongue.

He nodded. "That's true."

I gulped. "I don't blame you. I would have avoided a man running naked along a river who tackled me, too." I extended my hand. He held it. His hand was warm and hard, a little callused. He did not let go. "Hello, Governor Kendall, I am Jeanne Stewart. I met you when I was naked." I stopped. I felt nauseous.

Had I said that? Had I actually said, "I met you when I was naked?"

I tried to pull my hand away. I wanted to run.

He tightened his grip.

I was going to die.

I swallowed the giant boulder that seemed to have lodged in my throat. "I have recently moved to the area and didn't recognize you because I have not read the papers or been on the Internet because I am a head case. As working together would be impossible, I think I will refrain from wasting any more of your valuable time. Good-bye."

I stood. My legs shook.

Governor Kendall did not stand. I stood over him, my hand still trembling in his.

"Sit down, please, Ms. Stewart."

I hesitated. I preferred to faint outside of the state capitol, not here, and things were definitely getting fuzzy and wobbly around the edges of my vision.

"Please."

I sat. But only because my knees with the pancake batter in them gave out.

He released my hand. I made an unattractive gasping sound.

"There is no need for you to leave."

"But . . . but, *you know me.*" Ack. That sounded positively intimate. I made another unattractive sound in my throat. "You know about my anger management class. About Slick Dick. About my mountain bike. My mother. The farm I didn't get . . . you know I've taken a giant jump off my rocker."

I remembered how he felt on top of me. I remembered his warmth. I remembered how he listened. I remembered how he smiled at me.

I could tell he remembered, too. Probably remembered how I hit him, tried to bite him, complained of his "grimy hands," and how I called him an asshole and said "shit yourself" to him.

I shook my head, tried to breathe.

Good Lord.

I was going to die.

"So," he said after a very long silence, "I think a great deal of your brother. He's told me a lot about you, and how you'd make a great communications director."

That was alarming. The list of what this man could know. . . .

I groaned. "My brother is a dear and wonderful person." I kneaded my fingers in my lap. "I am positive you will always like him far better than you will ever like me. Also, for some reason he loves me dearly, so I'm sure he's exaggerated greatly anything he's said about me to make me look good. Please don't believe it."

The governor nodded. Those eyes were still soft. "Tell me about your qualifications."

"You're kidding."

He shook his head, hands clasped in front of him.

I felt the flush in my face. I was sure I looked like a fire engine. Vaguely I thought that it was reassuring I could still blush at the age of thirty-seven.

"You still want to interview me? Even knowing what you already know?"

"Yes. However, I would like your promise that you will not run naked along the river for the duration of the campaign." He stopped, pondered the ceiling, then back at me. This time his eyes were not so soft. "Actually, I would like you to agree *never* to run naked along the river. It's dangerous."

I nodded. "It wasn't on my list of things to do today."

"Good. How about if you take it off your list of things to do ever?"

I nodded. "That would probably be wise."

"Before we start I want to clear one thing up."

"Yes?" Could he read minds? Did he know that I had already made love to him in my head many times? Was he offended? Disgusted? Dear Lord, please don't let him be married. I did not want to be a mental-cheater with a married man.

"I told you I was going to come by in two weeks."

I nodded.

"It's only been thirteen days."

"That's right." I tingled.

"I have another day." His words were gravelly again, but kind, so kind. "I was planning on coming by tomorrow."

"You . . . you don't owe me an explanation."

"I think I do."

I blinked a few times. My eyes felt hot.

"You don't need to check up on me . . . I'm perfectly all right." How humiliating. I bet he thought I was suicidal. He seemed like the type of man who would care about people like that. "You don't need to worry. I'm sure you have other things to do." I glanced around the office. "Maybe about six-hundred-forty-seven-thousand other things to do. You certainly don't need any more projects."

"I do not consider you a project."

"Do you consider me a freak?"

"No." He smiled, slow and easy.

"There's no point to this." Dear heavens but there wasn't. I brushed a hand through my gold curls. It got stuck in a tangle. I pulled my trembly hand back to my lap.

"There is a point, Jeanne. Let's do the interview. Tell me about yourself, why you want to work on my reelection campaign, what you can bring to the campaign . . ."

I stared at the governor. Surely he was jesting?

I couldn't take this job anyhow, after my naked incident.

But I thought of my little wrecked she-home and that meandering river right outside my backyard. I thought of the enormous lawsuit launched against me by Slick Dick. I thought of having to pay taxes on the house whilst languishing in jail.

I collected my ping-ponging thoughts and I launched into my line of professional baloney and told him about my qualifications.

Well, I shouldn't call it professional baloney. In burying my pain after burying Johnny and Ally, I have worked my buttocks off and have many professional successes because of it. Slave away eighty hours a week, channel all of your energy and time and passion into your job, have no real life to speak of, be reasonably competent, and you'll make it big.

I made it big. I was the creative director of what became one of the most successful ad agencies in the nation under my direction.

At various times I have handled advertising, marketing, and public relations for companies and local and state governments. Twice I went out "on loan" for a couple of well-known national politicians. (They were both quacks. Both made passes at me. I threatened to damage their kidneys permanently, to say nothing of their careers, if they even looked in a slightly sexual way at me again. By pulling out a tiny recorder I had stuffed in my bra, brandishing said recorder, which played back exactly what the (married) quacks had said, things got squeaky clean in those offices.)

I have also given speeches and inspirational talks at business-type conventions catering to media, PR, and advertising nerds. I suffer from insomnia, and I have to read myself to sleep each night. I regularly read five top national newspapers, various academic magazines, and have plunged through hundreds of books on economics, history, politics, and business.

I am a miserable and solitary and lonely woman, but a knowledgeable one.

I had the governor sitting up and listening within about half a second. That soft, indulgent expression stayed gone as he took in my little speech.

At the end I said, "My only deficit is that I don't know Oregon as well as I should because I've never lived here. But here's what I know about it so far, based on the people I've met."

I linked my fingers together real tight.

"Oregon is quirky. The other day I saw a man bicycling down the street dressed in a pink sweatsuit. He was wearing purple glittering wings on his back. I found this fascinating and stared at him. No one else in the café where I sat looked at him for more than a second. They did not feel it was unusual. It was only me. That's Oregon.

"It is considered in bad taste to flaunt money, although some newly monied people don't get it and the ones with true money find them classless. Having a nice home, although not a McMansion, is acceptable. Cars should not flash. Bragging about your money is obscene. Being a snob is stupid. That's Oregon.

"Fleece, jeans, and raincoats of some casual sort are perfect attire for almost anywhere at all. Following fashion is considered shallow. One should have better things to do in life, like becoming an environmentalist or volunteering to build homes for disadvantaged people.

"People should not assume that the forty-year-old man stand-

ing on the sidewalk in ripped jeans and a ratty sweater is anything less than a retired computer executive. True Oregonians
don't like umbrellas, but are obsessive about coffee. Oregonians
do not want the federal government in their business. Ever."

The governor nodded.

I had another brief and graphic image of what it would be like
to have sex on the governor's desk, my sweet heels flying right
off, my tights only a small hindrance, but I did not indulge myself for long, this being an interview and all.

"Oregonians have a live and let live attitude—for the most
part. You have a large slice of the population that is liberal. That's
mostly in the city. You have an equally large portion of the state
that is conservative. Mostly in the rural areas and small towns.
But there are flaming liberals in Eastern Oregon and rock-hard
conservatives smack in the city, too. The two Oregons often
clash. The environment vs. jobs. Pro choice vs. antiabortion. Ac-
ceptance of gay marriage and loud opposition to it. My job will be
to figure out how you can reach both Oregons without compro-
mising your ideas and ideals, knowing full well that a certain segment of Oregon will vote for a zebra with toenail fungus for
governor if he labels himself a conservative Republican."

The governor nodded again. "Zebras have a certain appeal."

"Yep, they do. It's that striped thing they've got going on." I
thought of my faux zebra heels at home. They certainly had
panache.

We were silent. Why say anything more? He would be insane
to hire me.

"You're hired," he said. "Can you start next week?"

Surely he jests once again. "*What?*" The word came out too
loud but at least I did not yell "Good Lord!"

"I said, you're hired. Welcome to the campaign."

"I'm hired?"

"Yes. We need you. Desperately. Charlie was right."

I nodded once. Paused. Nodded again. Paused. Nodded once
more. The nod-pause routine quit when reality hit. Would this

be a good time to tell Jay Governor about those frisky assault charges? The pesky civil case pending against me? A tiny nervous breakdown in front of schmucky ad execs? A slight drinking problem? Nah.

I nodded again. Paused. I stood up to leave, that darn pancake batter still in my knees. I knew I would have a mininervous breakdown on my drive back to Rosvita's. I would shake and cry, but for now my goal was to escape before the governor came to his senses and told me I really didn't have a job.

He got up, too. I held out my hand and once again it became lost in the size and warmth of his. For some strange reason I went back to the weird "nod and pause" routine.

I turned to go, turned back, my hand still wrapped in the warmth of his. The pancake batter went squish, squish.

"Thank you," I said. It came out choked, but at least the words were there.

"You're welcome."

My heart fluttered like there were wings inside of it.

"There is one thing," he said. "We will not be able to go on our Beach Exploration Day until after the campaign."

I nodded. Dating campaign workers was not something that was done by an ethical politician. He was ethical. And yet I hung on to that last phrase: Until after the campaign. Did that mean later we could head for Le Beach? Oh, cease my fluttering heart!

He finally let go of my hand.

There was another long silence where our eyes locked and I knew we had an agreement. Silent, but there. Warm and earthy. Like hot chocolate and picnics by waterfalls.

Once again I displayed my great intellect. "How do you like my shoes this time?" I twisted my ankle so he could see my heels, knowing he would contrast them to my dirty running shoes.

"Very nice," he said, his voice quiet, eyes on mine. "Very, very nice."

This time his eyes wandered all over my face—eyes, cheeks, mouth—and my inside feminine parts started to quiver.

We stood smiling at each other for a while, smiling, smiling, smiling.

I spun on my pinkish heels with the gold buckles, wobbling only a tad because of the pancake batter, and headed out the door. I waved at the secretary with the polka-dot shoes.

"Did you get the job?" she whispered.

"Yes."

She clapped her hands together, gave me a hug.

Another school group chattered on by. A little girl was wearing a polar bear outfit.

I was beginning to like these Oregonians.

When I arrived in Weltana after my interview in Portland, I found a letter from Roy on top of my bed of blue heaven, which Rosvita must have placed there.

It was a copy of a letter from Jared's lawyer specifying exactly how much in damages Slick Dick was demanding in the civil suit he had filed against me.

I had already known of the amount but seeing it in writing had me fuming and sputtering and planning creative ways that I could damage him again.

I called Roy immediately. I very politely reiterated that I had zero intention of paying Slick Dick any money and to tell the prosecutor that I demanded a jury trial. I told Roy I wanted him to ask the jury to demand that Slick Dick give up his testicles in payment for his harm of me.

He said he had a meeting with Slick Dick and his attorney the next week and he would inform them of my decision.

Swell. I told him. Don't forget the part about his balls.

And, I added, when we're in court I want you to ask the jury to rule that Slick Dick should pay me back the nineteen hundred in cash he stole from me and give me back my mountain bike. Also inform Slick Dick and his attorney that we will be sharing with the jury Slick Dick's unemployment problem, how I paid off six thousand dollars in credit card debt and paid for all the food and supplies for us *and* his rat.

Roy agreed that Slick Dick had the right to know the full impact of what a trial would look like.

Splendid, I told him.

We ended our conversation with his assurance that he would decimate Slick Dick like a skewered hot dog in their next meeting.

"Thank you ever so much," I said, so polite.

"You're welcome, kiddo," he said. "I'm doing my best. But I will take this time, once again, honey, to inform you that a jury may very well find you guilty of assault against Jared and that we should plea bargain."

"Please call him Slick Dick at all times," I interrupted.

"Slick Dick. You did assault him, honey. There's no getting around that."

"And I enjoyed it."

"Please refrain from saying that on the stand."

"I'll try. But I must be honest."

"Not that honest, I beg you."

"I'm not plea bargaining, Roy. I want a trial. Bring it on."

I went out to the river and poured myself a brandy.

I did not drink a second one. I wanted to. I wanted to wash the stress away, but for a brief sane moment, I decided I was not going to let Slick Dick help me pickle my own liver anymore and I dumped it into the grass.

I did not wake up with a hangover.

I liked that.

"I'm going to kill that devil Dan," Rosvita pronounced that night as she whipped us up a Spanish omelet while I washed the lettuce for a Caesar salad. We were both on glass of wine number two. I would not have another glass after this one. "I can't believe you're working for a politician," Rosvita mumbled. "But at least Kendall's got a nice, clean spinal bone up his back, unlike most other politicians who have rubber bands running from their asses to their brain stems."

"What has the Migrant Devil done now?" I asked.

She slammed the spatula on the counter, then started chopping tomatoes with a vengeance. "I am going to kill Dan because he is an obnoxious pig who treats his migrant workers horribly. Have you seen the conditions those people live in?"

I knew it was a rhetorical question. Rosvita and I both dropped off goods at the migrant camps on a regular basis, sometimes together, but still she said to me all the time, "Have you seen the conditions those people live in?" before she launched into another diatribe.

"He treats them like cattle. Cattle!" She took a pink flower she was wearing in her hair out and smashed it on the floor with her feet. "I'm going to smash him like that. The other day, Juan Carlos got sick and couldn't work for two days and he fired him! *Fired him!* His wife had to put him in the backseat of their car with the two kids and go. I gave her five hundred dollars and she cried." Rosvita yanked opened the refrigerator door, grabbed the cheese, and slammed the door shut.

"And I know now what he does to the women!"

I felt nauseous. I knew something bad was coming down the pike. "What are you talking about?"

"I've seen several women from the migrant farm go into his house during the middle of the day. I've tried to talk to them about it, but those women only cry, *they cry and cry,* and won't tell me a thing."

A graphic image of the Migrant Devil rutting on top of one of the women I had met at the camp made me drop the colander. The lettuce flopped out onto the floor, looking wet and lifeless. I felt ill and livid at the same time.

"They go in for exactly one hour and they come out straightening their dresses and wiping their eyes." She cracked another egg against the bowl so hard that half of it landed on the counter.

"Those poor women. And worse, I heard that he is after the teenage girls, too. *Teenage girls!*"

Gall. I felt ill. Having sex with the Migrant Devil can only be compared to having sex with a huge, farting, violent warthog.

I picked up the lettuce, flinging it back into the colander. No, what was going on in the Migrant Devil's home wasn't sex. It was rape, plain and simple. I kicked myself for thinking even for a minute that it was sex.

I'll bet that in order for their husbands to keep their pathetic, back-breaking, pesticide-inhaling, frying-under-the-hot-sun jobs or to feed their kids, or under the threat of deportation, they allowed the Migrant Devil to rape them.

I shuddered. This type of crime has been going on for millions of years. It would be going on for millions more years.

Men are such shits.

"I'm going to kill him, Jeanne. I. Am. Going. To. Kill. Him."

Rosvita whipped the eggs almost into a froth and poured the mixture into a hot, buttered pan where they sizzled. "My brother, a famous criminal defense attorney, says that I should not commit a crime. He says he will protect me even if I am guilty, but he may not be able to get me off. But he is famous and rip-roaring successful so I bet he could."

"I would not risk it," I said, my tone mild.

"Dan will die," Rosvita predicted. "He must rot."

The thought of it whetted my appetite for our Spanish omelet and Caesar salad, but I really didn't think she'd act on her murderous intentions.

I was wrong.

And I had no idea she'd act so soon.

I woke at the crack of dawn for my first day of work and began trying on outfits. By the time I was done I felt quite smug. It took only six completely different outfits with completely different jewelry and, of course, completely different shoes, for me to decide what to wear to work today to Jay's reelection headquarters.

I showered and let my curls curlicue on down past my shoulders. I put on a little makeup—mascara, blush, lipstick. Not much. I have learned that in Oregon it is generally considered cheap or vain to spend a ton of time on your face. (Note: It is okay, however, even cultured and fashionable, to spend days, even weeks or years testing Oregon's home-bottled beers and lush wines before rendering an opinion on which is the best.)

On one hand I felt nervous and sick and scared and weak. Not at all up to going back to work, post-nervous breakdown. I still very much wanted to hide after working eighty hours a week for years.

And yet, on the flip side, I could hardly control the pattering of my little heart at the very thought of seeing Jay again. Patter, patter, patter. I reminded myself of what the last man in my life had done to shred my self-esteem. And the man before that and the man before him. Pissants, all of them. Careful, Jeanne, be careful, I told myself.

I pulled on a black suede skirt that dropped to about two inches above my knee, a white lacy shirt with a V that made my little boobs look bigger, and a textured suede jacket with beige and black threads that ended midhip. I added dangling earrings, a multistrand necklace, and three bracelets made with semiprecious stones.

Next I sat on the edge of my bed and pulled on my tights. They have little diamonds on them. I put on beige and black leather heels. I paused to give them an admiring stroke then grabbed my briefcase. I stood in front of the mirrors that doubled as closet doors.

My outfit was very cool. My jewelry added class and style. My shoes. Well, they were hot, hot, hot. I even loved my tights.

I watched as tears drowned my eyeballs and rolled down my only slightly made-up Oregon face like ministreams. I bent over for a second as this whizzing pain of fear zinged me in the gut, coming from out of nowhere.

When the pain died, I straightened my back up, sniffled and

snuffled, breathed in and out, grabbed a tissue on the way out the door, and forced myself to buck up. Next I shoved the keys into my roaring Bronco and drove from the mountains to the city.

On the way I noticed two spray bottles in the backseat from Rosvita.

CHAPTER 13

Governor Kendall has two headquarter offices for his reelection. One in Portland, where I would be based, and one in the state capital of Salem.

The headquarters of the reelection campaign is on the ground floor of an older building in the middle of downtown Portland, amid skyscrapers and well-preserved old buildings, the business people and the bums, and the requisite eighty coffee places within minutes of anywhere. The location was unusual—usually campaign headquarters is near the freeway with easy parking access, but Jay apparently wanted to be "near the people."

The windows were plastered with REELECT JAY KENDALL posters. I tried to avoid staring at those eyes in the posters, but I did note that they looked rather hard in the posters, not laughing and gentle as they were when he looked at me.

Before I dared myself to take the last few steps into the building I paused and tried to breathe away my fear.

I hoped that I could control the symptoms of my nervous breakdown.

I hoped that I didn't make a fool of myself in front of Jay.

I hoped I didn't feel compelled to tell everyone that they were "pointless . . . all pointless." I reminded myself not to mention how Baucom's vaginal creams were used by more women than ever before because of my efforts. I also pledged not to mention I was behind many of those lovely penis problem commercials.

I inhaled nice and deep and opened the door.

The first person I saw was my brother.

Charlie's face went from stressed and intense to relief and beaming joy. He engulfed me in a huge bear hug. I was so happy to see him I cried a droplet or two of tears.

The second thing I noticed was that I was way overdressed.

Way overdressed.

Most everyone was in jeans, casual shirts, and fleece sweatshirts. There were a lot of college kids running around, bright-faced and innocent. Not many women were wearing makeup. No one was in a suit. No one was in high heels. No one had tights with little diamonds.

I pushed back a handful of my curls and tried not to feel stupid.

I didn't fit in.

How typical.

"We should think of ourselves as The Decimators," the man said, pounding a fist on the conference table. "We will decimate any and all opponents of Mr. Kendall. *Any and all.*" He pounded the table again.

I looked at the second in command of the reelect Jay Kendall campaign (Charlie is the first in command). Damon Sturgill was sitting to Charlie's right. He is a short man with all the stereotypical complexes that implies. I had met him seven days ago when I started.

Bob Davis had had a heart attack two days after I'd talked to him. He had decided that it was of utmost importance to attend all of his grandchildren's birthdays immediately, so he quit his job, and danced into retirement.

There were only about twelve of us at the table, but through the office's windows I could see all the busy-bee campaign workers buzzing about busily.

Jay was renting space in the building. We had a huge room. The furniture was typical: Lots of foldout tables of all sizes, folding chairs, phones, wires everywhere, volunteers on the phones or in little meetings, empty pizza boxes, several TVs, a "THANK YOU VOLUNTEERS!" sign, and a huge timeline on one wall detailing Jay's public appearances, speeches, fund-raising events, when the voter ballots go out, and a countdown until election day.

I swung my eyes back to the Napoleonic short man, then snuck a glance at the faces of the other campaign people and saw various levels of disgust, disbelief, and irritation on their faces as they listened to him.

I had only been on the campaign a week, but I knew one thing: Everyone hated Damon.

Charlie was being attentive to Damon for the moment, but I could tell by the stillness of his features that he was about ready to jump up and strangle the man using his well-worn belt, a belt I had given him years ago with his initials carved on the buckle.

It would be a shame if he did that because I wouldn't want blood staining that belt. Still, I could always buy him a new one and it would please me to do so.

"This is not only about getting Jay elected. It's about debilitating our competition, destroying their infrastructure; it's about victory. *It's about war.* A political war." A few bits of spittle from Damon's mouth careened through the air. "Our candidate is our weapon. Our speeches are our bombs. Our battlefield is our political strategy. Our firefights are our debates—which we will control and win. Victory, people; keep yourself focused. *Fo-cused.*"

I tuned way out—I am so skilled at tuning out of meetings—and I studied my heels. They rocked. I was wearing black leather heels with a cheetah-print toe. I thought they looked splendid with my jeans (very Oregon) and black fitted sweater and chunky silver jewelry in my ears, around my neck, and halfway up my left forearm.

The first time I met Damon Sturgill he clasped my hand and shook it up and down as fast as if he was masturbating my hand.

I was several inches taller than him in my heels, and I knew he hated that. Made him feel out of control. Diminished. Teeny-tiny.

He had one of those salesmen hale-and-hearty type attitudes, everyone is his best friend, and he'll stab you in the back with a machete and a maniacal grin if it'll take him one step further up the ladder. He had freezing cold gray eyes that looked dead, as if any sliver of human compassion or kindness had withered away long ago, lost in too many nights with only his own dick for company.

It is a fact that I intensely disliked him on sight. I could not help thinking of him as the Walking Masturbator.

"Our strategy is to fire away at Kory Mantel like an AK-thirty-seven." He mimicked shooting a gun with his finger.

"Forty-seven," I said. "There is no AK-thirty-seven."

Damon glowered at me. "Whatever."

"Well, it's an important distinction if we're going to war," I insisted. "We should bring the right guns."

Damon glowered further. "Kory is a hard-core right-to-lifer. He's against assisted suicide; he's against civil unions for gays, he's against medically prescribed marijuana. He's against gays. We need to hammer on his poor voting record in the Senate, the fact that he takes a ton of money from special interests and right-wing conservative groups; and how he says one thing and then does another. We need to initiate quietly and carefully a public discussion on his son."

"His son?" Charlie's horrified voice broke through the black guck of Damon's murky lecture.

"Yes. He talked about his boy in his last speech, said what a great kid he is, that he's academically advanced, athletic. The paper picked it up and now we have to expose the situation for what it is."

"Which is?" Charlie asked.

"Hey, Charlie!" Damon spread his arms out like a vulture. "Charles, Charles, Charles!"

I decided to strangle Damon myself and save Charlie the trouble. Charlie had children and a wife to support and I had no one. Jail time would be easier for me.

"Kory's son is an addict." Damon said "addict" like this: Addick. "We can tell this whole state that Mantel voted to cut funding for drug treatment and isn't that ironic since his son is so . . . troubled. We can leak details of Mantel's son's criminal history, his addiction history, his expulsion from school to the press. How can a man with an addict for a son possibly run a state, when he'll have so many personal problems to deal with? How can he explain and excuse cutting the state's health care program for the poor? Don't the poor deserve drug treatment, too? He's a privileged man who can pay for rehab, but what about all the other families in Oregon who can't even afford a basic health care plan for their children, much less pay for mental health problems? Why, as senator has he not done more to fund antidrug efforts? In fact, he's voted several bills down. With his son so addicted (addick-ted), why doesn't he get it?"

"I don't agree," Charlie said. "We are not—"

"I don't agree," Damon mocked. "This is a tough campaign, Charles, a tough one. We have to fight Mantel with a blitz of strength and brutal force. Campaigns get bloody, buddy, and if anybody here can't stomach it, they should get out of the battle. It's brutal here on the front lines, but we gotta keep our focus. Winning, winning, winning. That's the goal. Right there, Charles."

Now I looked forward to strangling Damon. But first I would torture him by using a sandblaster on his large buttocks. I shot a glance my brother's way. I knew he was regretting allowing Damon to address the group, something Damon had been pleading with my brother to allow, Charlie had told me, from the first day he had joined the campaign.

My brother still had his composure, his dignity, but I could tell, as his sister, that he was pissed off beyond pissed off. My brother had years of experience running political campaigns and working for politicians. He certainly didn't need a lecture.

Before I or Charlie could speak up, Damon was at it again.

"We're going to attack. To the public, we'll look gentle, but we'll make our point, and let the media do the rest. We need to destroy Kory and"—he snapped the fingers of his hands three times in midair—"now is the time to discuss his marital history, too. There's a rumor of an affair with a former employee. This brings up not only his honesty and integrity as a person, it brings up the fact that he exploited—*exploited*—a vulnerable employee. We'll fry him with this and if we can get the girl to file a lawsuit against him for sexual harassment and intimidation, whoa, baby, we're on the right road. This is the way to do it, folks, this is the way to do it." He slapped one fist the size of a cow's head against the other.

For a millisecond there was a dead, decaying silence.

"Please tell me you're kidding," I said, leaning forward. My legs were crossed under the table and I circled my right ankle. *How I loved that cheetah-print toe!*

The stunned silence in that room almost blew me out of my chair. What did I care? I would probably be going to jail soon for assault and wouldn't be able to finish the campaign anyhow. I would miss Jay, though. I wondered if the prison warden would allow me to bring a REELECT JAY KENDALL poster to my cell?

Damon glowered at me. His lower lip dropped like a sagging sausage; his pig eyes narrowing into mean little slits. The slits reminded me of raisins. The type of raisin that has worms in it.

"Excuse me?" He took a couple of steps toward me around the table and I knew he was going for the ole intimidation trick.

I, however, do not intimidate.

"Your idea of bashing Kory's family is about as good as having the governor announce that he will not allow women to use their diaphragms anymore."

There was that silence again! What a group! I watched the cowhead-sized hands at Damon's side clench.

"Do you know what a diaphragm is?" I asked Damon, using my sympathetic voice. I tried to widen my eyes to appear innocent. He said nothing, but looked so furious I wondered if his head might split open. That would be quite fascinating. Bloody, but fascinating. "Well, let me explain it another way. Your idea of smashing Kory's family is about as good as having the governor announce that he will not allow men to scratch themselves while watching football. Ever."

"Ms.?" Damon paused as if I was so insignificant he couldn't remember my name.

What a mold-muncher.

"Teresa Mother," I told him. "My name is Ms. Teresa Mother."

Those pig eyes practically popped out. "This is a political campaign. I know you're used to advertising and public relations, but we don't deal with fluff here. We deal with real issues that effect real people in real life situations."

"Real life situations sometimes involve diaphragms, Dimon," I told him. The mispronunciation of his name came out well I thought.

"My goal—and it should be your goal, too, although I'm already getting concerned about your commitment level, Ms. Stewart—is to get Jay Kendall elected again. I am working very hard to do this. Now, I know your brother Charlie brought you on board—"

"Damon, you will stop right there." My brother stood up, the legs of his chair scraping on the floor. I could tell he was near the explosion point. Charlie hardly ever gets mad, but when he does, shut up, dive for cover, and hope it ends soon. He had a black belt in karate. I prayed he would use those skills on Damon before the end of the campaign.

"It's all right, Charlie," I said. I resisted the temptation to sneak another peek at my shoes.

I summoned up a glare for my brother. My glare said, Don't stand up for me, Charlie. Let me fight my own battles. "I'm sure Dimon was simply going to delve into the merits of certain birth control methods."

The silence was still very, very heavy, although I did hear some muffled laughter.

I waited.

Damon took a few steps closer, his face rashy red.

"Ms. Stewart," he boomed.

"It's Teresa Mother," I reminded him.

"I will not allow my time to be wasted on this conversation. You can be sure I will be speaking to the governor directly, but for now you should know that I am not interested in birth control—"

"No, I wouldn't think that you would have the need to be interested, in the slightest, or concerned with, birth control." I let my eyes wander over his heavy stout frame, right down to his shoes, pausing at his stomach. "Birth control is a touchy subject. Men don't like condoms. The pill makes many of us throw up at the first of the month. I feel queasy even thinking about the IUD. Spermicides cause yeast infection."

I heard my dear brother, Charlie, groan. I would need to buy him a stiff drink after this, I knew.

"But let me explain my point." I stood up so that I could tower over Damon. My butt had been falling asleep and the tingling was doing funny things to that area. I thought of Jay.

Stop, Jeanne, I told myself. No, Jay. No. *No, Jeanne.*

"So, we can go ahead and get down in the dirt and rip Kory's family apart." I looked down at Damon, straight into his dagger-throwing pig-raisin eyes. I started to amble around the table, passing him by on the left as I spoke. "But, you see, if we do that, people in this state will hate us. It's so simple. Everyone who has had to deal with a rebellious teenager or drug-using child—and they are legion—will jump to Kory's defense if we suggest, even in the slightest way, that his parenting, or lack thereof, caused his son to go temporarily to the bad side. They'll vote for Kory out of sympathy. Out of disgust with us for even bringing up his son's troubles."

I glanced down at my toes again. Roar!

"Even subtly attacking a candidate's child will backfire on us so hard we will be picking up our own molars off the ground."

My brother was not looking so ill now.

Damon clearly wanted to kill me.

"People with problems are very sympathetic when politicians get to deal with the same problems they do. Take Clinton. When people found out that he had to sleep on the couch after the Monica deal, they sympathized. How many men have landed on the couch before? Even the president of the United States, the leader of the free world, had to sleep on the couch. He got kicked out of bed by his wife. He was a man's man."

I heard one man chuckle. I had liked this one on sight. African-American. Big teeth. Small frame. A fellow loner, I would guess. His name is Riley.

"If we bring out these issues, we're fried." I stared at the ceiling for effect. "Think of a burning condom. I have never set a condom on fire. Anyone here?"

There was that stunned silence again for a few long seconds.

"This is a ridiculous conversation—" Damon sputtered.

"One time my brother and I put a condom on the faucet in the bathtub to see how big it would get," Camellia said, her voice quiet. Camellia is about twenty-five and an Earth Mother. She acts about sixty. She is hardworking and mentioned that she had been on her own since she was fourteen and her parents had left her and her thirteen-year-old brother to fend for themselves. She has a degree in biology and is working on a master's in political science.

Her brother is in med school.

They're both emotionally screwed, she told me, but they figured that in their screwedness they might as well get educated along the way.

"How big did it get?" asked Riley. He leaned back in his chair.

"Enormous. You would not believe it. Reminded me of one of those balloons that a clown will use to make you a balloon hat— only the condom was about three times that big."

"Did it eventually pop?" Ramon asked. Every day Ramon wears a fleece shirt and jeans. He is gay and is dating another campaign worker. I believe I am the only one who knows that tender secret, which I shall never reveal being the expert secret-keeper that I am. His boyfriend, Jerome, is a gentle and funny soul who looks like a football player.

"Popped with a bang. Water bursting out all over. We were soaked. But my brother, to this day, trusts a condom."

"And condom-trusters are useful people," I intoned. "But let's take this conversation seriously, people. Camellia's condom-blowing event provides us with a great moral: Do not blow something up so big that it bursts and you get soaked. Likewise, here today. If we blow up Kory's supposed affair and the son's criminal problems, we'll get soaked."

Everyone nodded in agreement—except Damon.

I looked closely at him. Yep. I was right. In another life he was the guillotine guy. You know, the one with the black mask, the huge stomach, and that scary, weird-shaped ax that removed people's heads from their necks with one neat slash.

"Ridiculous," Damon said.

I bet he had also been a cannibal. I could see him eating a leg or an arm, palm trees swaying above him as he burped and gurgled.

"This is a campaign, Ms. Stewart. A campaign." He said "campaign" like this: *cam-pain*. "It's not an advertisement for toilet paper or peanut butter or hemorrhoidal cream—"

"Well, there ya got me," I told him, wriggling my eyebrows. "I have written ads for toilet paper *and* hemorrhoidal cream for national TV. For the hemorrhoidal cream ad I suggested to my team that we show a half-naked woman smiling as she inserts the cream into her buttocks, her children smiling next to her, her husband caressing her back, the family dog and cat curled up near her feet. It was a phenomenal idea, but no one seemed to think it would fly with the pharmaceutical companies. Anyhow." I wiggled my eyebrows once more, to show how I took this situation seriously. "We have a moral obligation here."

"What?" Damon roared this. I could almost see toenails and tendons spitting from the cannibal's mouth now. "What moral obligation?"

"Haven't you been listening?"

"Yes, I've been listening to your drivel, your lecture on birth control, your insane ideas—"

"Not insane." I wagged my finger at him. "That's what I'm trying to tell you, Demon Damon. You must not use that word in this campaign. Ever. Even if it's against our opponent's son who has a few troubles. We'll lose if you do."

Riley nodded. So did Charlie. Camellia was definitely on-board. Ramon kept gazing out the windows of the conference room at his boyfriend, but I knew by how he'd nodded when I spoke that he was one hundred percent in back of me.

"Do not call me Demon Damon. I will not tolerate that disrespect, nor will I condone your unprofessional attitude. I will be reporting back to the governor."

I crossed my arms and decided to answer Damon as if he was but a fly. "We have a moral obligation not to humiliate Kory's wife publicly, who is innocent in this mess, or to exacerbate further the incredibly serious, life-threatening problems that his son faces."

Everyone nodded.

"Are you out of your mind?" Damon hissed. Whew! I could have sworn I saw an elbow bone fly from his mouth. "Kory knew what he was signing up for!"

"His son didn't," I said. "And I will not be a part of any campaign that allows an innocent teenager, one with problems already up the wazoo, to be exploited simply so that our candidate will win. It's wrong. It's immoral. I won't do it."

"Neither will I," said Charlie. He was still standing. "Sit down, Damon."

"I'm not into kid-bashing either," Camellia said. "Besides I knew a bunch of kids like Kory's son and it's by the grace of God that me and my brother aren't locked up in jail ourselves. I won't do it, either, Damon."

"Hell, no," said Ramon. "I'm not slicing and dicing any kid for a campaign. Or a wife."

"Not my style, man," Riley said. "Not my style. Plus, I have two aunts who have mental issues. My mother and I both look after them. One thinks she's a former nun and the other dresses like a garbage collector each day. Even wears a little black hat. There's no way I'm going to attack Kory's kid. No way. Besides, if I were Kory's son I'd probably be on drugs, too."

Damon sputtered. I envisioned teeth spitting from his mouth after a particularly tasty human meal. Finally he said the only thing he could think of and it came out like a hiss from a water buffalo. "You pussies."

After the door slammed we grinned at each other. Me, Charlie, Riley, Camellia, Ramon, and a bunch of other people. I did not know their views on various methods of birth control. Perhaps it would make for an interesting conversation over Reuben sandwiches at lunch today.

"Let's hear the condom story again, Camellia," Riley said. "That was funny."

I *must* get another pair of heels with cheetah print.

I ambled through the trees back to the river behind Rosvita's bed-and-breakfast wearing sweatpants and a t-shirt. I plunged straight into the cool miniwaves of the river, sat down on the rocks, bent my head on my arms and cried. I have found that my grief comes in waves. I suck it up and avoid it when I need to, but it always gets to me eventually and I cry.

So this is what I've learned about grief: You absolutely, positively cannot outrun grief. It will bring you to your knees and it will shove you to the ground face-first and there you will lay. You will not be able to get up until your tears are out, so cry and get it over with.

Later on that evening I spent about an hour in a hot shower, had several drinks alone in my room, curled up in a ball, and went to sleep in my clothes. When I woke up at 4:00 in the morning, I was holding the dolphin necklace from my father.

I felt sick from the drinking and leaned over the toilet. It was the first time in many, many days I was hungover. I had been doing so good.

I could almost hear my mother's voice yelling at me, begging me to quit drinking. I could see a huge cross before my eyes. It would be nine feet-by-twelve feet.

Her voice entered my head, like a bolt from heaven. "I'm slamming my cupboard doors at you!"

I knocked my head against the toilet seat.

"Get up and pretend you're a bird, Becky," Emmaline commanded, rising from her black beanbag in the middle of our circle and flapping those white arms.

Soman looked pained for Becky. Bradon groaned. I was about to protest when Becky spoke.

"I don't think I'd make a good bird." She pushed her blond straw hair out of her pale face. I did not miss the tiny crisscross scars on her wrists. Or on her upper arms for that matter. Each crisscross looked like a heartbreak to me. "I don't know how to fly."

"Fly, Becky," Emmaline shouted. She arched her neck like a bird, her graceful white hands above her head, then flapped vigorously. Becky jumped. I again wished that Emmaline wouldn't yell. It is so alarming to gentle Becky. "Fly! You need to fly away from your temptation of using drugs. Fly hard, fly quick. Fly with courage!"

"Right here?" Becky asked. "Now? Now fly?"

"Yes! Leave your nest of drugs and self-hate and criminal behavior here in your beanbag and fly away! Gather up your courage and zip around the room, soaring and dipping, and whizzing on by! Fly! Fly!" Flap, flap!

"Be a peacock," Soman said, rolling his huge shoulders back, as if getting ready to take flight. "A peacock is a bird, but he only struts about." I could tell Soman was trying to be helpful.

"Wrong, wrong, *wrong*," Emmaline argued. "A peacock can't fly like a bird. Becky needs to fly. She needs to fly with her heart soaring and free, lusting for a new life, craving the serenity that she, and she alone, has prevented herself from having. She needs to latch onto a lush life, a life filled with reds and oranges and yellows—not one littered with her own black and gray weaknesses. No one is leaving this room tonight, Becky, until we see you fly."

Becky glanced around. "That's not a good deal to make with me."

"What?" Emmaline squawked. (She sounded like a pissed off chicken.) Becky jumped. Bradon shook his bald head. Soman reached a hand out to Becky. Poor Becky. "What? This is not a class for rebellion. You've done enough of that!"

"Well," Becky's breathy voice caught. "I kind of like it here except for your yelling. I like punching the bags. I like the art stuff. It's warm. And I like these three." She nodded at us. "They're nice. They don't say mean things. They don't yell at me. No one here is going to offer me drugs. Usually I like you, too, Emmaline."

Emmaline was shocked, her white arms still pumping, albeit a little slower. "You don't *want* to leave anger management class?"

Becky blew the hair out of her face, then stared at all of us with defiance. "No. I don't. Why would I?"

Now that was tremendously sad. "I'll fly with you, Becky." Everyone looked at me. I had worked myself ragged at campaign headquarters for the last weeks, my mind constantly buzzing with increasingly amorous thoughts of Jay, and I needed a little flight in my life anyhow. "I'll run like a bird."

Bradon gave me the once-over, but it was analytical only, as if he were commenting on a banana. Or a bird. "You're a skinny bird."

"Yeah, girl, you gotta put on some weight," said Soman, his eyes narrowing on me but not in a suggestive way. "I mean ya got that classy bone structure going and ya gotta love those curls and all but, shit, ya ain't got nothin' to grab in bed."

I suppose I could have gotten offended at Soman's comment,

but I didn't. It was the truth. How can you get offended at truth? I am too skinny, and I ain't got nothin' to grab in bed. I didn't take his comment in a sexual way, either. Soman was about as likely to make a pass at me as he was to make a pass at Bradon. Besides, it was plain as day that Soman's heart beat only for Becky.

"I may be a skinny bird with nothing to grab in bed, but I wouldn't want to be a bird flying solo. I'm sure Becky doesn't either, even though she doesn't want to leave here because of the punching bags and cool art projects. This place reminds me a bit of kindergarten. All we need are blocks and cookies and milk and I could regress back real quick." I stood up. "Get up, Becky. You be a dove and I'll be a seagull. Based on my last boyfriend I seem to like trash."

"Heeeellll," Soman said. It sounded like "hail" the way he said it. "I'll fly with ya. I'm gonna be a vulture. Watch out for my wingspan." He stretched his "wings" way out and flapped as he got up. He made vulture sounds. I will not try to describe them.

Becky looked skeptical, but she soon made fluttering movements with her arms indicating her dove taking flight. "Coo. Coo. Coo."

I started zipping around the room with my arms out, swooping now and then down to the floor as if I was diving for food. I made cawing seagull sounds.

Bradon chuckled, then stood up. "If you all ever tell anybody that I did this, I will deny it." He flapped his hands real, real fast, and only his hands. "I am a graceful, African-American, proud, colorful hummingbird." He flitted from one corner to the next, making a hummingbird sound like this: Hmmmmm. He was quite a speedy little hummingbird, flitting about on the tips of his toes.

So Bradon flitted.

Becky fluttered.

Soman chased us (vultures like dead meat).

And I zipped and dipped hunting for trash and rotting food.

Emmaline blasted this great rock 'n' roll music and we birds danced and flew, twisted and whizzed on by each other, and took care not to get eaten by the vulture.

It had been a long and treacherous day at work in the city. Damon was pissy and I had had to tell him to get rid of his club and cavemanlike attitude and join the twenty-first century. He had not seemed to appreciate my wisdom. Especially when I drew a picture of a caveman and cavewoman, with the cave-woman hitting the caveman with a stick and hung it up behind his desk.

I had not seen Jay at the Portland office in way too long and my eyes were craving a glimpse of him.

Roy Sass left a message on my cell phone telling me that Slick Dick was not backing down. "Bring it on," I announced to myself. "Bring your sucky self on, Slick Dick. I will decimate you. And that's a promise."

In addition, Emmaline called and reminded me of our next anger management class. "You and Soman and Bradon and Becky are to wear shorts and t-shirts because you're going to slug the anger right out of your bodies until you can barely stand! Until you can barely stand!" She shouted those last five words. "I swear, you four are the worst, most incorrigible clients I've ever had. No one wants to relieve themselves of their insidious anger—so you're going to punch the hell out of it, then you're going to crawl through an obstacle course, and you're going to dance until I stay stop! Dance!" she'd shrieked. "Dance and punch!"

So, beyond a fourteen-hour workday and those particular calls, when I entered Rosvita's kitchen that night, I could tell that she was steamin' mad. About as mad as one can get without one's in-testines imploding.

"His time has come," she muttered. "I have had it."

"Had it with?"

"With Dan Fakue. He's done for. He's on his last days."

It took a little while to get to the guts of the story because Rosvita's hatred for Dan kept sneaking through the conversation, but apparently she had snuck over the previous evening to the Migrant Devil's farm with some spaghetti and meatballs for the tenants. Within hours she had to be restrained by the workers when she tried to storm the Migrant Devil's house with a table knife and wooden spoon in her hand.

Rosvita had taken it upon herself to get down on her hands and knees to inspect the floors of the sheds after providing the spaghetti dinner. Next she had sniffed the blankets. Tasted the water. Inspected the stove, cursed Dan and swore. She spent two hours with bleach and water and sponges cleaning the huts alongside the women.

After the scrubbings, she went out to the outhouse.

That's when the men had to restrain her.

"I worked myself to the bone over there, Jeanne, but when I saw that outhouse again, that miserable, overflowing, fly-infested, bubbling shack of excrement, I lost it. Lost it. I saw these cowering women and girls, these men who had been beaten down, who had been taken advantage of for months by Dan, who were not even allowed the dignity of a clean, safe home and a clean place to relieve themselves, and I saw red. Blood red."

I made her a cup of tea, laced it with brandy and lots of sugar and brought it to her while she ranted. "They might be afraid of him, but I'm not."

"I know you're not, Rosvita, but you're an American citizen with all the rights that entails. You're here legally. You have money. You make a living. Your brother is a prominent criminal defense attorney. If your rights are violated in any way, you sue. You have a voice and an education. You're best friends with the chief of police. They don't have anything. They're vulnerable. They're desperate for the money."

I sighed. Exhaustion almost did me in. "What happened after the knife and spoon scene?" I did not ask what she was planning on doing with the spoon.

"Carlos and Earl drove me home and walked back to camp. "No one, Jeanne, *no one*, and definitely not children, should have to live like that. And none of those women should have to put up with Dan's grimy hands on their bodies." She picked up several germ books she kept handy, thumbing her way through them, then recited to me several types of germs one can get from a pit toilet. "The world would be a cleaner, better, safer place without Dan, no question. I must enact the Elimination Plan."

She slid into her yoga position on the floor and muttered, "Die, Dan, die."

I joined her, settled my hands together, crossed my legs. "Die, Slick Dick, die."

CHAPTER 14

The next morning at breakfast I glanced at the front page and saw an article on Drake Windham. His company was under investigation. He had defaulted on a loan the size of Texas to another company. That company, which invested money for unions, crumbled to nothing in short order. Thousands of people lost their pensions overnight. The pensioners were mostly plumbers, electricians, and construction workers. Men and women who had worked hard for decades.

They had nothing.

It again detailed his arrest with the outraged hooker and the thrilling drive through the glass at the mortuary. The outraged hooker was suing him. His wife was divorcing him, the mortuary crash apparently the last straw, and she wanted the house, the kids, and a restraining order.

Drake was very unpopular.

If it were not for the lost pensions, I would have laughed.

A week later I picked up the phone around 8:04 at night and heard a deep, male, sexy voice. A voice that sounded like gravel and honey mixed. "Ms. Stewart."

My body froze and those nether regions started a slow burn.

"Hello, Governor." I tried to sound official, even though I was curled up in my bed of blue heaven, drinking—of all things—tea, and thinking about him. I was also wearing my favorite seafoam green silk shortie nightgown, one I never wore around Slick Dick, with all the lace around the bodice. I looked at my boobs and advised myself to gain weight so I could have a little more bounce to my boob.

"I hear things have gotten more exciting in the campaign since your arrival."

Oh, dear. Here it was. I was about to be fired.

"Excitement can be good. Stimulating." I choked. I put the teacup down. The river gurgled outside my window. I wanted a scotch.

He chuckled. His chuckle was low and straight in my ear. "Yes, it can be. Today I heard that during a meeting you said that a dead dog could have written a better speech than what Damon produced."

I bit my lip. I hadn't known my mouth was going to say those words until they were out. "That's correct. I did say that."

"And why did you say that?"

Honesty is the best policy. "Because it's true."

There was a flash of silence. "You must know some very clever dead dogs, Ms. Stewart."

"I know several. And each of them could have put more life and personality and warmth and Oregon charm and downhomeness into that speech. Please tell me that you're not planning on using Damon much for speeches."

"Damon has written very few speeches. It really isn't his role."

"I'm relieved to hear it."

"Damon works hard. He knows the numbers; he's been involved in many other campaigns. He has a huge array of contacts."

"I'm sure he does." I was going to say, but didn't, that all rats had a lot of contacts.

"I know you'll be writing most of the speeches, Jeanne, in future, so that should take care of this problem. You're very talented."

"Thank you."

"You also seem to have talent in terms of voicing your opinion," Jay said. "A few days ago, if I understand things correctly, you compared the opposing party with constipation. Is that correct?"

Dear Lord. "Yes, that would be correct."

"I see."

"No, you probably don't."

"No?"

"No. I'm a little unhinged right now in my life, Governor."

"I gathered that."

"You did? Gee. What was your first hint?"

He laughed in my ear again. That man could make me tingle, I tell you. The nether regions leapt with fire.

"Taken any nightly runs lately, Ms. Stewart?"

I was grateful for the change in conversation. "No, I have refrained from doing that again, although my fellow anger management companions were quite impressed with my daring."

I thought of Soman, who laughed so hard when he'd heard of my earthy exploit, he had to cross his legs to keep from peeing. "You was a skinny ass naked bird on the loose in the woods. That's good, girl, that's gooooodd!"

Bradon's comment was, "I wonder if I could get the school board to do the same thing. A little nudity at night along a river, their fat white asses fluttering about, might knock some sense into their boneheaded brains. Damn, but they are trapped in their own pampered white world. They're blind. They can't see it. They think there's no racism here because *they* haven't experienced it. Idiots."

Becky said, "That's the bravest thing I've ever heard," and burst into tears. (Call Becky, I told myself again. For lunch.)

Emmaline squawked, "You've raised yourself up, Jeanne, to a new and glorious level! You're stomping down your anger, forcing it onto a new road of peace. Pounding your anger into the dirt! Splendid!"

"I bet they could barely contain their admiration," Jay said, "and I'm glad you've stuck to our agreement."

"I usually do. Stick to my agreements, I mean. Would you like to go ahead and fire me now?"

There was a silence.

I thought about the firing. If I was fired from the campaign that would free me up to suggest a roll in the sack with Jay. Ever so politely I would suggest it.

"Why would I fire you?"

"Isn't that why you're calling?"

"No, not at all."

"You're kidding." I got out of my bed of blue heaven and stepped out onto my little porch so I could hear the river.

"No joke. Everyone thinks you're incredible. Blunt. Unusual. Dynamic. Strange. But definitely incredible. Except for Damon."

"Now that hurts. I idolize the man."

"He works hard. I'm giving him a chance."

I'd like the opportunity to give Jay a chance. A chance in my bed. But thinking about him naked at this moment would be inappropriate. Thinking about him naked in my bed of blue heaven would also be inappropriate. Thinking about him naked in my bed of blue heaven while I was wearing my seafoam green silk shortie nightgown while kissing him every which way would also be inappropriate. *I love inappropriateness!*

"I'm so glad I'm not being fired. I need the money to hire a plumber."

"A plumber? For your house?"

"Yes, indeed." And from there we dovetailed into the remodeling problems I was having on my house, including a charming family of bluebirds that had moved in, a living room floor that had caved in, and a bedroom wall that had tumbled in. Then we talked about the herd of deer I'd seen and the family of owls and how I loved to read books, too—what books was he reading now? Watching movies was also one of my favorite things to do—what were his favorite movies? I mentioned Rosvita, and her germ obsession, and he told me a couple of funny stories from the campaign trail.

Then I asked him what he did when he wasn't working and he said his life had been almost nothing but work. I told him that all work and no play would transform him into a gay man and he laughed and said he didn't think it was possible since he had run into one particularly naked woman on the river one night and it had not brought him any feelings of gayness at all.

We talked about many other things including national politics, favorite comedians, the San Juan Islands, families (I told him about my mother and the way she sent me crosses). He told me again that he was very sorry I lost my mother, and by then we had been talking for three hours. It was midnight.

"You probably want to hang up now, don't you?" he asked.

"Why did you call?" I decided to be blunt.

"I called to tell you to keep up the good work." He paused. It was a nice, long, friendly, pleasant pause. "Keep up the good work, Jeanne. This, by the way, is a professional call only, of course."

I laughed. "Of course."

"See you tomorrow. At ten."

"What?" This came out as a squeak. I was going to see Jay?

"Yes. I'll be at the campaign headquarters in Portland at ten for a meeting with the full staff."

I thought about this. Thought about being across the table from a man with bright blue eyes, a tough-lookin' chin, and a low rumbly sort of voice that made me quiver.

I thought of the little speeches in campaign headquarters I had given about spermicides, flatulence, whiny men, pathetic women, and stupid people when trying to make my point about certain campaign strategies. "I think I'm going to choke."

He laughed. "Somehow, Ms. Stewart, I don't think any situation would make you choke. None. Have a good night."

"You have a good night, too."

A suspended silence hung between us for long seconds. Heavy and warm, like holding the sun on your heart.

"Sleep well, Jeanne."

Another little image of Jay popped into my head. This time he was in my bed of blue heaven naked. I could tell he liked my seafoam green silk shortie nightgown. " 'Night, Jay."

I hung up the phone and did a little dance, complete with some moon-dancing moves and high kicks. I kissed the little gold dolphin necklace by my bedside. I decided to do what all smart women do when presented with an opportunity to sit across from a man who makes you tingle.

I swung open my closet doors. Goodness! What shoes to wear tomorrow, *what shoes to wear?*

On my way to work the next morning I reminded myself to keep looking for a contractor for my home. The roof resembled a diaphragm that King Kong's monkey girlfriend would have used and the stairs on the back deck were beginning to look like they'd been hit by a missile.

"I would like to thank everyone for their help and hard work these past months," Jay said to everyone at campaign headquarters.

Me, Charlie, Damon with his warthog face, Riley, Camellia, and Ramon stood with our older volunteers and about eighty college kids. Many of the students looked hungover because one of the rich kids volunteering for the campaign had had a big bash at his bungalow the night before with a bunch of big barrels of beer.

Jay was a born speech-maker. He stood confident; he spoke well, like syrup over pancakes; and he made everyone feel like an important part of the team, which was the goal of today's speech. He thanked them for all the canvassing they'd done around the state, for running the *Get Out the Vote* phone banks, for answering constituents' questions, organizing fund-raisers, sitting in endless strategy meetings, having the courage to voice their opinions, sticking to their core values, and for being "the heart of the campaign."

My, but he looked yummy. My, I wanted to plant a kiss on those lips.

The room was silent when he spoke, except for when everyone was cheering like wild banshees.

I did not cheer like a wild banshee because I am not a banshee, but I clapped my hands.

Jay thanked everyone, spending a lot of time on Charlie, as he should, because Charlie is a brilliant campaign strategist.

"Finally, I would like to thank a new member of our team."

My eyes locked on Jay's. If chocolate was blue it would look like his eyes.

"Jeanne Stewart." Jay motioned for me to come to the front. Those wild banshees started cheering again.

I could not move for many, scary seconds. Had Jay said my name? Riley and Charlie gave me an inelegant push from behind. *Good Lord.* Stand with Jay in front of all these people?

"Come on up, Jeanne."

I felt my feet moving, as if through the La Brea tar pits, although my brain was not moving at all.

As I headed up to the front, people patted my back and whooeeed. It would be silly to say that I was not affected by this. It was touching. I had no idea they even liked me. Even when I stood next to Jay, they didn't stop their junglish cheering.

I was later told that Damon looked positively ill.

"In the last few months, Ms. Stewart has surprised many of us," Jay intoned.

He paused and I dare say all those post-hangover banshees hooted and hollered.

"She has discussed certain subjects that many of us would never dare touch and related them to this campaign."

Those banshees seemed to find this statement even funnier than the last.

"Let's see . . . if I have it right, Ms. Stewart has compared our opponent's health care plan for Oregon to Viagra—good for a few minutes, but when you look closely, you realize it's all a fake.

"She said that the mothers of this state would appreciate the cuts in Mantel's budget for higher education about as much as they would appreciate the onset of early menopause and hot flashes.

"She treated you all to sundaes to remind you to tell voters I'm a proenvironment governor. The vanilla ice cream was representative of Mount Hood, the chocolate syrup all of our rivers, the whipped cream was snow, and the nuts were supposed to be Oregon's lakes."

More cheering. Sundae Day had been very popular.

"And she once stood on a table and danced an Irish jig to get her point across regarding social problems in this state. I believe she said that if we valued people in this state as much as the Irish valued their jig, we would all be living with a better beat."

Oh, he was so darn funny, wasn't he? Charlie was about ready to wet his pants he was laughing so hard.

"Further," Jay said, "I doubt that Mr. Mantel has anyone leading yoga in his office."

I had only done that twice with the staff. They had needed a good stretch. Riley had been able to get his leg behind his head. Camellia did the splits.

"Jeanne has been brilliant in writing press releases, answering reporters' questions, and helping to write speeches. It did make for an interesting newspaper article when she told one reporter that since Mr. Mantel so vehemently opposes Oregon's Death with Dignity law that she would personally stand over Mr. Mantel's deteriorating body during his last dying weeks and make absolutely, positively sure no one slipped him a drink to make his death more dignified or comfortable, no matter how grotesquely ill he became, no matter if he was vomiting through his nose and peeing in his diapers, and regardless of excruciating, uncontrollable pain. Further, her comment, 'I must be honest with you reporters about Governor Kendall's goals for Oregon or I will be struck by lightning, run over by wild pigs, and castrated as I've been told I have big balls,' was a real hit with the women voters."

Those banshees! They had a twisted sense of humor!

"So, thank you, Ms. Stewart, you have added life and energy to this campaign."

And all those hungover banshees hooted and hollered again, the meeting officially ended, and Damon, Charlie, me (not a banshee), and Jay went to the conference room and got down to business. My eyes kept locking with Jay's and my nether regions got so burning hot it was surprising they did not burst into flames, smoke billowing around the table.

I took the curve over the bridge real slow when I went home to ensure that my car would not leap over the side and drop the eight miles down (it appeared) from the bridge, and into the river and a swarm of yellow-bellied sea snakes. Would there be any life-saving dolphins down there? The car behind me honked. I tapped my brakes because people honking at me on bridges makes me even more nervous.

I flopped into bed around 12:00 that night, visions of Jay Kendall dancing through my head. Naked visions.

I interviewed a few more winners who claimed to be contractors who could remodel my home. I knew I would sooner hire a herd of possums than them. At my wit's end, Ricardo Lopez drove up. He was a short Hispanic man with broad features, tilted shy black eyes, and a thick chest. He came with his wife, Therese, his sons Roberto and Rudy, and his daughter Alessandra.

And from that moment on they brought me peace and laughter and friendship.

And a dead body. I can't forget the dead body. Or how difficult it is to yank a dead body up a steep incline of stairs. And they brought more secrets into my life.

But I'm jumping ahead.

Ricardo and Therese arrived on a Saturday in their rickety, creaking truck with their two teenage boys in the back, their sister between them. Sadness and hopelessness hung on those people like lead parkas.

At first I thought it was simply bone-crunching exhaustion from a life lived too hard, in fear, in desperation, and with no hope. But it didn't take long for me to figure out that something more was going on.

I gave them the tour of my home and they told me they'd heard through the grapevine at the migrant camp that I needed a contractor.

During the tour, Therese or Ricardo or one of the brothers had a hand on Alessandra's shoulder the whole time. Alessandra did not speak and often leaned heavily on Roberto. I thought I saw some discoloration on the side of her face, but she kept dipping her head, her hair sweeping down, so I couldn't be sure. Maybe she had a skin problem or birth defect, I didn't know, and I didn't want to stare.

I did not miss Therese's sharp intakes of breath as we surveyed each room or her muttered, "Mother of God . . . oh, Mother of God."

They were relieved that I spoke Spanish as we talked about the water damage on the ceiling, the carpet damage, and the kitchen, totally damaged. The bathrooms were damaged beyond belief unless one was a sewer rat. They would work well for sewer rats.

Still, I felt protective of my home by the river.

When the six of us were downstairs again, Ricardo and Therese looked at me, their eyes sadder still. Therese was about my age, only she had perfect skin and thick black hair. Plus, she had curves in the right places while I looked like an anorexic torpedo.

"Señorita Stewart," Therese started. She kneaded her hands. She was the sensitive sort, I could tell. "You would like us to fix this?"

"I need to hire someone who will fix her up."

Ricardo nodded. "But, Señorita, so much needs fixing, so very, very much."

"Oh yes. It's a rat trap."

"You think it traps rats?" Therese asked, her face anguished.

"Oh, I'm sure there are friendly rats here," I said with great cheer. "Ants, termites, bugs of all sorts."

Therese was distraught for me and patted me on the arm. "I'm sorry, Señorita."

Ricardo nodded again. "You see, Señorita . . ."

"Call me Jeanne."

Ricardo nodded but glanced at his children. "You will call her Señorita Stewart."

They nodded.

We were a nodding group.

"You see, Señorita. Jeanne . . . The house it"—he looked around, and back at me, his eyes begging for forgiveness—"perhaps it should be bulldozed? I can help you, but it will be, uh . . . it will be very expensive to buy the supplies, new carpets, new kitchen counters, paint, fix the ceilings—you know there's water damage? And the toilets . . . that's a project, those toilets—"

Therese grimaced. "The toilets are not sanitary at all . . ."

"Almost everything will have to be gutted and remodeled," I told them, still cheerful. I knew exactly what I wanted for the kitchen. Farm-style. White cabinets with handles shaped like coffee mugs. Original tile backsplash like no other. An island, painted blue, with a butcher-block counter. Open-shelving. Country-style white sink.

"And the bathrooms are so gross we'll probably have to use dynamite to blow up the toilets . . ."

"Not dynamite!" Ricardo held up his hands, instantly more worried. "That's not legal. We can't break the law, everything must be done right."

"I was joking, Ricardo. But you look very worried, if I do say so myself."

"He's worried," Therese cut in, "because . . . because . . . I don't want to . . . to hurt your feelings." She rung her hands. "But you see, Señorita, it will take a long, long time. This house is not going to be fixed in a week. It will be a long time. Many weeks.

Months. Probably months." She, too, seemed so worried I felt sorry for her.

"I know. It will take a long time."

They shared a relieved glance.

"It is good you understand this," Ricardo sighed. "But, please tell me, and no offense to you, but why don't you bulldoze it and start over?"

I thought about that. I'd thought about an ole bulldozer many times. But, nah. I wouldn't do that to her. Not to my house. I could not afford to replace the wood that was initially used to build this house. I wasn't even sure I could get it anymore. I loved the built-in shelving, china cabinet, original trim, and window seat in the living room. She was a classic. She was an original. She needed a makeover not a do-over.

"Nope. No bulldozer."

I asked them about their work history. Ricardo had worked as a contractor in Mexico, but things were tough there, work was sporadic. He had come to America so his kids would have a future and an education instead of a daily fight to survive.

Ricardo and Therese told me that they worked for Dan the Migrant Devil while waiting to become legal residents, but would no longer be working for him.

"I will be happy when he is dead because I know he will be in hell," I said to Ricardo and Therese.

They blinked. "Hell, yes," said Roberto, the first time any of the children had spoken since they were introduced. His fists bunched up, his face reddened. "He will go to hell and stay there. He deserves it. He—"

"That's enough," Ricardo snapped. Roberto closed his mouth, but he was clearly livid.

I glanced at Alessandra, the young teenager, who looked suddenly stricken and ill and terrorized, then to Rudy, the younger son, who looked ready to blow his top, and back to Therese who hugged her trembling daughter close and kissed her forehead.

Dear, dear God. What did Dan the Migrant Devil do to this

family? *What did he do?* "Yes, I am sure that Dan will go to hell and boil in oil."

Therese's eyes welled up with tears. So did Ricardo's. Rudy stalked away, out onto the bending back deck, while Roberto stared at me, nodding, with angry approval stamped on his face. Alessandra clung to her mother and her mother stroked her hair.

"I cannot work for him anymore, you see, Señorita," Ricardo told me, his voice quiet, weary.

"I understand perfectly."

Therese reached for Ricardo's hand. He gazed at her with such black, gentle eyes I would have choked up if I was a sentimental fool sort of person.

"You're hired," I told them. I offered them a salary sum and Ricardo and Therese's mouths dropped open. "Not enough?" I said.

"Too much," Ricardo said, waving his hand. "More than we deserve."

"Not too much. Fair pay for a fair amount of work."

Ricardo bent his head, tipped his chin back up after long seconds. His voice cracked. "We will make your home new again. You will love it. Thank you. *Gracias.*"

"*Gracias,*" Therese told me, holding both my hands in hers. "Thank you. We will work very hard for you. You will be pleased."

I knew I'd be pleased. I trusted them.

We agreed on what needed to be done first to the house. Which was: Make it sanitary so we would not be felled by vicious, crawling diseases.

"Where are you staying?" I asked them.

Ricardo looked down and away, so did Therese. "There is a place in town," she said.

"Well, if this home were livable, I would let you stay here. I'm sorry." I started searching my brain for somewhere they could stay in town that would not be expensive.

Therese and Ricardo looked around the house, then back at me, their eyes questioning and worried. I remembered the truck they were driving. The whole family was very thin. I had a real good idea that they had almost no money based on what Dan the Migrant Devil paid.

"You don't want to stay *here*?" I asked, aghast. They couldn't. There was mouse poop on the counters.

I did not miss the desperate look on his face and the panic on Therese's.

"You do?" I can't allow it, I thought. My sweet house is a wreck. No one should live in her at this point.

"We'll pay you rent," Ricardo said. "You take it out of my first check."

Therese nodded. "Yes. We'll pay rent."

I shook my head. "No rent. Absolutely no rent."

So what to do? I did a quick study of the furious teenage boys, the cowering Alessandra, the desperate Ricardo, the panicked Therese, and made a snap decision.

"Do you all know Rosvita?" I asked.

The Lopezes knew Rosvita. ("But I can't understand her Spanish," Ricardo whispered to me, his kind face anguished. "I try, I do, I try.") Rosvita greeted the family like long lost friends. I paid for the Lopezes to live at Rosvita's in two rooms for three weeks, meals included. I initially paid for a separate room for Alessandra, but Alessandra cried and looked ready to crumble, and her parents said it would be "best" if Alessandra slept in their room on a rollaway. So Rosvita brought the rollaway in.

Rosvita was delighted. She went through a detailed spiel about how clean her home was and, bless the Lopezes' hearts, they listened to every word, nodding appreciatively.

Before the Lopezes could move in, they arranged to have my house sprayed for bugs and all animals were asked to leave, including three members of a raccoon family, a possum, a community of termites, a mouse colony, a gaggle of spiders, gangs of flies, an army of ants, a bird, and a pair of snakes.

They tossed all the furnishings out, including the kitchen

counters and cabinets, and everything in the bathrooms, half-eaten curtains, and the dark paneling that made dark caves of several rooms. The carpets were ripped up and we discovered—oh, lucky me!—original wood floors throughout the entire home in perfect shape like they'd never been walked on. A plumber was hired (very expensive, don't ask) and the Lopezes and the plumber installed a toilet and sink in the bathroom. He would come later to help Ricardo install sinks, a shower, and a pool-like soaking tub upstairs, fit for two, in the new bathroom.

They cleaned the entire home again and again, nests were lifted from the two fireplaces, and the black goo clinging to the inside of the chimneys was scraped off. Therese made an appointment with a man in the city who would later install new windows and add two French doors downstairs and one upstairs in my master bedroom. A new roof was hammered on, too, by the Lopezes.

Before they moved in, I ordered a refrigerator and stove/oven, two queen-size beds and a single, plus bedding for each, and three dressers. I bought a couch and two chairs and a kitchen table with six chairs, basic kitchen utensils, and other items I cannot remember in my small brain.

While living in the house, the Lopezes would rebuild the kitchen and bathrooms, replace the ceilings, build mantels for the fireplaces, and shelving units on either side, repaint the trim, paint the entire inside of the house with bright cheery colors, and paint the outside yellow with white trim and a blue door. They would fix the living room floor that had caved in and the bedroom wall that had tumbled in.

They would build shelving units in all the bedroom closets, install all new light fixtures with an electrician from town, demolish and rebuild the front porch and back deck so that they wrapped around most of the house, and rebuild the deck off my master bedroom. Therese would sew all new curtains, among other things. I knew that when I was in jail for my wee assault on Slick Dick that I could trust them to keep the house up.

I gave the Lopezes another check the night they moved in. I did not miss the tears that flowed into Ricardo's eyes or the way Therese's whole body relaxed.

"We'll pay you rent," Therese said.

"No," I told her. "No rent. Absolutely not."

She hugged me, her body shaking in my arms.

That night at Rosvita's I pulled out one particular scrapbook from my scrapbook pile.

It had a pink cover.

I brought it out onto my deck and sat in the wicker rocker, the breeze caressing my face. My hands shook as I opened the cover. I shut it real quick when I saw the first photo. I imagined my arteries shriveling in shock.

I tried opening it again, then whacked it shut.

Tried a third time. The third time worked.

I stared at me and Johnny. We were at the beach and I could still smell the salt water, feel the hot sand. Johnny was crouched down, I was straddled across his waist, my old flip-flops dangling off my toes, my curls ruffled by the wind. His hair, longish, blondish, hung around his ears, his smile huge.

Johnny hadn't been very tall, but he'd had a great heart, a love of life, and people, and me. My mother adored him. Several times she'd served him dessert *before* dinner. That's how much she loved him.

I flipped through the pages, my heart pounding, my hands fluttering, my eyes hot.

There was me and Johnny with friends, fly-fishing with tie-dyed shirts. Me and Johnny in formal outfits at his sister's wedding, the bride grinning between us. Me and Johnny after a whipped cream fight. Me and Johnny camping, proudly holding up six skewered hot dogs each on sticks. Me and Johnny, in profile, black and white. Me and Johnny with marshmallows in our mouths.

The wedding photos about undid me. We hadn't wanted a

separate album; we'd wanted one to show the progression of our relationship.

Both our families were at the wedding, not a single family member was absent. Everyone was so happy. There were formal photos of me, and Johnny, and us together. Casual photos of us with our school friends, arms linked around each other. There was a photo of the whole laughing bridal party in a pyramid, another of the groomsmen standing on their heads. One shot, taken from above, of the wedding party laying on the floor in a circle, our heads together. Finally, a shot like the first photo in the scrapbook, with Johnny bending over, and me straddling him in my wedding dress, my flip-flops dangling off my toes, my golden curls cascading down my back.

I closed the photograph book, held it to me, rocked in the wicker chair.

It had been a pleasure and a privilege to be Johnny's wife.

That was the truth.

CHAPTER 15

"Only Jeanne has fulfilled her requirement to take herself off her path of anger," Emmaline declared, her arms outstretched, her face tight.

She was wearing white, as usual, and white heels. But tonight at our anger management meeting, she was also wearing a straw hat. She had bought all of us straw hats and insisted we wear them. After spending forty minutes at the boxing bags, she had instructed us to "art" our hats. Using different materials, we had all "arted."

"Bradon, you are still simmering with anger, like a cauldron full of soup that is burning on the bottom. You are still bursting with agitation, like a firework. You are still ready to let your antagonism sally forth, like a blowtorch. You are still ready to go off half-cocked, leaping onto tables and smashing chairs." Bradon had glued colorful pom-poms all over his hat. He pushed the hat off his head and ran a hand over his baldness.

"Roses, Bradon, roses. See the rose. Be the rose. Live the rose. This is simple, man. What do you have to say for yourself? What, what?"

"I say I suck," Bradon said. "I do. But I'm trying to make things up to my wife. I went to dinner and to the movies . . ."

"Roses!" Emmaline shouted. "Roses! Grasp this simple

thought, Bradon, grasp it. Don't you have one working brain cell? One?"

She flew over to Soman.

"Soman, you have not dressed as a woman and explored the city as your true self." Soman had tied tiny ribbons into bows and carefully attached them to the brim of the hat. It looked exotic and sunny. Soman was an artist.

"Hey, Emmaline, I'm a real man. This here is my true self. Manly. Studly. I'm a stud man. I got more testosterone than most men can dream of and that's a fact." He fiddled with the humongous pink bow he had wound around his hat and tied under his chin. His braids hung down his shoulders.

"Being a woman *is* you, Soman. At least some of the time," Emmaline insisted. "The reason why you're always getting into fights is subconscious and subliminal. You're fighting a fight within yourself, your alter-personality and you, and it's a psychological battle that you can't win because it's against the inner recesses of yourself."

"I got no idea what that psychobabble stuff means, Emmaline. Say what you wanna say."

"It means, Soman," Bradon said, "that she thinks what you want is to be a lady and your feminine side is aching to let the lady in you loose, but because the lady in you can't get out, you get ticked off and get in fights."

"Hell no, Emmaline, ya got that wrong. I dress up as a woman at home—and not hardly at all—to relieve my stress. To relax. Ain't nothin' weird about it. I ain't into porn, ain't into drugs or much drinkin'. And I like women." He snuck a peak at Becky. She bent her head. "That ain't right. I like one woman. One."

"Soman, stand up," Emmaline bellowed, standing herself, a vision in white and straw. Becky jumped at the bellow.

"What?"

"I said stand up!"

"I already punched the bag, Emmaline, and I made my flower hat, and I did the cartwheels to spin the anger out of my body and now I'm dog-tired, lady. My body's achin'." Soman said all this in a whiny tone, but he said it while he was getting up. Everyone does what Emmaline says. She's kind of scary.

"You aren't going to punch the bag, Soman. Stay right there."

Emmaline went off to a huge closet and grabbed the clothing bags.

She dumped them out in front of Soman. "Everyone, tonight is Soman's night to get off his path of anger. He's going to dress up like a woman, and we're all going to a bar."

"What?" Soman shrieked, his voice high. He tugged on the pink ribbon. "I ain't going to get dressed like a woman in front of you people and go to no bar. Hell, no."

"Hell, yes," said Emmaline.

"Hell, no."

"Hell, yes, big guy, hell, yes," Emmaline said.

"Hell, yes," I said.

"Yes, hell." Bradon laughed.

"This is going to be fun." Becky giggled.

Soman turned to Becky. She nodded encouragingly. He bent his head and sighed.

We helped him get his dress on. He did not wear his hat with the pink ribbon.

He wore a wig.

The bar we all traipsed to had a giant inflatable pink lobster attached to the top of the roof. It was at a busy intersection in downtown Portland. There were tables set up outside the restaurant and inside there was a long stainless steel bar and even more tables, all crammed with people.

Soman said Portland policemen hung out there, along with lawyers, businessmen and women, office people sick of their hamster-wheel jobs, movers and shakers and losers. And desperate people looking for a quickie or a spouse. Sounded like a typical bar.

But we were not a typical group. First, there was Emmaline,

who had changed into a slinky white silk shirt and white silk pants and gold heels. There was Bradon, huge and wealthy and successful and tough, dressed in the tailored suit he wore to work because he had a meeting with the bankers that day. There was Becky, tiny and fragile, her blond hair brushed and shining and tumbling down her back. (Emmaline had insisted on taking her ponytail out and brushing it.) She was wearing red jeans and a blue sweater. She looked worn-out and scared and stuck close to Soman, and yet she looked angelic at the same time.

And there was me. I was wearing a sleek black linen suit, sheer black tights with a black line down the center, and red heels.

But me-oh-my. I almost forgot to tell you about Soman.

Soman wore a very lovely blue cotton dress, a padded bra, and black shoes. He had on a long, black-haired wig, and pink lipstick. He was like a rather heavy woman with a beat-up face, but other than that, hey, he resembled a woman.

"You look like a woman, Soman," I told him. I put my hand on his arm. "In fact, if I had any gay tendencies I think I'd come on to you. Those breasts," I paused and gave him the once-over, "are fabulous."

"You think so, you skinny ass naked bird?" He grabbed his padded boobs with both hands, and wiggled his eyebrows, but I knew he was so nervous he could puke.

"I think."

"Baby, give me your arm," Bradon said. "It's you and me." Soman and Bradon sashayed to the door and in we went, me and Becky and Emmaline trailing behind, treasuring this unique scene.

And everything went fine for the first half hour. We found a table like normal people. We got our menus like normal people. Becky lost that panicked expression. Soman crossed his legs and relaxed a tad.

Bradon and Soman launched into a discussion about the professional basketball team in town and their disgust for the players who seemed to be endlessly in and out of court. I wondered aloud why men making that much money couldn't agree to stay away from pot, dogfights, speeding, and other illegal activities, but because I couldn't care less about sports, I engaged Becky and Emmaline in conversation.

We discussed the state of the Middle East, the healing influences of certain herbs, American Indians' usage of certain herbs, and witchcraft, to add a little zip to the conversation.

We received our drinks. Soman and Bradon had pop. I had coffee. Emmaline had a Shirley Temple. Becky had root beer. Out of respect for Becky, none of us ordered alcohol, although I was very, very tempted.

We got our mozzarella cheese sticks and sautéed mushroom appetizers. We were all talking and laughing, because Bradon was so darn funny and he was telling us about the people on the local school board and all their little quirks and habits and he described their faces in detail when he found himself on top of their table ranting and raving.

So I was laughing, Bradon was laughing, Emmaline was laughing, Becky was laughing, and Soman was laughing—when all of a sudden Soman stopped laughing and stared, frozenlike, not a muscle twitching.

And the rest of us stopped laughing midlaugh and stared at what Soman was staring at—which was a very large white man at the bar who looked like an ex-football player with the face of a hog.

Right about that time, Soman got up in his pretty dress. Bradon was quick and so was I, and before I knew it we were both standing in front of Soman and blocking his path.

"Soman, buddy, I don't know what's going on, but you gotta settle on down," Bradon said, nice and quiet.

"Soman, whatever it is, let it go. This is your night. We're here to have a pleasant dinner together." His arm muscles were tense under my hands, his eyes locked on the football player.

"Come on, sit down . . . sit down . . . there you go, man . . . relax . . . sit right back down," said Bradon.

"Please, Soman," I whispered. "Don't start a fight. It'll scare Becky."

That seemed to get his attention. Soman looked at Becky. Becky did, indeed, appear frightened, like a squirrel paralyzed by the gaping jaws of a shark, her eyes wide.

"Channel your anger," Emmaline demanded, holding his face in her hands. "Channel it. You're on a new path now, Soman. You're not going to be pathetic, not going to let anger take your life hostage, not going to ask for pity or attention or make excuses anymore. You are who you are. A real man who is comfortable expressing his spiritual feminine side. Be proud of it. Your life has not an inch left of space for your anger. Do away with it."

"Nope, there's no space, Soman," I said. "You're more than that. More than your anger."

He looked at me and I naïvely thought he heard what I said.

"Don't screw this up." I glanced meaningfully at Becky.

Soman blinked, nodded.

"There ya go, man. We're cool, we're cool." Bradon said. "Here comes our food. You ordered a chef salad and diet pop, right?"

"Okay, I'll sit down. But if that one starts somethin', I'm gonna take him out," Soman huffed, but quietly, so Becky wouldn't hear. "I know him and I hate him. Stupid white man. I seen him with women, grabbin' one one night, another the next. Trying to pick on black boys here, startin' stuff, always startin' stuff. He started crap with me two times and both times he regretted it. I don't take no crap from him or anyone else."

Bradon nodded. I nodded.

"You are a most difficult client, Soman," Emmaline announced, stabbing her fork into the table. "Sit your brown ass down in your pretty dress, and fix your wig like a man, or I'm going to flunk you and you're going to have to take my class again. Do you like flying around like a vulture?"

Soman sat. I believe it was the thought of flying around like a vulture that probably got to him.

And everything was so soft and peaceful again. We ordered more drinks, we started eating like normal people, and then Soman said he had to go to the bathroom and he slipped out before we could stop him.

I dropped my spoon. I knew, at that point, that we were done for.

Before even Bradon could spring to his feet, Soman was speeding toward the bathrooms, which happened to take him past the bar and past the man with a hog for a face. And wouldn't you know it, but the object of Soman's affections shifted his position at about that time and I could tell that the two of them locked eyes like two magnets.

Keep on truckin' to the bathroom I thought, Soman, keep on truckin', baby, come on now.

"Oh, shit," Bradon said.

Keep on truckin', Soman. Come on, keep on truckin' . . .

"He flunks," Emmaline said, flapping her white arms about. "He F. L.U.N.K.S. Flunks. Soman has flunked anger management!"

"Oh, shit," Bradon said again.

I saw the football player give Soman the once-over. He smiled this smirky smile, and when Soman passed the hog-faced football man, I saw his hand reach out and cup Soman's solid butt.

The football player uttered something out of the corner of his hog mouth. I have been in enough bars to know that it was suggestive and about Soman's body which, of course, the football player thought was the body of a woman with overly large breasts. Soman whipped around, his pretty dress pinwheeling at the bottom, and by that time me and Bradon were up and flying over to Soman—but not before Soman took a step up real close to the football player who was smug and sleezy, exactly the type of man you warn your daughters away from. Soman ripped off his wig, his braids flipping to his shoulders, and the football player's eyes got all buggy with shock and then Soman threw the first punch.

And that was how the bar fight started.

My arrest came about twenty minutes after that.

It did not end up being a pleasant evening and Emmaline was not pleased.

She told me so when we were all thrown into a paddy wagon—except for Bradon, who took an alternate route out the back-door—and were taken to the downtown Portland precinct.

No, she was not pleased at all. Not one steaming, arm-flapping, cartwheel-pinwheeling, dancing, arting, punching, flying, vulture-soaring bit.

Because there were about twenty people involved in the fight, the police had to bring in the new and improved paddy wagons to haul all of us criminals on over to the police station.

On the way, Emmaline ranted that people in America today were on "pathetic paths of anger," in particular her current anger management group, which consisted of a "bunch of raging lunatics." Becky cried, her shoulders shaking. Soman and the hog-faced man were taken away in police cars. Everyone else in the paddy wagon was yelling and bad words were bantered about like ping-pong balls. "Don't swear," I instructed the woman next to me in the paddy wagon, who was shrieking.

"Shut up, you pussy bitch!" she screeched at me.

We both had our hands handcuffed behind our backs and that forced us into awkward positions. At least I had not lost my red heels in the ruckus. I remembered the last time I had handcuffs on. These handcuffs matched no better with what I was wearing to-night than they had in Chicago. It is unfortunate that one can't pick out a different color of handcuff depending on what one is wearing.

I eyed the woman who called me a pussy bitch. I had not taken offense.

Sometimes I definitely am a pussy bitch.

"I like your shirt," I told her. It was a pink shirt but it was too tight. "It's too tight, though. You're showing too much boob. Your style is too obvious—like you're searching for sex, not a relation-ship."

She made a screaming sound through her teeth, swore again, then raised up her foot and tried to smash mine. Beside me in the paddy wagon, Becky whimpered.

I moved my foot right in time, and stomped her smack in the middle of her right foot with my high, spiked red heel. "Please don't swear. I was only trying to help you."

She made grunting sounds as I squished down harder. When she tried to kick my other leg with hers, I deflected it as well. Things went on like that for a while and she called me a "cactus cunt" and a "lesbian freak" and a "cock-cuddler," but I won our battle and she finally dropped her foot back down where it belonged.

"I've been where you are, and I think that you'll attract the wrong kind of man with that outfit," I told her, panting a mite from our altercation. "You look like you're easy, like you'll pop into bed in a heartbeat. You'll attract men who are cheap and shallow, who only want sex and are incapable of having a decent relationship. You need to hide more of your body. You need a classier, more expensive look if you want to find a nice man." Unneeded information, I told myself.

"What the hell! Did I ask you for fashion advice, Madonna?"

I shrugged. "Those black leather pants of yours? They scream of bondage and whips and chains and that sort of perverted stuff. Don't wear them unless you've got them paired with a classy-looking blouse and heels that don't look like they're used for strutting on men's backs. Plus, your boobs are hanging out too much. What are you, a dancer searching for a pole? And you need to take off almost all your makeup. Your face is too hard, much older than I think you really are."

She swore. "Okay, smarty shit, how old do you think I am?"

I looked her over. "I think you're about twenty-eight, but you look forty and like you've been ripped through the bar-hopping grinder and have had too many drinks and too much smoking and too many one-night stands under your belt."

She sucked in her breath. I do believe she would have hit me had we not been handcuffed. Instead she raised her foot again, I smashed it back down. She grunted. The paddy wagon hit a pothole and we were all thrown about like human marbles.

"Anyhow, underneath it all, I can tell that you're young and fairly beautiful. Change your look. You need to look richly stylish instead of richly slutty. That's the key right there—style, not slutty."

Her eyes were about to pop from her head, but I could tell she was listening.

"You see, in a bar you'll only meet narcissistic, selfish, penis-loving perverts who are there for sex. Go to church."

"Church?" Her eyes opened wide.

"Yeah. Find a big church, go and get involved. Or take up a sport. Or do volunteer work. Volunteer work is a huge male market, trust me." The paddy wagon lurched to a stop, then started again. "And if some big corporation is sponsoring a fund-raiser— the men will be hoppin'. They'll recruit their employees to help out. But for heaven's sake, don't wear clothes and makeup like that if you ever want a future with a husband, kids, soccer games on Saturday, camping vacations, that sort of thing. Men in corporations do not want wives who look slutty. They want class. Good for business, you know. I don't remember hitting you in the bar, hope I didn't?"

She looked further stunned at the quick shift in conversation. She shook her head. "No. You didn't." She nodded behind me. "I hit her, though."

I glanced over my shoulder and cringed. Emmaline. Emmaline, the ultimate in anger management counselors, had a black eye. Quite a shiner, too. She was almost hyperventilating, she was so steamin' mad.

"That's Emmaline. She's my anger management counselor."

"Your anger management counselor?" She laughed, not too nicely. "She's not very good."

"We're all trying to manage our anger. Emmaline doesn't have to." I glanced over at her. She was pounding her feet into the floor of the paddy wagon and yelling, "Shit! Shit! Shiiiittt!!"

"Me and Becky do have to work on it. So do Bradon and Soman." I nodded reassuringly at Becky. She still looked scared to death, like she was collapsing in on herself and shutting down. I'd take her out to lunch soon.

The woman who was too slutty snorted and said, "I don't think you're doing a very good job of managing your anger."

I nodded. "You could be right on that point. Soman took a swing at a guy—"

"Was Soman the guy with all the braids wearing a dress and a black stuffed bra?"

"That would be our Soman." The football player with the hog face had ripped the dress in the tussle. Out had popped one of Soman's boobs, encased in a black bra and stuffed with tissue.

She looked up at the ceiling of the paddy wagon. "I didn't like that dress very much."

"It's not my type, either, but Soman seemed to feel comfortable in it. The heels were a real problem, though."

The woman sank back against the wall of the paddy wagon, her face exhausted and drawn. Too old for her youth. "I can see why."

Indeed, the heels had been a problem because Soman wobbled a bit after the football player recognized Soman and hit back. Soman pummeled him again and the football player's friends jumped in and Bradon and I jumped in to help Soman and somehow I ended up on top of the hog-faced football player's back pulling his hair, and he flipped me over and I landed on my butt.

Becky gallantly tried to help Soman, too, who was plum in the thick of the fight, swinging those huge fists and holding his own. Emmaline whacked someone with her shoe, and Bradon took it upon himself to crack a couple of heads together, and throw someone halfway through the air who had been attacking Soman, the man/woman.

Anyhow, the next time I looked up, the police were there, and I was splayed on the floor like a loose lobster, and being hauled up and out to the paddy wagon by a young man wearing a blue uniform. I saw Bradon gathering up our purses at the table and sneaking out the back.

I did not blame him for it. Bradon was a businessman who didn't need any more bad publicity after that little stunt he pulled at the school board meeting. Plus, I was glad that he had my purse. I would not want to be the victim of identity theft if it got into the wrong hands and, more important, I did not want to lose my favorite lipstick. Berry Merry, it's called.

"Was the man that our friend Soman hit your boyfriend?" I asked the girl who wore too much makeup.

"Yep. Sort of. No." She got tears in her eyes. Underneath the caked makeup she seemed sadly vulnerable. "I hate him."

Hmmm. "Let me guess. He makes you feel like an afterthought. You try to dress sexy to keep and hold his attention, but it never works. You can see his eyes wandering around and over every other woman with two legs without white hair. You always feel like you want more from him emotionally, you want him at the very least to be kind to you, but he never is, so you and he end up fighting a lot. You're not happy with him, not comfortable in the relationship, and your self-esteem is in shreds because you can't figure out why you stay with someone who makes you cry all the time. He drinks too much, is totally cheap, never listens to a damn thing you say, is incapable of a real conversation, talks to old girlfriends and lets you know about it, has a ton of secrets, and you know he's hiding something but you don't know what, and he expects you to do all the work during sex."

Her eyes about flew out of her face she was so surprised.

"Did you date Morgan?"

"No, I didn't. But I have dated many of Morgan's twins."

"He has twins?"

"No, silly." We hurdled around a corner and my shoulder met hers. "I mean that I have dated many men like Morgan. Drop him. He's a loser. Get a classy look, a classy life, and you'll get a classy man." Listen to me. Like I know what I'm talking about.

A few tears spilled over her eyes, making black tracks of her thick mascara.

"He does drugs," Becky said, her voice quiet. "That's the secret. One of them, at least."

"What?" she whooped. "How do you know?"

"Because I've seen him," Becky said, a little more with us again. "Pot. Coke. Pills. I know because I used to buy from the same dealer as him."

The woman groaned. Obviously, she was a tad overwhelmed. "I want to go to bed. I want to get into my flannel pajamas, have some tea, go to bed and pull the covers over my head and pretend none of this shit ever happened. I really want some tea. Peppermint."

I nodded. Peppermint tea was ringing my bell, too, and my bed of blue heaven had never called me so loud.

"And I want to smack all of your heads together," Emmaline rapped. "I have never, ever been arrested in my life and here I am. In a paddy wagon. With handcuffs around my wrists. And I have a black eye because I was in a bar fight! A bar fight! With my clients! *My clients!* Me!. Emmaline Hallwyler! I'm an anger management counselor and I hit a man over the head tonight with my purse!" She yelled that part. "How pathetic is that? I ask you, how pathetic is it?"

"Pretty pathetic," Becky said, her shoulders curving in as though to protect herself. "Pretty pathetic."

"Please don't yell, Emmaline. It scares Becky."

Emmaline rolled her eyes. She pounded the floor of the paddy wagon with her feet again. "Shit! Shit! Shiiiiiiiiiit!"

I cannot say I enjoyed my stay in jail, but it was a learning experience. I learned that precincts are loud and emotional places. I learned that jail is stiflingly cold and lonely and you feel like an animal that no one likes and no one wants to touch. I learned that paper-processing takes a long time and it is fortunate there are not enough jail beds for people like me because of budget cuts, or I would have had to stay in the slammer. I learned that there are scary, scummy people in jail who look like they've been molting and gelling and decaying for a while. I also learned that jail smells like fear and vomit and pee and drugs and sweaty people completely out of control of their lives.

I filled out their paperwork and when it said, "Employer" I wrote down "Jeanne Stewart, advertising." I had tried incredibly hard not to think about Jay and the campaign as I was leaping on the football player's back, stumbling to the paddy wagon with my hands trapped behind my back, and resting my ass on the floor of a cell, but I could no longer ignore it.

I was scared to death of what Jay would think. Scared. To. Death. Dare I hope that he wouldn't find out?

Bradon came right away and bailed us all out as soon as possible. Me, Emmaline, Becky, and Soman, a man who dressed like a woman, were released on an unsuspecting public. We would be given our court dates at a later time.

It was 7:00 in the morning and the five of us stood outside the precinct—me, relatively intact except my mascara had streamed down my face and hardened, Emmaline and her shiner, Soman in his dress, for which he said he took a lot of harassment inside the jail, and Becky who looked like she was withdrawing into herself an inch at a time and closing up (*Note to me:* Call Becky and go to lunch with her.), and Bradon in his fine suit who handed us our purses.

"You have all flunked my class," Emmaline said, her voice booming, her white arms pumping up and down like an agitated white turkey.

We nodded. None of us could blame her. We were poor students. Very poor.

"All of you." She flapped again.

We nodded again.

"I will see you *tonight* at anger management class." She spun around on her heel and charged down the street making disgusted sounds.

"Tonight?" Bradon protested, "But it's Friday night!"

"That's right, you pathetic people," Emmaline's voice echoed off the tall buildings all around us. "Wear shorts and do not be one iota of a second late. Not one." She stalked back to all of us, her white bird-arms pumping, her face livid. "And bring umbrellas and peanut butter."

"What?" Soman said, adjusting one cup of his bra.

"You heard me!"

I groaned. I didn't even want to think about it.

"Shit! Shit!" Her words tunneled between the buildings, her white arms flapping as she sped down the sidewalk having a nail-spitting tantrum. "Shiiiitttt."

CHAPTER 16

I didn't know that Jay was going to be at headquarters that morning.

As he had been there the day before with his sexy blue eyes and very solid, grippable hips, I assumed he would be back in Salem doing whatever good governors do in Salem.

I was wrong.

After Becky declined a ride home from me, Soman and Bradon and I split up to collect our cars. Soman declared he was calling in sick, while Bradon and I were going straight to work.

I drove toward campaign headquarters, then ducked into a local coffee shop after grabbing a silk scarf from my glove compartment. I washed my face and hands and pits with their soap, brushed my teeth with my handy-dandy miniature toothbrush and toothpaste, put on deodorant and perfume (miniature bottles), added makeup, and studied myself for a moment.

I needed to change my outfit. Can't wear the same thing two days in a row to work. In my past life, I would often go to a bar after work, have way too much to drink, and spend the night in a hotel in town so I didn't drive home. I learned to carry all the toiletries I needed and how to change my outfit without changing my clothing.

This time I didn't have much to work with. Off went all my

jewelry. I opened the tiny side pocket of my purse and took out my "emergency silver dangly earrings and bracelets." I pulled all my curls into a loose ball, buttoned my suit jacket all the way up, and flipped the scarf over my shoulders. I yanked off my tights because they had ripped.

I looked only slightly like death when done. I bought a double espresso and a roll, and headed to work.

I had my briefcase in one hand, my coffee in the other, and the roll in my mouth when I entered headquarters. It was still quiet in the offices.

The only other human in there was Jay.

I was so shocked to see him, I opened my mouth to speak and the roll bopped out and onto the floor.

I stuttered a hello, trying not to think of the bar fight, the cacophony in the paddy wagon, and the fact that I was now a criminal two times over. I bent to retrieve my roll and, of course, I spilled my coffee, much of which landed on my leg. It was piping hot.

I dropped the briefcase, grabbed the roll, gripped the cup, then kicked hot coffee off my legs, much like you might see a dog shaking himself off after peeing.

"Ms. Stewart," Jay drawled, a smile tilting his lips.

"Hello, Governor." I straightened. A curl fell into my eyes. I blew it up. It settled back down across my cheek. This was not good. Not good that I hadn't had a shower. Not good I'd been in a bar fight. Not good I'd been arrested. Not good that I was the liaison to the press for Jay's reelection campaign. Not good my face was red and I felt sweaty.

Jay's blue chocolate eyes traveled down my outfit, from my silk scarf, now unraveled, to my red heels, and back up again to my face and hair. I had the crazy suspicion he knew I wasn't wearing underwear.

By the time his blue eyes got back to mine, they were cold.

Cold and hard. Like blue Jell-o that had petrified over two hundred years.

Oh, double shoot. *He knew.* Gall. But of course he knew. He probably had contacts all over—including the police station.

"Aren't you wearing the same outfit today that you did yesterday?"

I couldn't believe it. He'd noticed. No one ever had.

"Uh." I felt nauseous. "Yes. Uh. I am. It's the same. Uh. Tiny changes."

There was a tense silence. I could hardly breathe. "Do you want to explain why?"

Triple shoot. Some lieutenant or captain or, heck, the police chief, probably called Jay at home and told him about his barfighting, chair-flinging, tackling media spokeswoman.

Another tense and terrible silence followed while he glared at me, his jaw rigid. For the first time, I sensed a boiling anger beneath the control.

"It must have been a long night, Ms. Stewart."

"Yes, it was a rather long night." Jail cells are not relaxing.

Silence. He rocked back on his heels, hands in his pockets. "I called you a couple of times last night. At home and on your cell. I guess I shouldn't have bothered."

"No, I'm glad you did—"

"Did you enjoy yourself?"

He had to be kidding. I decided to make light of it. "There were parts that were enjoyable, parts that were wild and crazy, parts—"

"I get it," he clipped, his face a rigid, tight mask.

I felt nauseous.

Why didn't he come out and say it: Why the hell did my top PR person get arrested last night? What the hell were you doing? Do you know what this could do to the campaign, *to me*? How could you do this?

"I can explain, Jay. You see, my friend Bradon and I and—"

"I have no interest in hearing about your goddamn friend, Bradon!" His voice thundered in that room.

I swallowed. My leg was no longer burning from the scalding coffee. I felt deathly cold. Cold and scared witless.

"Things got out of control. We didn't expect things to happen as they did, certainly not that fast, it caught us off guard . . ."

A pulse was jumping in his temple, and he took a few steps toward me. "These things happen," he said, his voice a pissed-off whisper. "I understand."

"I don't think you do."

"You're a busy lady, Ms. Stewart, aren't you?"

I had no idea what that meant. "I have stayed busy working on your campaign, if that's what you're talking about, however I will quit if you'd like me to. It would probably be best if I did." Communications directors, after all, shouldn't hurdle chairs in bars even if a man with a hog-face is assaulting your male friend who is wearing a pretty dress.

Jay's face flushed and I saw that he was about ready to lose it.

"I'm not asking you to quit," he snapped. "Your personal life, is that. Personal."

I was miserable. "But my personal life affects you." I thought about what would happen if the newspaper got the story. I could see the headline: *Governor Jay Kendall's communications director arrested in bar fight. She did not lose her high heels.* "How will this affect you?"

He closed his eyes for a second and I could tell he was clenching his teeth together. "I thought we had an understanding, Jeanne, but I guess I thought wrong."

"This is my fault completely, and I'm so sorry, Jay, so sorry." I thought I would die. My nauseousness was running from head to foot. Even my toes felt ill. I had tried to protect Soman in his pretty little dress and I wasn't sorry for that, but I was tremendously sorry about the fallout this could have on Jay and the campaign

"I thought—" He stopped, looked away, his face more pale now than flushed.

"You thought?"

"I thought I knew you." His voice whipped through me like an arctic blast. "I thought I understood *us*. I made a mistake, didn't I?"

"Please, Jay." I felt my heart shriveling up. I had so looked forward to getting to know the Pacific Ocean with Jay.

"For God's sake, Jeanne, don't 'Please, Jay' me. It's not going to work with us, obviously. You do your work; I'll do mine. We'll finish the campaign and that'll be that. No hard feelings."

But I could tell, because I know men, that the "no hard feelings" part wasn't going to happen. He was furious. Absolutely furious. And he was probably hurt by what I'd done, because he trusted me as a person and as an employee to be professional and aboveboard and I'd blown it. Big time.

I felt like crying. "I'm sorry," I whispered. I let myself cry.

He studied the street outside the window for a while, then slanted that blue-eyed gaze back at me. I could see that he had tears in his eyes. "I am, too."

I wiped the tears off my cheeks.

"Tell your brother I stopped by. I'll catch him later."

I grabbed Jay's arm as he strode by me and he shrugged it off. "So that's it?"

We were inches apart, his heat going right through my arm to my heart that had now shrunk to a tight, lonely ball. "Yeah, Jeanne, that's it."

And that was that. Out the door he went.

I made it on pancake knees to my office as if nothing life-shattering had happened, closed the door, threw the coffee and roll away, pulled the blinds, leaned my head on my desk, and cried my eyes out until I could barely breathe.

That night at anger management class the floor was covered with black plastic. We were not allowed to talk. First Emmaline made us watch her go to the screaming corner. She did not bother to put a pillow over her face. She screamed, loud and piercing. 'Bout blew my eardrums out. "I have a blaaack eye! Because of you four! GET OVER HERE!"

We put pillows over our faces and screamed.

"I can't hear you; I can't hear you!" Emmaline kept yelling as we screamed. "I can't heeeeaaaaar you."

When we were red and all screamed out she roared, "This peanut butter is an emblem of your anger. You're going to cover yourself in peanut butter because your anger is sticking to you like peanut butter. It's pitiably pathetic! You're pitiably pathetic! Then!" She pointed both fingers up in the air and stood on tip-toe, "Then you're going to throw it at each other. You're going to throw your anger."

"You're kidding," Bradon said.

"You have lost it, Em," Soman said. "I said I was sor—"

"I don't like to throw things at people," Becky squeaked.

"This is a bit too weird for me," I started.

"Shit! Shit! Shut up! All of you, SHUT UP! SHIT!"

I changed into the shorts and t-shirt I'd bought after work.

We covered ourselves in peanut butter.

Then we threw it using our umbrellas as shields.

By the end we were covered in each other's anger.

Late at night, several days later, I sung along at the top of my lungs with a number of hard-rock singers all the way home to Weltana so my tears wouldn't choke me.

My nervous breakdown was back with a vengeance.

Working at campaign headquarters had fried my cerebellum and nary a brain cell seemed to still be working in my head. In addition to writing speeches, talking to reporters, organizing staff, and strategizing, every time I turned around Damon seemed to be spying on me, like a viper watching prey. I knew he was plotting something. In every meeting he tried to cut me down, although he was careful not to do it in front of Jay. That Jay still looked at me with ice crystals in his eyes had me contemplating driving that ole Bronco into the ocean again.

Would I do it? I mulled this one over. Probably not.

But the ice crystals had rapidly chipped away at the fragile and newfound happiness I had had with Jay. I knew I had sunk into a black and sticky place and I was unsure when, or if, I would be able to climb myself out of this particularly black hole.

The climb seemed insurmountable and I was tired of climbing.

I usually loved the part of my trip where the city seemed almost instantly to disappear and the beauty began, the trees tall and graceful, endless above me, and I suddenly couldn't wait to get home to my bed of blue heaven and hide. Or hibernate.

The one good thing was that my house was coming along at quite a clip. I definitely wanted it completed before I went to jail. The Lopez family had installed my new, farm-style white kitchen cabinets, with handles shaped like coffee mugs, open-shelving, and were working on an island, which would be painted blue, with a butcher-block counter. My country-style white sink was in already.

The new toilets and sinks never clogged. With help from an installer, the Lopezes had replaced all the windows in the house and had added three sets of French doors—two in the great room, one in the master bedroom. The boys had been working on the stairs when they weren't in school, and Therese was sewing curtains. We were in the process of choosing paint colors for each room.

While we talked about colors, Therese told me about her life growing up in Mexico. Her family lived in a hut. She has five siblings. Her father lived apart from them for most of the year and sent money back home to his exhausted wife. They had no medicine, no running water, no electricity. Her grandfather had had a gun and she and her siblings used it for target practice. Therese was the best shot in her family.

"We had no real life in Mexico. I can't have that for my children. I want them to go to school, to learn, to help other people. I want them to be safe. That's why we came here. There is no hope there, Jeanne. No hope, no jobs, no future. Life should be more than worrying about whether or not there's enough food to eat tomorrow, don't you think? It should be more than worrying about your child getting sick and not being able to get to a doctor. It should be more than nothing. Right?"

"Right, Therese. You are right." Life should be more than nothing, of that I was sure.

Therese was very sure which color would look good in each room. She is a very gentle woman, and she loves her family, but she runs a tight ship.

I like tight ships.

A few nights later Rosvita's bed-and-breakfast was ablaze with lights when I got home which was very abnormal. Every night Rosvita cleaned her kitchen with bleach and water and a host of other cleaning materials for a good hour. She read books on germs or romance, depending on her mood, and snapped out her light exactly at 10:00 so her body had plenty of time to rest and rejuvenate in her bleached white sheets to fight off all future germ attacks.

Tonight, however, I entered and found her on her hands and knees with a dry toothbrush scrubbing the corners of her kitchen floor.

"Greetings," I said tentatively. "Rosvita?"

"Hello, Jeanne." Her words came out in a pant. "Did you have a good day at work?"

I paused. She went immediately back to her scrubbing, her movements vigorous.

I saw a stack of cleaning supplies on paper towels in the kitchen. "Everything okay, Rosvita?"

"Yes, it's fine, Jeanne. I was reading about germs that hide in nooks and crannies; germs you can't see, can't smell, but they're there."

"I'm glad to hear it." She kept scrubbing.

"I've also learned about three new diseases today: One is hirsutism, mostly found in women and children. Its main symptom is a speedy and excessive growth of too much body hair. I studied—"

"Rosvita!"

She stopped midsentence. "Yes?"

"Rosvita, you seem . . . Is everything okay?"

"Yes, yes, of course. Well, go on to bed. I know you have to work tomorrow. I'll be happy when the election is over so you can live a healthful life."

"Are you sure, Rosvita—"

"I'm well, very well, no problems, all is well."

She scrubbed. I watched her. I contemplated helping, but then decided I could barely stand and had to go to bed. "Okay, well, I'm glad all is well. Go to bed soon, will you? Rejuvenate yourself and all that."

She nodded, wished me a good night, went back to her scrubbing.

I trudged up the stairs, not bothering to flip on my light when I got to my room. I dropped my clothes on the floor, washed my face and teeth. I glanced out at my house and noticed that all the lights were on there, too.

I checked my watch: 12:30 at night and the Lopez family was still up? I thought about going over there to make sure everything was okay, but thought that would be prying. Plus, my body ached, my head ached, and my heart ached for Jay.

I crumbled into bed and lay listening to the river until I fell asleep and ventured into my lonely, cold dreams.

The next two days passed in a blur of work.

I was sleeping about five hours a night, getting up early to run along the river, working fifteen hours straight through, ignoring Damon, driving in a stupor back to Weltana and collapsing into bed, sleeping to the sound of Rosvita scrubbing downstairs.

I had no idea what was up with her and she would not tell me.

Work was a repeating nightmare. I would quit except that I had promised my brother I would work until the campaign was over, and I had promised Jay the same thing. Even though Jay would hardly look at me on the two days that week he was, briefly, at campaign headquarters, even though I wore my sexiest heels.

Plus, except for having my nervous breakdown months ago, I had never quit anything in my entire life.

Still, it would have been easier if I had simply cut my own heart out with a table knife and put it atop my desk, than to see Jay but not be able to chat like we used to, laugh like we used to, joke like we used to, and shoot each other private looks and smiles like we used to.

I wasn't sleeping gently through the night, and even though I saw the dark circles under my eyes and the sick pallor of my skin, I still took a great deal of care with my clothes. I figured I might as well look as good as I could to entice Jay to change his mind. Plus, my shoe fetish was back with a vengeance. When I felt hopeless, I glanced at my shoes. They gave me a little antisuicide lift. Shallow, I know, but one does what one needs to do so one does not jump off a skyscraper and split one's head open like a melon.

When I was in meetings with Jay he treated me with respect and almost always implemented every idea I had, and accepted every speech, and approved of all my interactions with the press, but there was zero warmth or friendship.

When he left the last meeting, looking drawn and tight, Charlie glanced my way and said, "Jay's wiped out. Fried." He'd known from the start about me and Jay.

Riley nodded. "Hell, I would be. He's the governor. He's gotta deal with all these incompetent people in the legislature who simply want him to fail because they want their candidate in. Mantel is flinging all kinds of crap his way, and he works constantly."

"But he looked haggard," said Camellia. "Wiped out. Something's wrong. He's not even joking around anymore."

We all nodded. I tried to appear concerned, but mystified. Better that than banging my head against the wall whilst whimpering.

I ignored the driver who sat right on my tail as I drove across the bridge carefully and slowly over the Willamette River that night to avoid all lurking sea monsters and arrived in Weltana at midnight.

When I arrived, all of Rosvita's lights were on. I looked at my house. The Lopezes had the lights on, too.

What the *heck* was going on?

"I wanna say somethin'," Soman announced at anger management class when we were all slouched in our beanbags after taking time out to scream in the screaming corner.

"I wanna say somethin'." He stood up. "I want to apologize to all of you, but especially to Becky and Jeanne, and you, too, Emmaline."

"All right, go ahead, Soman." Emmaline crossed her arms, her face tight, her shiner healing. "You need to take personal and emotional responsibility for the flare-up of your inner molten rage. You need to take on the consequences for your actions, and own what you did and how that effected all of us. You need to explain how your anger monopolized your thoughts, retracted your reasoning, and eclipsed all rational thought."

"I told ya, Emmaline, I don't really understand all that psycho stuff, but about the bar fight . . ." Soman cleared his throat. "I gotta apologize. That should not never have happened. It was my fault, Soman's fault. I got outta control. I let my anger roll over my head, my fists, I could feel them achin' to hit, the blood rushin' in my head when I saw that prick, my whole body, I dunno, man, it was tingling like, *tingling*, and then I was up an' at him."

He sighed, flipped his braids back. "That's all I can say about that. I'm sorry. It was s'posed to be a nice night out for all of us angry people, and it wasn't. It ended up being scary for Becky, that's the worst. I'm sorry, Becky." He was about ready to cry

"It's okay, Soman."

I didn't ask why Soman didn't think it was scary for me and Emmaline and Bradon here. I think I already knew the answer.

"The men in my family," Soman went on, wiping his eyes, "we don't hit women. We don't hit in front of our women. Ever. And there I was. Hittin'. Stupid, stupid, stupid. I apologize from deep and deep in my heart, especially to Becky. I didn't mean to scare ya none and now you probably won't go to dinner with—" He stopped right there, coughed a little.

"Anyhow, that was a bad night and I'm sorry, you guys, Becky." He looked her right in the eye. "I'm real sorry, that should never have happened. It was all Soman's fault, and I scared you, put you in a bad way, that was bad, and the rest of you, too, and Becky shouldn't have even had to see that kind of stuff."

Bradon gave him a manly side hug; Becky blushed; Emmaline nodded and floated her arms out to her side, peacefullike.

"No problem, Soman," I said. "I thought it was exciting."

Everyone's head bobbled over to me.

"What?" I asked. "It was. It's not every day I tackle someone the size of an SUV with a mouth like a pit bull."

"Yeah," Bradon said. "I don't do bar fights. I prefer to do my chair-throwing at school board meetings."

"It was out of line, out of line!" Emmaline hollered, wriggling. "Out of line, Soman, it will not happen again! Never! Look at my face!"

We regarded Emmaline's purple and now, greenish, shiner on her eye.

"Lookatthis!" She pointed with both fingers in case we were unable to find her eye. "All because of anger!"

"Yeah, Emmaline, that's a doozy. It's gonna get more green and blue and it'll be yellowish green, then yellow, I think that's the order. It'll go away, don't you worry none." Soman cleared his throat, lifted his braids off his neck for a second. "Hey, everybody. I'm sorry, man, I blew it, but hey, thank you for helpin' out, jumpin' in, tryin' to get me back on a peaceful path and all that."

We said, "You're welcome."

"You know, all of you, you're true friends to me. You're true." He wiped his eyes again. "I took a swing at a guy and what happens next but you alls jump in there with me, flailin' around, sluggin' people. I saw Bradon chuck a guy right off my back and you, Jeanne, you were spinning around on the bad dude's back not lettin' go, and Emmaline, I saw you whack two guys who were after me with your tiny little wee fists there and Becky," his eyes shone, "honey, don't you ever stand in front of me again to protect me when some guy wants to pop me one and give me a shiner. You promise me, baby, don't you never do that, I don't want you gettin' hurt, never do I want that. No tryin' to protect Soman again."

"Okay, Soman," she said, still shy around him.

"Good, honey, good. That's good."

Love is sweet. So sweet.

At first I attributed the tense and tight silence at Rosvita's candle-lit dinner the next night to my own tense and tight mind. Surely I was projecting how I was feeling?

Rosvita was silent though, too, which had me worried in a big way. Any time there was even a sliver of silence Rosvita entertained us with information about diseases.

The Lopezes looked positively deathly. They didn't come in chatting like they usually do. They hugged me and slumped into chairs at the table, Ricardo burying his head in his hands.

Ricardo said grace and asked for God's mercy, his grace, forgiveness, mercy, protection, guidance, mercy. Amen.

I tried to make small talk, but no one seemed the slightest bit interested.

I knew I was dead-on right that something was wrong when I sliced open my chicken. It wasn't quite cooked. My silverware clattered to my plate, my hands freezing in fear.

Rosvita usually cooked chicken into an embalmed state.

I swirled my wine, studied this very strangely solemn crew and said, with great politeness, "What the hell is going on?"

The words cracked into the room, the candles flickering between us. I wanted to switch on the lights because the atmosphere was freaking me out.

No one said anything.

"Ricardo?" Nothing.

"Rosvita?"

My eyes snapped back to dear and sweet Alessandra who was silently crying over the fresh-baked garlic rolls. She was so skinny and tired and pale.

Therese got up to hug her, and prayed to God to help them. Her father patted her hand. "Give us mercy, Lord," Ricardo said. "Mercy."

"He deserved it," Roberto suddenly burst out in Spanish, his fists bunched on the table. "He had it coming to him and he deserved it. I'm glad he's dead."

Rudy stalked from the table, tears streaming down his face as he shouted, also in Spanish "No one can do that to anyone, especially not to—"

"Sit down, Rudy," Ricardo ordered, his voice hoarse.

"I won't sit. I hate him, hate him, hate him!"

Rosvita stood. "He is gone now, son. He's gone, you have no need to worry further."

Even through my own blinding grief over Jay, even through my own exhaustion, all these little pieces clicked and clicked and clicked, right into place. Rosvita had finally done it. She'd carried out her threat.

"Dear God," I whispered, in Spanish.

"That is right, Jeanne," Therese said. "Dear God, have mercy on us . . ."

Me and Rosvita tried to be as silent as possible as we snuck down to the rundown guest house on my property, the night dew clinging to our ankles. We tried to be as silent as possible as we opened the wobbling front door. We tried to be as silent as possible as we descended the stairs into the pitch-dark basement.

Why? I don't know. Perhaps it was because I thought a murderess and her accomplice should be quiet. We flipped the flashlight on. There, in the middle of the floor, dead as a doornail, eyes open wide, foul mouth gaping, stomach jutting into the air, staring at the ceiling, was the Migrant Devil.

"You didn't." Oh, but dear God, I felt my whole body freeze up. He had one bullet hole in his head. Nice and neat.

"It had to be done," she told me. "He was filled with germs."

Please deliver me from this madness, I thought, my insides twisting like an intestinal tornado. "So because he was filled with germs, you killed him?"

"He was filled with germs and he spread his germs!" she declared, flailing her arms around her, white gloves whipping through the dark.

I would get very drunk, I assured myself. I deserved it. But first I would figure this all out. "His migrant camps were hideous, Rosvita; he was abusive and horrible. I know that. I hated the man. We all did. But dare I say that you should not have killed him? What happened to sticking to spraying him with bleach and water!"

"The bleach and water was not going to do the trick. He spread his germs further than where I could reach."

I leaned against the wall of that dank, damp, dark, dreary basement.

"What do you mean he spread his germs?" I asked. My, if it wasn't hard to breathe!

"He spread them to a person."

I tried to inhale like a normal woman. "I know the women were sleeping with him at the camp, Rosvita—"

"You certainly couldn't call it sleeping with him, Jeanne."

I put my fingers to my temples, nodded my head. "You're right, Rosvita. I didn't mean it like that—" Those poor women. Helpless, hopeless, stuck.

Rosvita put her hands on her hips. She looked defiant and, was it, proud?

Darn it. I knew there was more. "There's more here, Rosvita. Care to share it with me?"

"I can barely speak of it," she whispered. "I just found out. I can barely think of it. That dear, dear girl . . . that dear, wonderful girl . . . and those germs. All over. Inside."

"Those germs? What girl? What are you talking about?"

Rosvita took a deep breath, then started to cry. Both gloved hands flew to her mouth. "Dan raped Alessandra. *He raped her.* That's why the Lopezes left the migrant camp and came to work for you."

I was going to be sick. A visual image of Dan on top of Alessandra, with Alessandra screaming and crying flashed in my head. I shut down the vision, covered my mouth, tried to inhale. *Breathe in, breathe out, breathe in.*

"Therese told me last week that one day when they were still working for Dan, he told Alessandra to come to his house for their eggs and milk. Therese wasn't in their shed at the time, she was working in the field. When Alessandra got to Dan's house he grabbed her by the neck, shoved her against the wall, ripped off her pants, and raped her. She said she tried to fight, but he hit her in the face. I told the Lopezes to go to the police, but they're afraid of the police and they're afraid they'll be deported."

I bent over double, feeling bile rise in my throat. That was why Alessandra kept her head down at my house when I first met her.

"You just found out?" I whispered, not trusting my stomach.

"Yes. Therese and Ricardo were worried that Alessandra might be pregnant, so recently they took her to a clinic hours away from here. The doctors checked her, ran some tests, and said she is not pregnant but that she had chlamydia. Chlamydia is linked to an organism, a tiny thing, called *chlamydia trachomatis*. It's curable and she's already on the medication so she is pure and clean again, but he raped her, Jeanne. She is fourteen. He had to die."

I crumbled onto the floor of the basement, thinking of sweet, scared, shy, well-loved Alessandra shaking like a leaf in my family room, pale and scared to death. I thought of that potbellied, pig-eyed, vile-smelling, dangerous brute of a Migrant Devil rutting on that thin girl—Alessandra crying and petrified, and in grave, bone-piercing, psyche-smashing pain.

I pictured Ricardo and Therese, their endless, intense pain, the tears they must have shed.

I buried my head in my arms until I could breathe right again, then looked back up at Rosvita.

"You're right," I said, now feeling quite calm. "He had to die."

She nodded.

"So what are we going to do with the body?" I asked.

And there it was. A profound little question. A question that made me an official accomplice. A criminal accomplice.

Had I known that this was to happen on my first day in The Opera Man's Café under the fir trees in Weltana, I would have run like I was being chased by rabid leopards. How I would have run.

I thought of Alessandra.

I thought of Rosvita. Eccentric, outspoken, kind, loud, germ-obsessed Rosvita, who loved the Lopezes.

I thought of Therese and Ricardo. I thought of Alessandra again.

I would not run.

CHAPTER 17

I decided to go home and drink on the problem of the Migrant Devil. When I lived in Chicago "drinking on the problem" meant that I drank until I cried or passed out.

I got out a bottle of kahlua and some cream and mixed a drink in a long, tall glass.

I took my drink onto my porch, my hands shaking. The river gurgled. A few problems had cropped up in my life and I needed to dissect them.

First, I missed my mother more than I would miss my arteries if someone took them out and borrowed them for a couple of months.

And, second, Jay Kendall, the first decent man I'd met since Johnny, was no longer speaking to me and probably never would again, and I couldn't blame him. Who wanted to hang out with a woman who got arrested for fighting in bars?

Third, Rosvita, a new but lovely friend, even though she had a little fetish for diseases and germs, had knocked off the Migrant Devil and his corpse was now dwelling in the basement of a small and dilapidated house on my property.

I raised the glass to my lips. I would get drunk.

No, you won't. Those words came from a voice in my head.

But a good drunk will take the edge off of my life, I told the voice. It'll take off the corners of the pain that are jabbing my heart like steel rods. I need things to be a little fuzzy.

You need a clear head, the voice said. I figured it was my rational self, finally breaking through. *You said you were going to stop drinking, stop getting drunk.*

I don't want to stop drinking. A nice drink is a nice friend.

Get a grip, Jeanne, the voice said. *It's been twelve years. Twelve long years. You need to try life without alcohol.*

I put the drink up to my lips. I wanted to suck down that kahlua and cream so bad I could cry. In fact, I wanted to bathe in it.

My legs might start hurting again if I don't drink.

Please. You know your legs are better. They won't hurt you.

But my baby isn't there anymore. I might be reminded of that if I stop drinking.

You remind yourself of that every day, you know that, even without the alcohol, the voice said. *Let it go, Jeanne. Let the past go. Let the pain go. Stop being pointless. Live a life that is worthy and honest.*

I don't want to let Johnny and Ally go.

Never, the voice said. *Johnny and Ally will always be with you. But now you have to find the courage to find peace.*

Peace? I almost laughed.

Yes, peace.

I put the glass down on the railing, bent my head.

Peace.

Okay. I would find the courage to find peace. The courage to keep my Bronco out of the ocean. The courage to help Rosvita and the Lopezes. The courage to keep standing upright like a human.

I tipped the kahlua and cream into a pot of geraniums on the deck.

There. At least the flowers could get drunk.

It was 2:00 in the morning when I crawled into bed cold, stone sober.

I drove to Portland through the pounding rain and worked with my brother on all sorts of campaign stuff that had to be done immediately, if not yesterday. I tried not to lust over the posters of Jay.

He called several times that day. He was speaking in various towns to various groups and I was feeding him interesting tidbits about each town and each group to make it personal. He was the health care/education/environmental governor and we stuck to those themes pretty hard.

Each conversation ended like this: "Thank you, Jeanne."

"You're welcome, Governor."

There would be a hesitation, a loaded pause, and he'd hang up. I never hung up first. I would scramble to get back to work. If I was having a particularly bad day, I would shoot out for twenty minutes and buy a pair of shoes. So far, I had bought six pairs of shoes. I quietly gave them to the ladies in the office. Mrs. Ederson, who was eighty if she was a day, wore her black zebra-striped heels to work every day from then on out and Camellia loved wearing her new red slingbacks with her ratty jeans.

Seemed like I didn't actually want them for myself for once in my life, I only wanted to buy them.

Don't ask.

At 9:00 that night I finally drove back to Weltana.

I drove over the Willamette River slowly, cautiously, with care. When an SUV built like a small house came zooming up behind me real fast, I slowed down. He honked. I flipped him off. He flipped me off. I ignored him.

I hate bridges. Why did I move to a city with so many bridges? Bridges here, there, everywhere. And there was a whole bunch of water under the bridges, too. Probably electric eels way down there. And man-size squid. Sheesh. They should clean that river out.

The darkness in the basement of my guest house could not hide the pain of despair on Rosvita's features the next night.

"We can't wait any longer to get rid of the body," Rosvita said, her white gloves glowing in the darkness. "You see, after someone dies, rigor mortis sets in and the body freezes and hardens. He'll dry out like a prune and eventually his skin and hair and nails will fall away. The smell of rotting flesh will awaken the dead and it will surely bring on the authorities."

"Thank you, Rosvita, I think I've got it," I said.

She closed her mouth, fussing with the sprigs of jasmine she had stuck in a clip on her head. She had shoved a sprig of jasmine down my shirtfront to lessen the scent of Dan the Migrant Devil and his decomposition.

I stared down at the Migrant Devil's body and tried to decide how to get rid of it. The river behind my house wasn't deep enough to put him in. Those waves with the whipped cream tops wouldn't cover him. He couldn't stay here. We certainly couldn't go to the town cemetery.

"Why don't we bury him out in the forest?"

I peered out the darkened window, seeing only the lights of Rosvita's home. There were huge trees and mountains and open space out there. Surely there was some logging trail we could take way out into the boonies? We could drag his body out and dig a nice, deep, cozy grave.

Rosvita nodded.

I nodded.

Sounded like an easy plan.

But life is full of surprises.

How was I to know that we were going to get shot at that night?

We wrapped the Migrant Devil in black plastic and duct tape. He was very difficult to maneuver. Rosvita had brought gloves and masks but it was still icky to touch him. His head was remarkably heavy and unfortunately I had to deal with that end. Even in death he had an evil expression plastered on his face.

When we had him all wrapped up, I felt better. He couldn't escape now. Then I remembered that dead people can't escape.

We tried to lift the Migrant Devil, an enormous monstrosity of a male.

We heaved. We sweated. We grunted. Rosvita used bad language.

We were halfway up the stairs when Rosvita lost her footing and darned if the Migrant Devil didn't tumble all the way back down with a lot of thumps and whumps.

It was deathly silent in that basement while we pondered our options.

"We're going to have to rope him up like a dead cow and pull him up the stairs," I said.

My co-conspirator nodded at me. We found some old rope, secured it around his ankles, and pulled. The rope broke.

The Migrant Devil went tumbling down the stairs again with more thumps and whumps. I sat on the steps of the basement, my head in my hands. Why could I not have kept driving to the Pacific? Why oh why? I liked the beach. I liked sand. I liked seals and fish and seaweed and seafoam and taffy and clam chowder.

I looked at Rosvita who was near tears.

"I know you didn't get him down here by yourself," I said. "The Lopezes helped you."

She wiped her eyes with her gloved hands. "That's true."

"We need to get the Lopezes," I said. "We can't lift him ourselves. We can barely get him up the stairs. They helped you get him down here, now they can help us get him out."

"No," Rosvita said. "They have their own nightmares to deal with. I want to spare them this part. They can't be a part of this. We cannot risk their arrests."

"And you can risk mine?" I asked, aghast.

Rosvita had the good sense to become agitated and tearful. "I don't want anybody to get arrested. No one. But they don't need any more pain. Alessandra Lopez can't stop crying; the boys are about ready to explode, they're so furious; and Ricardo is pulling further into himself each day. It's like he's leaving the planet, Jeanne, his pain is suffocating him."

"We need help."

"Not from them."

"Yes, them. Who else? Your best buddy, the chief of police? Or, perhaps your friend, Beatrice McConnelly, the judge in Portland you're so close to, could whip on over here one afternoon between criminal cases? You mentioned a bacteriologist pal the other day, too. He available?"

She sputtered and harrumphed. "All right, fine. But I don't want Alessandra here. She's been too traumatized."

That was an easy one.

I left to get Ricardo, Roberto, and Rudy.

The bullets whizzed over our heads, crashing into the trees around us, bark flying off in all directions. Later I was to think that the scary, swearing men wielding guns probably weren't intending to kill us, but we did not stick around long enough to inquire about their true intentions.

Ricardo, Roberto, Rudy, Rosvita, and I had quickly lifted the Migrant Devil up the stairs and into the back of my Bronco. We drove out of Weltana toward Mount Hood, then veered to the left. We got onto an old logging road that Rosvita knew of because at one point she had dated a logger and they used to enjoy the view at the top.

"I always made him use a condom," she announced to us in the darkness of my roaring Bronco. "And, before we had intercourse, I always made him shower with me so that I knew he was absolutely clean. He had to brush his teeth twice, and floss, and run a wire over his tongue so that I knew the germs in his mouth were at a minimum. He didn't seem to mind my ministrations . . ." Her voice faded.

"Of course, we only dated about three months. He told me I was a warm, sultry siren in bed, but too much of a germ-freak." She shrugged her shoulders. "That was acceptable. Getting him cleaned up for sex eight times a week had gotten tiring for me, too. I needed a break."

Eight times a week? I stared out the window into the pitch-darkness. Here we were, delivering a dead body to a grave after

Rosvita had offed him, and she was focusing on a past lover. A lover she had sex with eight times a week.

Gall. How exhausting.

I turned off on a dirt road where Rosvita indicated, stopped and switched off the lights. For a few minutes, we all sat quietly, still as the night, as they say.

We got out of the car as quiet as only petrified, clumsy criminals can. Ricardo, me, and the boys grabbed the Migrant Devil and yanked him out. Rosvita marched in front of us down a small embankment. There wasn't a hint of light. It was our intent to carry him as far as we could, then dig a grave deep enough to meet the roof of hell.

But about thirty-five yards into our little burial procession we felt those bullets whizzing past our heads.

"Get the fuck off my property!" someone yelled. He ended his statement with another hail of bullets.

Now, I must say that I was tempted to drop the dead body and take off. In fact, Rudy did that before his father ordered him back.

Rosvita whimpered, "Mother of God, help me, help me, help me."

I gurgled in dry panic, and we hightailed it back to the Bronco through the blackened night, hauling the Migrant Devil, his body flipping and flopping about.

Another deep voice shouted at us, "I'm gonna kill ya, I'm gonna kill ya."

Whiz, whiz, whiz.

"Here I come! I'm gonna get ya!"

We grunted and groaned and whimpered as we hauled butt up that embankment.

"You come again to my land and you are dead meat. Ya hear me? Deeeaaddd meeeaattt!"

The bullets went flying all around us.

I am confident in saying that no five people, carrying a dead man, at any other previous time in history, outside of a war zone, ran faster than us. We flew up that embankment, keeping our heads low. We tossed the Migrant Devil into the back of the Bronco like one might toss a sack of rotting potatoes and sped away from those bullet-blowing bastards as fast as we could.

We co-conspirators had had enough for one evening and were stone-cold with fright, so we headed home. We pulled up to the guest house on my property, brought the body back in, and lugged it down the stairs with the expected amounts of awkwardness, stumbling, and poor language.

"Now what?" Rosvita asked.

I shook my head. Ricardo looked like he was going to cry. Roberto and Rudy were exhausted and pale. Rudy looped his arm around his brother's neck and Roberto bent his head and sobbed. Rosvita hugged the boys, told them she was taking care of everything, everything would be fine.

I leaned against the wall, feeling quite ill. Vomitous, actually.

I looked at the bagged body. "Let's meet tomorrow night."

We trooped up the stairs and out the door. I made sure I locked it, then laughed at myself. As if the police wouldn't knock down the door if they wanted.

Getting rid of bodies is such hard work, I'm telling you.

The next night about 11:00, me, Rosvita, and the Lopez men met at the river and whispered like a bunch of Mafia bosses to each other in English and Spanish, as usual, although no one could understand Rosvita's Spanish and I didn't think she understood us.

Rosvita suggested we burn the body in a huge bonfire. She raised her hands high to indicate the height of the fire.

I informed her that it was not burn season and I knew a black cloud of smoke would gather too much attention.

Roberto suggested we put the Migrant Devil in a chest, nail the lid down, and dump it in the ocean.

That was a good idea, clichéd, of course, but it was worth consideration.

"The problem with that is for the rest of my life I'm going to worry that the chest is going to bob to the surface," Rudy said.

Yep. That bobbing would be a worry.

"We could bury him under concrete," Ricardo said.

That would be a good idea. It worked for the Mafia, perhaps it would work for us. We could get the concrete at a local shop, find a hole, dump him in, pour the concrete. "But where will we bury him?" I asked.

We all thought of our exciting evening the night before.

"We could drive to another spot," Rosvita suggested.

That was a possibility.

"Life will be so much better for the people in his camp now that he is gone," Rosvita said, entwining her gloved fingers. I rolled my eyes. Surely this was a time to focus on the problem at hand? "I'm sure whoever buys that land will bulldoze those sheds full of germs and vermin and plagues. No one, *no one* will have to use that horrid excuse of a toilet again. In fact, I think I'll push that toilet down myself!"

A wave of bone-crushing exhaustion overwhelmed me. I didn't think that Rosvita truly understood her own predicament. She had killed someone. Did he deserve it? Yes. It was unfortunate he was not murdered before this. But still. If she was caught she would be looking at a very long jail sentence, despite extenuating circumstances. So would I, for aiding and abetting a crime. So would the Lopezes. The boys were old enough to be prosecuted as adults.

I held my head in my hands, rocked my brain back and forth.

"That toilet was a sick disgrace," Rosvita went on. "We should tear that toilet down and have a party to celebrate!"

A toilet party.

I thought I would scream.

And then it hit me.

I looked at Rosvita. She was listing again all the germs that could possibly lurk in a toilet like that, including snakes and rats that could bite an unsuspecting bottom.

"I know where to hide the body," I whispered.

Oh yeah.

I knew exactly where to hide the body. It would be a fitting burial site.

Fit for a giant germ.

The invitations Rosvita made read, "Potty Push-Over Party." They were light brown with a photo of Dan the Migrant Devil's potty on the front. They invited everyone to Rosvita's for a potluck party after the push-over segment of the party. Donovan, the ex-opera singer, would sing for entertainment. Ricardo assured us that he would get everyone in the migrant camp to come. I had to have every living person out of that camp that night so no one would see us.

All invitees would meet at the Migrant Devil's place, but not too close to that stench-filled outhouse. I knew exactly who we would ask to bulldoze the potty: Tory Blankenship. Tory was a neighbor of the Migrant Devil's. Tory hated Dan because he had run over two of her dogs in a drunken rage with his giant pickup and told her that animals were meant to be eaten, hunted, and tortured, not played with.

You might be wondering how we could legally bring a bulldozer onto private property without the owner's permission? This is where a little fraud and forgery came in. I wrote a letter to the chief of police, Rosvita's kindergarten pal, Paul Nguyen, citing concerns about Dan the Migrant Devil's farm from a sanitary perspective from the Oregon Department of Health.

If I do say so myself, I replicated the letterhead from the Department of Health quite well. I looked on their website, magnified the design, and transferred it to paper. It was signed by their top official who—drat—happened to be hiking in the Himalayas on vacation so was, sadly enough, unable to confirm or deny the order.

I mailed it from Portland. Three days later, I called Chief Nguyen to complain about the condition of the potty on Dan's

property once again. "Well, hell's bells, Jeanne, you won't believe what I got yesterday in the mail regarding that shit-hole,"
Paul said. "The state wants it to come down and they're insisting
that Dan put in regular facilities. I've called about that steamin'
outhouse for years and nothin' happened. Wonder why they're
doin' this now? Not that I give a rat's ass, I hate that fuckin'
thing. Since Dan's not here to yak his mouth off, and no one
knows what hole he's crawled into, I'm taking action. That shit
piece is comin' down."

I pretended surprise and said that maybe I'd give Tory a call
and she could bring her tractor, and wouldn't it be nice to get this
done before Dan got back in town and where did the chief think
he was anyhow?

Paul said he didn't know where the fuck that prick was and he
didn't care if that son of a bitch never came back and if I would
give Tory a call that'd be whoppin' great. He was going to see
that lovely lady later tonight for dinner (I did not inquire further
about those plans) and he would confirm with her, by God and by
damn he would.

I hung up with the chief, waited ten minutes and called him
back. Chief, I said, as sweet as I could, we should make it a community event, shouldn't we? Wouldn't it be cool, I told him, especially for the Hispanic community, to see their chief taking
action against this monstrosity? Taking a stand against a crime
committed against the Hispanic community, against all of us?

I could almost see that kind, albeit blowhard, man puffing out
his chest on the other end of the telephone wire at the thought of
the attention. And wouldn't it be stupendous if we had a celebration afterward, I asked? In fact, I had been on the phone with
Rosvita and she had offered to host a Potty Push-Over Party by
the river tomorrow, wouldn't that be fun? People could thank
him, the chief, for curing such a scourge on the community.

Puff-puff.

The chief told me it was the best damn shittin' idea he'd
heard in a long time and he would barbeque some of his friggin'

famous ribs to bring to the party after getting rid of that devil bastard's shitty-hole.

And that was that.

Next I called Tory. She couldn't wait for the Potty Push-Over Party and asked if we couldn't have the party that night as it would give her such "scintillating pleasure." I told her, no, we couldn't, but the invitations would be delivered that day. She thought about it for a second and said, disbelief in her voice, "I will anticipate this as I used to anticipate Christmas morning as a child."

On my way home from work I paid cash for extra bags of dirt at a local building supply store after ripping my hair back in a bun and wearing big glasses.

I almost felt like a Mafia woman. Dig a hole. Dump him in. Cover him up. Done.

People started arriving on the Migrant Devil's property an hour before the scheduled event on Tuesday evening in a festive mood. Everyone stayed well clear of the potty because of the stench. Rosvita and I had arrived early to meet with Tory and discuss the best angles for the push-over part.

Most of the town came and all of the migrant workers. Rosvita passed out plastic gloves to everyone, "in case a germ popped from the potty." She also provided white paper masks. In the spirit of the party, we all donned our gear.

"Germs are insidious here," she bellowed through a bullhorn, milling through the crowd. "Put on your masks and gloves! *Put on your masks and gloves!*"

The police chief had opened the Migrant Devil's home the day before, so that the migrant workers could use his "facilities" as, he said, the Department of Health had declared the shit-hole completely unsanitary and unusable.

When it was time for the Potty Push-Over, Paul got on his bullhorn and addressed what looked to be most of the town.

"Ladies and Gentlemen, I want to thank all of you for coming out today. Today is a great damn day! Today Tory's going to bull-doze over this horrible excuse of a toilet. I got permission from the state after years of work. We're going to dig out the crap and, Rosvita told me, we're going to plant a cherry tree there. A frig-gin' pink one with friggin' pretty pink flowers!" A cheer went up from the crowd. "Dan's not gonna be happy, but I don't know where the hell he is, so he's gonna have to deal with it when he gets back. Tory!"

Tory stood up on the front of her tractor. "You ready, honey?" she called.

Chief shouted through his bullhorn. "Are you ready, Weltana?" he repeated.

Weltanans cheered their readiness.

"Are you ready, Weltana?" he repeated.

Oh, how they cheered again.

"We're all ready, Tory!" the chief yelled, one fist up in the air and pumping. "Let her roar!"

Tory made a big V with her arms for victory while everyone yelled and clapped, and tipped her head up to the heavens as though thanking God. She spun into the seat of her tractor with great flair and revved the engine, and backed her tractor way up to increase the drama of the situation. As the crowd clapped in unison, the tractor roared forward. By the time Tory smashed into the outhouse she was driving along at quite a clip, hooting her joy into the clear blue sky.

The outhouse collapsed at the first hit.

I would have to say that the crowd went wild.

Tory waved at everyone, backed way way up again, then shoved that tractor throttle up and smashed the outhouse again. And again. You could tell she was almost orgasmic as she kept rollin' that tractor right over that outhouse.

Way orgasmic.

An hour later the party was in full swing at Rosvita's. People had brought tables and chairs and they'd lined them up on the lawn by the river. The tables groaned with the amount of food.

Rosvita seemed to be having the time of her life, as if oblivious to our planned criminal activities. Donovan followed her around, a very sweet grin on his face. His opera would keep everyone fully enthralled and occupied while we made our great escape.

Rosvita had collected everyone's gloves and masks, then stapled them to a giant bulletin board that she labeled in black marker—"The Germ Bulletin Board." She tried to reel people in to discuss the germs that people carried on their hands—day to day and also germs found in outhouses—but when there was not much interest, she gave up, swapped her old gloves for a new pair, and got herself a plate of food.

The Lopezes were there, although they were pretty quiet. Ricardo tired, Roberto withdrawn, Rudy sad, Alessandra scared, and the mother, Therese, haggard, as if she hadn't slept for days. And yet . . . there was some other emotion stamped on her face, too. Pride? Strength? A lack of fear? I didn't know. Didn't have time to figure it out, either.

When it was dark and Donovan began his opera concert, me, Rosvita, and the Lopez men faded into the shadows.

We changed into black pants and shirts in the car, including black ski masks and black gloves. We drove to the Migrant Devil's property in the dark. During the drive, none of us spoke. I don't think we even breathed. We couldn't. We were so scared our bones were shaking.

The darkness moved in on us, closer and closer as we drove, so close that if the night sky could suffocate a person, we would surely be suffocating. I began to feel like I was in a moving coffin.

When we arrived, Ricardo made sure none of the workers were in their sheds.

The truth was, none of the workers would have called the police on us anyhow. That I knew without a doubt. But I didn't want to put any of them in jeopardy if things got bad with the police. Lord knows, I was already panicked enough about Roberto and Rudy being involved.

When not a blade of grass bent or moved or shuddered we slipped out of the Bronco.

One of the doors squeaked and we all froze. Rudy made a gasping sound, like a spider might make if spiders could gasp in fear. We all spun around in the darkness, and froze, our eyes searching for anyone, any living person, who might be watching us grave-diggers.

We searched the trees, searched the dark horizon, searched the farmworkers' sheds, and when our hearts stopped hammering we stealthily tiptoed toward the back of the Bronco.

I clicked open the latch to the back, which again set all of us off on a spinning/freezing tailspin as we searched for suspicious people peeking over at us. When no peeping persons were located, we got back to work.

In the back lay the Migrant Devil's body. I must say that he smelled like dead fish and decaying meat and disintegrating flesh mixed with leaking eyeballs.

We could not help ourselves as we covered our faces with our gloved hands. Rudy went to a tree—on tiptoe—and vomited. Rosvita patted him on the back when he rejoined our crime scene.

I indicated that everyone was to grab the Migrant Devil. No one moved for long seconds and the darkness moved in another two feet, the silence screaming loud.

I moved toward the Migrant Devil, and finally everyone else did, too. We each grabbed part of him, but Rudy made the spider-gasping sound again and had to let go. We pushed the corpse half-way back in the Bronco/hearse, all of us stepped away, and listened while Rudy lost what was left of his stomach.

I could feel bile in my throat, but I willed it down. Nothing like a jail sentence to make you take control of all your bodily functions in a hurry.

When Rudy was back, I grabbed the Migrant Devil's right shoulder area, Ricardo the left, and everyone else took a spot. We lifted, dropped, then pulled him feet first over to the hole. For a second we paused. The smell of all that petrifying potty poop was particularly potent and overpowering as it perfumed the air. Combined with the scent of the Migrant Devil, it was a wonder that we were still upright.

"Right now, his body is breaking itself down, gnawing on its own bones, its own organs . . ." Rosvita whispered.

"Shhh . . ." Ricardo shushed. Rosvita shushed.

Tory had dumped the whole outhouse into a Dumpster (charged to Dan) and had dug out much of the waste and dirt inside the hole. We had a nice deep hole.

There was no way of getting all that waste out though, and it reeked like you wouldn't believe. It smelled like despair. It smelled like hopelessness. It smelled like the death of souls. This was only one of the horrendous things the Migrant Devil had done to people like my mother's mama.

I shook my head in disgust. Ricardo and I looked at each other. I knew he understood what I was thinking.

The five of us picked up the Migrant Devil and dropped him into that dark hopeless pit. He landed with a thunk.

The darkness moved in on us, another foot, I think, and the silence blistered my ears once again.

Rudy and Roberto went back to the Bronco/hearse and got the flowering cherry tree and the rest of us hauled out the bags and bags of soil I had bought to fill in the hole.

I used my hand to open the bags, as did the boys and Ricardo. We dumped bag after bag of soil down on the Migrant Devil who we couldn't even see, wrapped as he was in black plastic and duct tape. I knew I would never forget the smell of that rich topsoil.

When all the bags were almost empty, we put the ball of the cherry tree in, then covered it up with the remaining soil. Finally we stomped down on the dirt.

Before we left I took a look at the tree.

I knew it would be beautiful in the spring, probably in March.

And I knew that every time I looked at it I would think of the decaying Migrant Devil.

I wiped off my hands on my black pants. As much as I didn't like this dark darkness and the screeching silence I know that we, as a whole human community, are truly better off with certain people planted in the ground.

Dan the Migrant Devil was one of those people.

The drive back to the party was as cloyingly quiet as the drive out. We had to pull over once so Rudy could puke, and soon Ricardo joined him. We drove with all the windows down, the rush of the cool wind eliminating most of the stench of the Migrant Devil.

When we arrived, I stopped the Bronco/hearse and we all sat in silence.

"Dan committed a heinous crime against Alessandra and other women," Rosvita said. "He is now in hell talking to the devil."

"He was punished," Rudy said, his voice harsh. "He deserved to be punished for what he did to Alessandra."

Ricardo nodded. "Yes, he did. But we will not speak of this again." He stared at his boys. "To anyone. Ever."

For once, even Rosvita was subdued. "To no one," she said.

We all nodded our agreements.

No one here would tell, I knew. We all had too much to lose.

But our secret would shift and change in the months to come.

Secrets do that type of thing, you know.

Shift and change.

CHAPTER 18

We all changed clothes, knowing if we all arrived in black with black stocking caps that people would become suspicious. We mixed back into the party, one by one, so we wouldn't look as if we'd been busy burying some body under a cherry tree. Donovan was still singing, his audience on their feet giving him a standing ovation after each song. When I saw the bright hanging lights and the tables laden with gourmet food and Donovan's soaring voice, I finally felt the black night back off, letting me breathe again.

After burying a body, deep in the moist earth, where an infested outhouse once stood, most people would be inclined to sleep in the next morning and relax. Enjoy. Perhaps get a pedicure.

I was up by 4:00, running by 4:05 by the river, out the door by 5:30, and in my office at campaign headquarters by 6:20. Because of the time I had had to take for the Migrant Devil, I had a ton of work to catch up on at the office.

Press releases.

One speech to finish, another to begin crafting.

About two-thousand-three-hundred calls to make, meetings to prepare for, e-mails to answer, jobs to delegate, phone calls to take from Jay.

Plus, I couldn't sleep. Being an accessory to a felony does not induce sleep.

I tried not to gaze into Jay Kendall's blue eyes in all of the posters plastered around the office. It was better for me that way. I was training myself as well I could to think of Jay as a product I had to market, not a person that I'd wanted in my life, lusted after, and lost. It made things less bone-jarringly painful.

The election was three months away. I could rein it in, suck it up, live, I told myself. Couldn't I? I fought back the black thoughts that had sent me tumbling down into my deep pit recently. Mustn't go deeper into the pit. I don't like it there.

On my way to the copy machine, I wobbled a little bit on these very chic navy blue heels with rhinestone-studded buckles which matched perfectly with my pants and a short jacket of the same color and a white lacy shirt I had bought on my lunch hour the other day.

But those very chic navy blue heels with rhinestone-studded buckles came to an abrupt halt when the front office door opened and in stepped Jay.

First emotion: Loss.

Second: Lust.

Third: Want.

At rare moments, you can catch people in an unguarded moment. What they think and how they truly feel about you shows on their face for the briefest of brief milliseconds.

And I knew, in that glorious millisecond, how he felt about me. I knew.

Inside and out. I felt like crying with relief.

I was so happy I damn near clicked my above-mentioned heels.

"Jeanne," he said, his voice very gruff. And sexy.

"Jay," I said. I smiled at him.

"How are you?"

How was I? Not good, not really, I thought. I'm clinging to the sides of a black pit. And yet, I was good. At that moment, I was. Here with him alone, I was good. "I'm doing good."

He nodded. "Glad to hear it."

"And you?" Oh, I am good at polite chitchat.

"Fine."

We stared at each other. Full-on, raw, honest, aching stares.

The door opened, two noisy college students burst in, and the moment was over.

How I love my navy blue heels with rhinestone-studded buckles!

Campaign headquarters was a barely controlled madhouse for the next few weeks. We lived day to day, hour to hour, minute to minute with mind-crunching chaos. We were adding people all the time who wanted to get involved with the campaign. Most of them were there simply because they believed in Jay and wanted to be a part of the campaign. Others wanted the experience of running a campaign. And more than a few were volunteering because they hoped they would meet someone.

For many, the experience was successful in the love department. Romances had spread all over the office and it amused me to watch them when I had a spare moment. On the flip side, tempers had also flared on more than one occasion. Stress, exhaustion, constant excitement, and being in incredibly close quarters with other people will do that. Often Damon would yell at various people until he saw me coming to protect the poor person and he'd tone it down. Needless to say, many of our volunteers quit after one episode with Damon.

Damon and I continued to nurture a silent and intense dislike for each other. Actually, he detested me and I disliked him as I disliked red-dotted boa constrictors high on cocaine. In strategy meetings we would often clash and I would have to illustrate my point using colorful images. I referenced strippers, my strong desire for daily chocolates, bad dates, lousy husbands, pineapples, breast implants, and Botox to get my points across.

This infuriated him and we went at it.

On his end, though, Damon seemed increasingly and overly interested in everything I was doing and where I was. It was rather obsessive and I told him that. On a couple of occasions he asked if I was dating anyone. I told him I would discuss my personal life with him as soon as Pluto came to lodge in the parking lot.

I had, however, no more lucky encounters with Jay.

Such a bummer.

I talked to Roy. My trial was upcoming and the depositions were going well.

Slick Dick's deposition had been taken for days in Chicago. Roy sent me copies. I read them for entertainment purposes only. Oh, what a liar Slick Dick was, what a fruitcake, what a delusional doofus.

I would soon have to face him. For some strange reason, I relished the thought.

Emmaline was slowly getting better in terms of her free-flowing frustration with us. The bar fight and paddy wagons had not gone over well, but at anger management class that week we only had to hit the boxing bags for the first fifteen minutes, Afterwards, we sat in our colorful beanbags, arms outstretched, fingers touching each other, eyes closed.

She switched off the lights. "Envision peace," she said.

I envisioned.

At least, I tried to envision. But my body was wiped out from the long, frantic hours of the campaign. My mind was fried with worry that the Lopezes and Rosvita would land in jail. I was being sued by Slick Dick for an obscene amount of money. My heart was in a twist over Jay and yet at the same time Jay was making me think of Johnny and Ally and that farm and the multitude of noisy kids I'd always wanted. I missed my mother, too. Like I'd miss the ventricles of my heart should they ever be removed. Peace was not part of my picture.

I had not had a drink for a long time, and that was hard, hard, hard, not being able to soften the edges, dull the pain, unfrazzle the mind, that sort of thing.

It was about at that moment I broke finger contact with Soman and Bradon and bent my head down between my legs and sobbed like a female water buffalo might cry if she got real hormonal. I felt Soman's arm around me and he murmured, "Skinny ass bird, you're gonna be all right."

And Bradon said, "There you go, Jeanne, you cry and cry and cry. My wife cries sometimes, too, although she doesn't quite get this shaky . . . hey, take it easy, honey, you need to breathe, deep breaths." He cupped both hands around my mouth. "Breathe in deep or you're gonna hyperventilate, breathe in, breathe out, breathe in."

Becky, didn't say anything, only put her face right by mine. I felt her tears on my face. (*Note to self:* Call Becky and invite her to lunch.)

Emmaline patted my knee. When my sobs finally stopped rising from the grief lodged in my heart, she said, "What is it, Jeanne?"

"I can't visualize peace." The very thought of not being able to visualize peace sent me off on another round of crying and gasping.

"Think of a garden full of roses," Bradon said, trying to be helpful. "Climbing roses, tea roses, miniature roses. I know about them now. They're peaceful!"

"Think of the river behind your house," Becky said, her voice urgent.

"Think of a quiet place filled with white clouds and a rainbow," Emmaline intoned.

"Shit, baby, that's why you crying?" Soman said. "I'll give you some peace to think about. Peace is when you know you got in a good shot right at the face of a man who you've hated for years and his blood is on your face, baby, and stuck in your fingernails, that is one peaceful feeling! And if you a badass island man like me and you dressed like a woman with a wig on and you shock the shit out of him, that's all the better, damn, but it's all the better!"

Becky snorted. Emmaline rumbled, growled in her throat. Bradon said, "I'm never going to a bar with you again, no offense now, Soman."

And that struck me as absurdly funny so I laughed. I remembered the hog-faced man's completely bewildered expression when Soman ripped off his wig and stood there in full glory with his swinging braids and lovely dress and heels and punched him right in the face.

I laughed and laughed.

Crying and laughing. Why do they so often go together?

On Friday night I drove over the bridge slowly, as usual, ignoring the honking behind me from another car. (These Portlanders treat their bridges like raceways.) I snuck a quick peek out my car window at the city and I had to admit it was beautiful. Way too many high and scary bridges and I wish they would get rid of the Willamette River, home to scary Loch Ness–type monsters and giant squid, or at least reroute it through Boise or something, but other than that . . . it's lovely. Cool buildings with different shapes and colors, but nothing too intimidating, a river with an esplanade, tons of trees, and a whole bunch of unique and funky areas in town to visit that have their own sort of Oregony style.

Once out of the city and connecting suburbs and twinkling lights the road gave way to the trees and hills, and Mount Hood greeted me like a mound of whipped cream. I parked in my usual spot at Rosvita's and made a beeline for the peace of the river. The moon was shining right down on it; the owls hooting to each other; the trees offering up a whisper of a cool breeze.

I slipped out of my brown velvet high heels, rolled up my brown velvet pant legs, and stuck my feet into the river. The river water was cold and refreshing and my brain finally defried from work.

I swished my feet in the water.

I had tried to suck it up the last few weeks about Jay, but had found that it would probably be easier to swallow a fire-breathing dragon headfirst. The more I knew about him, the more time I spent with him, the better I liked him.

I had never met anyone who was as compassionate and honest as Jay. The campaign staff had dug up some good dirt on his opponent, Kory Mantel. Mantel's a screaming antiabortion guy and we had found an ex-girlfriend who Mantel had pressured into an abortion before Mantel had met his wife. The woman bitterly regretted it to this day and had been in counseling for years over it. In fact, she worked for an antiabortion organization and used herself and the emotional trauma she endured from the abortion as an example as to why women should not follow in her path.

Mantel was also vitriolic in his condemnation for gays, gay rights, gay marriage, and yet his brother in Colorado was gay. The brother had not told the candidate of this particular thing, and Jay decided that we would not be the ones to haul him out of the closet.

Finally, Mantel's affair with an employee, who was a worldly twenty-one-year-old, had also been confirmed, but Jay declined to bring it up in the campaign.

That had not gone over well with Damon. Damon confronted Jay with all of these issues and Jay, looking exhausted but still yummy, had decimated Damon. Jay had no desire to drag the poor woman who had the abortion into the political ring, and she had expressed, quite clearly, her refusal to be a part. He didn't want to drag the brother in because he thought it was wrong to do so. As for the affair, Jay, like me and Charlie and the others, was against bringing a personal, private, family matter out to the public for their consumption because he was concerned about the impact on Kory's already troubled son, and on his wife, who Jay had met and respected.

I am smart enough to know when someone is smarter than me, and I knew that Jay was smarter. He was also more self-assured and, well, flat-out more kind. He was a kind man. Tough, and he didn't tolerate wimps or weakness, but he was kind. And he had a hard, muscled, nice bottom. No flopping around at all. That butt looked confident and cocky and I sure liked it.

I kicked the cold water up toward the stars. The owls hooted again and I figured I was their evening entertainment. I twirled my way toward the center of the river, holding my arms out, and watched the stars spin. I wondered where Jay was at that very moment.

When I came to a stop I indulged in a little entertainment of my own and wondered what it would be like to marry Jay. Splendid. Bliss.

And a total disaster for him.

I thought of my past and my problems and how I would be a totally unsuitable wife for the governor of Oregon.

The only less suitable girlfriend for the governor of Oregon would be an ex-hooker.

I laughed. Nah. Scratch that. The very large and noisy liberal contingent in the Portland area would be fine with that. It would be seen as exotic and sexy. The Christian coalition would praise God for the hooker's redemption and change of heart. The conservatives would make an issue of it for a while and let it go as soon as the ex-hooker threatened to get out her little black book and name names.

It would become a quirky side note and men would envy Jay his nights.

But me? Someone who was involved in bar-fighting, creative assaults against a past boyfriend, and body-burying, who also had a drinking problem, a public nervous breakdown, and a loud mouth might be a slight problem.

I felt that depression settle over me again, black and heavy, like sticky goo, and I decided to sit in the river, so it could defrazzle my entire weary body. I went back to the grassy bank, pulled off my brown velvet pants and my tank top and silk sweater, then waded back into the coolness. I sat down in my red lace underwear and matching red lace bra.

The water froze my rear end, making it tingle all over, and a little high-pitched squeak escaped from my mouth, but as soon as my butt got accustomed to it, I relaxed. The fir trees did their fir thing, the owls hooted, the moon shone, and I leaned back on my elbows and let that cool river flow.

I tried not to drip on Rosvita's floor when I snuck up to my room carrying my clothes, my purse, and my briefcase from work. I had a steaming hot shower, and changed into jeans, and an oversized black sweatshirt. I checked my cell phone, which I'd switched off at the river. I had no expectation that Jay would call me to chat, but I hoped, dear me, how I hoped.

There were six messages, five having to do with work, none from Jay.

The sixth was from Soman. "Jeanne, baby, we got a problem . . . shit, baby . . . come on down to St. Eileen's. I can't believe this . . . she's gonna be okay, I know she'll be okay . . . this'll all get better, there was blood, God, Jeanne."

Fear jangled about my insides like pinballs as I listened to Soman pant and cry and suck in his breath. "Oh baby, oh baby . . ." I knew he wasn't talking to me but to someone else.

"Jeanne, Becky's hurt. She's hurt real bad. She tried . . . oh baby," he cried more. "Becky used the damn razors . . . she used the damn razors on her skinny little wrists, tried to kill herself, come on down and help me. Bradon and Emmaline's comin' too."

I snapped the phone closed, shoved my feet into the nearest black boots in my closet, grabbed my purse and flew back to Portland.

I whipped into a space in the parking lot of St. Eileen's hospital and sprinted to the admissions desk.

"Becky . . ." I paused, panting. I couldn't remember Becky's last name. Had I ever known it? *I would have known it,* I told myself, *if I had taken her out to lunch. Like I had planned, like I had told myself I would.*

I should know Becky's last name, for God's sake.

I bent and leaned my forehead on the counter, still panting. I am a mean and selfish person.

A lousy friend.

Why hadn't I ever taken Becky to lunch?

The woman, African-American with huge dark eyes, patted my shoulder. "It's all right, honey, it's all right . . ."

I sucked in air so I could speak. "I need to see my friend, Becky. I don't know her last name. I can't believe I don't know her last name." I panted and choked. "But I know her, I know her inside, her true self. I know that loud noises make her jump, and she's too thin and I'm beginning to think she might be homeless and she's clean and sober now and when Soman got hit she actually leaped onto the back of a man who was clobbering him, she was so brave, even when he shoved her off. She got right in the middle of them again to protect Soman—Soman, who's huge." I stopped, gulped in air. "And I know that she is a good flying bird and she can sculpt clay into art, and she can box like you wouldn't believe someone that small can box. . . ."

For someone who was herself contemplating a trip into the ocean with a very large Bronco, I was appalled and unbearably saddened at what Becky had done.

I called Soman on his cell phone. He told me Becky's last name. "I'm gonna come down to get ya, Jeanne. Shit, Jeanne, I can't believe my girl would . . ." He whimpered, his voice muffled. He told me where to meet him. I took off running.

The receptionist yelled, "You hang in there, hon, you hang in there."

I waved. Ran faster.

"Hanging in there" was what I'd been trying to do for twelve years. Frankly, I felt overly old and sick to death of all this "hanging."

Becky looked like a white skeleton covered with a sheet. Her blond hair was pulled back off her forehead and an IV ran into her arm like a clear-colored snake. Machines beeped and blipped all over and nurses rotated in and out of the room to check on her.

I held one hand, Soman held the other. Emmaline, dressed in bright white, perched at the end of the bed. Bradon, along with his wife, Olivia, an elegant woman with stylish hair and strong features, sat together near the window overlooking the city.

I blamed myself.

I should have stepped out of my own troubled world and helped Becky.

I should have paid her more attention in class.

I should have insisted on driving her home from anger management so I could have figured out where she lived.

I should have helped her more, should have taken an extra step and tried to find out if she had a job and, if so, what she did.

I should have . . . should have . . . should have . . .

And now, here she was. In a hospital after letting her own blood out, on purpose, because she did not care to live anymore.

"Becky?" Soman whispered.

Becky moved her head back and forth, her eyes closed, her skin pasty.

"Becky?" Under his dark skin, Soman looked pale. His hand shook in Becky's. "Becky, girl, wake up for me, honey. Ya can't let life get ya down like this."

But she had and it did.

"Life's gonna be better," he whispered. "A lot better, girl. Hell, it's got to. Anything is better than being in the ground, baby, anything."

Becky stirred, opened her eyes.

The first person she saw was Soman.

Her eyes opened a little bit more. Even under the layers of exhaustion and sedation I could tell she was surprised. "Soman?"

Her voice was weak, like a drugged kitten's.

"Yeah, baby, it's me."

"What are . . . what are you doing here?" She coughed.

"Where the hell else would I be when you're here?"

She blinked.

"Damn, girl, why'd you go and do something like this?"

"I don't think she needs a lecture right now, Soman," Emmaline said, in pseudowhisper.

"Emmaline?" Becky looked more confused, but another emotion broke through. That emotion appeared to be pathetic gratefulness.

"Yes, Becky. I'm right here." Emmaline rubbed her leg with her hand, up and down, up and down. "Stay relaxed. Stay calm. Focus on serenity, on peace, on light."

For a second I focused on Emmaline. Emmaline, strong and demanding and quick to criticize, was rattled. Rattled and upset. Her whole body was shaking, her hands like little white doves having panic attacks.

Becky's tiny head rolled toward me. I saw her eyes skitter over to Bradon, who was now leaning over her.

"Hi, Becky," I said. My voice cracked. I was so glad to hear her voice. The woman and I had been such good blue jays together in class one day. We'd attacked Soman, a vulture again.

"Hey, sweetheart," Bradon said. He bent down and kissed her on the forehead, then introduced his wife.

"It's nice to meet you," Becky said, ever the polite one. "How are your roses?"

Olivia did not seem surprised by the question. "They're beautiful," she said. "Do you grow roses?"

Becky closed her eyes for a second. "I used to."

Olivia nodded. "Perhaps you'd like to see our roses soon?"

Big fat tears started rolling down her cheeks. "I think I would enjoy that. What type do you have?"

"I have many types. Bradon has recently and surprisingly taken a sudden interest in roses and we've planted so many varieties together in the last couple of months. He couldn't help himself at the last rose show we went to." Olivia patted Bradon's arm. "He bought eight new rosebushes, two of them climbing roses for a trellis he's building me in our backyard. Plus, he's going to enter an annual rose contest with me this year. Last year I got fourth place, but this year we're going to get first, aren't we, Bradon?" Olivia started listing the names of her roses.

Becky asked what her favorite roses were and Olivia said that she and Bradon had decided they liked the tea roses the best, after studying a number of books on roses and viewing a few rose gardens together.

"Well, let's stop with all this rose-shit," Soman said, shaking his big head back and forth, his braids flying. He seemed angry, but I knew he was simply being a typical man. When men get scared, they get angry. When they're scared it infuriates them and they snap or yell or minimize what's going on. "You tell us why the hell you tried to take your wrists off with a razor, Beck. For God's sake, don't you like your wrists?"

Soman hadn't meant what he said to sound funny.

It wasn't funny. Nah.

Nothing about it was funny.

And yet, Becky's mouth wobbled into a smile.

"What the hell's wrong with you, girl? You're laughing about taking off your wrists? No fun in that, girl, and I'm pissed off at you. I don't mind telling you that none at all. I. Am. Pissed. Off. You keep your wrists right where God put 'em."

Becky closed her eyes again, she was so weak, and laughed, harsh and raspy. And because Becky was laughing, and the thought of someone not liking their wrists was, for some reason, amusing, in that macabre and horrible situation, we all laughed.

And our laughter filled that room like warm bread and cinnamon rolls, filling up all the corners even though the IV loomed like a scary, stiff tentacle and the white bandages seemed to shrink Becky all by themselves.

Emmaline bent down and hugged Becky, her face wet when she straightened, then hustled away to the window to hide her crying. Olivia gave her a hug; Bradon held both of her hands in both of his and said something like, "We all love you, Becky, don't do this to yourself. Please, honey." Soman towered over her and shook his huge head, his braids swinging around, telling her again and again that he was, "So. Damn. Pissed. So damn pissed," at her.

Becky started to hiccup-cry and Soman gave in, sat his huge body on the bed and gathered her up in his arms and hugged her close and Becky almost disappeared in that embrace.

"Now you promise me, Becky—" he said.

"I know, Soman, I know . . . I'll keep my wrists on. Right where God put them."

And I knew, with that bizarre comment, that we'd all pull through, even though Becky, at least earlier in the evening, had not shown a bit of liking for her wrists.

CHAPTER 19

Soman and Bradon almost came to blows in the hospital corridor several days later as they fought over who would take Becky home with them. Me, Olivia, and Emmaline positioned ourselves carefully between the two giants.

The problem here, as we found out those terrible days, is that Becky did not have a home to go to. She lived in a shelter, sometimes, and on the street, other times. Hard truth was, Becky was homeless. We called the shelter she stayed at and the woman who managed the place said that Becky always left if a mother with kids needed a place to stay. That gave them a roof. She'd head for another place, but often there would be no beds. So she'd be outside.

Now if I had taken her out to lunch I might have known that. I wanted to kick myself in the teeth until they popped out of my head. Why could I not have seen that Becky was in a desperate situation? Why hadn't I tried to see the truth?

"She's coming home with us," Bradon roared at Soman, his bald head getting a little shiny with sweat. "We've got a whole huge rose garden that Becky can help my wife with. She likes roses, you heard her. A garden will be therapeutic. We've got an extra bedroom. We've got a *family* environment . . ."

"That's right, man, ya got a bunch of kids runnin' around

there," Soman yelled. "I been at your house, brother, and I love it and I love everybody there but it ain't quiet—"

"And your place is? You've got that stereo blaring all the time—"

"I'll keep the damn stereo off!"

"And you've got your band!"

"I'll tell the band not to come over!" Soman's braids went flying around his head as he whirled around and back again to face Bradon.

"And you're a single man and she's a single woman! It's not appropriate!"

Soman's mouth opened and shut, opened and shut again, and he looked plain hurt. Soman was huge and muscled, but I tell you that man had a very sensitive woman inside of him who came out even when he wasn't wearing a dress and heels.

He cried sometimes at anger management class; he sang; he talked about his emotions. I loved the guy. I could talk to Soman like I could to a best girlfriend, if I had had a best girlfriend. "Well, ya got that right, I am single and so's Becky, but I woulda thought that you would know that I wouldn't hit on Becky. Hell, I wouldn't hit on no woman who's been through what she's been through. She don't need none of that in her life right now."

Bradon ran a hand over his bald head, eyes down on the floor. "I'm sorry, man, I didn't mean any offense."

Olivia shook her head in exasperation. "Forgive him, Soman. Bradon always says what he's thinking no matter what."

"I do not," Bradon said, but he said it on automatic like they'd had this conversation many times before and it was a rote denial.

"You do."

"I don't. I'm thinking that Becky might feel uncomfortable staying there alone with a man."

"I ain't *any* man, brother! *I'm Soman! Soman!* I'm in anger management class with the woman. We're friends! We do bird-flying shit together. I sit by her during arting time. We screamed together in the screaming corner. Hell, she tried to save me from a man the size of a bull with breath worse than a rabid dog!"

"I'll take her home with me," I said.

Four heads swiveled toward me.

"But you don't even got no house, Jeanne," Soman said.

"And you live forty-five minutes out of town," Bradon added.

I nodded.

"I'll put her up in the bed-and-breakfast. The country will be good for her. She can relax and get away from all of this. When I'm at work, Rosvita, the woman who owns the house, is always good for conversation."

She would love mothering Becky. Perhaps it would give her something to do now that she didn't need to run around town spraying the Migrant Devil's goodies with a bleach and water mixture.

I nodded at both men. "It's the best solution, at least for a while. Bradon, I'm sure your house is great, but you do have five kids there, and Soman, I think . . . I think that because what's going on here . . ." I let it trail off.

"What's that supposed to mean?" Soman put his hands on his hips, but I saw that he knew what I was getting at.

Bradon nodded. "Man, you should do your courting properly. When she's better and healthy and whole again. You've got to show her respect. You've got to show her you're in this for the long haul by being a friend to her until she can meet you at an equal level as an equal partner."

For the first time in at least eight minutes, Emmaline spoke, "Your heart needs to wait until Becky's heart is beating with openness and strength. Becky has no openness and strength now. Becky needs to find Becky. She needs to fight off her demons; she needs to make a choice to save herself. When there's joy inside of her again, when she's whole, Soman, you can be together, not now."

Soman dropped his arms to his side. "I wouldn't've done nothing outta line. Nothin'."

"We know that," I said. And I did. Soman wanted to help Becky, wanted to be with her. He would have treated Becky with that same gentleness and tenderness.

Still, Emmaline was right.

"You can always come out to my place and see her, Soman," I said. "We'd be glad to have you out there."

I knew he wanted to argue, but he knew better. He knew that we were right. And he wanted what was best for Becky. The woman in him was an unselfish woman.

"All right, baby," he told me. "But I'm comin' out to Weltana, you can bet your skinny ass bird booty on it."

I hugged him. He hugged me back. His braids smelled like vanilla-scented soap.

Soman, Emmaline, Bradon, and Olivia all came out to visit me and Becky in Weltana the weekend following her discharge from the hospital. We went to The Opera Man's Café and had stacks of pancakes. A week later they all came for a spaghetti dinner and Bunco at the local church. Soman absolutely loved Bunco. Linda, Margie, and Louise were especially fond of him, although Margie said he was an "abysmal" player (I think that hurt Soman's feelings.) and Louise asked him to braid her hair like his. (He kneaded together about ten braids for her. She was the belle of Bunco.)

Soman started coming to see Becky by himself. He would often bring her books, sweets, or a craft project for both of them to do together. Once they made several nature-themed frames using pinecones and sticks and moss and stuff they found by the river. Another time they painted a long mural of the main street of Weltana at sunrise which Soman had framed and gave to Becky. The next week they painted lamp shades. And still another time Soman brought out white pajamas for both of them and they tie-dyed them in white buckets.

They were both incredibly talented artists, no kidding. The mural was this rich blend of colors and the lamp shades looked like illuminated modern art. I figured they could market the tie-dyed pajamas.

Becky got a little better every day. I had rented a room for her at Rosvita's and Rosvita cooked up a storm and lent her the truck for anger management nights. "She's sad. Her soul is sick," Rosvita said. "It breaks my heart."

One night, about 11:30, when I got home from work, Becky and I sat together on Rosvita's back deck on Adirondack chairs, the river rolling on by.

My nerves were shot from working and I had a ringing in my ears, like the Liberty Bell had lodged in my cranium.

"I didn't think I could go on for one more day," Becky said to me, her voice ragged.

I nodded in the dark. I knew the feeling.

"I didn't want to fight anymore, didn't want to deal with all these withdrawal problems I was having from the drugs, didn't want to fight against taking drugs anymore, didn't want to think about all the pain I've caused so many people who loved me." She leaned her head back against the chair.

"I have six brothers, Jeanne, six. They all tried to help. They would show up, all of the sudden, in one drug house or another that I was in, one shelter or another. They'd haul me back home, put me in rehab, and I'd escape as soon as I could. They kept trying. I rejected them and my parents. I don't even know why. I love my parents and my brothers. We always got along. I can't even remember having any fights with my parents at all before I tried drugs. But from the day I tried meth at seventeen, I was hooked. Absolutely hooked. Nothing mattered but the next hit from there on out."

I nodded. I understood that desperate need for a mind-altering chemical that would suspend reality. Alcohol had worked on me like a giant, invisible suction, pulling me toward it every night, toward one more drink, and another one, and another one, until it blurred the pain in my life. It took the edge off, but it also took me away from me.

I was, however, winning the battle against my drinking cold turkey, as they say. It hurt but it worked. I wanted Becky to win, too.

"When I think about . . ." Becky set her glass of lemonade down, then hunched over and buried her head in her hands.

I reached over and stroked her hair.

"What Becky?"

Her bony shoulders shook.

"When I think about what I have put my family through, especially my mother . . ."

The tears slipped through her fingers, like miniature streams.

I waited for her to stop crying, but it took a long, long time. Meanwhile, I patted her back. It's such a simple gesture, patting a back. But it means the world to people, doesn't it?

"They don't even know where I am. I don't even call my mother on her birthday. I have ruined my life. I have probably ruined theirs. I have so many secrets, Jeanne. So many horrible things I've done, to me, to other people. I close my eyes and I have all these flashbacks. They keep tearing away at me. It's like my secrets don't ever want me to be happy again. I am such a screwup, Jeanne."

I didn't argue with her. I was not in a position to judge anyone. But, yes, Becky had screwed up mightily, to argue that would have been pointless and counterproductive. She was a screwup; I was a screwup. So there it was.

"That's why I did it," Becky said, sitting up. "I've been clean for almost a year and at first I didn't think about my family. I concentrated on getting clean and not getting sucked back into that lifestyle. It's why I moved from California to Portland, to get away from all the people I knew pushing drugs."

"I didn't know you were from California."

She nodded. "But the longer I've been sober, the more meetings I've been to, the more counselors I've talked to, the more I've realized how I've . . ." she started back in on the crying jag. "The more I realized how badly I've hurt everyone in my family and I couldn't . . . I couldn't . . . couldn't live with myself anymore, so that's why I . . ." She rubbed her wrists.

So Becky felt guilty. I knew guilt, not the guilt of causing someone grievous pain, as she did, but I had wrestled with survivor's guilt, which is also wretched.

She pulled her knobby knees up to her skinny chest, her stringy blond hair falling over her legs. "I remember my mother crying by the fireplace when I was eighteen. She was sitting on the hearth and I came in about two in the morning, and I was high and she looked up at me and her whole face—*her whole face*—it was like she collapsed or something. She started rocking back and forth, hugging herself and crying. I went over to her and tried to comfort her, but I was so stoned I fell and I must have passed out because I woke up and she was still crying only she was cradling my head in her . . . in her lap and her tears were all over my face."

Becky started hiccupping while she cried. "My dad, too, when he knew I was doing drugs, he kept me home from school. They even tried to homeschool me, but I snuck out of the house. Getting drugs was all I could think about. At eighteen I left home, six months before graduation. My father had gone from grounding me because of the drugs, to lecturing me, and finally to pleading with me. All my brothers were on my case, too. But I wouldn't listen. I couldn't listen. Drugs were stuffed in my body up to my ears. I remember the last thing my dad said to me before I snuck out of the house for good: 'I'll always love you, Becky-girl,'— that's what he called me—'I'll always love you, Becky-girl.' "

She pulled her thin legs closer. "I wonder if they still love me? It's my mother's birthday tomorrow."

I missed my mother, too.

Becky missed her mother.

But there was only one of us who could do anything about it.

I thought about Ally and how I missed her every day. I knew, without ever spending any time with her outside my body, that no matter what she did, I would always love her, always ache for her. Surely Becky's mother would feel the same? Surely she longed for a call from her daughter every day, but especially on her birthday?

"Tomorrow morning, Becky, bright and early, we're calling your mother to wish her a Happy Birthday."

"No."

"What?"

"No, I couldn't. I'm a mess and a wreck."

I pondered that one. "You've been a mess. You've been a wreck. You have screwed up big time, Becky. No doubt about it. You've let the drugs rule your life and you've damn near lost your soul. But you've been clean for a year. You can have your family back, Beck, but you can't have the drugs back. You know the next time you're on them, you'll die."

Becky nodded. "I do. I do know that."

"Tomorrow morning then?"

It was 7:00 in the morning when Becky knocked on my door. Wrapped in a robe, I had showered and was putting on makeup for work.

She opened up her cell phone. We settled on the bed together, our heads against the headboard. I pulled the covers up over us.

"My mom always gets up at five A.M. She was raised on a farm."

"Call her, Becky, do it. Before you think for one more minute, give your mother a call. You're going to be clean for good and you can be a good daughter to her again. She deserves that."

"Do you think so?"

"I do. You'll do it, Becky. You'll stay clean. You know you can." I put my arm around her. "Call your mom."

She nodded. Hands shaking, she dialed a number. I heard a woman say hello. Becky hung up.

I made a groaning sound in my throat, whacked her with a pillow, snatched the phone from her and hit redial. I handed the phone back. "Rule Number One," I said, "do not ever, *ever* hang up on your mother."

Becky's big eyes filled with big tears.

I heard the mother on the other end say, "Hello?"

"Momma?" Becky said, her voice shaking. "Momma, it's Becky. I, well, I only . . . I, Mom, I wanted to wish you a Happy Birthday."

And then I heard it, a woman's voice, shaking like Becky's, but so relieved, the relief ringing through every syllable like a giant bell. Becky's mom yelled, "Bertie, quick get the phone! It's Becky! *It's Becky!*"

From my deck at Rosvita's I looked across the dark night at the twinkling lights of my home. In about two weeks, after months, I would be moving into my home. The kitchen was almost finished and darned if it didn't look like something off the pages of a magazine with its blue, butcher-block island, white cabinets, and open-shelving. Therese had applied an eclectic mix of tiles for the kitchen backsplash and my kitchen now looked like a work of art.

The need for those eclectic tiles had necessitated yet another lunchtime trip over the treacherous Willamette River, which is filled, I'm sure, with undiscovered gaping-jawed monsters, sharks, and barracudas. I slowed way down over the bridge, willed myself not to shut my eyes in fear, and bravely drove on.

But the trip was worth the fear. At a huge warehouse, I bought tiles with painted dragonflies. Tiles with butterflies. Tiles with carved mountain scenes. Copper tiles. Tiny tiles made from glass. Stone tiles. Oversized tiles. Bright blue and sea green and red tiles. I bought them all and brought them home. Therese Lopez studied them and nodded. "This will be beautiful, Jeanne, this will be beautiful."

And, under Therese's artful hands, it did. She seemed to know exactly how to balance the array of tiles around the kitchen. She used the extra tiles across the room around the surround of the fireplace so—miraculously—the whole room tied together. She is so darn clever.

The boys had painted the walls a buttery yellow and the wood floors shone. On either side of the fireplace, I had had Ricardo build me shelves so I could display dried flowers from nearby fields, local artists' work, and framed photos of my nieces and nephews.

In the garage of my home, in the wee hours of the night, when my insomnia plucked at my brain, I painted an old table white. The next night I opened the box I had packed very carefully for my escape from Chicago to Oregon. Inside the box were individual tiles that formed a blue bowl overflowing with fruit. My mother and I had bought those tiles on our last shopping trip before she became too sick to shop again. After I had grouted the tiles I leaned down and kissed them, tracing the outline of the fruit.

The home renovation had cost a fortune. I would probably have to sell one of my kidneys, but I loved it. People in town who had seen the transformation of my house were already calling the Lopezes for help with their own homes, so I knew they were set for work in future.

I thought about Charlie's family and took a deep breath.

They would be the first people I would invite to my new home.

Thinking about Charlie's expression when I asked him made me happy.

The next morning I got into the Bronco and it roared to life.

I was not happy that Becky decided she did not like her wrists and yet, from this whole miserable process she had taught me something about family and what a lousy sister to Charlie I had been, what a lousy sister-in-law to Deidre and, worst of all, what a lousy aunt I was.

Depressing, but true and, like Becky, hopefully fixable.

Charlie's oldest daughter, Jeanne Marie, would be about the same age as Ally. It was certainly high time I met Ally's cousin.

I was still not solving my problems by "drinking on it."

I felt a lot better, too.

One's day starts out so much calmer when one's head is not infused with Jack Daniels or scotch, straight up.

* * *

I moved into my house three weeks later. I gave the Lopezes a bonus and helped them find a nice rental house to move into. I gave them the beds and dressers and table and chairs. Ricardo already had other work lined up. Therese, too, had sewing work. That woman could sew anything and had done a beautiful job with all my curtains, tablecloths, and a beautiful light blue comforter with white flowers.

"You and I will be friends forever, Jeanne," she'd said one evening after the Lopezes and I had eaten Chinese food together at my house. "I can never thank you enough. For everything." She wrapped the comforter around my shoulders and hugged me tight. "You'll be happy here. I have prayed in this house every day that you will have a happy life and I know God heard me."

For the first time since arriving in Weltana, I fully unloaded my Bronco and the trailer I'd hauled behind me from Chicago and had kept in Rosvita's garage. There were boxes of books, art, embroidered pillows, my grandmother's teacup collection, my mother's china, all my scrapbooks, the rest of my resplendent shoe collection, and all the small, medium, and large crosses my mother had sent me over the years, which I nailed up on a wall in my living room.

So. I was home.

Finally.

"Okay, Jay, you've got the chamber of commerce speech in about forty-five minutes. The car's out front," Charlie said, flipping through notes at the conference table, as he pulled on one of his curls. "I'll send with you the recent phone stats from our poll and the draft of a speech Jeanne's writing for tomorrow's mind-numbingly boring Metro Business League's event at the Snobby Center (that's what Charlie calls an elite, old club in Portland), and here's a list of three phone calls you need to make this morning. Right away."

We were getting to the final stretch of the campaign, and I was whacked out with exhaustion, but still not whacked out with alcohol, which was an impressive feat. Things were definitely clearer to me when my arteries weren't flooded with tequila.

In the past weeks, I had written speeches, handled Jay's schedule, calmed the staff, dealt with the press and a picky reporter, followed Jay to an endless number of brain-gelling dinners and a few debates where Jay smashed Mantel, shook the hands of people I knew I would not recognize four minutes later, and had a series of nail-scraping disagreements with a surly Damon—who had forced me to tell him upon one occasion, because he's such a prick, that he *is* a prick, and he was not appreciative of my opinion.

He kept watching me.

I was rip-roaring tired. Even my teeth felt fatigued.

But, at the same time, I was *delighted* to be in the same room with Jay, with only Charlie, no one else.

Deeee Lighted.

I grinned at him. I'd already been dumped, so it couldn't hurt, could it?

"Tonight is the big shindig across the river. I know you hate those, but it's a huge group of women voters who are sponsoring the event. We will not win this election without women voters," Charlie continued.

Jay nodded. I knew he would suck it up and wow everyone, as he always, always did, but I thought he looked wiped out. I wanted to hug him and kiss those lines on his face.

"And when you get home," I quipped, leaning a little forward. Perhaps Jay would like a wee glimpse of my lacy, black bra?— "You can call the eight hundred people that have called you this week, review the speech I wrote you for Thursday night's event, prepare the key points you want me to hit for the Rotary breakfast speech, get ready for the meeting with the city council, and continue to run the state of Oregon. Did I mention the looming crises in health, education, and fish that must be addressed?"

"You did. I know this is grueling. Thank you both for all you've done. You're both," he paused, "more than I deserve."

"Nah," Charlie said. "Jeanne's more than you deserve, but not me."

Jay's eyes dropped for a millisecond to my lacy, black bra.

"We have only six more weeks. That's it," Jay said. "This will all be over. We'll be done." His blue chocolate gaze captured mine.

I felt like I'd been kickboxed in the stomach. I got what Jay was saying loud and clear. It could only have been louder if he'd used a bullhorn.

We'll be done.

Lickety split I became immersed in studying the fine grain of the wood conference table so he would not see the heart shreading devastation I was feeling.

I figured that Jay would win. He was doing well in the polls, clever parts of his speeches (written by *moi*) were always in the paper, and the crowds coming to see him were large. It might be close—Oregon's got a conservative contingent—but I thought he would win.

And that would be that. I'd have no job. No money coming in and a trial in Chicago coming up. Worst of all, there would be no Jay. There would be no reason to see him, talk to him, call him, laugh with him.

We'll be done.

"You need a break," Charlie said to Jay. "Why don't you go out to your house in Weltana this weekend? Get time off and . . ." Charlie sat up and snapped his fingers. "Hey, Jeanne invited me and Deidre and the kids to her house for dinner Saturday night. She moved in last week and we can't wait to see it. You should come, too."

I felt my mouth drop open, hit the table, and roll out the door. Had Charlie invited Jay to dinner? *At my house?* Had that happened?

I turned to Jay, knowing I looked ridiculous without a mouth. I pictured my mouth opening the door of the conference room and rolling right out to the street, where it would get hit by any number of light-rail trains and trolleys that seem to run through this city.

The corners of Jay's mouth tilted up. Darn but that man was gorgeous. Tired and exhausted-looking, but so gorgeous.

"I couldn't impose like that." His deep voice caressed my ear, but I heard the humor in his tone.

I would have spoken but my mouth was still gone, probably out on the street trying to buy a decaf coffee at a café.

"You're not imposing," Charlie said. He kicked me under the table.

"I'm sure Jeanne already has her guest list planned." He tapped a pencil against the table.

"No, she doesn't," Charlie said. "It's only us. And you."

Jay nodded. "Escaping to Weltana has great appeal."

"Good Lord, do you really want to come to my house for dinner?" I heard my tone. It was shocked and disbelieving. Surely he didn't?

But he did. He nodded. "I do."

"You do?" But what about that bar fight?

"Yes, I do."

"*But why?*" Now, this was a stupid question, but my mouth, being absent for many seconds, being as it had been out on the street corner, had not quite gotten into the swing of speaking properly again.

Jay leaned back in his chair and studied me. Tingles started racing down my body and back up again real quick, before diving back down. "I'd like to see your home."

"What for?" Drat that mouth of mine. It would be so good at doing something else to Jay, but talking was not now its forte.

"I want to see it because you've been telling us how you've had it remodeled. Maybe I'll go running, too, while I'm there. At night. Do you like to run at night?"

"You're funny," I said, feeling my throat tighten. He had seen every inch of me naked. Running and naked. Running and naked and flopping around in the places that flop. Need he remind me?

"So, it's settled," Charlie said, clueless about the jogging-at-night reference. "We'll be there about six, Jeanne. Super. Deidre and the kids can't wait. We'll bring the dessert."

And up he got and left, closing the conference door. He was very careful not to meet my eyes.

And there I was. Across a table that I wished would morph into a bed so that Jay and I could have a frolicking romp.

"Good Lord. You're coming to dinner?" My mouth squeaked. *"At my house?"*

"Yes." There went the corners of his mouth again. "I'm looking forward to it more than you can imagine, in fact."

"Um. Hmmm. Ack." I thought about my home. Not furnished. Not unpacked. Therese had the curtains up and they looked absolutely amazing and all the paint colors—the coffees and creams and chocolates and golden sun and blues—added a whole ton of cheer and color, but the rooms were empty and barren, resembling what a cave would look like if it was painted a cream or golden sun or blue color. "Good Lord." I heard my mouth mutter again. "Um. Hmmm. Ack."

Jay laughed. "I don't know why you keep getting me confused with the Lord, Jeanne, but I'll take that as a compliment. See you Saturday. I'll bring the wine." And up he got and left.

Just like that.

Good Lord.

The next four days passed in a blur of work . . . and more work . . . and more work after that. My brain was blitzed since I was in constant contact with Jay as we juggled the campaign. I wanted Jay to win. I was on a mission to accomplish that goal.

And when he won it would be my mission to stop listening to the radio, watching TV, and reading the newspapers because I could not imagine seeing and hearing Jay, knowing that I was never going to wrap that man in a giant hug and tell him his eyes reminded me of blue chocolate. In fact, I would become a hermit. A hermit that never asked about the outside world until Jay Kendall's term was up.

Because that would hurt way too much.

I sped off on a long, long run along the river on Friday evening, running until I could barely move, then limped back to my new house, where I'd left several lights on. For a few minutes, I stared at my yellow house with the blue shutters, new roof, and upstairs and downstairs decks that were sturdy and strong.

I loved it. It was small and perfect and old-fashioned and new all at the same time and it had cost me a huge fortune, but it was perfect.

Five minutes later I sunk into my soaking tub built for a gang of people. Rosvita came over about ten o'clock and we played cards for a while on my wraparound deck, jackets and hats on, gloves off, as we listened to the river.

I lost $8.62.

I watched Rosvita shuffle the cards, making a bridge of them, fluffing them down, cutting and cutting again. She had spent some time when she was younger working at a casino in Vegas. She had many secrets, that Rosvita. I sensed them. But there was only one I really wanted to know the answer to.

"Rosvita."

She put the deck down. I cut it and she went back to her expert shuffling. "Yes?"

"You never told me what happened with Dan."

"Dan put those migrant workers through hell, that's what happened!" She slammed the deck on the table, which made the fake white daisies in her hair flutter about.

"But, Rosvita, I thought you hated guns. How did it happen? Where did it happen? When?"

"It happened when Dan decided to rape vulnerable young women and girls, giving them a disease and psychological problems that will chase them their whole lives like devils on motor-cycles." Her silver bracelets jangled.

"Rosvita." I covered her hands with mine, her huge rings cold under my palm. "Tell me. What happened?"

She clasped her hands together and eyed me without speaking before saying, "What happened is that Dan got what was coming to him."

"I know it. I hated the man, but did you go to his house?" I knew a little about the legal system so I prodded her this way and that. "Perhaps you went to his house after finding out what happened to Alessandra and he started to get violent with you and you had brought the gun with you for protection purposes only and you had to use it in self-defense?"

Rosvita's eyes widened in surprise. "I did not carry a gun to Dan's house."

"But Dan was shot, Rosvita."

Rosvita nodded. "Yes, he was shot."

"Shot by you," I said, my voice so quiet.

She laid down the cards. "You're a good woman, Jeanne."

I noted the change of subject and felt rather nauseous. "Dan was shot by you, wasn't he, Rosvita?"

She shuffled the cards. "Yes, Dan was shot."

"Rosvita?" Sheesh. Could my heart take another shocker?

"You're a good woman, Jeanne," she said again. "I see no germs on your heart or in your soul."

"That's a pleasure to hear, but can we talk about this?"

"You're a good friend to all of us. I'm glad you live here."

"Thank you, Rosvita, but—"

"You are germless," she said.

"Yes, germless, but you—"

"Germless in spirit and virtue."

"You told me—" I sputtered. "It was my understanding from our conversation that you shot—"

"Let's end this conversation, Jeanne. You are my dear friend and there's no need to drag you further into this conversation than you've already been dragged. No need at all."

I thrummed my fingers on the table between us. Perhaps she was right. The less I knew, the better. All I knew was that Rosvita had shot Dan and a violent man was gone and buried under a pink cherry tree. The Lopezes helped her get him to the basement in the guest house and we all disposed of the body.

She shuffled the cards again, her black hair glinting in the moonlight, the white daisies bobbing.

Right. So she shot him. That was that.

That's how it went.

Probably.

That was most probably right.

That was right.

It didn't feel right, though.

There was a secret here. My nauseousness notched up a notch.

I lost another $1.24

CHAPTER 20

As soon as I knew Jay was coming to my house for dinner, I started "midnight-shopping" online at my house each night at local stores. I spent a treasure-sized fortune but, by golly, my bare house was going to be transformed.

The morning of the dinner party, an eclectic mix of over-stuffed couches and chairs in rich blue and green and striped fabrics, a plethora of oversized pillows and rugs, and several old-style lamps with colored-glass shades arrived. I also scooted down to a small town outside of Portland that sold antiques and bought an armoire, sideboard, rollback desk, a pew from a church, and a long wood table with chairs. The Lopezes came over to help unload.

Upstairs, I'd had the Lopezes paint one of the bedrooms pink, the other blue. I bought two sets of bunk beds. I bought the girls' bedspreads, shiny purple with fringe, and I bought the boys' bedspreads made out of denim. Each room also had a white desk, a dresser, matching beanbags, and a huge shelving unit for new books and stuffed animals and games I'd bought the kids.

I hoped so much the kids would like their rooms.

I hoped so much I would not leap on Jay as soon as he entered my home. Children being present and all.

* * *

Jay arrived first with several bottles of wine.

I was so nervous to see him, and the kids, and Deidre, that I felt like pouring the whole lot over my head.

Jay was wearing jeans and boots and a dark blue shirt.

For a second I stood in my doorway, speechless. The last time we were in Weltana together I had been running naked.

"At least I'm not naked," I breathed. Might as well go for broke, I thought.

I will never regret going for broke with that little flirtatious comment. Jay smiled, full and deep, his blue eyes completely unhardening, and after many, interminable, miserable weeks, I knew I'd reached him. "And that's a good thing?"

I laughed, he laughed, and we stood for a moment, in peace, with the sound of the river, and a few sweet chirping birds.

"Come on in," I told him, opening the door wide.

Jeanne Marie, age eleven, looked exactly like me, but she did not have my abrasive attitude. She was tall and skinny with curling golden hair. She was gentle and fascinated with my antiques, especially the rollback desk. She writes poetry. We wrote a depressing poem together when she was here. "That's life you know, Aunt Jeanne. Life sucks sometimes so poems don't need to be all happy and goo-goo like. We gotta write about what's *real*."

Tommy, even at nine, was taller than Jeanne Marie and he let her know it by periodically patting her on the head. "Smunch," he called her, short for "smaller than me and a munchkin." He brought his basketball and a football and a soccer ball. We played soccer while they were there. "You're not too slow for an old person," he panted at me, a glimmer of respect in his eyes, before I scooted around him and kicked a goal through the trees.

Theo looked like his mother, Deidre, with a spray of freckles across his nose, two dimples in his cheeks, and eyes that tilted up when something astonished him. He is seven but acts fourteen and wanted to know my "political leanings." He loves math and does it for fun. He brought his math workbook. We did six-digit multiplication problems together. I missed three, he pointed out, but would get better if I practiced more. "Math takes time." He pushed his glasses on his nose. "Don't push it."

Julie Anne is almost three. She does not look like me; she looks like Charlie. But she has my temperament. She is strong-willed and stubborn and does not like the word "no." She came dressed in purple and red flowered pants, a red and yellow striped t-shirt, and a yellow tutu rimmed in black. She wore a green frog hat on her head. The frog had a six-inch-long pink tongue that kept getting in her eyes. Halfway through dinner, Julie Anne escaped into the house, stripped off her clothes, and insisted on wearing only her tutu and the green frog hat the rest of the evening because she was hot.

And there was Deidre. The woman I have snapped at and been rude to and dismissed her stay-at-home-mommy life and isn't she *screaming* to get out of her narrow and dull domestic life?

Deidre looked terrific, thin and athletic. When she saw me, she did a little dance, flung her arms out wide and wrapped me up in a tight hug, swinging me back and forth. "I've missed you," she said.

I cried all over her.

Me, Jay, Deidre, Charlie, and the kids sat at my new glass-topped table outside on my deck under a huge red umbrella. I had Donovan cater the whole meal: Monster-size, layered club sandwiches, pink lemonade, two types of salad, purple Jell-o for the kids, chips, chocolates, root beer floats, and coffee.

We ate dinner while Julie Anne danced around the table and Jeanne Marie braided all of my hair. I felt like Soman when she was done.

We discussed very important topics like: How many whales pass by the Oregon coast each year? (Julie Anne said six. Theo said four million.) How does the moon stay up in the sky? (God uses gum to attach the moon to the sun, Tommy said.) What is the sun made out of? (Rock, said Jeanne Marie. Boiling butter-scotch, said Theo.) Is it true there are fairies out in the woods like Aunt Jeanne said? Should Charlie's family get another dog? What about a hamster? Can they have a monkey, why not? What do you get if you cross a zebra and a leopard? (A zeepard.)

Later in the evening Tommy announced, chocolate still on his face, "I want to stay here overnight!"

"I stay, too!" Julie Anne jumped up and down. "I stay Aunt Jeanne I stay Aunt Jeanne I stay Aunt Jeanne!" The frog tongue bopped about.

"Me, too! Please, Mom?" Jeanne Marie said.

"I didn't bring Pinkie, but I can sleep without her tonight, Aunt Jeanne!" Theo said.

"Not tonight, guys," Charlie interjected, fighting down all arguments.

"Well," I said, flipping my braids around a bit. "I do have a place for you all to sleep when you do spend the night. Want to see it?"

"Is it in that old building?" Tommy asked, eyes big, as he pointed at the old guest house, home to a corpse for a while.

I laughed. "Nah. Not unless you're bad."

The kids looked nervous.

"I'm kidding. Come with me."

So everyone, including Jay and Charlie and Deidre trooped upstairs. With all the excitement, I had not actually shown everyone up there, yet. Although Jay, Charlie, and Deidre had oohed and ahhed about the rest of my house, Deidre went on and on about how she loved it.

I put Tommy and Theo in front of the door of their room and the girls in front of their door.

"All righty, say the magic words, and open up the door," I told them.

"What are the magic words?" Jeanne Marie asked.

"Bumbblee-umbbelllee-boo!" Julie Anne shouted. "Bumbblee-umbbelllee-boo-boo-boo-boo!" She shoved open the door.

Not to be outdone, Theo and Tommy charged into their room. Their laughter and screams told me all I needed to know.

Charlie toured both rooms with Jay and Deidre, and gave me a hug, his body shaking a little. "Jeanne, honey, thank you."

"Daddy," Julie Anne said, flipping her tutu up and down. "Why are you crying?"

"Because you have such a wonderful aunt, such a wonderful, wonderful aunt."

Deidre joined the hug, her cheeks wet, too.

"I have always thought of you as the coolest person I know, Jeanne," Deidre told me as we sat by the river under bright-white stars.

"How could you possibly think that?" Talk about a comment torpedoing me out of the blue. "I have been nothing but rude to you, dismissive, unkind. Deidre, how come you're even talking to me?"

Deidre put an arm around me. This is why everyone loves her.

"I've rarely seen you. I've been a miserable failure as a sister, sister-in-law, and aunt."

"I understood why you didn't see us, Jeanne. I really did. But you've never failed us. You've been there for us in many ways and I always knew you'd come running if we were in a real jam."

"That's real gracious of you, Deidre, but it's not true."

Deidre paused for a few seconds and we listened to the river. "Remember when Jeanne Marie split her head open? Who was the one who sent her a giant striped five-foot stuffed unicorn? It was the only thing that made her happy. When I had pneumonia, you paid for a nanny to be at my house for two weeks. The kids were so young, Julie Anne was a baby, and I have to tell you it was almost a pleasure to have pneumonia because all I did was read romances and eat chocolates in bed." She looked far into the distance. "I still desperately miss that nanny."

Poor Deidre. She had been so sick. I couldn't imagine having four kids, pneumonia, and a husband at work full-time.

"When we went to Yellowstone last year for a week, we got to the hotel and found you'd already paid for us. You did that when we went to Jackson Hole and Yosemite, too."

I bent my head between my knees. "I did that because I liked the thought of you—" I coughed as I started getting emotional. "I liked the thought of all of you, your whole family, on vacation."

"I know. But that's what I mean, Jeanne. You do things because you like the thought of someone else's family having fun and being together. Plus, Charlie told me that you donate huge amounts of money each year to your mother's school."

That made me laugh. "My mother made me. I didn't have a choice. Every year my mother would call me on the phone and say, 'This is an official call, dear, not a mother-to-child talk. Now I know, Jeanne, that you're making a lot of money and you are blessed and here's a good way to bless others.' She'd tell me about the playground that needed fixing, or an after-school science program that every kid in the school must take, or an art teacher who needed to be partially funded. She'd tell me the amount, and I'd write a check.

"To thank me she'd send me another cross, often with a note like, 'I thought your shirt was too low cut the other day. Pull it up over your boobs next time,' or, 'Eat. You look like a scarecrow without the goofy face.' Or, 'See you on Friday. Don't forget you're going to help me in my classroom and don't forget to bring enough clay for the art project for all thirty kids.'

"And every note was signed like this, 'I love you I love you I love you'."

"She didn't make you, Jeanne. You did it because you wanted to help kids. Like you help my kids. You've paid for the older kids to go away for a week of Bible camp each summer for years."

"Well." I brushed my hand through the air. "I loved summer Bible school. Except for the time I got bitten by wasps."

"Charlie and I always tell the kids that you paid for it, that it was a gift from you to them."

"Deidre, you know of a few of the good things I've done in my life, you know extremely little about the other sick stuff. The not-so-good stuff. And, please realize, there's a lot of not-so-good stuff. Truckloads full. Too much drinking, too much desperation, too much noise and cacophony in my life of the wrong sort. Too many mistakes."

She hugged me close. "I know all I need to know, absolutely all I need to know. You are the best, the best of the best, Jeanne Stewart, and don't you forget it." She kissed my cheek.

See? What'd I tell you? This is why *everyone* loves Deidre.

"You didn't have a date here tonight."

When Jay spoke, my stomach flipped over and about, like a salami that's being flipped in the air. Charlie, Deidre, and the kids had left and it was him and me. Him and me alone. On my deck, side by side on cushioned lounges, in the dark, except for the candles flickering along the rail.

"Why would you think I would have a date here?" I asked. A date? I barely had time to pee anymore.

"I thought you would have your friend here."

"What friend?"

I could see, even in the dark, that those frosty eyes were back. It was cold enough to freeze the tits off a woman. "Your gaze is frosty enough to freeze my tits off."

He glanced down at my boobs for a millisecond. I resisted the urge to stick them straight out. In my deeply V-necked lavender silk shirt, I thought they looked quite good. Small, but evident.

"I certainly wouldn't want that to happen."

"Why?" Such a daredevil I am with my queries!

"Why?" A smile finally lurked across that chiseled and square and kissable jaw.

"Yes, why would you not want my tits to freeze off because of your frosty gaze?"

"Because that sounds rather painful. I think you'd miss them."

"Well, I don't think you'd miss them."

"Why do you say that?"

"Because of your cold crankiness as of late."

He stared into his wine.

I let the silence between us lay right there. Sometimes silence is the only thing that can bring two people together.

"I had never had a conversation like the one I had with you the first night we met." Jay's voice was quiet, somehow blending in with the river water and the inky night.

I remembered that conversation, rolling around on the dirt, naked, telling him about my anger, raw and blunt. "Naked, running women telling you all their problems are a rarity in your life then?"

"You're a rarity in my life, Jeanne." I saw a pulse leap in his temple. "I thought . . ."

"You thought what?" Please say what I want you to say, Jay.

He rolled the wineglass stem. "Jeanne, I hired you to work on my campaign because of your background and experience. I hired you because I knew you would be able to help me get reelected."

Disappointment blasted through my body like an exploding glass pitcher filled with freezing margaritas. I had so wanted him to say something about us *personally*, not about us campaign-wise. I tried to recover before my heart shriveled up into a prune. "You didn't hire me for my naked boobs then?"

The corners of his eyes crinkled up. "No. Believe it or not, no. Had I thought for a second when you were sitting in my office in Salem that you were not competent and brilliant, I would not have asked you to work on the campaign."

"That's good." But what I was thinking along thousands of brain synapses was: This whole conversation sucks.

"But I thought," he said, his voice getting the cranky tone again. "I thought we had an understanding and I would like to know what happened to that understanding."

"An understanding?" Gee, what would that understanding be? That I wouldn't get in bar fights and get arrested?

"I'm sorry about that, Jay, I am. So sorry." My heart felt even more sick than it had in these last barren weeks. "My friend was getting pounded and I jumped in to help. It's that simple. I thought he'd be able to control himself that night—he was dressed like a woman for God's sake, heels and a dress and everything—but I was wrong."

"What are you talking—"

"Wait a minute." I put up both hands. "Let me finish. I'm not sorry that I helped Soman, Jay. I'm not sorry I got arrested, although Emmaline was sure ticked off about it. But I am sorry for the trouble it could have caused the campaign, I truly am, Jay. I know it could have put everything at risk, *you* at risk. And I'm grateful it was never in the papers. It could have shifted the focus onto me and my bar fight and that would have reflected so poorly on you. I am so sorry for that, Jay."

I stood up and gripped the railing of my deck. I was scared to death. Humiliated, too. I hunched my shoulders. I felt so stupid.

I heard the scrape of his chair, the thunk of his feet, and he spun me around, his face showing complete confusion. "I have no idea—none—of what you're talking about. Who is Soman? Who is Emma—what's her name? And what the hell is this about a bar fight?"

And there went my mouth again. Off. Off on its own. Like it had in Charlie's office when Charlie invited him to my humble home. I pictured my mouth rolling off my shoulder, onto my deck, and down the stairs as it headed for the river. I tried to speak, but I couldn't. I had no mouth, I was sure of it. It was on its way to the river.

"You got arrested?"

I still could not speak. No mouth! He knew I had been arrested, that's why he wasn't kind anymore, why he didn't call at night, why he didn't smile; at me, slow and sexy, like we were making visual love.

"Jeanne!" He shook his head as though he was trying to shake in a few clear thoughts. "Can you answer me? When did you get arrested?"

He knew though, he *had* to know. I saw him that morning. He was so disdainful, so angry. . . .

"Jeanne." He grabbed my shoulders and I tipped my head back to look into the blue chocolate. *"What are you talking about?"* *What are you talking about?* "I'm talking about the bar fight." My voice sounded so small. (That's what happens when your mouth rolls off your face and heads to the river.)

"When did you get in a bar fight?"

Surely he jested. I got in a bar fight and lost Jay. It was a horrible and pivotal moment for me, making me rethink a mad dash into the Pacific Ocean. "Weeks ago. I don't . . . I don't understand, Jay."

"I don't either. *I know nothing about a bar fight.*" The words came out of his mouth and hung there between us, heavy and noisy and so deeply troubling. I started to shake a bit.

"But, that morning, at campaign headquarters, when you said I was wearing the same outfit as before . . . I thought someone had told you that I'd been arrested and that's why . . . that's why . . ."

"That's why what?" He spread his arms out, totally frustrated. "That's why what?"

"That's why you were so ticked off. You didn't call anymore at night; you didn't tell me any jokes; you didn't ask me how my house was, or what movies I liked, what books I read. . . . You were civil, but barely."

"I was furious." His voice rang out in the night. "I was furious and hurt and I felt like you'd kicked me in the stomach. I thought we were putting us—you and me—on hold until after the campaign."

"Me, too. The day after the election, I would kick off my heels, officially quit working for you, and we would go to the Pacific Ocean together. See some whales, walk on the sand, find shells. Like normal people."

"That's right. I would show you the Oregon coast. And, I was hoping, the California coast, the Mexican coast, and the Canadian and Alaskan coasts, too. But that morning, I thought you'd been out all night with another man. And by being out all night that told me that you and I were off. I knew it was a long time to ask a woman to wait, Jeanne. I knew it was going to be hard on both of us, but I could not, *cannot*, date someone who is working for me."

An owl hooted. Another hooted back. *How could this have happened?* "I was not out with another man, Jay. Well, yes, I was. There were two men," I bumbled along. "I was out with friends. A friend named Soman, another named Becky. Bradon was there. Emmaline. Soman is in love with Becky. Bradon has been married forever and has five kids. Emmaline is an anger management counselor. I don't think she has a husband or boyfriend, but I'm not in love with her so don't worry."

A little puff of wind meandered by and the candles flickered enough for me to see that my words had knocked him into semi-shock. He looked up at the sky, then right back at me, and I saw all I needed to see.

"Why on earth did you think that I was on a date with another man?"

"Because of our conversation that morning! And because of your clothes. You were wearing the same outfit you'd worn the day before. You'd switched things around. Charlie had mentioned you had to be somewhere that night. I assumed it was a date." His shoulders sagged a bit. "Jeanne, I dated someone who used to do that. I didn't know she was cheating on me for months. She wouldn't make it home to her apartment before work. I'd see her at work, and she'd take off her suit jacket for the day, or use a different scarf, change out jewelry. That's the way she hid her boyfriend from me. And I leaped to the wrong conclusion with you. God, Jeanne, I'm sorry—"

"The only man who's been in my life since the day I ran into you is you, Jay." I took a step closer to him, close enough to smell wine and aftershave and fir trees all mixed up. I put my hands on his arms. "In the bar I jumped on top of a guy who was pummeling Soman, who was dressed like a woman. Soman was dressed like a woman because he was supposed to get to know his true self, accept his true self, so he could get rid of his anger. Things got a little out of hand. Other people jumped into the fight, including Emmaline, Bradon, and Becky. When the police came, I was handcuffed, shoved into a paddy wagon, hauled to the police station, and released on bail. In the morning I ducked into a café, did the switcheroo, and headed to the office. I was sorry it happened. I *am* sorry it happened."

"I can't believe this," he said, running a hand over his neck. "I can't believe we've missed out on all this time because of my own stupid, stupid assumptions. For months, I'd been thinking you were with someone else—"

"There's been no one else. Are you dating anyone?" Please no, no, no, no, no.

"I've found someone I would like to date, but she is currently unavailable."

"Ah." Dare I hope? Dare I ask? I dared. "Is it someone who remodeled her house recently? From Chicago?"

"I see you know her." He smiled. My heart flipped.

"Yes, I do." I did know her! I did! Cease, my fluttering heart. "Hopefully she will become available again. The campaign will be over soon. That might be a good time for you to ask her to go on a drive west with you. I hear she has not yet seen the ocean."

"I think that's an outstanding idea."

"Perhaps though, you should take care not to freeze her tits off with your coldness in the meantime."

"I'll endeavor not to do that." He glanced down at the aforementioned area. "I would certainly not want her to lose her breasts."

We shared one of those long looks that heats up your vagina so hot you fear flames will burst from it, and we both grinned goofily. Smiled like tomorrow there would be no more smiles to smile. He lifted one hand and wound my hair around his finger, studying the curl.

I could feel my heart racing and my breath shortening in one delicious second as I watched those strong fingers play ever so gently with my hair. My curl wound around his finger like golden silk, round and round.

He leaned one arm on either side of me, his palms on the railing of my new deck. His face was so close to mine I couldn't resist it. I lifted one hand and cupped his jaw. Underneath my hand his skin was warm, and rough, and sexy.

"I'm sorry. I am so profoundly sorry." His low voice rumbled through me. "I feel like an idiot. And the hurt I caused you, caused both of us. It's inexcusable."

"It's excusable, trust me, Jay." He was so sexy. I stared at his lips. He moved his head and kissed the inside of my palm.

I closed my eyes for a second. I could feel his heat, his tension, the attraction between us absolutely sizzling. I love sizzle. I haven't felt sizzle since Johnny, but I felt it.

Only a few inches separated me from that huge chest and those muscled shoulders and a slip into orgasmic delight. I put my hand on the back of his neck, feeling the softness of his hair.

Even though I could barely stand I wanted that man so much, I tilted my head up and kissed his cheek. I stepped close enough so he could feel those small but evident tits of mine.

He sighed and I felt him tremble.

I didn't move, only held my kiss on his cheek and he moved his head a few centimeters and our lips found each other's, and I will tell you it was bliss. Pure, pure bliss.

A warm and possessive kiss to end all kisses with promises for more.

Jay pulled away from our kiss under the stars for one second. "I have never kissed anyone who worked for or with me or even anyone within the vicinity of my work at any time, I want you to know that, Jeanne."

I kissed him, tasted that bliss again and again, and felt liquid love sliding through my body, like honey and chocolate blended, as his arms held me close. "You're not kissing me, I'm kissing you. See how I'm forcing you?"

He laughed, and his lips came down on mine again, and I wrapped both of my arms around his neck. I leaned in, chest to chest, thigh to thigh.

I kissed him and kissed him and soon began to wonder if I could have an orgasm standing there so innocently on my deck under a few shooting stars. If I did I vowed to call it My River Orgasm.

And things got quite hot and heavy and hands started to wander and a millisecond before My River Orgasm over-rivered me, he pulled away and I was left leaning against the rail and panting.

Jay groaned in frustration and put some space between us. I heard him taking huge intakes of breath. He leaned on the rails and our hot and heavy glances caught and held. It was quite evident that a river orgasm had almost over-rivered him, too. "Jeanne Stewart, we have very little time left on this campaign."

"Yes, I know." I could hardly get in any oxygen and certain areas on me were steaming.

"At the end of it, you will be without a job. You will not be working for me at all."

"Yes, I know." There was no air flowing into my lungs, but it was so delightful.

"We could officially date."

"Yes, I know that, too." Joy! My heart did a jig! Could he hear the tapping?

"I haven't dated anyone seriously in years and years."

"I haven't dated anyone in twelve years that I've cared about in the slightest," I told him, my voice full of cheer. "Also, I am slightly unhinged."

He nodded. "Recently, I have discovered that I have a thing for unhinged women. One in particular."

"You should also know that I have a rather colorful past." Was this the time to mention the assault charges? The wandering speech? The buried body? Nah.

"I have also recently discovered that I have a thing for women with colorful pasts."

"And the bar fight?" I inquired, getting a hold of my panting. "We can forget about that little snafu?"

"I have no problem with a woman who knows how to fight in a bar to protect a male friend dressed as a woman." He crossed one ankle over the other. I liked his thighs. "Would you like to go to breakfast with me the morning after the campaign?"

I pretended to puzzle that one out. "Lemme think. I think so. Perhaps. I'll memo myself to analyze your proposal, make some strategic suggestions, issue a plan of attack regarding said breakfast date, and let you know."

"You do that." He had such nice lips!

"But if I say yes, let's go to The Opera Man's Café. I love their pancakes."

"The Opera Man's Café it is."

His face had grown so amazingly dear to me. A face that I could look at every morning and every night and every second in between for a million decades, and I would still love everything about it.

"I like you, Jay Kendall." I didn't have the courage to say anything else.

"Good," he said as an owl hooted. "Because I am completely in love with you."

I would have kissed him but these sloppy tears filled my eyes and they ran down my cheeks like they couldn't wait to escape my eyes and Jay strolled back to me and cupped my face with his warm hands and wiped away my tears with his thumbs. He kissed me and even though my lips trembled a bit and I made this little sobbing sound in my throat, it was like kissing love.

Bliss is the best.

And everything went splendidly for about a week.

I kept replaying in my head those kisses on my deck. I had already dubbed them The Deck Kisses.

Jay called me all the time. We went to sleep each night talking and laughing on the phone. The laughter curlicued through my dreams, and my insomnia danced away.

I worked my derrière off for his campaign. He spent a lot of time at the Portland campaign headquarters. I trailed him around to one speech after another, working with him in the back of his SUV on his speeches, discussing answers to debate questions and questions that reporters might ask, and I tried to refrain my ever-hottening body from jumping atop his in the backseat.

He didn't kiss me again, but every time I saw those eyes I knew he was thinking about The Deck Kisses. The memory followed us everywhere, every second, every moment. The Deck Kisses being like Mozart and Van Halen and cupcakes and milk shakes mixed together.

And, of course, when we did actually brush up against each other it was all I could do not to wriggle out of my clothes and flick off whatever heels I was wearing that day.

Controlling oneself can be so dreary.

In the midst of all that pulsing heat between me and Jay, on a late Friday afternoon, with the rain coming down like heaven had a plumbing problem, Jay fired Damon.

And that caused all hell to break loose at campaign headquarters. In fact, all hell broke loose, swirled around, crashed into a bunch of stuff, and exploded onto the front pages of the newspapers.

Nasty.

CHAPTER 21

It was a simple thing, *simple*. Damon, Charlie, and I had long since drawn our feud lines. Charlie and I couldn't stand Damon, but we all worked together because we're (gag) professionals and because Jay asked us to. To be fair, Damon worked all the time, he hustled the phones, he hustled the volunteers, he hustled. That's why he was kept on.

But Damon secretly loathed Charlie because Charlie was his boss and he wanted to be the top doggie. He did what he could, at first, to undermine Charlie, but it didn't work, not with the staff, who loved Charlie, and not with Jay, who understood Charlie's brilliance.

Damon couldn't stand me, because a) I am a woman and he has a thriving, insidious short man's complex and hates women; b) I am not a woman he can control; c) He knows I am smarter than he is (I am not bragging when I say this. Damon has the intellect of a spider without the web-making skills.); and d) He is attracted to me.

And he hated himself for being attracted to me because he knew I thought he was fresh puke.

But a few days before all that swirling hell broke out at campaign headquarters Mr. Puke decided he couldn't stand it anymore. I got into work very early that day, as usual. I was wearing a pink silk V-neck shirt, black pants, and these fabulous, I mean you would love them, black heels with these pointy-pointy toes that killed my feet. Plus I had strands of necklaces on me, gold with these black and pinkish beads and rocks and matching earrings and about ten gold bangles.

Anyhow, I was in a back room working, my curls veiling my face, when Damon toddled in.

"Jeanne," he intoned.

"Damon." I stood and opened up the top drawer of a file cabinet. Every time that man squinted at me I knew he was ripping my clothes off with his filthy sewer mind and I wanted to reach in his head, grab those membranes, and toss them out.

"We need to have a meeting with the full staff and discuss the strategic goals for the continuation of the campaign. We gotta discuss how we have to hit hard, hard, hard, if we wanna win. We need to recruit more volunteers for door-to-door pamphlet drop-offs, and we need to get more lawn signs out there, more lawn signs. The more the better. Every damn lawn needs a damn sign."

"You'd better get to it, Damon. Time's a' wastin'."

He put his hands on his hips. He had gained about twenty pounds since I'd met him and those hips were large and fluffy. "I think that's your job."

I shut the drawer of the file cabinet, opened another one, fiddled around. "Gee. I don't. You want it done? Go do it."

It was my mistake to turn my back on Damon. Never turn your back on an arching viper. I could hear him huffing and snarling and staring at my ass.

"What is it, Damon? Today is Monday. Monday is Don't-Tell-Me-What-to-Do-with-an-Imperious-Tone-or-You'll-Be-Sorry Day." I whipped around. His eyes did the Boob-Waist-Butt thing, coming to rest for several seconds on my boobs. Men do this to degrade women. It's a power trip; they're trying to reduce women to a sexual "thing," not a person.

"Hey, Jeanne. Can I ask you something?" He studied me in a creepola way.

Like we were friends. How strange. I went on instant alert.

"What's going on between you and the governor? I know there's something. I'm not stupid. Is it what I think it is?"

I paused, fiddled with one of my rock-and-bead necklaces. "What's going on with me and the governor?"

"Yeah. What is it?" He crossed his meaty arms.

I leaned toward him a little. He leaned toward me.

I leaned a little farther in. He leaned a little farther in.

I whispered, "I'm making mad passionate love to him every hour, every day, most often on the conference table. Sometimes we do it on top of these filing cabinets. One time we did it under your desk and guess what? You were actually sitting there at the time and didn't even notice."

I leaned away from Damon, wriggled my eyebrows a few times.

First Damon looked stunned. And then royally pissed.

"Last week we made love in front of the full board of the Rotary Club. They enjoyed it and promised their complete financial support. The week before we went to Portland State and let an art student film us making love for her film class." I pantomimed filming. "The students loved it and promised to help you deliver lawn signs. Every lawn needs a sign, doesn't it?"

"Funny, Jeanne." He was all red. Like an enflamed infection.

"When he calls me I breathe as heavy as I can and I lick the phone. It helps him to relax before speeches."

"Dammit, Jeanne—"

"Please don't swear. You asked a stupid question on 'Don't-Tell-Me-What-to-Do-with-an-Imperious-Tone-or-You'll-Be-Sorry Day,' and I was good enough to answer you."

"You're always flapping your big mouth, aren't you?"

"That's my job, Damon. I'm the communications director. I deal with the media. I write Jay's speeches. I flap my mouth and get paid for it."

He ran his eyes over me. He's vile. So vile, like a black eel with pointy teeth slithering down one's body. Damon took a deep breath. I knew that cunning son of a gun so well. He was going to try to get to me from another direction. Men are so easy to read.

"All right. So you do. And maybe you do a good job of it."

"No, Damon. *I am good*. Real good." I stared back at him. Men try to give women crap all the time, and I'm so sick of it. They are the Masters of Mental Crap.

"Shut up, Jeanne."

"No." I said that quite loud, as if I was addressing a mob. "I will not shut up. I will never *shut up*. Get out of here, Damon, you gross pig."

For a gross pig he moved quick. He grabbed both my arms and pulled me way up close to him and I knew he'd snapped and lost it. "I don't take orders from women, particularly orders from women like you. You—"

"You have got the worst breath I have ever smelled in my life, Damon. It smells like vomit and ant poop."

He was so ticked I thought his eyeballs would bulge out of his head. "You think you own this office. You think you're running things here. You think that you're the queen-fucking-bee."

"Don't swear. Let go of me now or you are going to get hurt." I saw Camellia behind Damon in the office door. Luckily, Damon didn't. She took off running. Later I found she'd gone flying in to Charlie's office, where Charlie and Jay both were, almost detaching the door from its hinges.

He focused his gaze on my mouth an instant before those slimy pig lips slammed into mine and one hand grabbed my buttocks. I did not hesitate, although his beefy arms held me so tight against his pig body I could hardly move.

I stabbed my right heel down on his foot. This made him pull away. Then I jammed my knee straight up into his groin as hard as I could. He groaned and bent over.

Next, I fisted my right hand and knocked him as hard as I could in the chin. I heard something snap.

I thought he'd back off but he drove right at me, shoving me against the file cabinet. My head whacked back with a bang. "You fucking bitch," he panted, his hot breath coursing over me like boiled cabbages.

I shook my head because everything was all blurry and Damon looked like he had two heads. I heard Jay's voice and he was swearing quite vociferously. He hauled Damon off of me, his face tight and furious. My butt slid to the ground because my head felt like a coconut whacked in two.

I saw Jay's fist flying through the air and Damon hit the table. Charlie came from nowhere and tackled the slimy-lipped pig to the floor, when he tried to struggle his potbelly up. Everything went blurry again and out I went.

Whew! What a morning.

We had another titillating day later on in the week after every household in Oregon had been delivered a mail-in ballot for the gubernatorial race and other state and local offices.

On that same *precise* day, a photo of Jay and me landed on the front page of the newspaper. We had been at another tedious outdoor ribbon-cutting celebration by the Willamette River when it was taken. I was wearing a sexy sage green suit, my curls floating a bit in the wind. Jay was in a sexy blue suit. We were both smiling.

I stared at the photo by my own river very early in the morning while drinking black coffee. I was a little disappointed that my high heels did not show in the photo. They were a matching green with an embroidered lion. Still, it was a lovely shot of me and Jay and I would get a reprint ASAP.

The text of the article ripped along my tattered nerve ends, but I will get to that momentarily.

My head still hurt from Damon tackling me into the file cabinets, but at least the bump was down and the hospital had determined I did not have a concussion. My knuckles had been scraped from my right hook, but that was healing well. I did not know how Damon's testicles fared. I do know he had a shiner when he left the campaign offices.

I must mention that all that raw rage and fear for my safety on Jay's face when he finished the job of demolishing Damon made it splendidly worth it. He'd slammed Damon to the ground and yelled, "You're out, you son of a bitch. Get out! Get out!" Then he'd been all over me, along with my brother. Although first Charlie had to get in a yelling fight with Damon, which Jay joined as soon as he realized I wasn't dying. Ramon and Riley had to restrain Jay so he wouldn't hit Damon again.

I could tell at one point when I was slumped on the floor that Jay was going to kiss me, but I clamped my nails down on his wrist so he wouldn't. By that time the room was packed with people and they didn't need to see me and Jay making out, rollicking on the floor.

But I digress from my morning read of the newspaper and the article with its titillating news that ripped along my tattered nerve ends.

The article detailed my tiny problem with Slick Dick and the pending criminal and civil cases against me, and it also mentioned the recent bar fight and my subsequent arrest and release.

It helpfully explained my past executive status in the advertising world and how all those months ago I'd called exactly eight-hundred-thirty-four people "pointless schmucks" during my speech about how there had to be more to life than Tender Tampons. They quoted me as mentioning that people in advertising were working so a "few thick-headed (expletive) white men with limp (phallic word) at the top can become richer."

The article continued, noting that I lived in Weltana, my home near to the governor of Oregon's vacation home.

And, oh yes! I won't forget to tell you this juicy part: The most important thing it said was that I was working on Jay's campaign as the communications director. They did not call Jay "Jay" though. Nor did they call him Naked Run Man. They called him Governor Kendall.

It did not take a genius to figure out who had tipped off the press.

It was not a smooth way to start the morning. Did I mention my head hurt?

"I'm worried about you, worried about this, but I think you're going to have to talk to the press, Jeanne," Charlie said to me later in the morning. He ran both hands over his haggard face.

"No," Jay answered. He was sitting across from Charlie and me in the conference room of the Portland office. As a reporter friend of his had called him early that morning, he had had a heads-up of what was coming down the pike.

He called Charlie second and me first.

I had still been standing on my deck, numb and feeling like I'd been hit by a Mack truck, as I read the article. His phone call had been brief. "You've seen the newspaper?"

"Yes."

There was a silence.

"I'm sorry, Jay." I felt so sick. And guilty. And scared to death. Jay would probably have had it with me by now. Worse, his campaign was about to take a bitter, perhaps irrecoverable, blow.

There was another silence.

"I should have told you about the criminal charges." I wiped a tear.

"Yes, you should have."

"I should have told you about the civil case." Two tears.

"Yes, you should have."

"I probably should have told you about my little speech at the advertisers' convention, too." Three.

"Yes, that, too."

"I did tell you about the bar fight."

"You did."

More silence. Heavy and full of words that weren't being said.

"I'm so very, very sorry, Jay." And, my God, I was. More sorry than I'd been about anything I'd done in my life ever.

That sad, heavy silence hung between us and I heard him sigh.

"Jay, I . . . I didn't think that any of this would come to light."

"You still should have told me."

There was no argument there except the obvious. "I should have. Although you would not have hired me."

Silence.

"You're right. I would have skipped the hiring part altogether and asked you out to dinner."

I wished he had. We could have been sleeping together by now, I thought. "We could have been sleeping together by now," I said. I started to cry thinking that I would never get the chance to be naked with him in a field of wildflowers and I suddenly couldn't talk, so I muttered something about seeing him at the office. He said, his voice gruff, "Any more secrets?"

I hesitated.

"Jeanne?"

Should I tell him about Dan the Migrant Devil? No, that would make him an accomplice.

"Jay, I shouldn't have stayed on the campaign. I didn't know you at first, had no idea that things between us . . ." I wiped my nose, told my heart to quit pounding. "I should have quit, but I wanted . . ."

"You wanted what?"

"I wanted to be with you."

I heard him say, "Dammit," and I could picture him running a hand through his hair.

"I didn't know when to tell you about everything."

"How about months ago? That would have worked."

What else could I say? He was right. So right. "I'm sorry, Jay. I am so truly sorry."

"I am too, Jeanne. I'll see you in an hour downtown." He hung up.

I hung up. My own selfishness poured down on my head. I should never have been a part of Jay's campaign to begin with. I hadn't thought that my criminal and civil charges would ever become public here in Oregon and, as I'd had little respect for politicians of any sort before meeting Jay, I hadn't been too concerned anyhow.

But I had met Jay, fallen in love, and that's when I should have told him the truth.

And I hadn't.

I had so wanted to be with him, so hoped he'd never know.

I buried my head under my arms. I was the most selfish person I had ever met. Staying on the campaign had been all about me. Yes, I had worked my tail off for Jay, but I should have left. I had hurt Charlie in the process, too. He'd known about the breakdown, but not about the assault charges. I'd risked his integrity, his reputation, his trust. I wanted to jump in the river and float away to the Pacific.

Hell and damnation.

Please don't swear, I reminded myself.

The river rushed. The birds tweeted. My phone rang again.

"Jeanne," Jay said.

"Yes?" My tears were gushing like a flash flood.

"We'll get through this."

"We will?"

"Yep. We will." He hung up.

The flash flood continued.

"I'm quitting," I told Charlie and Jay.

"No, you're not," Jay snapped, leaning toward me across the campaign table.

"Yes, I am." Inside the conference room it was quiet. But it was quiet outside of the conference room, too, as though everyone who worked there was waiting. Waiting, waiting, waiting. "Look, officially I'll quit. Unofficially, I'll still work for you, still write press releases, your speeches, still work as an advisor. . . ."

"No. Don't argue with me, Jeanne. You're not quitting."

I looked at Charlie for support.

"I agree," Charlie said. "You're invaluable to the campaign. This will pass."

It would pass? "Charlie, this is not going to pass into the night like a comet. I have pending criminal and civil charges filed against me. I was in a bar fight. I told eight-hundred-thirty-four advertising executives that their jobs were useless, their profession utterly ridiculous. I'm thick into this campaign. You think our opponent isn't going to use it against Jay now that it's all out in the open?"

"He'll use it," Jay said, his tone clipped. "And we'll deal with it."

Charlie looked pale, his face somewhat ghostlike.

"I guess we don't have to ask who gave this information to the press," Charlie sighed. "The reporter got it correct then?"

"Yes." Damon had probably had me checked out minutes after I'd bamboozled his balls. "Yes, it's correct."

Charlie pulled on a curl. "I'm worried about all of this. About you, the charges, everything. I love you and I'm worried about you."

"I'm sorry, Charlie. I had hoped it wouldn't come out. I was so stupidly, stupidly wrong, on so many levels, so many times. You helped me, and I . . . I ruined everything. I'm sorry."

I studied my hands, my fingers twined tight together, and felt like a self-centered, mean and careless, overly skinny, no-boobed loser. I thought of Camellia and Riley and Ramon, who had worked so hard on the campaign, as had all of the college students, a huge group of senior citizens, and hundreds of other people.

I had undermined Charlie and everyone else, and I may have ruined Jay's chance to get reelected. All by myself. All by my selfish self.

"You're not quitting, Jeanne," Jay said again. "I won't let you."

That was sweet. Impossible, but sweet. "I am. There's no other way, Jay, and you know it. The focus will be off you and on me. You can make a statement saying that you didn't know about the charges and that now that you do you have fired me. You regret that these particular issues have taken away from the in-

tegrity of your campaign and you praise the people on your staff
for their efforts. You can flip this around to your credit by taking
swift and decisive action—"

"I said no, Jeanne." There was that authoritative tone again.

I thought about asking Charlie to leave the room, but I knew
he knew everything anyhow about me and Jay.

"Jay, you're letting your personal feelings about me—about
us—color your judgment. You've never let emotions get in the
way of your decisions and you shouldn't now."

"I'm not letting my emotions get ahold of me, Jeanne." Those
chocolate blues rammed right into me. "You and Charlie and I
are running this campaign together. We're going to the end together, too. And, we're going to win. Oregonians are notorious for
their forgiving attitudes, their liberal leanings, and their fair-
ness."

Riley stuck his head in. "Governor, excuse me, we've got a
bunch of reporters outside."

"We'll be out in a minute." He thrummed his fingers on the
table. "You are not quitting. Follow my lead out there and we'll
be fine." He reached out and put one hand over mine. "Trust
me. Take a deep breath and trust me."

I held his hand, warm and strong.

I needed a drink. A huge one. The size of the table in front of
me.

But I knew I wouldn't have one. I had given up my drunkenness, my hangovers and the guilt and remorse and disgust that
followed.

I would not allow myself to go back to the me I had been for
twelve years. I didn't like her.

I peeked at my shoes. They were wedge shoes with polka
dots. Go down looking good, I always say. Go down looking good.
I wobbled toward the door, my knees gooey.

Jay tilted my chin up, and smiled softly, as if he was trying to
give me strength. "And, for the record, Jeanne, I think the advertising profession is ridiculous, too."

I felt laughter bubble in my otherwise paralyzed-with-remorse body.

"They're pointless schmucks," he muttered as the door opened. "Pointless schmucks."

"Jeanne Stewart is a valuable member of my campaign staff," Jay said to the mob of reporters and cameramen jammed into campaign headquarters. His voice was firm, decisive and impatient—as if this matter was trivial and he was irritated he had to address it at all. "She will not be leaving our team. She has a past—we all do—and we'll let the justice system work its way through this particular issue."

I stood to one side of the podium, Charlie on the other. I stared at my polka-dot shoes for a second. Loved 'em. They hurt, but I loved 'em. I glanced at Jay. Loved him, too.

"Her ex-boyfriend is suing her in civil court for damages," a fat lady reporter with long blond hair and dandruff said. I had never liked her. She hadn't liked me, either. "Won't her legal problems take away from her ability to serve your campaign?"

"Of course not. Ms. Stewart has been working with me for months. She's a professional. She's brought new ideas, vision, and focus to my campaign, and she will continue to do so."

"What about her speech at the convention in Chicago? Aren't you concerned that she won't be able to stand up to the pressures of the campaign here?" The fat, blond, mean one again. She had always ogled at Jay like she wanted to eat him up.

Jay laughed. It was one of those dismissive laughs. "Ms. Stewart's speech had zero to do with not being able to stand up to pressure. We all have our own opinions; Ms. Stewart simply had the courage to express them. She is well qualified to stand up to the pressures of this campaign, and has done so since the day she started."

"What about the bar fight?" This from a male reporter I had dealt with often. He was young and hip and liberal.

Jay was about to speak before I cut in.

"I think I can explain." I sidestepped and shared the podium with Jay. I tried to get him to move over but he wouldn't budge, our shoulders smashed together. "A man reached out and grabbed the rear end of a friend of mine. My friend swung at him in self-defense. The man swung back and I went to defend my friend. I had no desire to be in a bar fight. Lord knows I certainly wasn't dressed for it—bar fights should not be fought in high heels—but I wasn't going to stand by and let my friend get pummeled. Friends do not let friends get pummeled in bar fights."

The reporters chuckled. Bent their heads and scribbled.

"But wasn't your friend a man and wasn't he dressed as a woman in a dress?" Blond, mean, dandruffed reporter here.

Jay tried to speak again, but I wouldn't let him. He certainly did not need to take the heat here. The heat belonged to me.

"My friend is a man and he has every right to dress however he wishes. He studies male and female roles in society and was dressed like that to see how it felt to be a woman in a bar. He told me he felt very vulnerable and sexually harassed when a man reached out and grabbed his butt. For those of us women who have had that happen to us, we know how he feels. We know how scary and sickening and threatening it is. My friend simply fought back, which many of us women are too afraid to do because the man is usually so much bigger and stronger than we are. This time the man who grabbed my friend's butt was knocked over by someone in a dress and heels. He deserved it. He should have kept his hands on his own butt."

Those reporters chuckled again. Scribbled.

"Ms. Stewart, how do you feel about the assault charges filed against you in Chicago?"

"I think that's the end of the questions, people," Jay started.

Thinking of Slick Dick brought out my fighting spirit. I again leaned toward the microphone. "I feel fine about them."

"Fine? Can you elaborate?"

The words fell right out of my mouth before I could stop the rush. "I found out that my boyfriend had cheated on me with a truckload of women for a period of two years, creating a health risk for me that entire time. I was hurt and furious and scared to death." I stopped and tipped my head as if I was curious about something. "Will any of you be calling Jared Nunley to ask him if he agrees that he put me at risk for all sorts of sexually transmitted diseases, including AIDS, and will any of you be asking him if he feels guilty for playing Russian roulette with my health?"

"Ms. Stewart, it doesn't sound like you regret what you did to your ex-boyfriend." This from a different reporter. Bald. Skinny.

I thought for a moment, ignoring the fact that Jay was kicking me, softly. "I regret what I did only in so far that it has embarrassed Governor Kendall. Governor Kendall knew nothing about this incident before this morning. As for Jared Nunley (how I delighted in saying his name in front of reporters who would print it!), he should have kept his pants on and his goodies inside."

Those reporters guffawed and went a'scribblin' again.

"Ms. Stewart." This reporter had black curly hair. I could tell that behind her glasses she had found sheer enjoyment in my attack of Slick Dick. "It's my understanding that Mr. Nunley has asked to settle the case, with you paying him a substantial sum, but you're refusing to settle and have insisted on a jury trial, is that true?"

"Yes, that's true."

"Why? Why not settle?"

Even thinking of settling ticked me off. "Why should I settle? I should be suing him. I should be suing him for emotional battery. I should be suing him for his careless disregard of my health and life. I should be suing him because cheating is wrong. I should be suing him for stealing nineteen hundred in cash and my mountain bike. I miss that mountain bike."

I could tell the reporter wanted to laugh out loud. "He's asking for an enormous sum of money in damages."

The thought of having to pay Slick Dick made my blood simmer. I had even bought his pet rat special food. Don't get me started. "Jared Nunley will get money from me as soon as the moon becomes purple and Canadians adopt Swahili as their national language. If I lose the civil case, I will instantly liquidate my assets into one dollar bills, rent a helicopter for an hour, fly over the city of Portland, drop the dollars out one by one, and declare bankruptcy. I will announce when I'm going to do this so that those who are in need of money can take to the streets."

I did not smile when I heard the reporters laugh. They bent their heads. Scribble, scribble!

"Did Mr. Nunley require medical care after the incident?" Bald reporter.

"Very little. I believe he was given rash medicine and a tranquilizer because he was so upset about his . . . *pistol*, shall we say? There was no lasting damage. He'll live. Unfortunately," I muttered under my breath.

The reporters laughed again. Now why hadn't I been a stand-up comic?

"In his lawsuit he's claiming he suffered emotional trauma." Black curly-haired reporter.

I gritted my teeth. My blood went from simmering to boiling. "One might say that I suffered emotional trauma when I found out there were about sixteen other women in our relationship, and in our bed, that I knew nothing about. When you multiply that by how many men those women have probably been with, we've got half of Chicago in our bedroom. Now that's emotional trauma."

"Do you think that a jury will find you guilty or not guilty of assault?" Young, hip liberal reporter.

"Guilty."

There was a unilateral inhale of breath.

"Why do you think they'll find you guilty, Ms. Stewart?"

"Because it's true."

There was that inhale again.

"Do you deserve to be punished for what you did?"

"No."

My brother tried to speak. I held up my hand slightly. He knew what it meant: Let me handle this.

"Is it also true that you told almost one thousand advertising and PR executives that they are pointless, their careers are pointless?" Black curly-haired reporter.

"Yes. But that would be eight-hundred-thirty-four boring people."

"Why did you say that, Ms. Stewart?"

"Because it's true."

"Would you like to elaborate on that?"

"Sure. No one who works fourteen hours a day trying to sell trucks the size of small houses, black thongs, and hot dogs can honestly go home at night and feel good about what they've accomplished. They haven't accomplished anything. Nothing."

"Ms. Stewart, the election is very close right now. Do you think that your past will taint the results?"

Jay finally spoke before me. "I think the people of Oregon will make their decision on who to vote for for governor based on my record and the very serious issues that are facing our state today. I highly doubt that they will be distracted by what's happened here. Thank you all for coming. That's all."

Jay grabbed my arm, his fingers pinching me, and the three of us made our exit.

"Ms. Stewart, do you have anything to say to Mr. Nunley?"

I thought about it for a second. "I want my mountain bike back."

CHAPTER 22

The next morning there I was again on the front page of the newspaper next to Jay. This time we were standing together at the news conference along with Charlie.

We weren't smiling this time and my heels didn't show, which was a shame.

The reporter had quoted me exactly, and I was impressed with her work. It must have been a very slow news day because the news on TV covered the issue as well. I was on TV again and again, each segment showing a different quote. Every time I was on, a shout would go up at campaign headquarters, all work would stop, and there I'd be on the screen. The only one not watching it was me.

I was horribly depressed when I arrived home that night. Not for me, but for the extreme damage I believed I had done to Jay's campaign. I had apologized again to Jay who had pulled me into my office, tugged the blinds shut and pulled me close to him. I had cried on his shoulder while he soothed me, which was ridiculous. I should have been down on my knees begging for his forgiveness.

Charlie had been great, too, hugging me close, telling me that Jay would still win, not to worry, that he, Charlie, was entirely to blame, which was so ridiculous I cried again and apologized and felt truly terrible.

The staff had been unnecessarily fabulous, too. I must have apologized, however, for way too long after we'd shooed all of the reporters out of campaign headquarters because when I was on my third extensive apology Ramon yelled out, "We get the picture, Jeanne, okay, we got it. Got it. Got it good. Let's move on. Can you repeat what you said about dumping money out of the helicopter? That was hilarious."

For a second, I forced my abject misery aside. I looked out at the campaign workers. They were all smiling, many of them laughing.

"Yeah, and can you tell us what you said at the convention? I definitely wanna hear that one," Camellia said. "What about those schmucks?"

More laughter.

Surely this wasn't happening, was it? I shook my head, laughed, and wiped a whole bunch more tears from my flaming red cheeks. Those crazy people did the unexpected—but I am learning to expect the unexpected from Oregonians.

They clapped for me.

I went home that night, changed into shorts, and grabbed two bottles of liquor, and three beers from my fridge.

The old me would have guzzled them down, head propped up on a pillow while I watched a sappy movie.

The new me dumped them out in the river, then tossed the bottles into my recycling bins. The fish could get drunk.

I ran and ran along the river, listening to the owls sing. When I was done, I waded in to my neck, clothes and all. It was freezing cold. I did not stay long.

Drink had destroyed me for too long.

Me and my booze were done.

For good. Forever.

The next day it appeared that many people in the state of Oregon were clapping for me. Several newspapers ran follow-up stories about my misadventures with Slick Dick. It was the topic of talk shows on TV and on radio. Miraculously, it appeared that many Oregonians thought he deserved the stealth assault I had inflicted.

"He had it coming," one woman from Canby said. "Too bad she didn't put something in there that would permanently disable his pecker."

"If a man cheats on his woman, God will find a way to punish him," a minister from Portland intoned. "This was his punishment."

"*He's* suing *her* for a million dollars because he's romping around with his pants off and doesn't like the consequences?" a man from Lincoln City asked. "What's become of our court system to allow a suit like this?"

My comment about wanting my mountain bike back endeared me to hundreds of Oregon bike riders. My comment about not giving the cheating Slick Dick a cent and wanting to drop all of my money dollar-by-dollar over the city of Portland via a helicopter endeared me to thousands of people who didn't think they should have to pay partners who had cheated on them. And my comment on keeping your "pants on and your goodies inside" became a statewide joke.

Jay Kendall's popularity went up fourteen points.

I woke the next morning and drove to campaign headquarters in the rain, slowing as I crossed the bridge over the Willamette River—a deep river, home, probably, to man-eating piranhas and prehistoric sharks that really belonged in Boise. When I arrived, the place was mobbed with reporters. Unfortunately, they were there to see me, not Jay. I plowed through them, answering shouted questions as I went.

"How do you feel about your trial coming up next month, Jeanne?"

"I feel bright and cheery," I announced.

"Do you think you'll have to spend time in jail?"

"It's a probability. I'm bringing my own handcuffs," I answered. "I was disturbed with how the Chicago police department's silver handcuffs clashed with my outfit last time, and I want to make sure that I'm led from the courthouse to jail in style."

"You don't seem to be taking the assault charges against you very seriously," another reporter observed.

"I take them very seriously. I would rather not go to jail. I've heard they will not allow me to take my shoe collection. That is a serious shame."

"We talked to your ex-boyfriend the other day, Jared Nunley."

I stopped and raised my hand. "Please don't say his name to me."

The reporters looked baffled. "What would you like us to call him?"

"I prefer you refer to him as Slick Dick."

Those reporters. They get such a kick out of tiny details. "Please stop laughing," I told them. "The name suits him."

"Jeanne, one more question. You've admitted to your crime against Jar—" he stopped when I held up my hand "—and the creative nature of said crime." He laughed. "Is there a chance the jury will find you not guilty?"

"Yes. Women are sick of being cheated on. Men, too. Slick Dick himself should be found guilty of being both slick and a dick. That's it. I have to go and get a governor reelected."

It was a busy, busy day. Governor Kendall was giving speeches around the state, calling me on a regular basis. At each town, I fed him statistics and stories about the place so he could personalize each speech and address the problems and issues that town had. He used the uproar with his top communications director (*moi*) as fodder for the initial jokes. His audiences loved it, and his speeches were crammed with people, like never before.

Having Jay Kendall's voice off and on in my head all day was a pleasure. Having his body off and on mine all night would have been an even greater pleasure.

* * *

Several nights later, worn out to the bone, I dragged myself to anger management class. We had almost finished our sessions. As usual, Emmaline had us whack our anger into punching bags.

After we had the usual amount of sweat pouring down our faces, Emmaline had everyone line up in the middle of the room.

We stood there, panting. Hot and sweating, but invigorated by our hitting.

"You're ready," she said, her voice quiet, her white arms raised above her head. "Thank God, you're finally, finally ready. My most difficult class is ready. We don't even need to go to the screaming corner."

She gave us paints. Squishy paints in tubes. Red and blue and green and yellow. Some with glitter.

"Finger painting again, Em?" Soman said. "Man, I am a good finger painter, if I ever met one—"

"No, not finger painting," said Emmaline. She twirled, strange for Emmaline to do. Her white silk dress made a bell.

"We're making another mural to chart our colorful progress through life?" asked Bradon.

I remembered that activity. Emmaline had unrolled this huge piece of white paper. Using only our fingers we had to paint a mural, together, without speaking. We had to communicate through body language only and the mural had to progress, each scene different, each scene indicating change.

We had painted a mural of a ghetto maturing and growing and morphing into this cool city block with a town center and library and fountain and a coffee shop and natural foods market. Plus it had a community center with a pool and gym.

Darned if we shouldn't have been city planners.

The mural was supposed to reflect our desire to change and how we were when we first entered anger management class and how we now are.

"No, we're not making another mural," Emmaline said. "Take off your shirts."

I rolled my eyes. I was wearing my dark purple bra with black trim. I had brought gym clothes, as usual, but had forgotten to bring my running bra. Becky cringed.

Bradon and Soman were shaking their heads.

"Give me a break!" Emmaline shouted. "For God's sake, you've been sweating together, crying together, telling your life stories, fighting in bars and getting arrested. Plus, Becky and Soman are dating. Not much to hide here, pathetic people, so let's go."

She had a point. I pulled off my shirt, so did Soman and Becky and Bradon.

Soman and Bradon are well built, tons of muscles. To my surprise, Becky had on a very pretty pink bra with lace. I caught myself. How silly of me to be surprised. Whenever a woman starts dating a man, or even thinking about or dreaming about dating a man, she always buys new underwear and bras.

"Whoa, girlfriend, that is some boobie trap ya got on there," Soman said to me.

I stuck out my chest. With pride.

"Purple? A purple bra," Bradon shook his head. "Your bras are like your shoes, aren't they? Making a statement. A statement about life and style, right?"

"That bra rocks," Soman said. "Although I prefer Becky's. It's like my woman here: Soft and sweet and pink."

"What?" I pretended to be angry. "I'm not soft and sweet and pink?"

No one said anything. They looked like cats who had mice in their mouths. You could darn near see the tails swinging out of their lips.

"Give me a break," I said. "I can be nice and sweet and pink, whatever the pink part means."

There was that silence again. The mouse tails swished.

"You're a red-hot piece of ass with attitude," Soman said. "You got a great right hook; you don't take no shit from anyone; you smash people who get in your way; and you ain't have no patience with anything but honesty. And people love you, you skinny ass bird. But you're not sweet like my Becky here."

"I love you, Jeanne," Becky said. She looked so much better than she had after she'd tried to remove her wrists, and so much better than she had when I'd first met her. Her eyes didn't have that dead, despairing, I'm-outta-here-look anymore. "I wish I were more like you."

"Shit, woman, I'm glad you're not," Soman protested. "Jeanne here can scare the balls right off a man, you know. She can shrivel his manhood. You, sweetheart, are soft and cuddly and—" Soman hugged Becky to him and talked real soft in her ear until she giggled.

Bradon looked at me. He tried to be serious, but I saw that glint. "I think you're soft and cuddly."

"Very funny, Bradon." My voice sounded snappy. "Very funny."

Bradon guffawed proudly. He finds himself so amusing sometimes.

"Come together!" Emmaline clapped her hands. "Come together."

We came together, although I could tell that Soman and Becky would like to come together more privately.

"You will use these paints to paint your bodies."

"What?" Soman squealed.

"Put paint on my chest? This here huge chest?" Bradon protested.

"Paint yourselves."

"My *whole* body, even my brown ass?" Soman squealed again.

"Paint your whole body, even your brown ass," Emmaline ordered. "Stand in front of the mirrors. Use your imagination. Use your creativity. Paint who you were. Paint who you are now. Paint who you want to be. Paint who you will be when you're eighty. Paint. Paint. Paint."

"I want to be a warrior," Bradon mused.

"I want to be a rock star," Soman said. "Rock out, baby, rock out!"

"I want to be an artist," Becky said. "An artist who knows

something about people and terrible things and who can show hope through her art. Everybody needs hope or we might as well die now."

Now that was a bit of philosophy for me.

"I want to be a mother," I said, my voice so quiet. Something in my heart opened up, and grieved, but then softened, and for the first time those words were freeing to me, instead of tying me down under a cloak of black, suffocating grief. "I want to be a mother."

Bradon, Emmaline, Becky, and Soman studied me.

"You'd make a damn good mommy," Soman said, some astonishment in his voice. "Damn frickin' good mommy."

"You definitely could do it," Bradon mused. "You'd be tough, but you'd be good."

"Your children would be really lucky, Jeanne, to have you as a mom," Becky said, soft and sweet and pink. "I'll paint for them."

"All of you, quit this!" Emmaline swiped at the tears on her cheeks. "Quit it! Don't be so touchy-feely. Get to work and paint your bodies, sluff it on, slide it on, throw it on. I don't care, but get painting, dammit. What are you waiting for?" She flapped her white arms.

What the heck. I grabbed several tubes and headed toward the mirrors.

Becky, Bradon, and Soman followed.

Red, blue, green, yellow, purple, magenta, glitter. All over. Head to foot.

About an hour later the four of us stood in front of the floor-to-ceiling mirrors.

Bradon had striped himself purple and yellow with glittery stars all over his chest. "Purple is the anger. Yellow is peace. The stars are for who I'm trying to be."

Soman was red. All red. "My heart's on fire, man, for Becky, so I gotta be red. Red for love. Shit, I'm in love."

Becky had painted circles, small circles, big circles, medium-size circles all over herself. "I'm changing," she said. "Sometimes I feel small, sometimes I feel big. But I'm seeing color in my life for the first time and all I used to see was black."

I looked like a cross between Cupid and Van Gogh. I mixed all the colors and swirled them around my body with an overabundance of pink and hearts. "Pink for hope," I told the others in explanation. "And the mixed colors are for the messes I've made in my life."

"Girlfriend, you got some pretty colorful messes. I'd be damn proud of those, I would," Soman said.

"Fixing our messes is the only way we grow, Jeanne," Emmaline said. "We don't learn through success, we learn through mess. We don't learn through joy, we learn through hardship. We don't learn through the easy times, we learn when we're at rock bottom, flailing around, trying to stand up again." She crossed her arms in front of her chest and stared at us, looking especially bright white tonight. "I'm proud of all of you," she said, her voice quiet. "For once, you edgy, explosive, crazed group of people, I am proud of you."

I was so exhausted after anger management class I didn't want to drive home that night. I rented a room in the same bed-and-breakfast I visited before. Short One and Tall One hugged me like I was an old friend.

I do believe they were grateful that I was not stone-cold drunk that night or the next morning. We all went out to breakfast together. My treat.

First thing I did when I saw Jay Kendall at the office was to tell him that I had been too tired after anger management class to go home and had rented a room at a bed-and-breakfast in town.

The corners of his eyes crinkled up in the corners. "Was it a nice room?"

I wanted to kiss that man, kiss him 'til I could kiss no more. "It was a nice room."

"Good."

I wanted to have dreams next to him and hum rock songs together as we hiked in the mountains. "It was a nice enough room."

"Sounds like you had a quiet night."

"It was a quiet but lonely room," I said. I wanted to dance through snowflakes holding his hand and make love in a cornfield.

"A lonely room?" He arched an eyebrow. I wanted to kiss the eyebrow.

"Quite. It needed a friend." I wanted to be a mom with this man. A mommy. A mommy of many.

"When is this darn election over with again?" I asked him.

This time he laughed out loud. I wanted to kiss the laugh.

The election would be over in two weeks. The polls had us ahead, but you never know.

The entire campaign office was in a frenetic tizzy. We were working sixteen-hour days. I wrote speeches and handled the press. Charlie managed and strategized. We had college kids working the phones and pounding the streets. It was only slightly controlled chaos as people yelled, argued, cried, laughed, hyperventilated, fell in love, fell out of love, and worked to exhaustion.

It was barely controlled pandemonium. And yet, in a weird way, I felt like I was thriving. Living. I had been sucked right into the middle of life and I liked it.

That night I ordered lingerie over the phone. Such fun. If only I could get my boobs to grow a teensy bit so they would have some bounce. . . .

"So do you feel ready?" my dear attorney, Roy Sass, asked me over the phone.

Did I feel ready for the Slick Dick trial? I leaned back against my new four-poster bed with a lace canopy in my new house, only one vanilla candle flickering in the darkness on my classy antique dresser.

The criminal charges had been dropped as there was no lasting physical damages. The prosecuting attorney declined to prosecute because he thought it a waste of the state's money and time and didn't think he could get a conviction anyhow due to the "extenuating circumstances of Jared Nunley's rampant cheating and extraordinarily poor moral character," but the civil case was alive and kicking.

"I'm ready," I said. My deposition had been taken months before by video conference by Slick Dick's attorney who sounded and looked as slick and as dickish as Slick Dick was. Roy had a lawyer friend in Portland who had let me use his conference room.

I said to Slick Dick's lawyer often, "Okay, Slick Dick Two, let me explain this again to you," or, "Slick Dick Two, we will be presenting Slick Dick's W-twos to show precisely how much he did not make during the years of our relationship," or, "Slick Dick Two, I think you should understand that I will never pay a penny to Slick Dick One, so you are not going to get paid here. Nothing. Nada. Zero."

The attorney always objected to being called Slick Dick Two.

"You'll have a few days to wind down after the election, then you'll need to fly out here," said Roy. "I want to practice your answers with you before the trial starts. I have real concerns about your attitude on the stand and of your ability to control your mouth."

"I know, Roy, I get it. I'm to be sincere. I'm to be likable. I'm to be demure and answer the questions with short and polite answers. I am not to let opposing counsel trip my temper. In fact, I am to show no temper. Tears would work. I am not to call Slick Dick's attorney Slick Dick Two. I am to be kind and thoughtful in my answers and honest about how terribly, tragically hurt I was to find out that my one and only beloved was repeatedly cheating on me. I am the victim here and I am to stress that I knew that Slick Dick's physical reaction to my teeny-tiny assault was going to be minor."

"Right. And you are to stress that you lost it. You were hysterical. Hurt. You thought you had a future with this man, you thought he was as loyal and faithful to you as you were to him, and you were blindsided by his deceit."

"Exactly. I will be sweet and sorrowful. Downtrodden. Defeated. Weak."

I could tell by Roy's silence that he did not have much faith in my acting abilities. "You do not have much faith in my ability to be a sweet and sorrowful defendant, do you? Not to mention downtrodden, defeated, or weak."

"That's correct. None of those traits are the slightest bit in your nature." He muttered something. It sounded like, "Goddammit." I did not call him on his poor language.

"Quiet, demure, and subdued people are dull. But I will become demure and subdued, Roy, I will. And dull."

He sighed, long and heavy. "I wish I had confidence in that."

I said what I've already said a hundred times. "Thank you, Roy, for all you've done. I love you."

I heard him make a little choking sound deep in his throat. "I love you, too, kid. And I'm happy to help you, honey. Helping you is something your mother would have wanted me to do and you know my only goal in life was to make that woman happy."

I let the silence be for a minute while we both got emotional over losing my mother. She was the best. The very, very best. "From the minute I met you Roy, I could see why my mother loved you."

"I loved her more than life, honey, more than life."

We said good-bye because there was nothing more to say. Grief can be a silencer. A deep, pervasive silencer. And left hanging in the silence is a bleak, lonely void.

After an evening listening to Rosvita, who discussed various African diseases in depth, by region, and complete with all the symptoms, I craved the serenity of the Salmon River. I stood staring at it from my balcony. It is a beautiful river, natural and

clean. It's like water poetry. It reminded me of Vivaldi and
Monet and whipped cream.

And when I was envisioning whipped cream, I thought about
those police officers coming to my highly fashionable town house
in Chicago where I was dressed in a highly fashionable outfit.

I remembered how the two officers entered my home. Both of
them were trying not to smile, their lips twitching and pursing
like guppies caught on a hook.

Within seconds, as the river rushed by, and the trees rustled
overhead I couldn't help it.

I laughed.

Laughed at the way the police officers laughed as one at-
tempted to read me my rights. Laughed at the way one sounded
like a giggling bulldog after I readily admitted to my crime and
told him that I didn't regret it in the slightest because Slick Dick
deserved it and I was sorry to hear there was no permanent damage. By the time I was done telling the policemen precisely how
I had committed my crime both officers were laughing so hard
they were crying.

I laughed remembering how one of them called the station
and reported they had the condom criminal in custody and were
bringing me and my latex in. I laughed at how the dispatcher inquired if they had frisked me for other dangerous condoms. I
laughed at how the police officers said they had made sure I was
not "packing a condom," nor did I have any dangerous peanut oil
on my pretty person.

"There are no glue guns onboard," one officer intoned to dis-
patch. "Repeat. No glue guns onboard."

In fact, I laughed so hard I wet my pants a little bit.

And for a second, I felt it: Life.

I was rejoining life.

Rosvita's lights were on when I came home from work several
nights later, so I went to her place, hoping for a game of cards.
The music was on so loud she didn't hear me. I watched her

waltzing alone around her family room in a frilly party dress and white gloves. She was drunk. I had never seen her drunk before. She was a friendly drunk, thank heavens. I let her swing me about the room a few times.

"I had bur-bur-burrrrrritos with the Lopezes. They were loaded with onions and garlic, which kills cancer cells." She froze and stared into the air, her arms gracefully poised in the air. "My aunt Courtney told me that years ago. Aunt Court-Courtney had a wooden tooth. Her own wood wood wooden tooth. She lived to be one hundred and six. That is o-o-o-old."

She spun me around the room, insisted I dip, then flung herself into her comfy flowered couch, her feet flying over her head. "I am as delighted as a singing canary for Ro-Rob-Roberto. To know that he will not be exposed to all the bacteria and viruses of jail makes my heart dance for j-j-joy." Her head lolled back and her eyes started to shut. "Poor, poor, poor, poor boy. He didn't deserve that at all. Imagine him being punished for clearing the world of a living cesspool." Her eyes fluttered closed.

I froze. "What?" I shook Rosvita as my insides went cold and clammy. "What are you talking about?"

"Roberto," she slurred. "Poor Robertoooo. He was so scared he was going to have to go to jail. He's young. He's good-looking. Lord, if the plan hadn't worked he was going . . . going . . ." I shook her again. "Going back to Mexico, he was. Fast. Like a gazelle. Like a cheetah. Fast to Mexico. All of them, he said, all of them were going to make a run for Mexico."

Gall. "Why would Roberto be worried about going to jail?" Well, obviously Roberto would be afraid of going to jail for helping us hide Dan the Migrant Devil's body, but there was something more here, I knew it. The pounding in my head told me so. I sunk into the seat next to her. I knew this wasn't gonna be good.

Her eyes started to shut. "Wake up, Rosvita! Wake up! Why was Roberto worried he was going to jail?"

She shifted in her seat, then reached over and patted my hand. "He thought he was going to have to go to jail and wear those striped pajama clothes because he shot Dan dead. Dead dead dead. Dan dead. Dead Dan, la-la-la."

"Roberto shot . . . shot . . . shot Dan? *Roberto did it?*" It felt like a shovel was being spiked against my cranium.

"Dan . . . Dan raped the lovely Alessandra. I love Alessandra. Alessandra. She's the nicest girl I've ever met." She patted my chin, my nose, my forehead. "Except for you, dear Jeanne. You are nice, too." She burped, and put her white gloved hand over her mouth. "Alessandra makes the best pastries. Such a talent."

Her head rolled back. "La . . . La . . . LaLa."

I leaned my head over my knees and breathed deep. The shovel seemed to be lodged in my forehead, the makings of a headache coming on like a mental tornado. I was so tired of secrets being sprung on me. When I could breathe I shook an almost-passed-out Rosvita. "I thought—stay with me, Rosvita, only for a minute more—you said you killed him." I swallowed hard.

"Me?" She lifted her head and laughed. "I never said that. I didn't kill Dan. I never would hurt anyone. Too violent. I abhhh-hhhhhhor all forms of violence. Plus, all the body fluids and blood. Dan's body was a very real threat to me and my virile, clean health. I liked to talk about killing him. I liked to plan it. But no, you silly silly, I didn't do do do it." She shook her head, fixed me with a blurry gaze. "I thought you knew that in your heart of heart of hearts?"

"How in heck would I know that?" I said. "How would I know? You said you did it."

But Rosvita was going out for the count, her white gloved hands clasped in her lap. "I never ever never said that, honey. Roberto ran to my house . . . crying . . . crying . . . shaking one night. He was so scared I could barely understand his Spanish! He told me there was a bullet bullet bullet in Dan's head. You were at your I-Am-So-Angry class. He cried. I could hardly understand his Spanish, he cried so much and kept talking about his mother, poor mama Therese. He said his whole family would go to jail now. He hated Dan that Devil, and said the man deserved to die for raping his sister and, Jeanne, Jeanne! I felt bad, bad, bad for him. Very bad, bad, bad, so I helped him."

"What do you mean you helped him?" My voice sounded strangled, like a giant lobster was manipulating my vocal cords with his claws.

She yanked herself up, like a puppet on strings, leaned over and whispered in my ear, "I mean that I told him that I would help him get rid of the shot body. I told him to tell his family not to tell anyone else, to keep it a secret secret, and I would take the blame if I had to." She leaned heavily into me. "Blame, blame, blame."

"But, Rosvita . . . Rosvita, why?" I gave her a little shake. "Rosvita, why would you take the blame?"

"Because of Domino," she slurred, eyelids closing.

Domino? "Domino who?"

"My brother. I knew that Domino would protect me, but no one . . . no one would protect Roberto. No one. He would go go go to a cement block teeming with putrid criminals. Roberto is not a criminal."

Domino her brother, the famous criminal defense attorney. That Domino.

"So Roberto killed Dan, not you . . ."

"Roberto told me he was the one who saw Alessandra running from Dan's house . . . poor Alessandra." She burped again in my ear. "Roberto said that she was crying and hys-hysterically hysterical. Her clothes were ripped, her face was swollen where Dan had hit hit hit her. She was bleeding, he told me. That poor girl. Roberto went to Dan's house and hit him and Dan fired the Lopezes. Fired. Fire! Fire!" She waved weak hands in the air. "That's when the Lopezes left the camp and came to work for you. Roberto told me everything Dan did to his family when he lived here. Dan is a piece of human cholera."

I shook Rosvita before she sank back into her alcohol-fueled oblivion.

Rosvita hugged me closer. "Dan was very bad, bad, bad." She whispered in my ear, "Dan was bad . . . but Donovan—you know, Donovan, Jeanne? You do? The pancake man who sing sings? La la la? He's good. A good man, that Donovan. Sing sings . . . Songs sings . . . handsome Donovan . . . la-la-la . . ."

She toppled back into her chair and passed out completely.

I paced for a few minutes, then flicked off the lights and lay flat on her immaculately clean floor.

Life is a stunning mess.

CHAPTER 23

The revelation that Rosvita had not killed the Migrant Devil kept me up for most of the night. When I drove to work the next morning, it felt like someone had driven an eyeliner pencil between my ears when I wasn't looking. I drove slowly over one of the bridges over the Willamette River and again thought: Go home to Idaho, river. No one honked. No one was behind me. Normal people are asleep at 5:00 in the morning. I'd had two hours of sleep, neither of the two hours good, by the way.

I thought over all of the conversations I'd had with Rosvita. She'd never actually *said* she'd killed Dan the Migrant Devil, but that wily woman had implied it. And, because of her hatred of him, and the many times she'd told me she was going to kill him, I'd assumed she'd whacked him off.

And it was Roberto all along. Rosvita had kept Roberto's secret.

She had lied by admission to protect Roberto. I pondered that one awhile. There were not many people who would take the fall for someone else. The Lopezes had neglected to tell me the truth. I was a little steamed about that at first, but I understood. The Lopezes were protecting Roberto, and parents will do anything to protect a child.

Rosvita had only known the Lopezes for a few months, but her big heart had opened up wide and the Lopezes had fallen in.

Rosvita's plan was brilliant. She would have known that the first person accused of killing the Migrant Devil would be her. Her constant harangue around town against him would have been a clue, but the very public spraying of the man with a mixture of bleach and water would have done her in.

Rosvita would have denied it, of course. And when, or if, she was arrested, she would have hired her nationally known brother, a criminal defense attorney, to defend her. He would have forced the prosecutors to come up with real evidence, not circumstantial, that tied Rosvita to the murder.

Rosvita, given her social schedule, probably even had a valid alibi.

The authorities would be unable to prosecute because Rosvita hadn't killed Dan.

And Rosvita knew this.

In the meantime, the Lopezes would have quietly left town and no one would have suspected them anyhow. Rosvita, at the very least, would have deflected attention.

With one person off the hook for the murder, a bum trial, and no other obvious suspects, the police would have been forced to drop the case.

My, she was smart.

Stupid, but smart.

Smart as a tack.

A little, irritating voice in my head told me something wasn't adding up here, but I couldn't figure out the problem, so I gave up. It was surely nothing.

I would have to discuss with Rosvita the merits of never getting drunk again.

Yes, that discussion would have to take place immediately.

I'd rather everything stay a secret among her, I, and the Lopezes.

A doozer of a secret, one we would all take care never to speak of.

I rubbed my face with my hands. I was getting a wee bit tired of secrets.

* * *

The election night party was in full swing downstairs in the ballroom of a high-class hotel in downtown Portland. There was food and drinks, balloons, confetti, odd campaign buttons, the works. Me, Jay, Charlie and Deidre, Ramon, Riley, Camellia, and a number of other people were holed up in an upstairs room. All mail-in ballots were in, all ballots were now being counted, and we would have the first results in about thirty minutes.

The mood was festive. I believe the main emotion running through that room was relief. Relief it was over. Either way, we were done with this campaign. It was a wrap.

Jay pulled me outside on the balcony and said, "You haven't forgotten our breakfast date tomorrow, have you?"

I assured him I hadn't.

"Win or lose." He wrapped an arm around my waist. A whole bunch of stars in the sky gave me a little star wink.

"Win or lose, we're eating pancakes," I told him.

I didn't care who saw us. Neither did he. I reached my arms around his neck, pressed myself close and kissed him on the smackeroo. He kissed me back.

Bring on the pancakes and smother 'em in syrup and butter.

I could taste them already.

We trooped down the stairs, me at Jay's side, before the first televised results came in. Jay was greeted by the expected over-the-top screaming and cheering by everyone there. 'Bout blew my ears out. He was gracious and kind and shook about six thousand three-hundred and thirty-four hands.

Minutes later, a newscaster with lots of big teeth and red hair read out the results of the initial votes: Jay Kendall was winning by a landslide.

By 10:00, Kory Mantel graciously acknowledged defeat and Jay was up at the podium addressing hundreds of screaming people and a horde of reporters. I stood at the very edge of the stage, behind three rows of people. I'd had enough of the spotlight for a few lifetimes.

After each sentence the crowd exploded in ecstasy. Jay could have said, "Today we will leave the planet earth as the sun is hurtling toward us. We have spaceships awaiting you outside and are hoping to find a habitable planet to land on before we run out of fuel. Remember to fasten your seat belts, keep your tray compartments up, and we'll be around with peanuts shortly," and everyone would have spun a few rapturous back flips and continued their yodeling.

"I want to thank all of you for your support and dedication to this campaign." Blah, blah, blah. "I want to thank . . ." and then he listed people. Blah, blah, blah.

"Finally, I would like to thank my campaign manager Charlie Mackey. We would not be where we are right now without him. Charlie is . . ." Blah, blah, blah.

"I would also like to sincerely thank his sister, our incredible communications director, Jeanne Stewart."

And I'll tell ya, at that second the cheering almost shot my eardrums straight out of my ears. Jay dropped an arm around my waist (that would be the photo on the front page of the newspaper the next day. My heels did not show. Again!) "Jeanne has added energy and color to this campaign, hasn't she?"

How they screamed and laughed.

"She has not only helped to write most of my speeches and handled the press, she has come up with a number of . . ." he paused here, "interesting quotes about our campaign. When she became the focus of attention weeks ago, she handled the matter with grace and style. I personally would like to thank her for all of her efforts and time and wish her the best of luck in the future. I know that, starting tomorrow morning, Ms. Stewart will be embarking on another adventure." Blah, blah, blah. I did not miss the meaningful look shot my way.

Jay went back to his speech and we partied 'til 12:30.

By 1:30 Jay and I were at my house in Weltana, sitting on the deck, watching the river, holding hands like long-married people do.

"I love you, Jeanne." His face was completely serious. "Loved you at first sight and I'll love you forever."

"Me, too, Jay. I'll love you forever, too."

Jay liked my new bed. In fact, we liked the bed so much we did not emerge for pancakes at The Opera Man's Café until 3:00 that afternoon. We were up late the next night and the night after that. We went for runs by the river and made love in the exact spot I tackled him. We also made love out on blankets on my deck under the owls and fir trees and on the original wood floor in my kitchen. We did not make love on the table with my fruit basket tiles, because I would not do that on the memory of my sweet mother.

We also talked and laughed and cried and ate chocolates and shrimp and steak and more pancakes and ice cream, and I enjoyed all of my orgasms immensely.

On the fourth morning, when it was still dark, I got up quietly, grabbed a suitcase I'd packed when Jay was on the phone one afternoon, and snuck out the door.

I left my note to him on the table with my fruit basket tiles.

I knew he would be furious at the way I left Weltana, and him, and I was right.

He blew his stack.

"We agreed that I was coming to this trial by myself, Jay."

"Dammit, Jeanne, you couldn't even say good-bye before you left?" His frustration thundered through my cell phone like a series of shooting cannonballs.

I laid back against the headboard in my sterile hotel room in Chicago. Why do all hotel rooms seem to scream, "This is a lonely place!"

"You were asleep. I didn't want..." I choked up. I already missed him so much my body ached.

"You didn't want what?" He sounded snappy.

"I didn't want to argue with you again about this. I don't want to involve you in this part of my life. I want us to be . . . *us*. Not this mess. Not this problem."

"We have already fought about this, Jeanne." He shouted. I held the phone away from my ear. "I don't want to get into it again, but I agreed to stay away from the trial because my presence will cause even more of a circus than it's already going to be. But for you to sneak out, to not even tell me you were leaving, to leave me a note, for God's sake. Jeanne, you should have told me!"

"I'm sorry, Jay."

"Jeanne—" He raved for a few more minutes until he ran out of words.

"I love you, Jay."

There was that silence again.

I heard him groan. "I love you, too, Jeanne, but you are a pain in the butt. A royal pain in the butt."

"The Honorable Judge Sheldon Pitman presiding. . . . All rise."

I could not believe that my trial had started. I snuck a glimpse at the packed courtroom. Too many people. Too many reporters. Too many cameras.

And across the little walkway, at the plaintiff's table, sat Slick Dick, looking arrogant and cocky; his hair pushed back and glossy; his expensive suit making him look like a male model. I bet his daddy with his enormous trust fund had bought him that new suit.

I glanced behind him. A woman sat in the front row. She was young and well made-up and wore a dress with a plunging neckline from which her bulging, bouncing boobs burst forth like big bombs (note the alliteration). She also wore a short jean skirt and high heels. I sniffed. Her shoes could not compare to even my worst pair of shoes. I know my shoes, I do.

I peeked down at my feet. Now you will be surprised to know that I was wearing a dull pair of blue heels. The heel was thick and one-inch high and it was scuffed.

Why, you ask, was I wearing such dull, scuffed heels?

First, let me tell you about my blue suit. I was wearing a dull, ill-fitting blue suit with a white shirt underneath. The skirt came to the middle of my knees and flared a bit.

Why, you ask, were you wearing a dull, ill-fitting blue suit?

First, let me tell you about my hair. Instead of letting my hair do its own curly thing, I had pulled it back into a loose, sloppy-looking ball.

Why, you ask, did I pull my hair back into a loose, sloppy-looking ball?

First, let me tell you about my makeup. I was wearing no makeup. None.

Why, you ask, was I dressed like a frump?

Easy.

My dear lawyer had explained it to me. "The jury will be much more sympathetic to you if you don't look..." Roy coughed into his hand.

"If I don't look?" I had prodded.

"If you don't look... as you do. You know. The fashionable clothes, those wild shoes of yours, all that hair. Most people don't look like you and you need to make the jury relate to you, feel sorry for you, understand your plight. You're to look helpless, not like you're daring the world to take you on. Get it?"

I nodded. I got it.

So there I was, in court, in front of all those cameras and reporters and blowhard lawyers looking like a major frump. I adjusted my nonprescription glasses with the big, circular frames that kept sliding down my nose. I felt the little gold dolphin from my father against my chest.

It had been a delightful pleasure seeing Slick Dick's face when I stood within two feet of him. He had looked right past me, hadn't recognized me a whit!

When he realized I was me, he did this huge double take, forced to take a look at the person blocking his imperial path.

His Slick-Dick face went slack with shock. "Jeanne?" he said, his voice hoarse.

I nodded, gave him a tight smile, then pushed my glasses onto my nose and peered up at him. "Good to see you, Slick Dick."

When he was done being shocked, a flash of petulance struck his limp, pretty little face. Why had I never seen how truly ugly he was behind the surface beauty?

"You're looking as pretty as ever," I added. "What do you think of my blue suit?"

He opened his mouth to speak as I twirled before him, but no words emerged.

I laughed, wiggled my glasses on my nose. "How do you like my shoes?" I raised my scuffed heel up, twisting it a bit so he could see all sides. "So stylish, don't you think?"

He got it. Comprehension dawned over that man's face with sickening clarity. He knew why I wasn't dressed to the nines. Knew why I wasn't wearing my usual kick-butt high heels. He knew. And he was, well, the word for it would be "stricken." Stricken like a snake.

"You bitch," he hissed, his face getting more puce-colored by the second. "You total bitch."

I chortled merrily and Roy grabbed my arm and pushed me toward our table. "Do not swear at my client again, Mr. Nunley, or I will have to inform the judge of your harassment."

"My harassment? We're here because she assaulted me—"

"Jared." Jared's lawyer, Slick Dick II, put a hand on his arm.

I eyed Slick Dick II and resisted the temptation to snort. I had a glorious feeling the jury would hate them both.

"We're here to try the case in front of an impartial jury, not to try it in the aisle." He glanced down his nose at me. I recognized the smirk. It said, "I am better than you, female. You are nothing."

"I'm William Sheridan Stanton the Third." His voice was well modulated, snobby.

"Fab," I said. "So fab. I'm Jeanne Stewart the First. This is my attorney, Roy Sass, I believe he's the First, also, and does not include his fancy-schmancy middle name when being introduced to others for fear of being seen as elitist and smug, isn't that right, Roy?"

William Sheridan Stanton III narrowed his eyes.

"That would be correct, Jeanne. No need for pretenses," said Roy, running his hand over his graying ponytail. "No need to pretend we're someone we're not simply because our daddy has money and was able to buy us into elite schools that we would otherwise not get into. Thank you, Daddy!"

William Sheridan Stanton III's face froze like white lead. "And where did you attend law school? Hope you're not out of your league here."

"Yale," Roy said. "Graduated second in my class. A woman beat me. It was a fair fight. She was smarter than me."

Slick Dick II blinked. Shocked. How could a man with a ponytail have attended Yale?

I noticed that William Sheridan Stanton III's, aka Slick Dick II, hair was slicked back with gel. I wondered if it would move if someone touched it. "Does your hair move at all or is it stuck in that beastly glob all day?"

His eyes widened, before narrowing to slits. Like a mean weasel. He definitely looked pissed.

"And are you as priggish as your suit suggests?" I peered at him, cocking my head slightly to the left like: I must study you, you freak. "What did you say your name was? Something Something the Third of Something Special?"

Slick Dick made a hissing sound through his bright white teeth. "You haven't changed, have you, Jeanne?"

"But I have changed!" I enthused. "I have! I'm worse than ever!" I leaned in close to him. He smelled like rotting sour cream. "You smell like rotting sour cream."

He hissed again, livid. "You tried to kill me, Jeanne Stewart!"

"No, I didn't, Slick Dick."

"You put peanut oil in my condoms! *Peanut oil!* He raved. "In my condoms! And you know I'm allergic to peanut oil; you knew I would have a severe reaction! You are one sicko-freak woman and you're gonna pay for it. You are going to pay and pay until you don't have a nickel to stick up your little ass!"

"Slick Dick, I would never stick a nickel up my bottom. It's unsanitary." I turned and wiggled my butt at him, shooting him a wink over my shoulder. "I want my mountain bike back."

When the bailiff said, "All rise," I rose.

And in tottered an old, white, male judge. Old. White. And male. Possessor of a penis, undoubtedly.

Some of my confidence whooshed out of me. Roy stiffened beside me.

From the start, things did not look good. Not good at all.

Jury selection took two full days. My lawyer and Slick Dick's lawyer asked many questions, all of them intended to sway the possible jury members over to their side:

"Has your spouse/partner/girlfriend/boyfriend ever cheated on you? How did you react? What was your mental state?"

"The defendant has admitted to her crime. Does that make her guilty?"

"If someone cheats on you, does that give you the right to assault that person, putting their life in danger?"

"Is it right to take the law into your own hands?"

"When someone cheats is it always their fault? What if their partner never paid any attention to them? Was never home? Treated them like, well, a neglected pet. Is it acceptable for them to cheat?"

"How would you feel if you found out someone had possibly exposed you to numerous sexually transmitted diseases? Should that be considered a crime in itself? If not, why not?"

"Is revenge okay?"

"How much money should someone who has endured a
grievous injury receive from his perpetrator?"

"What makes a criminal?"

"Should someone be monetarily rewarded for cheating?"

During jury selection on the second day I wiggled my glasses
at Slick Dick when he glanced over and mouthed to him, "I want
my mountain bike back." My only problem was that I did not
like my outfit. It was a beige suit fit for a homely mouse worn
with brown pumps. Plain. Brown. Pumps. Urgh.

Still, I would do anything I needed to do to avoid paying Slick
Dick a dime—even if I had to wear ugly heels. My sacrifice at
this trial, I told myself, was enormous.

By the end of the second day, we had a jury.

There were twelve jurists.

There were only three women.

And nine men, possessors of penises.

Nine men who had the exact same plumbing as Slick Dick.

Who probably felt that the sun rose and set on their jewels.

We also had an old, white, male judge, possessor of a penis.

Did I mention that things did not look good?

Each day after court I was accosted by the media. My small assault on Slick Dick was both scintillating and entertaining to the
press. That I was also an ex-communications director and had
helped run Governor Jay Kendall's reelection campaign in the
fine state of Oregon (note: It's not Or-EEE-gon) and because it
was a very slow news week, I had become a person of "extreme
interest."

The media people had questions like this for me:

"Is this a feminist statement?"

"Do you condone violence against men who cheat?"

"Should men take this as a warning?"

"Jared is allergic to peanut oil. Did you intend to kill him?"

"How does the governor feel about his campaign spokes-woman being arrested for assault?"

"Do you think the jury will find you innocent or guilty?"

"Do *you* think you're innocent or guilty?"

"Jared wants one million dollars in damages. How do you feel about that?"

So I answered their questions like this:

"No, it is not a feminist statement. All women, feminist or not, have a right to take action against condoms that are worn by cheating men."

"I do not condone violence against men who cheat. I condone revenge."

"Men do not need to take this little incident as a warning. They should take it as a threat."

"I did not intend to kill Jared. I knew he would have a mild re-action. He has always had performance issues and problems, even though he has stated in his complaint that this was not the case. I do hope, however, that he decides to get counseling so he can overcome this problem. Sometimes there are deep-seated sexual issues that go along with sexual dysfunction that people don't want to face." I paused delicately here.

"What . . . what do you mean deep-seated issues?" a reporter from one of the news magazines asked.

"Well, I can't say in relation to Jared, of course, because the man could sue me for slander, but we all have to come to grips with our sexuality and there is nothing wrong with being gay." That one caused a lot of chatter among the reporters, so I held up my hand for quiet and refused to answer any more questions on that subject.

I continued:

"As for the governor of Oregon, it is true that he would have preferred that I had avoided this particular problem and subse-quent arrest."

"I think the jury will find me guilty."

"I will not give Jared one million dollars. Ever. Please remember to capitalize the word 'Ever.' "

"I have to go back to my hotel now. I'm getting hundreds of e-mails from women who are asking for creative ways to get back at their cheating men via a condom and I must attend to those questions. You all have a good day now." I spun away on my heel, but addressed the media once more. "However, if you are cheating, I might suggest you check your condoms."

How those silly reporters love to laugh!

That night, alone in my hotel room, I flipped off all the lights and crawled into bed wearing my favorite pink high heels with tiny red flowers painted on the sides. They would come off when I slept, but I needed the spark they offered me.

I glanced out at the skyline of Chicago, the lights twinkling, and I missed my river.

I missed my home by the river under the trees. I missed the Lopezes and Donovan and his opera-singing and Rosvita and my friends at the café. I missed Margie, Linda, and Louise who waited up 'til 10:00 one night so they could have a vodka tea party with me (I declined the vodka). I missed seeing Becky and Soman doing their art projects together. I missed Emmaline and her temper tantrums and Bradon.

I missed Weltana.

I missed my pancakes.

I missed my mother.

And I missed Jay.

The tears started again, pouring out of my eyes like two tiny rivers, and I pulled the blankets over my head and let 'em flow.

It is so tiring being a smart-ass.

CHAPTER 24

Roy and I were followed to court the next day by a bunch of cameramen and reporters from our hotel to the courthouse, all spouting out questions. Even though Roy, at six-foot six-inches tall, was an imposing figure, we still had four armed policemen escorting us. They were handsome chaps and I told them so. They thanked me for the compliment and off we went. Roy waved his hand at the reporters saying we would not be answering questions at this time.

The jury filed in first thing of course. We all rose for the old, white, male judge.

I looked at the jurists as we sat down. Two of the people were Hispanic. Both men. One wore a crisp white shirt and a tie with champagne glasses on it; the other had a goatee and work boots. Three jurors were African-American: One older man with white hair; one younger very stylish man with light green eyes; and one stunning woman who looked like she'd stepped off the pages of a magazine. Two were Asian—one older man with a black leather jacket and red scarf and one young woman wearing a striped dress that made me dizzy when I looked at it. The other five were white and in their midforties or fifties, four men, one woman. One man was very fat, another skinny as a skeleton, the third looked like a professor complete with a bad hair day, the fourth was in his fifties and attractive, and the woman looked tired. I figured she was a working mom.

I again wished there weren't so many men, possessors of penises.

I snuck a glimpse around the courtroom. One row of women caught my eye. There were about eight of them. They all appeared mighty ticked off, their faces set. They ranged in age from early twenties to late thirties. It did not take me long to figure out that they were Slick Dick exes.

Two of them peered over at me, then nudged the women next to them. When I had their attention, I winked. They all grinned back. Two gave me the thumbs-up sign. One flashed her middle finger and pointed it at Slick Dick.

I knew I had a cheering section.

The gavel came down and my trial began.

Slick Dick's lawyer got up to speak in his million-dollar priss suit.

"Good morning. My name is William Sheridan Stanton the Third."

Gag. I thought. *Gag.* He reminded me of mucus.

I studied the jurors. About half of them sat back and crossed their arms as soon as William Sheridan Stanton III addressed them. Must be the mucous effect.

"Today you are going to hear about one woman, a woman utterly consumed with jealousy, who attacked my client when she found out their relationship was over." He ran a hand over his globby hair. (The glob did not move.)

"But this trial isn't about my client, Jared Nunley, and a broken, difficult relationship that he was gently, carefully, trying to extricate himself from." He spread his arms wide. All he needed were whiskers and he'd look like a weasel. "It's about Ms. Stewart and her vengeful assault on Jared. Her diabolical, premeditated assault and the harm that came from it."

William Sheridan Stanton III whirled around and stabbed a finger at me.

I made myself jump a smidge in perceived fright and my glasses slid down my nose and hit the table. I fumbled around for them.

I heard Slick Dick groan.

William Sheridan Stanton III paused, flustered. "Miss Stewart," he semishouted, "deliberately opened Jared Nunley's condom wrappers with an Exacto knife, pulled out the condoms, and put several drops of peanut oil in each one! Peanut oil, people, and she knew that Jared was highly allergic to peanut oil! She used a hot-glue gun to reseal the wrappers and cover up her secret! When he used a condom, he had a severe—*severe*—reaction to it and ended up in the emergency room overnight. *Overnight!*"

The lips of the skinny white guy on the jury twitched. The Hispanic man with the work boots snorted.

William Sheridan Stanton III paced the courtroom, as if he couldn't bear to keep still with such evil swirling in the air. "Her assault damaged Mr. Nunley physically, emotionally, and mentally. We will call witnesses, including medical personnel, who will detail the appalling effects on Jared from this assault. And do you know what, ladies and gentlemen? Ms. Stewart has already admitted her guilt. She admitted it to the police officers who arrested her, to my client, to me, and to her own lawyer, among others."

He fisted his hands and popped them against each other.

"Now, I won't tell you that my client, Jared Nunley, is a saint. He's not. None of us are, are we?" A creepy smile slithered out. I could tell he was trying to be ingratiating.

The jurors did not smile back.

William Sheridan Stanton III cleared his throat. "In fact, during this case you might hear things that make you doubt my client needs to be reimbursed for his pain and suffering. You might find that you don't personally like him. I understand." Pompous tone was back. "But remember that whether or not you like him is *irrelevant*. Your opinion of him personally is *irrelevant*. Your feelings about his relationships are *irrelevant*. What's important is that justice is served here."

The chin went up of the juror with the black leather jacket and red scarf. The attractive white guy set his jaw tight. I didn't think the jury liked being told they were "irrelevant."

"When someone is assaulted they deserve to be compensated and at the end of this trial, I will ask you to put a dollar amount on Ms. Stewart's unwarranted, hateful, damaging attack on my client, and I will ask you to be generous. Thank you for your time."

Roy took his own time getting out of his seat. He stood in front of the jurors, looked 'em square in the eye, said hello, thanked them for coming.

I have to tell you, Roy was a man to watch and a man to love. During his opening statement the jurors leaned forward when he spoke, they nodded, they laughed a couple of times. He started off with telling the jurors about the homeless dog shelter he runs on his property outside Chicago and how he tries to find those dogs good homes. Told a few funny one-liners about the quirky, insecure, temperamental, slobberingly affectionate dogs he's taken in over the years, and related the whole thing back to humans and their emotions.

"Humans are unpredictable in so many ways, folks. You know that. But I'll tell you all something, they're also extremely *predictable*. They want loyalty from the people who profess to love them."

Several of the jurors nodded.

"They want faithfulness."

The fat white man mouthed, "Yes."

"They want to know that the person they love will not sneak around and hurt them."

The professor tipped his head heavenward in agreement.

"They want to know that their life and health will not be deliberately put in danger by the person they sleep with at night."

The working mother looked like she might cry.

"My client," he waved his hand back at me and waited a few seconds so the jurors could get a good look, "will not deny that she put peanut oil in Jared Nunley's condoms. She won't deny it. I won't deny it. We're going to be straight-up honest with all of you people during this trial." He paused, let the jury see how honest he was. "Mr. Nunley slept with many women during his two-year relationship with Jeanne Stewart. This fact is not in dispute. When Ms. Stewart found out, she was distraught, hysterical.

"You will be asked in this case to think about Ms. Stewart's mental state and to think about the real damage that was done here to the plaintiff—which is miniscule." He faced Slick Dick, raising up his fingers so they were about two inches apart. "Miniscule. Little. Tiny. Insignificant."

I bent my head real quick. I knew what he was getting at. So did the jurors. The guy with the goatee sucked in his cheeks to keep from laughing. The young man with light green eyes raised his eyebrows. The model smirked. My cheering section laughed. One of Slick Dick's exes stage-whispered, "Miniscule. You got that right."

The old, white, male judge did not crack a smile, but he did bang his gavel for order.

"You will hear from a number of women who were sleeping with Jared at the same time he was living with Jeanne," said Roy. "You will hear from Jeanne herself, how she supported Mr. Nunley during the two years they lived together. You will hear how she trusted him. How she believed they had a respectful, faithful, committed relationship. You will also hear how she was scared beyond belief when she found out Mr. Nunley had been cheating, because she feared for her life, for her health.

"Cheating, as you all know, can have life-threatening consequences. Mr. Nunley could have contracted AIDS and passed it on to her. He could have contracted herpes, which also is a lifelong, painful disease. He could have given her any number of other sexually transmitted diseases, a couple of which could have made her infertile, unable to bear children.

"Jeanne Stewart was beside herself." Roy paused. "And, at

the end of this trial, despite her admission, I believe you will find that she does not owe Mr. Nunley any money. Not. One. Cent."

I sat up straighter, pulled at my beige shirt tucked under a brown, tired-looking suit jacket. My hair was in a sloppy ponytail today. No makeup. No jewelry.

I looked pathetic.

I was darn proud of myself.

It was Slick Dick's time to take the stand.

He looked so pretty my stomach cramped up. Did I ever sleep with him? Did I ever live with him? How could I have been attracted to him?

Yuck.

Yucky mucky yuck.

I stared down at my shoes. Today they were dull brown and scratched. I had found them at a used clothing store. Three dollars.

I raised my eyes back to the stand where Slick Dick was taking his oath to be honest, then switched my gaze back to my shoes.

Since shortly after Johnny and Ally died, I had felt almost naked without an eye-catching pair of heels on, yet today it felt different. As if my whole life had boiled down to this. As if my feet were naked, I was naked, and here we were together. We had made it this far and we were still kickin'. I clicked my heels together.

"Mr. Nunley," William Sheridan Stanton III said, his voice pompous. "Please tell the jury what happened to you on the night of April 28, 2007."

Slick Dick turned an eager face toward the jury, as if he was dying to tell the truth, and nothing but the truth, so help him, Mr. Devil.

He reminded me of a used-car salesman, toothy and cheesy. I watched him carefully. He let his gaze linger on two of the women in the jury—the mother and the one who looked like a model.

Sheesh. Like they would be swayed by that. Double sheesh.

"I was with my friend, Gabrielle Smythe. We had gone to dinner and dessert in town and then we went back to her place."

"Yes?" the III said.

Slick Dick tried hard to seem embarrassed, as if he couldn't bare to talk about his sex life. "One thing led to another and we . . ." He smirked again, looked at the jury as if for help and understanding.

They stared back. No expression.

Gag.

"We started to, you know, mess around, and I reached for my wallet, because that's where guys keep their condoms, isn't that right?" He cocked an eyebrow at the jury. Isn't this funny, guys?

The guys on the jury were not amused.

Slick Dick looked rather befuddled by this lack of warmth.

"So I opened it up, you know, and I take it out and she, my girlfriend, she puts it on, you know, and we start messing around again and then we're having . . . you know."

He cleared his throat, shifted in his seat.

"And?" the III asked.

"In the middle of it I feel like . . . well, it feels like I'm going to explode, like my, you know, like my penis is going to explode."

"Explode?" Slick Dick II curls a hand around his chin. *Fascinating!*

"Yeah, explode in like, you know, a bad way. And it hurts and it itches and I'm, like, what the hell's going on? And my friend, she's, uh . . ." He laughed, the big he-man on campus, all caught up in his little moment.

"Yes, Mr. Nunley?" the III asked, trying hard to look innocent.

"She's enjoying herself and I don't want to stop anything, of course. Women don't like that." He smirked at a couple of the male jurors, as if to bond. They apparently were not interested in bonding. He coughed. "Uh . . . yeah, well, you know, pretty soon, I could barely move. I'm so big and Gabrielle's liking it but I'm getting worried and I start to hurt. I start to ache, I start to . . . throb . . ."

"Your penis . . . throbs?" the III arched those eyebrows again.

"Yeah, it's aching and it's getting so irritated and itchy . . ."

The jurors looked disgusted. The model looked like she might gag.

"Thank you, Mr. Nunley," the III interrupted, after a quick glance at the jurors.

"And, my girlfriend, she's done and all." He glanced again at the men in the jury and grinned like, "Hey dude, we all have women in common, don't we?"

Apparently the jurors did not feel that commonality.

Slick Dick's head jerked back to his attorney and the man-to-man smile disappeared. "But I'm feeling short of breath and I'm in pain and I try to pull out. My girlfriend had a great time, but you know, it's time to go, and I . . ."

"You?" the III prompted.

"I can't move."

"What do you mean you can't move?"

"I mean, I can't leave her, can't get out of her. I'm stuck."

The skinny white guy shifted in his seat. The woman in the dizzy dress laughed, stifled it, and pretended she was coughing. Two more jurors leaned forward, their faces stunned. The cheering section laughed. The gavel came down.

The III waited for silence, his expression awestruck. "You're stuck?"

"Yeah, that's how swollen I was. I'm stuck."

Like two dogs, I thought. "Like two dogs," I whispered to Roy.

Roy looked down at his papers real quick.

"So what did you do?"

"Well, Gabrielle wants me off so she's pushing at me to get off and I'm trying, but I can't move because I'm in a ton of pain and I'm still feeling like I'm going to explode." He raised his eyebrows. "A ton of pain."

"Mr. Nunley," the III said, his eyes all concerned and weepy. "We realize this is difficult for you as you're a very private man, but what happened after that?"

"Well, I finally pulled out but I can't even recognize myself. I mean I've always been larger than average, women have told me that and all." He shrugged and tried to appear sheepish, but you know he's proud of that statement.

The older white-haired man on the jury shook his head, real slow. The man with champagne glasses on his tie looked disgusted. The model rolled her eyes. She'd heard it before.

"But now I'm huge and I'm red and there's all these welts all over me."

The jurors looked like they wanted to barf.

"So what did you do?"

"I told Gabrielle to call an ambulance."

There was a silence in the courtroom. One of the jurists snorted. Another laughed, smothered it quick.

Slick Dick called an ambulance for his dick, I wrote on a piece of paper to Roy.

Again, he bent his head and stared at the papers in front of him. He did not look up for a good minute, but I felt his body shaking with laughter.

"And when you got to the hospital?" the III asked.

"I felt like I was going to scream I was in so much pain. The doctors came in to help me and they're all shocked, I can tell you that. Shocked. Absolutely shocked."

"Objection," says Roy. "It's hearsay. The plaintiff does not know that the doctors were shocked."

"Sustained," the judge said.

"Go ahead, Mr. Nunley," the III said.

"So they asked me what happened and I told them and they asked me about allergies and I told them about my severe, severe allergy to peanut oil."

"How long have you had this allergy?"

"Since I was a child. I can't even touch peanut butter. If I do, whatever part touches it gets red and swollen and hives form."

"Then what happened?"

"The doctors were extremely worried. They were about flipped out, running all over the place, panicked almost."

"Objection," Roy said. "Hearsay again. How does he know the doctors were worried about an allergic reaction?"

"Sustained," the old judge croaked.

"I thought I was going to have to have surgery or something. I mean, I'm big down in that region to begin with, but I'm not *that* big."

The jurist with the light green eyes stared up at the ceiling, as if he wished for deliverance. The fat white man tightened his lips, disbelief stamped on his features. The cheering section laughed. The gavel came down.

Jared glanced at the jury, wanting to share the moment of his bigness, even as his face became a magenta color.

They stared back with no apparent fondness for sharing time.

"So what was your treatment?" William Sheridan Stanton III asked with grave concern.

"They had to give me powerful allergy medication *and* cream to spread on and I had to stay overnight in the hospital to make sure there were no further serious complications."

I rolled my eyes. Slick Dick was such a worrier. Any time he got sick he assumed he had anything from malaria to leukemia to a tumor and back again. And he always laid himself in bed for days on end and pissed and moaned.

"Mr. Nunley, tell us how you figured out what happened?"

"I recognized the rash. I knew I had gotten it from peanuts and I knew who did it. *I knew it.* She's like that. Vengeful. Hateful. Jealous. Angry." His face twisted up.

"Who is she?" the III asked.

"Jeanne Stewart. Right there at the defendant's table." He pointed a long finger at me, as though no one in the courtroom would be able to find the defendant's table. I resisted the urge to stand up and wave like a princess.

"Did she admit what she had done?"

"Yes, she did. She admitted it to me when I called her that

night. She laughed. Laughed so hard she could hardly talk." And here he glared at me. "Jeanne Stewart put peanut oil in my condoms and tried to kill me."

Roy was up next. Me oh my, this would be so much fun. I used one finger to push my glasses right up my nose.

"So, Mr. Nunley." He stood and crossed his arms over his chest. "Let me get this straight." He looked down at his notes. "You were having sex with your, uh . . ." he fiddled with his glasses. "You were having sex with your *other* girlfriend, your second girlfriend, I should probably say . . ."

"Objection!" the III yelled.

"Overruled," the old, white, male judge drawled.

"You were having sex with your *second* girlfriend—my client, Jeanne Stewart being your *first* girlfriend, although she had no knowledge you had a *second* girlfriend—and during *intercourse* your penis became red and swollen and you noticed welts on it, is that correct?"

"Yes, that is correct," Slick Dick said, his voice sounding strangled.

Roy let the silence hang for a while. "So. Am I correct in saying that you called an ambulance for your penis?"

It took quite awhile for everyone in that courtroom to get all that pent-up laughter out. Especially when one of the women in the cheering section mimicked the sound of an ambulance siren.

"Mr. Nunley," Roy began again, after being admonished by the judge to control himself. "Who was Jeanne Stewart to you at the time of this incident?"

"She was my ex-girlfriend."

"Ahh, I see," said Roy. "How long had you been together?"

"Two years."

"Would you call it a serious relationship?"

Slick Dick shrugged. "We were together."

Roy nodded. "You were together."

"Uh. Yes."

"You were living together. Correct?"

Slick Dick froze up.

"Correct?" Roy asked. "You have to speak up for the court reporter. She can't write, 'He nodded churlishly.'"

"Objection," the III said.

"Withdrawn."

Slick Dick glared at Roy.

"Yes, we were living together, but the relationship had ended."

Roy looked perplexed. "Did Ms. Stewart know that the relationship had ended?"

Slick Dick paused and coughed. "Yeah, she did."

Roy nodded. "How did she know?"

He shrugged again. "She knew. I knew. We were over. It was only a matter of time before we split up."

"I see. So you never said to her, 'I want to break up with you'?"

Long pause. "No."

"You never said, 'We need to go our separate ways'?"

Slick Dick shifted in his seat as if something was itching his bottom. "No, not in a big conversation or anything like that . . . we didn't have a break-up talk . . ."

"You never said, 'I need some space'?"

Slick Dick swallowed hard. "Not exactly."

"Not exactly? Yes or no, Mr. Nunley."

He shifted and itched that butt again. "Ah, no."

"Did she know that you were sleeping with other women?"

Slick Dick squirmed again.

Roy raised his eyebrows. "Did she know that you were sleeping with other women?"

"Uh. Urgh. Uh. No." He whispered.

"Mr. Nunley, what do you do for a living?"

"I'm a consultant."

I laughed. My laughter rang through the courtroom. The

judge whacked his gavel, glared at me. "The defendant will control herself."

"What, exactly, does that mean, Mr. Nunley?" Roy asked.

"It means . . . it means that I help people get their businesses up and running. I provide them with expert financial advice. I help them build their portfolios. I devise forecasting and plans, and I . . ."

"You sound very successful, Mr. Nunley."

"I do fairly well." He crossed one leg over the other.

"You do?" Roy raised his eyebrows. "Mr. Nunley, how much did you earn each of the years that you and Ms. Stewart were together?"

"Objection," the III yelled and stood up. He blathered on about that not being relevant, that it had nothing to do with the assault. The old, white, male judge overruled him.

"Mr. Nunley, I'll ask you again, how much did you earn in each of the two years that you and Ms. Stewart lived together?"

Slick Dick mumbled and jumbled. "It was hard to track . . . I had big payoffs at certain times, then I'd go a couple of weeks without money, later I'd get a huge lump sum . . . you know . . ."

"No, I don't know. Mr. Nunley, I'm going to ask you one more time. How much money, working as a coonnnsssulllttannntt did you earn?" He strung out the word consultant in a way that suggested consultant was quite questionable.

"About . . ."

"Sorry, sir, you're mumbling. How much did you earn last year when you were living with my client?"

"About . . . about . . . nine thousand."

Roy let that amount hang in the air for a while. "Nine thousand for the year?"

Slick Dick said, "Yes."

"Ahhh. *Big* payouts then. Did you ever apply for welfare?"

"Objection!" the III screeched, all red in the face again.

"Sustained. You will not make sarcastic remarks," the judge told Roy.

Roy nodded. "Mr. Nunley, is it true that you actually made closer to seventy-eight hundred last year? It is? Can you also tell us how much you made working as a consultant the year before?"

Slick Dick looked furious. He mumbled a sum. I heard it, but Roy pretended not to.

"I'm sorry. I didn't hear that. How much did you make the year before working as a consultant, Mr. Nunley?"

"About ten thousand."

That amount hung in the air for a while, too, nice and heavy.

"Ten thousand?" Roy whistled. "Hmmm. Is it closer to eight thousand? It is? So, who owned the home you lived in?"

Slick Dick flushed. "Jeanne did."

"Did you pay rent?"

Slick Dick glared.

"I would like to ask that the judge direct the witness to answer the question. The court reporter can't write, 'The plaintiff made a grumpy face.' "

"The plaintiff will answer directly," the judge clipped.

"No, I didn't. Jeanne made about thirty times more than I did so she paid it. It was her house, too."

"Did you pay for groceries?"

Slick Dick glared.

"Did you pay for the utilities—gas, electricity?"

Slick Dick glared.

"Your Honor," Roy whined, "must the court reporter be forced to write, 'The defendant pulled his grumpy face again'?"

The jury laughed.

Your Honor didn't wait. "The plaintiff will answer the questions or be found in contempt of court."

"No," Slick Dick said.

"Nothing? You contributed nothing to the household expenses, is that correct?"

"I guess."

"You guess? Yes or no, answer the question. Did you contribute in any way to the household expenses?"

"No, but—"

"Mr. Nunley, isn't it true that you have a large trust fund given to you by your father?"

"Yes, that's true." Slick Dick looked relieved. And proud.

"So, you did have the money to help pay for the household expenses, didn't you?"

"Jeanne was working—"

"I didn't ask that. I know she was working. On an easy week, she worked seventy hours. You have a multimillion dollar trust fund and yet you did not contribute to the household expenses, is that correct?"

"I contributed a little."

"A little? But you did not contribute to rent, utilities, or food? What about vacations? No? Thank you, Mr. Nunley. At what point did Jeanne know that you and she were not together?"

"She had known for a long time. Before I even met Gabrielle."

"Gabrielle being the woman you were having sex with when you got, uh . . . stuck and had to call an ambulance for your penis?"

There were the usual objections.

"So, you were still living with Jeanne when you were having sex with Miss Smythe and had a reaction to the condom, correct?"

"Yes. But we had broken up."

"I understand that you thought the two of you had broken up by that time," said Roy. "The question is, did Jeanne?"

Roy cruised along in that vein for a while, "Mr. Nunley, how many people did you have sex with while you were still living with Jeanne Stewart?"

"I am not a perfect man. I am not a perfect Christian. I made mistakes."

"You're not a perfect Christian?"

"No, I'm not," Slick Dick snapped.

"Well, thank you for offering that up. I'll pray for you, but that's not what I asked. The question was, how many people were you sleeping with while you were living with Jeanne Stewart?"

"I don't know."

"That many?" asked Roy, eyebrows raised.

"No. I strayed because Jeanne worked all the time. I was lonely. I was alone, she was neglectful—"

"Can I read off some names for you?" Roy asked, pushing his ponytail off his shoulders. "Do you know Marisa Kube? What about Nancy Tettler? Anisha Cable? Kristi Rottendam? Leesa Buddler? Bethy Sattleson? Carrie Mortenger? Bam-Bam Wham, who works as a stripper? Susie Come, also a stripper? Latisha Corrinne? Are those names familiar?"

Slick Dick looked like he wanted to morph into a rat and disappear. "Yes," he choked out.

"Did you have sexual relationships with all of these women?"

"They are all . . . friends of mine."

"I'm glad you have so many friends, Mr. Nunley, but, again, that's not what I asked. Did you have sexual relationships with all of these women?"

"Yes," a squeak, a little squeak.

"Did you have sexual relationships with all of these women while you also had a sexual relationship with my client, Jeanne Stewart?"

"Your Honor, he's badgering my client," the III said. I peered at the III. I bet he did not get laid very often. It would be like having sex with a robot. He would probably quote tort law during the encounter.

"He's not badgering your client; he's trying to establish Ms. Stewart's motives for what she did and her state of mind at the time. You will answer the question," the old, white, male judge croaked to Slick Dick.

"Did you have intercourse with all of these women while you were living with Jeanne Stewart?"

"Yes." Squeak. Squeak.

"Did you sleep with any men?"

"No!" That got Slick Dick. He sat straight up.

"No? You're not gay?"

"No, I'm not a fag!" He squirmed in the witness chair, his face getting red and angry. "I've never been gay. I've never even been with a man! I'm not gay!"

"You're not gay? You never had a gay experience?" Roy furrowed his brows at him, as though he didn't believe him.

"No! I am not gay!" He shot a quick look at one of the more stylishly dressed male jurors who was studying Slick Dick with disdain.

"So you will swear, at this moment, that even though you say that you're not gay, you've never had a gay experience?"

Slick Dick was beside himself, his voice pitchy. "Yes! I will swear! No! I haven't! Never!"

Roy sighed, his shoulders sinking as if it truly bothered him personally that Slick Dick had lied. "Did you stop to think that when you were having intercourse with all these *people* that if Ms. Stewart found out you were cheating on her she would be upset, even frightened? Panicked because of the diseases you might have brought home?"

Slick Dick slunk down in the chair. I could almost see his rat tail hiding between his legs. "I always wore condoms."

"Always?" Roy let that word hang, too. "So we're to believe that you always, always wore condoms?"

Slick Dick twitched again. Must be that itchy bottom, I surmised.

"Mr. Nunley? You always, always wore condoms?" Roy asked.

Gracious. How glad I was that there were a number of Slick Dick exes in the courtroom. Two of them snorted. Two snickered. Another said, "Sure. Yeah. Right. Okeydokey."

"The spectators will control themselves," the judge said, whacking that gavel, "or I will have you removed from the courtroom."

"Most of the time I wore condoms." Whispered.

"Most of the time?" Roy spread his arms. "Aren't you aware

that by not using condoms all the time, in fact, even with wearing a condom, that you could have exposed my client to a variety of sexually transmitted diseases, including but not limited to gonorrhea, chlamydia, herpes, and AIDS?"

Slick Dick got redder. "No one had any of those diseases . . ."

"None of the women did? Did you get the women checked out at a doctor's office before sleeping with them?"

One woman said, "Hell, no," but luckily the old, white, male judge didn't hear her.

"Speak up, please, Mr. Nunley," Roy bellowed. "Did you have all of the women go to the doctor to be checked for all STDs before sleeping with them?"

"No. But I knew they were safe. I would never, ever do anything that might hurt Jeanne."

The professor having an extraordinarily bad hair day shook his head back and forth. The skinny one leaned back in his chair, his lids lowered and fiddled with a pencil. The tired mother folded her arms and shot Slick Dick a scathing stare.

Slick Dick smiled a shaky smile at the jury.

The jury glared.

CHAPTER 25

After lunch we began again. First witness: Jared's girlfriend who, to be crystal clear, was not the same girlfriend with the bursting boobies and short jean skirt who was sitting behind him.

This girlfriend had lots of blond hair laying all over her shoulders and was wearing a tight pink t-shirt over a formidable bosom and black shiny slacks and cool heels. Ms. Gabrielle Smythe was about thirty-five and did not appear to be in a good mood.

Slick Dick II was up first to question Ms. Smythe. He did not appear comfortable with this particular duty. In fact, he pulled on his tie as if it was strangling him like a serpent.

"Ms. Smythe," William Sheridan Stanton III said, with caution.

"What?" she spat out, curling her lip. "*What?*"

"Ms. Smythe, you were with my client, Jared Nunley, when the attack took place, right? Could you tell us what happened. "

"What attack?" Ms. Smythe crossed her arms under that formidable bosom. "There wasn't no attack."

"Yes, there was. My client was hurt on the evening of—"

"He wasn't hurt. He's a baby. He's a cheater." Her voice kept rising in volume with each word. "He's a liar. His thingie got red and rashy. That ain't hurt."

"Ms. Smythe." William Sheridan Stanton III gave his tie another tug. I could almost hear that serpent hissing! "You are under oath. Do you understand what that means? Are you clear that if you don't tell the truth you could, potentially, serve jail time?"

"Oh, shove it," Ms. Smythe ordered, leaning forward on the witness stand. "I understand what 'under oath' means. Do I look that stupid? Do I? Yeah, I was with Jared Nunley the night his dick turned red. He wasn't hurt at all and look at him. He's sittin' right there, ain't he? I don't see no damage!"

Mr. William Sheridan Stanton III choked out, "No further questions." He sat down, pulled on his tie. Coughed.

Wait . . . I hear a snake hissing!

"Ms. Smythe," Roy said, nice and calm. "Can you tell me about your relationship with Jared Nunley?"

Oh, could she.

"I'm a hairstylist. Jared was my client. The first day he came in, he asked me out. I said no. Not a chance. I was off men. He came in the next week with flowers. Asked me out again. I said no. Same reason. And, by damn, he came in the next day with more flowers and the day after that. Now I was at the point where I thought all men were assholes, but he kept coming on to me so I finally decided to give it another go, and said yes. I thought," she glared at Jared, "I thought that maybe for once this guy wasn't a jerk."

"When you were dating him did you know that he already had a girlfriend?"

"Absolutely not. Jared told me that he didn't have a girlfriend or a wife. I specifically asked him, because I don't mow other women's grass, you know what I mean? I don't cheat with cheaters. I'm not no home-wrecker. I thought he was single because he lied and said he was, and he didn't wear a ring." She flipped her hair back, glared again. "So we started dating."

"Can you tell us what happened that night when Mr. Nunley had a reaction to his condom?"

She was going to love this part, I could tell. Gabrielle Smythe sat up straight and smirked at dear Slick Dick. I could only guess what happened. He had slept with her, had some performance issues, and blamed them on her.

"Sure can. I'll tell you everything. We went to dinner, which he made me pay for because he 'forgot' his wallet. This had happened before. In fact, I almost always paid. The only food Jared ever bought me was chicken nuggets. In my head I called him, 'The under ten-dollar man.' He was the cheapest . . ."

"Objection!" cut in the III.

The old white male judge paused for a second then creaked out, "Sustained."

Ms. Smythe rotated in her seat and smiled at the judge, her tone changing from red hot rage to quiet respect. "Pardon me, I don't know what that means, Your Honor."

The judge said, "It means I agree with the other attorney's objection and you should stick to answering the question."

"Sorry. I'm very sorry." Ms. Smythe was genuinely contrite.

"It's all right," the judge said. "Don't worry."

Roy indicated she should start again.

"Anyhow, we went back to my place, and I was going to break up with him because he's not very nice to me and our sex life was lousy, but he starts coming on to me, nibbling on my neck like a squirrel might. Do you see how he's got big teeth?" she asked the jury, jutting out her own top teeth for example and pretending she was a squirrel nibbling on a nut.

"Objection!" shouted the III.

Roy said, "Keep telling us about that night."

"So he's nibbling on my neck, squirrel-like, and I'm thinking, I'm tired and I don't like this guy, but what the hell. His hands are sticky from all this pop he drank and he's running them all over me and it's gross, but again I think, what the hell. We're naked and on the floor and he's on top of me and I can barely breathe and he's panting in my ears so loud I'm wonderin' if I'm fucking a freight train . . ."

The jurors laughed.

"Objection!" the III bellowed.

"Sustained," the old, white, male judge said. "Now let's not use the f-word," he admonished Ms. Smythe.

She faced the judge again. "I apologize, sir. I need to watch that, don't I?"

"You do." He raised his eyebrows, not unkindly. "Go ahead, miss."

"Thank you." She nodded at the judge. "And I am sorry for my language." When she faced us again, the same disdainful anger was stamped on her face. "I moved my head because he smelled like a hamburger that had been out on the counter too long . . ."

"Objection!" from the III.

"Sustained," the judge said. "Let's proceed onward here."

She caught the judge's eye, her tone respectful, sorrowful. "I apologize again. My anger is getting the best of me." When she glared at Slick Dick, the same blistering hate reappeared like magic. "Jared rolls off of me and crawls to his pants and gets a condom out of his wallet and he can't get it open so I have to open it for him. I'm wishing this was all over but Jared's sweating and I know he's all geared up in his head. Jared has had problems with getting the old man up and so I had to deal with that for a long, long, looooonnngggg time and I'm thinking I sure would rather be in the bath reading my horoscope, but I keep working and working and working on it."

I snuck a peek over at Jared. His face was splotchy red with humiliation and he was shaking his head as though denying everything.

Ms. Smythe sighed. "So *finally* Mr. Friendly gets up and Jared starts doing his thing and my head keeps banging onto the floor and the freight train's back, but I'm thinkin' he'll be quick, he's *always* quick." She rolled her eyes.

I put a hand over my mouth so I wouldn't laugh. Roy coughed beside me. The cheering section snickered.

One of the jurors, the heavy one, laughed, then clamped his

mouth shut. The juror next to him, the one with the work boots, caught the laugh, but managed to muffle it by staring at his hands clasped in his lap.

"We were having problems with that, too." Ms. Smythe pushed her platinum blond hair back over her shoulders.

"Objection!" The III was positively outraged.

"I'll allow it," the old, white, male judge intoned. "Mr. Nunley is claiming that this incident with the condom caused him permanent damage in that department and that he was not having any issues before this. Her testimony is relevant."

"What problems did Jared have?" Roy asked

"You know, problems with him being so quick. He comes, he deflates, and it's over in seconds, I mean *seconds*, but this time I'm thinkin', as my head keeps hitting the floor, 'This is the last time I'm gonna do this. I've had it. Small dick, small mind, small wallet.' So all of a sudden, he stops pantin' and I'm thinkin' good, he's almost done. I can read my horoscope and still catch Letterman. I'm a hairstylist. I work, you know. I work hard, and this guy, he never ever has to work, so he can sleep-in all morning, but I can't as a workin' girl. So Jared, he stops panting in my ear and makes this gurgle in his throat. I look at his face and it's all red like it is now. See how his face looks now? That's how it was that night, and I say, 'Are you havin' a heart attack or somethin'?' and he shakes his head."

"What happened next, Ms. Smythe?"

"Well, he tries to pull out and he can't. It's like we're stuck. Like someone put glue between us. You know, super glue or hot glue, something you would use on a craft project, like makin' a potpourri ball or something. Only I'm not doing a craft project. I wished I was doing a craft project, but I'm having sex—*bad sex*—and he won't get out."

If suppressing laughter could kill a person I would be dead by now.

But I am better than the jurors. Seven of them gave up and laughed out loud. Those naughty jurors.

The judge pounded that gavel of his. He looked quite miffed. "Stop. Get control of yourselves," he said, his white head quivering. "Ms. Smythe, you may proceed."

Ms. Smythe was pleased to do so.

"So we're like, stuck, like someone put glue between us, did I say that already? I did? So, I'm yellin' at him, 'Get off of me!' and he says in this weird voice, 'I can't!' Finally, it seems like *hours* later, he's *finally* out and I looked at it." She wriggled in her chair, her face contorted with revulsion.

It was so quiet in that courtroom, if a spider farted we would all have heard it.

"What do you mean, you looked at it?" Roy asked.

She rolled her eyes with total exasperation. "I looked at his dick. His penis. His thingie, you know."

"Thingie-wingie," I heard one of the ex-girlfriends mutter in the rows behind me.

"And what did you see?" Roy acted like he'd never heard it before.

"It's all red and swollen—I mean it's a hell of a lot bigger than he's ever been before. I don't even recognize it, it's so big. And I'm like, where did this come from? I used to think of him as Jingly Jared, he was so small. Anyhow, the worst of it is it's got all these welts over it and it's bright red and rashy-looking and I'm pissed off thinkin' he's got some disease or something and he's given it to me! He gets up and stares down at himself and I'm so furious I throw a vase at him."

Now that did it. Laughter burst out of those naughty, naughty jurors. Their laughter was drowned out only by the laughter of the bystanders and press.

"So, let me get this straight, Ms. Smythe," said Roy. "After you and Mr. Nunley made love—"

"There was no making love," Ms. Smythe said, her face furious. "That was sex. Bad sex. Noisy sex. Head-banging sex in a migraine-causing sort of way, if you know what I mean, but it wasn't making love."

"All right, so afterward, you're on the floor, he pulls away, and you see that he has some welts on his penis?"

"Shit yes!" She sucked in her breath, twisted ninety degrees and faced the judge. "I am so sorry for my language."

The judge nodded. "Apology accepted. Carry on."

She addressed Roy, so livid. "I've never had no disease and I don't ever wanna get one and I'm thinkin' that this jerk has given it to me."

"Then what happened?"

"Jared stands up and he's holdin' his thingie with one hand and with the other he grabs my mother's glass candlesticks and throws them across the room and they break all over my fireplace and he yells, 'That bitch!' " She glared at Jared. "You owe me for those candlesticks. My mother is furious with you."

"Who do you think he was calling a bitch?" asked Roy.

"It was Jeanne. He was calling Jeanne a bitch. 'Jeanne, you will pay for this,' he's screamin'. 'I'm going to take every cent you ever had, you cold bitch.' "

"Ms. Smythe," Roy said, so friendly. "I understand that Mr. Nunley had some problems with his penis, but did you notice any other physical problems after that? For example, was Mr. Nunley having trouble breathing?"

"No."

"Was he having trouble standing up straight, walking around?"

"Nope. He was walkin' around, holdin' his dick, and screamin' at Jeanne."

"Ms. Smythe, was Mr. Nunley sick at all?" asked Roy. "Did he vomit? Did he say he had diarrhea as a result of this reaction?"

"No. No barfin' and no poopin'. He kept swearin' and screamin' that he was going to 'kill her.' "

"He said he was going to kill her? Do you mean Jeanne?"

"Yes, I do."

"So what did you do next?"

"Well, the big baby hollers at me to call an ambulance. 'Call an ambulance, my dick's on fire!' he's yellin'. 'Call an ambulance, my dick's on fire!' God. Like the doctors are going to want to see a red and swollen dick with welts on it. He kept screamin' that he was going to sue her."

"Sue Jeanne?"

"Yeah, he said she was going to regret it, that she was a rich bitch, but she wasn't going to be a rich bitch when he got through with her, that he would take every penny. And I said 'Who's Jeanne?' but I knew. I figured she was his wife so I started screamin' at him and he's holding his thingie and hoppin' around and yellin' for ice and for me to call 911, but I won't do that."

"You won't call an ambulance for the problem with his . . . uh . . . penis?"

"No, I won't. So he crawls over to the phone, hangin' on to his dick with one hand. He gets a bunch of ice in my favorite dish towel—you owe me a new dish towel, too, asshole," she informs Slick Dick. "He lays down on my couch and I'm swearin' at him because I think he's given me a disease."

"When the ambulance arrived what happened?" Roy looked properly interested.

"Well, these three paramedics come in and I light a cigarette and show them where Jared is lying on the couch cryin' over his thingie, holdin' it like it's a baby. These three guys lean over him and when he takes the towel with ice in it off his dick, they back away real quick, like they think it's gross and one of the paramedics goes, 'Ah, that's sick, man, that's sick.'

"And they tell him they think he's got a disease or something and he tells them to take him to the hospital damn quick, assholes, that's what he says to them, 'Take me to the hospital damn quick, assholes.' The paramedics stand back and ask him not to swear at them. One of them says he can probably drive himself, that they don't usually take people to the hospital for sexually transmitted diseases, but Jared's yellin' at them and threatenin' to sue, so they tell him to pull on his pants, and they'll take him, and they're all rolling their eyes at each other."

"And after that?"

"The paramedics tell him to walk on out to the ambulance, but he insists he can't walk, so they bring in the stretcher and help him up and he's still holdin' ice to his dick using my favorite dish towel, you pissant," Ms. Smythe directs to Slick Dick. "He's fussin' and whinin' and they take him to the hospital, but first the paramedics fight about who has to sit in the back with him, and the short one lost and wasn't none too happy about it."

"Did you go with him to the hospital in the ambulance?" Roy asked, his eyes wide with curiosity.

"No, man, I did not go to the hospital."

"No? He was your boyfriend. Why didn't you go?"

"Three reasons." Ms. Smythe held up three fingers and glared at Slick Dick.

"What are those three reasons?"

"One, he wasn't my boyfriend. He was a mistake with a capital M. Two, I didn't want to hear him complainin' any more about this Jeanne lady or how he was going to 'kill her,' because I didn't even know that he had a wife or girlfriend in the first place and I was pissed off about that."

"And the third reason, Ms. Smythe?"

Ms. Smythe sat straight up, seething. "The third reason was that he was bad in bed, had a tiny, limp dick, couldn't hold it for more than four seconds, and I didn't want to go out with the cheap shit anymore anyhow."

The jury had a tough time with that. All twelve heads suddenly bent down as they found a sudden interest in their shoes, their notepads, or the floor, but none of us missed the way some of those horribly naughty jurors' shoulders shook with laughter.

The old, white, male judge did not crack even a tiny smile.

And that about wrapped up the first testimony.

After Ms. Smythe's testimony, we had a little break. At this time, Slick Dick's young girlfriend with the gaping blouse and burgeoning breasts whacked him on the head with her purse and stormed out. He called her name in a strangled, pleading voice, but she didn't stop, her skinny hips swaying her good-bye. My cheering section laughed, and one of them called out, "Want to join our 'I Hate Jared' group?"

Jared caught my eye and I could see hatred in them. I gave him a big ole grin, then jiggled my glasses.

The next witness was the doctor who treated Slick Dick. Dr. Bernard Wilson was about six-feet two-inches tall, skinny as could be, and African-American. He wore glasses and had white hair mixed in with the black. His gold wedding ring stood out against his skin. When William Sheridan Stanton III approached him and reintroduced himself, I could tell that the III and Dr. Wilson had already gone a few rounds and the good doctor did not care for him.

Perhaps it was the way the good doctor crossed his arms across his chest when the III approached him. Perhaps it was the way he leaned back in his chair and lowered his lids, as if speaking to a spoiled schoolboy. Perhaps it was the way Dr. Wilson insisted on calling William Sheridan Stanton III "young man" in his deep, authoritative, baritone voice that clued me in.

It's but a humble guess on my part.

I glanced at the jury. They were nice, normal people. It was not hard to deduce who they would like better between the good doctor and the snobby III.

"Dr. Wilson, can you tell the jury here what you saw when Jared Nunley came to your hospital, Saint John's, on the night of April 28, 2007?"

"Of course. Mr. Nunley's penis was slightly red."

"Slightly red?" William Sheridan Stanton III almost choked. "*Slightly red*? You said in your deposition that Mr. Nunley's penis was '*red*.' "

"That's right, young man, I did," the doctor said.

"Now, sir, you're saying that his penis was *slightly* red." The III looked flustered. Poor the III.

The doctor stared at William Sheridan Stanton III. Waiting.

The jury stared at William Sheridan Stanton III.

Waiting.

"Well?" he said to the doctor.

"Well, what, young man?" the doctor snapped.

"You said in your deposition that Mr. Nunley's penis was red, now you're saying that it was 'slightly red.' Which is it?"

The doctor shook his head in exasperation. "Must we engage in an argument over a red or slightly red penis?"

The III looked like he would blow his top and he was now *slightly* red, too. "Judge, please direct this hostile witness to answer the question."

"He answered it, counselor, didn't you hear it? Red, slightly red. We got it. Now move on."

The III's head would soon fly off, I was sure of it, he was so mad. "Dr. Wilson, please tell the jury about the *extensive* welts on my client."

"The welts?" The good doctor raised his eyebrows and stroked his jaw, as though he couldn't remember something so insignificant. "The welllllts. Hmm."

The III flushed more than *slightly* red. I wondered if that was the shade of Slick Dick's penis? Perhaps I could point that out to the jury? Look, I could say, Slick Dick's dick was about the color of his attorney's face. There. Does that help?

"Yes, the welts!"

The doctor pursed his lips. "Yessss, the welts. There were welts." He paused. "I think."

"You think?" the III almost shouted this. He got control of himself by breathing like a dragon through his nose. "Can you elaborate?"

Gross, I thought. Must we hear about a welted penis? Two of the jurors took a moment to wrinkle their noses up.

The doctor explained. "The welts on Mr. Nunley's penis were minor."

The III made a sound as if he'd swallowed his tongue and it

was tickling his intestine. "Dr. Wilson, may I remind you of your testimony in your deposition. You said that there were welts, and I quote, 'covering, covering,'" he almost shouted that word. "'*Covering*' Mr. Nunley's penis."

"That's true, young man," the doctor said.

The III gasped and gurgled. "How can you now say they were minor?"

"Easy," the doctor said. "I said the welts were minor, because they were. Welts are caused by any number of things. Allergies. Exposure to certain plants. Stress. They rise, they flare up, they go away. People have different reactions to welts. Mr. Nunley's physical reactions were minor. He did not go into shock. He did not lose his ability to breathe. He did not vomit. He did not have stomach problems or stomach upset. He had little pain—"

"Thank you, Doctor. I didn't ask you what did *not* happen to my client—"

"But you obviously needed to know, young man."

"Ask that that be stricken from the record," the III almost shouted to the judge. He ran a hand over his glob of hair.

The judge said, "The jury will not discuss further what the plaintiff's lawyer needed to know in regard to the welts on the penis."

Roy snickered. I heard myself making these little gasping sounds, because I thought my laughter would sneak out of my mouth.

"You said in your testimony," the III accused the doctor, "that Mr. Nunley's penis was swollen when he arrived in your emergency room."

I noticed that several jurors had their arms crossed in front of them now, too, copying the good doctor.

"Yes, his penis was swollen."

"How swollen?" the III said, his voice high. Beads of sweat outlined his hairline.

"Well, it's hard to tell. Mr. Nunley is not particularly well endowed. I determined the next morning that his penis size is somewhat below average. And when he arrived there was some swelling of his penis. It was about . . . I'd say . . . maybe . . ." The good doctor stared up into the air, as though trying to remember the size of the below-average penis. "I'd say he was swollen up about seventy-five percent larger than normal by the time he got to the hospital. He complained that he couldn't urinate."

"Couldn't urinate?" The III grabbed onto that one real quick. "That must have been painful, Doctor. To have an allergic reaction so strong he couldn't urinate."

The doctor looked at William Sheridan Stanton III as if he was speaking to a dim-witted worm. "I think he was uncomfortable. When we can't urinate it is *uncomfortable.*" He said that last sentence real slowly.

"But for Mr. Nunley, who couldn't urinate for hours, that would be painful. Mr. Nunley—"

"That wasn't the case, young man, as I have told you three other times during my very, very long deposition." The good doctor paused here and bent his head a bit to emphasize this, as though he was reprimanding the III. "We offered Mr. Nunley a catheter for his urination issues, but he refused. A catheter would have relieved any discomfort, and I stress the word *discomfort,* that he had in that department."

The III decided to change tactics.

"So he was in pain," William Sheridan Stanton III said. He sneaked that word in super fast. "If I could ask you one more—"

"Excuse me," the doctor rapped out. "Mr. Nunley was uncomfortable, as I've stated before." He leaned forward at the podium and pointed his finger at the III. "*Uncomfortable, young man.* He was not in pain. And, the swelling went down almost immediately, as did the welts, after we gave Mr. Nunley a dose of allergy medicine and a little over-the-counter cream. He was able to urinate and we told him to go home. People have allergic reactions all the time. They go home, they rest, they're fine."

"That's all, Dr. Wilson." William Sheridan Stanton III cut him off, sat down and started scribbling. I imagined he was writing,

"Slick Dick had an allergic reaction in his penis. Doctor says he was uncomfortable, *uncomfortable, young man.*"

My dear Roy spoke to the doctor next. You could tell the doctor and Roy were buddies. Roy got him to say three more times, that Slick Dick had no, no, no permanent injuries, that the swelling went down almost immediately, almost immediately, almost immediately after the medication was administered, that the welts disappeared, disappeared, disappeared and that there was no pain, no pain, no pain.

"But, Doctor," Roy said. "Jared Nunley stayed overnight in the hospital. Overnight."

The doctor sighed. "Jared Nunley *insisted* on staying overnight in the hospital. Insisted. We told him repeatedly that it was unnecessary, that he could take the cream with him and take an additional allergy pill with him, but he refused. Because the patient was so unglued mentally from this event and, fearing a lawsuit of some sort because he kept threatening it over and over again, we wheeled him down the corridor in a wheelchair, as he also insisted, and put him in a room for the night."

"Were there any complications during the night?"

"None," the doctor said. "However, he called the nurses in about every fifteen minutes to check on his genitalia because at various points he thought he was, in his own words, 'relapsing.'" He also ordered green Jell-O four times."

"But there was no relapse?"

"None. He was even able to urinate. Therefore, he was not even uncomfortable."

"Thank you, Doctor," Roy said. "You have a nice day."

The doctor nodded at Roy, the judge, and the jurors, and left the stand. When he passed me, I kid you not, he winked at me.

Next up were several of Slick Dick's girlfriends that he had slept with during our time together. William Sheridan Stanton III had objected to their presence on numerous occasions during pretrial events, but was always overruled. The III protested again but Roy convinced the judge that I had temporarily lost all rational thought and reasoning after finding out about all these girlfriends and that we had a right to establish that there were, indeed, other women, which went to my mental state at the time of the alleged peanut oil incident. Plus, we needed to establish that Slick Dick had had physical problems with sex before this particular incident, as he was asking for money to compensate him for this "new" problem.

The judge nodded his old, white head and we proceeded.

In fact, we proceeded through seven women over the next few days. Seven. Most of the cheering section.

Roy established the women's names, ages, occupations, and how they met Jared. My, was he sexually busy! He met one at an art gallery, three online, one through a sleezy friend, another through a dating service.

One of the girlfriends called him a "raging prick" on the stand.

Another tried to kickbox him on the way out and only missed because William Sheridan Stanton III stood in front of Slick Dick and got kicked himself.

The third gal detailed how he told her he worked for the CIA which is why he couldn't see her for weeks at a time. "He even told me about a couple of secret missions he had been on in Guatemala. That he had to run through jungles, hide in caves," she snorted. "One time he claimed to escape a firing squad."

The fourth said Slick Dick told her he'd studied to be a priest for two years before quitting because he wanted a wife and kids.

All of them said they had asked him if he were married or involved with another woman at the time and he had said no. No. No. No. There was no other woman in his life.

Roy established that he had been sleeping with, on average, three of us at any one time and only sporadically wore condoms. I had had myself tested again for all STDs and had tested negative. I had dodged a bullet—many bullets here.

As Slick Dick had alleged in his complaint that I had caused him physical harm, that his sex life had been adversely affected, Roy asked all of the women about Slick Dick's "prowess" in bed.

All of the women had the same complaint as Ms. Smythe. An attorney said she'd had more fun writing legal briefs than she'd had with sex with Jared. An electrician said she'd wished for one of her electrical tools to give him a longer "spark." "It takes less time for me to cross two wires than it did for Jared to . . . how shall I say it? . . . *fulfill* himself."

But the last witness summed it all up real tight: He had penis problems. Problems getting it up and keeping it up. Problems with ejaculation. Way too soon ejaculation. The jury also heard that, in every situation, he blamed the woman. She wasn't as experienced as he was in bed. Too fat. Didn't have big enough boobs. Couldn't sexually excite him like the other women he'd been with before.

"It would have been easier to have sex with a raccoon than with Jared Nunley," she seethed. "A *rabid* raccoon."

The jurors gave up, as did everyone else, except the old, white, male judge who did not crack a smile. Laughter filled that courtroom, ricocheting off the floor and the ceiling and back and around again. My cheering section made hissing sounds like raccoons. When I looked back one of them had her hands up like paws with a crazed expression on her face like a rabid raccoon.

Wanting to continue to appear to be the wronged but stoic and saddened victim, it took all I had not to laugh. In fact, to ensure that I didn't, I stared down at my blue flats. Yes, flats. I had reduced myself to wearing flats with my frumpy suits.

But here is the truth: I thought the whole thing so funny, I darned near wet my knickers.

CHAPTER 26

During a break in the trial, Roy and I retreated to a small room inside the courthouse. He made notes in his folder and made a few calls, while I stared out the window.

It had been fascinating to hear the testimony of the women. What a complete loser Jared was.

But I had to face the same hard questions I'd been wrestling with for months: Why had I hooked up with him in the first place? Why on Earth had I stayed with Jared as long as I did? Why hadn't I realized he was cheating?

But I knew the answer. I stayed with Jared as long as I did because I was lonely and tired of being alone. I hadn't realized he was cheating, because it never occurred to me that he would. Not because I trusted him not to cheat. Not because I thought he loved me dearly. No, it never occurred to me that Jared would cheat because I didn't really put that much thought into him in the first place.

I worked a seventy- to eighty-hour week and I traveled extensively for my job. I had hardly been home long enough to get a good look at him. I wasn't in love with him, hadn't even loved him as a friend. He was a break for me, someone to sleep with, someone to go to dinner with and a few trips. But I had never looked to him for anything else. It had never occurred to me to open myself up to him emotionally. I hadn't paid attention to him. Hadn't carved out time for him. In that particular area, Jared had been right. Did it give him license to cheat repeatedly? No. Not at all, but I certainly hadn't been around to make sure it didn't happen.

That made me a cold person, didn't it?

I thought about Jay. He wouldn't cheat on me because he simply wasn't that type of person. But even the thought of him cheating made me feel like crying a river of tears.

I stared out at the city again. If there was ever the remotest chance I could be with Jay, I would not make the same mistake. I would not work long hours. I would not ignore him. I would not put him last. He would be first. I would let him know every day that I loved him and always would love him.

The next day at the trial, Slick Dick appeared deflated and defeated. I wondered how much his attorney had charged his lavish trust fund so far. The very idea amused me to no end. I fiddled with my beige blouse and tugged it over the waistline of my long blue skirt. How I missed lipstick!

The police officers who arrested me took the stand next, one by one.

Officer Marychek was first. When William Sheridan Stanton III asked if he recognized anyone in the room, he indicated me.

"I recognize Ms. Stewart over here." He wiggled his fingers in a hello.

Officer Marychek is an African-American man, over six feet tall, with a giant smile. He wears a gold cross around his neck and is a stand-up comic in downtown Chicago clubs. He had asked me for more details of my condom crime as we zoomed to the police station in the squad car because he said he needed new material for his routines. He'd had to pull over when we were halfway there because he couldn't see through the laugh-tears in his eyes.

"Officer Marychek, when you questioned Ms. Stewart did she admit to putting peanut oil into Mr. Nunley's condoms?"

I could tell that Officer Marychek liked William Sheridan Stanton III about as much as the good doctor did. Police officers are not known for liking snotty, rich daddy's boys with globby hair who think they're special and better than everyone else.

"Yes, she did."

"Can you elaborate?"

He shrugged, like the incident was a nonincident in his mind. "Not really."

"Not really?" the III hissed.

"No, not really," Marychek said again, raising his eyebrows.

"I want it noted that the police officer is not cooperating," the III said.

"He's cooperating," the old, white male judge said. "Question asked, question answered. Continue."

The III glared at Marychek. "What happened after she admitted her crime?"

"My partner and I didn't call it a crime, counselor, but we did read her her rights." He paused. "Sort of."

"What do you mean, sort of?" the III huffed.

Marychek squirmed a bit and smiled big. He was such a nice man. "We read her the rights, but we kept laughing. I mean, the line, 'You are entitled to an attorney' was funny because we started making jokes about Ms. Stewart hiring an attorney because of a penis attack."

The jury laughed.

"My partner called her a Condom Criminal. That was so darn funny." He chuckled, sat back up straight and tried to look stoic, but it didn't work. That smile beamed out again. "We talked about whether a hot-glue gun could be considered a weapon and should we call the SWAT team in to have it confiscated from Ms. Stewart's house."

"We got it, Officer," the III said, through clenched teeth. "What happened after her rights were read?"

"My partner and I, Officer Tobiason, had a problem with Ms. Stewart at that point."

"A problem?" For the first time, the III looked delighted. Obviously, the officer had not shared this in his deposition.

"Yeah. Officer Tobiason and I were laughing, I mean, we were *really* laughing. I thought Tobi was going to wet his pants. I called her the Peanut Oil Princess and the Lubricant Lady and Eerily Excellent Eyedropper Woman. Ms. Stewart here had used an eyedropper to get the oil into the condoms, isn't that clever? Women are so smart, they think of things men never could." Out popped the beaming smile again, and a laugh. All of the men on the jury nodded in agreement. "So Tobi starts pretending he's shooting me with an eyedropper."

The jury liked that image. I heard chuckles.

"We had a tough time getting the handcuffs on because we were laughing so hard. Tobi couldn't even stand up. Fact is, Ms. Stewart here had to put them on herself."

Clearly William Sheridan Stanton III was expecting a different answer than the one given, judging by the way his chiseled jaw dropped.

"But she admitted to assaulting a man. That's not funny," the III bellowed.

"You had to be there," Officer Marychek said. He nodded at the jurors who grinned back. "It was funny hearing about how she used that Exacto knife on the condom wrappers, trust me. She had to make a teeny-tiny slit to extract each condom and the hot-glue gun zipped it right back up and—"

"Objection!" III yelled.

"Objection sustained," the judge drawled.

"Did Ms. Stewart admit that she knew Mr. Nunley was allergic to peanut oil?"

"Nope. We did not discuss Mr. Nunley's allergies or any past sexual performance problems."

The III looked so furious I thought the top of his head might detach and explode through the ceiling. "No further questions!"

Roy was next up. "So, Ms. Stewart cooperated with both you and your partner, is that right?"

"Yes, sir, that's right. She was very polite. Offered us coffee and juice when we arrived, and cookies." He nodded at me. I noted his look of approval. "They were sugar cookies. Delicious."

"So she put up no resistance then?"

"Nah. She was very polite, friendly. If I wasn't arresting her, I'd have her over to my house for a barbeque and to meet my mother. She said she had recently found out that Mr. Nunley had been cheating on her for two years with a bunch of gals, which is so dangerous, man, trust me. In my line of work I hear about this all the time. It's threatening someone's life when you cheat on them, *threatening their life*. You could give them herpes, AIDS; people freak out, I'm tellin' ya, they freak—"

"Objection!" the III was bright red and livid.

Slick Dick covered his face with his hands.

"Anyhow," Marychek continued. "She was scared to death. The plaintiff also took nineteen hundred in cash and left with her mountain bike." He turned to Slick Dick. "She wants the mountain bike back."

Officer Tobiason nodded at me after he was sworn in. Officer Tobiason is huge, Hispanic, and looks like a street thug in uniform. His mother is Hispanic, he told me, dad is English. I had had time to chat with him while other perpetrators were being checked into the police station. Seems he loves clothes and loved my shoes. This launched us into a discreet discussion, in Spanish, of shoes and style and evolving fashion in this country and have you looked at the spring styles on the runways recently! Fabulous, we both agreed, positively fab.

His testimony didn't take long. "Let me tell you something, counselor," Tobiason growled at the III, leaning forward and pointing at him. "We're talking peanut oil here, buddy. *Peanut oil*. We're talking about a man who got a rash on his dick. Hell, a rash is a small price to pay for a man who cheats on his lady. I got a wife and seven kids. If I cheated on my wife I wouldn't even have a chance to say, 'boo.' She'd have a hit man at my house that afternoon, so give me a goddamn break. Got it? Give me a goddamn break."

The court took a goddamn break.

It was time for my sworn testimony first thing the next morning. I pushed my chair back when I was called to the stand and deliberately got a little bit stuck trying to get out of my seat. Next I banged into the table, and tried to open the little gate to the witness stand the wrong way. I clunked up to the witness chair and fumbled with my glasses.

I raised my right hand, made it tremble a bit, swore to tell the truth, and nothing but the truth so help me God, and I swore to myself that I would never again in my life wear a yucky green suit and clunky shoes with nylons that I had deliberately run a little bit in the back. I did swear that.

I also had my hair back in a badly done bun and wore no makeup and no jewelry except a cross.

The III stepped up and I wiped the tears from my eyes and tried to look scared to death of the III. I could tell by the way he and Slick Dick were glaring at me that they saw through this whole thing. That delighted me further. I was told later that I looked exhausted and flushed and very victimlike.

William Sheridan Stanton III asked me the usual questions for a while. He was almost wet he was so slick. Again, I thought of mucus. I stole a glance at the jury. At least half of them had their arms crossed on their chests again.

He placed one hand on the jury box, one hand in his pocket.

"Ms. Stewart, you have admitted to putting peanut oil in my client's condoms, is that true?"

I tried to look confused. "Yes, I admitted it."

"Well, we know now that he is not mildly allergic to peanut oil, his allergy is severe. He ended up in the hospital—"

"He is *mildly* allergic," I snapped. "The hospital tried to send him home after giving him allergy medication, but Jared refused to leave." I shut up quick. I reminded myself to stay victimlike. I bent my head, as if the lawyer intimidated me.

"Your Honor, please instruct the witness to answer the question!"

His Honor was on it. "I didn't hear a question, counselor."

The III opened and closed his mouth like a piranha might.

"Ms. Stewart, are you sorry about the mental and emotional anguish that you caused my client?"

Oh, dear. An easy question, but I could not be honest in my answer. "I am sorry that Sli—" Whoops! Mustn't screw up now. "I am sorry, yes. It sounds like this incident has caused Jared further sexual dysfunction and performance issues. It also sounds like he was terribly frightened because he needed an ambulance to take him . . . his . . . him to the hospital and he insisted on a wheelchair. And I'm sorry that he was not able to pee for an hour. That would be uncomfortable. Very *uncomfortable*." I paused on that word. "Still, I was acting out of fear. Stark fear. I could have gotten AIDS from him. I could have been stuck with a lifelong disease. I could have been sterilized myself—"

"That's all," the III said hastily and retreated.

I wiped two tears away with the palms of both hands, careful to pull on the corners of my eyes so that I looked particularly miserable.

I peeked at the jury.

They smiled with such sympathy at me.

I smiled a wobbly smile right back at 'em.

Roy was up next. Where had I met Slick Dick? How long had we dated? What did we do together?

"Had you and Mr. Nunley broken up before the incident with the condom?"

"No." Snuffle, snuffle.

"But Mr. Nunley said you had broken up."

"Mr. Nunley never told *me* we had broken up." I was so proud of the tremor in my voice!

"When did you find out that Jared had sex with Ms. Smythe, plus Marisa Kube, Nancy Tettler, Anisha Cable, Kristi Rottendam, Leesa Buddler, Bethy Sattleson, Carrie Mortenger, Bam-Bam Wham, Susie Come, and Latisha Corrinne?"

"I didn't know their names but I found out that Sli—" I coughed. "I found out that Jared had been repeatedly unfaithful to me the day after I found out he was cheating on me with Gabrielle Smythe. We had a huge fight. He seemed proud of cheating on me. He told me he had had sex with other women in my house, too, in my bed, and several times in my car when he would borrow it for the night, or when he took it for the weekend, supposedly to go and visit his family. It wasn't a big car, either."

"How did you feel when you found out that Jared had cheated on you?"

"I cried. I couldn't stop crying. I cried for days."

That wasn't quite true. I may have dropped two tears of frustration and humiliation. Tiny detail.

"Were you worried?"

"No."

"No?" Roy looked nervous. This was not the answer we'd practiced.

I allowed my voice to raise an octave. "I was petrified. Jared and I had both been tested for all STDs before we began sleeping together. I thought we were in a committed relationship and I was on the pill. We didn't use protection. I was petrified that I had contracted a disease—possibly AIDS or herpes. I am hoping to one day have children and I was scared to death that if I was already infected with some sexually transmitted disease I might be sterilized. I was crushed, humiliated. Furious."

"What did you do?"

"I told Jared to leave and he said he would, but he needed a couple of days to find a place to live and refused to get out of the house."

"What happened when he refused to leave your home?"

"I faked being sick the next morning and when he left, I used an Exacto knife to open the wrappers of the many condoms he had in his wallet. I put peanut oil into them using an eyedropper. I glued the condoms back up with a hot-glue gun, and put them back in his wallet."

"You admit that you put peanut oil in his condoms?"

"Yes, I admit it. I was so . . ." I managed to cry here. I was so proud of myself. Why had I not become an actress? "I couldn't believe he had cheated on me—especially not with that many people. I thought we had a great relationship. I paid for everything. I took care of the house, his laundry. I cleaned up after him, took his rat to the vet, gave him birthday parties, let all of his relatives stay in our house whenever they wanted. . . . I was good to him, so good, and I couldn't figure out why he cheated." I let my voice go up sort of pitifully here, bent my head, and pushed my messy hair back from my cheeks.

"Did you mean to hurt Jared?"

"I didn't hurt him. I've never hurt anyone in my life. I can't *believe* it still. I thought he was f-f-f-faithful. I couldn't see straight, I was so upset and hurt and all those women. *All those women*," I gasped.

"But you knew he was allergic to peanut oil, didn't you?"

"I knew he was slightly allergic to peanut oil, and his reaction had always been mild. One time he touched peanut butter on a cruise I took him on to celebrate his fortieth birthday and his finger got a little red and irritated. Another time, when I took him on a skiing trip, his favorite thing to do, he ate a cookie with peanut butter in it. His lips became a little red and a welt appeared."

"So you knew his reaction would not be serious."

"That's correct."

"How much peanut oil did you put in each condom?"

"Two drops." Okay. Maybe there were three drops. Maybe there were four. Or five. All right, all right, you got me. There were seven drops. Another wee detail not worthy of mention.

"That's it. I was so mad, so upset, so scared that I might have contracted a disease . . . I thought my whole life was falling apart . . . I was so emotional and wanted to get back at him a little bit for what he did. I thought his—" I paused so delicately as if my moral-self struggled valiantly and couldn't get the word "penis" out of my innocent mouth. "I thought his penis might get a little itchy, a little irritated, and that would be that." I sniffed.

"Thank you, Ms. Stewart," Roy said.

And that was that.

Roy called Slick Dick up to the stand again.

"Mr. Nunley, is it true that you had no lasting physical problems after this event, that the swelling of your penis went down, and the welts disappeared within two hours of contact with the peanut oil, and the hospital staff told you to go home?"

Slick Dick shifted in his chair. His left eye started to twitch. "Well . . . uh . . . well . . ."

"Will the court direct the witness to answer the question?"

"Answer the question," the old, white male judge demanded.

"I'll ask it again. Mr. Nunley, isn't it true that the swelling of your penis went down and all welts disappeared within two hours of your coming into contact with the peanut oil?"

"Yes."

"Is it true that there were no lasting physical side effects at all."

"Uh, yes." Shift, shift. Itchy bottom again.

"Mr. Nunley, you have admitted to cheating repeatedly on my client during your relationship, correct?"

Shift. "Yes," said so quiet.

"Mr. Nunley, you are asking my client to reimburse you an ungodly sum of money for performance problems supposedly caused by this incident, yet isn't it true that you had potency issues and erectile dysfunction before this particular problem with the condom?"

"Only a little," he whispered, then twitched. "Guys do, you know."

And that's when Roy went over the testimony of every single gal he'd already had on the stand, repeating word for word what they'd said about Slick Dick's potency and that rabid raccoon.

Buried, I thought. Slick Dick was buried.

"So I'll repeat the question, sir," Roy said. "Is it true that you had potency issues and erectile dysfunction before any of this happened with Ms. Stewart?"

"Yes," Slick Dick gasped. Twitch. Twitch.

"I'm sorry. I couldn't hear the plaintiff in regard to his erectile dysfunction. Could he repeat his answer?"

The III did not even bother objecting.

"Yes," Slick Dick said. "Yes." He leaned back hard against the chair, his face red and pale at the same time. Twitch.

Slick Dick, in open court, had been humiliated. Filleted. Ripped. Destroyed.

What a prick.

The judge gave the jury instructions. The jury left the room.

I snuck a look over at Slick Dick. He was clearly ill and vomitous.

He got up to leave with the III. On cue, his ex-girlfriends stood all together in one row, and held up the middle fingers of both hands.

I leaned back in my chair and raised my fist.

They raised theirs.

To victory.

Roy and I chatted a bit. I told him that he had been brilliant, that I knew he had done his best and I loved him.

I figured the jury would come up with a bunch of money I'd have to hand over to Slick Dick, but I was still glad I was here. There was no way I was going to pay a penny to him without a fight. Sometimes you've got to stand up for yourself, even if you know you're going to get nailed. This was the time to stand.

A couple of Roy's lawyer friends came up to chat with us. We decided to go to lunch together and headed for the courtroom doors.

We were stopped by the bailiff. He put his cell phone back in his pocket and said. "Jury is back. Good luck, ma'am."

I stood there, stunned.

Roy didn't move. He shook his big head, his ponytail scratching his back. "Shit," he said.

"Damn," said one of the lawyer friends, patting him on the back. "You tried it well, though, Roy. You did a great job."

"I'm sorry, Jeanne," another one of the friends said, whose ponytail was longer than Roy's. "I'm real sorry."

I had stood. I had been nailed. That's life.

At least it was over.

CHAPTER 27

"**A**ll rise," the bailiff called.

We rose.

The old, white, male judge came in and sat down. "You jurors don't mess around, do you?" he croaked. "Well done. I hate to waste time. You have a verdict?"

The jury forewoman rose. She was one of the three African-Americans. Good, I thought. They had elected a woman. "We, the jury, find that the defendant, Jeanne Stewart . . ."

I held my breath. Roy held his breath. I swear I could hear Slick Dick's girlfriends holding their breaths.

She smiled at me, her teeth shiny and white. "Not guilty."

Pandemonium. Absolute pandemonium.

The noise was deafening. People were hooting and hollering and clapping. The cheering section was on their feet, arms flying in the air, hugging each other. I figured after this they'd all go to lunch together and become best girlfriends.

I sagged against my chair.

"Holy shit!" Roy whispered. "*Holy shit!*"

The judge banged his gavel again and again. "I will not have disorder in my courtroom! Sit down! Sit down!"

"Further," the forewoman said, when the noise lessened to a dull roar, "we find that Jeanne Stewart owes nothing to the plaintiff, Jared Nunley."

It was like being in the middle of a pack of hysterical football fans whose team had just won the Super Bowl. I could hardly hear myself think through the rollicking waves of noise. Roy hugged me tight.

Slick Dick's shocked face was even pastier than before. The color of white glue, in fact, and his body looked as if it was shrinking inside his expensive suit. He rubbed two trembling hands over his drooping face, and glanced over at me. I grinned like a Cheshire cat, took off my glasses with a flourish, and waved them in the air. "I want my mountain bike back," I shouted with glee.

"Order, order!" The judge pounded the gavel down until the courtroom came to a semblance of order.

"Ms. Stewart." The old, white, male judge gazed down at me, real serious and all, but I saw his eyes twinkling. Humor ripens with age, me thinks.

I stood up. So did Roy.

"I will caution you against blending peanut oil and condoms together again, young woman."

I agreed. "Out of respect for you and this system I promise not to mix peanut oil and condoms together ever again."

I grinned at the jury.

They grinned back. The professor with the crazy hair gave me the thumbs-up. The skinny-as-a-skeleton juror flipped me the victory sign with two fingers. Two of the women raised their fists and shook them.

But the old, white, male judge, possessor of a penis, wasn't done. He slowly moved his old head until he was glowering at Slick Dick, the twinkling eyes now hard and cold, his old voice crackling with indignation. "Mr. Nunley!" He paused, his face rigid. "Mr. Nunley, sometimes we make very bad decisions. You, son, have made an atrocious amount of bad decisions. Currently, however, your worst decision was to take this case to court. I order you to pay all of Ms. Stewart's legal fees within thirty days and all court costs. If you appeal this ruling, and lose, you will pay Mr. Sass twice what you now owe him." Another cheer went up in the courtroom. I could hear the girlfriends cackling and high-fiving.

"My fees have skyrocketed," Roy whispered. "*Skyrocketed.*"

The judge pounded the gavel. "Further, Mr. Nunley, you will return her mountain bike."

That old, white, male judge addressed me again. "Ms. Stewart." His crinkled lips parted, his white dentures shining. "Enjoy the rest of your life."

Wham! That gavel came down for the final time.

Before I left the courtroom and faced all the cameras and reporters I slipped into a bathroom and changed my clothes. Off went the dull suit, the dull heels, and the dull blouse. On went a bright red bra and a gauzy blouse with a cool pattern that hinted at the red bra. On went these way cool jeans and three strands of shiny gold and red necklaces and dangly earrings and eight, count 'em, *eight* colorful jangly bracelets.

On went mascara and bright red lipstick and, finally, the shoes.

Bright red heels of course, with spirals of gold.

Victory is red hot. Red hot, I tell you.

I smiled before the cameras and reporters and answered their questions, throwing out answers like:

Women must always fight for their mountain bikes.

And: Welts, redness, and rashes—cheating men should watch their asses.

And: Long live peanut oil.

And: Women unite!

And: Remember! Exacto knives are not only for crafts!

And: Every woman needs a hot-glue gun!

But while I was smiling, I thought of my dear mother.

My heart ached for her. I knew it always would. But I smiled brighter because that's what grieving people have to do. They have to cover their grief up and pack it away and not burden everyone, but I ached all over.

I missed my mother. I missed how she smoked a cigar each year on her birthday to remind herself that she was still a wild and crazy gal. She'd get about one-fifth of the way through before she'd "had enough" wild and crazy stuff and tell us to bring on the cake.

I missed how she gave me crosses throughout my life and how she'd yell at me about how I worked too much, looked too thin, and that my taste in men was "abominable." "The men you choose are fit for one thing, Jeanne: Licking their own toes." I missed her dedication to her students, and how she railed on them if she felt they weren't giving their all. She did not believe in being politically correct and coddling children's self-esteem. She believed in truth and honesty and discipline.

All the parents wanted their child in her class.

I flat-out missed her.

And I knew I always would. It would never, ever leave me.

The flight back to Oregon was uneventful.

The white bald guy sitting next to me, with a booming salesman-like voice, and rancid breath who initially told me about his wife and *highly* successful children and how he was a "pillar—a *gigantic* pillar both financially and morally," in his home town, and a man who stood for "family values, and *traditional* families, with a wife who knows her place at home and none of this gay stuff," tried to pick up on me, but I told him that, gee, *I* was gay, and I couldn't wait to get back to my girlfriend and get naked with her.

He hardly knew what to do with that one. I'm sure he wanted to tell me that I was immoral, but, hey. Hard to do that when you're a moral pillar and hit on someone with a wife and kids at home.

"Do traditional family values include cheating on your wife?" I asked him. I glanced down. "I think you have a tiny pillar."

He looked like he was going to choke on his own rancid breath, and I was left to read my book, write in my journal, and think, as I watched miles and miles of open land pass below me like a beige and green quilt.

I thought about Jay and my mother and Becky and Emmaline and Jay and Soman and Bradon and Jay and Rosvita and Jay and the Lopezes.

I thought about my life.

How things had gone fairly well for me for twenty plus years, with the exception of my beautiful father dying.

I had crashed and burned in a mighty emotional fire with the loss of Johnny and Ally.

I had gone from living a life to merely surviving for the last twelve years.

I had crashed again, and yet . . . this time, I had managed to crash, burn, and find friends. Find a home. Find a purpose. Find depth. Find a life.

And I had finally found my soul. It was battered and exhausted and I knew a part of me would always be lonely because of losing Johnny and Ally and my sweet mother, and father, but there it was. I had, despite my initial desire to drive my Bronco into the Pacific Ocean, created a life for myself. A real life. With all the mess and joy and laughter and hysteria that life is about.

Now all I needed was Jay.

I awoke to Rosvita and Becky hovering over me, the sun slanting through my newly formed skylight in gold tunnels.

"I hope that you are not diseased," Rosvita said, a worried look creasing her features. A red flower half the size of her face was tucked behind her left ear. She put her white gloved hands on my temples. "There are certain diseases that are defined by exhaustion. For example, bird flu, latent measles, Legionnaire's . . ."

I stretched, loving the feel of my own sheets and my own light blue comforter from Therese. It was so delicious to be back in my little house. That I would not have to give it up for a cold jail cell and a roommate named Madge made every nook and cranny and tile all the more precious to me. "Rosvita, I don't think I have a disease."

"Maybe. Maybe not."

"Here, Jeanne, I'll help you get up," Becky said. She did not look like a human death stick anymore. She'd put on a little weight which made her look a lot healthier. Even her eyes were clear and there was a tiny sparkle in them. Love'll do that to you, I thought. Love and Rosvita.

"Are you ready?" Rosvita asked.

"Ready for what?" I asked. Gall. I braced myself. What did I need to be ready for this time?

"Your welcome-home breakfast," Rosvita said, her silver bracelets jingling on her wrists.

"Welcome home, Jeanne," Becky said. "We missed you."

Rosvita and Becky had set a table on my back deck with pink plates, crystal glasses shaped like giant roses, five miniature daffodil bouquets and a dozen pink candles.

The ladies had outdone themselves. We put on our jackets and hats and had eggs Benedict, squared and spiced potatoes, fresh orange juice, chocolate muffins, banana bread, and carrot soup (a recipe that Rosvita had wanted to try for months).

We held up our crystal glasses for a toast.

"Cheers to our friend, Jeanne," Becky said. "She soared, she flew, and she did not let herself get eaten by a vulture."

"To victory," Rosvita said, her eyes getting all filled up with tears. "To victory over a scum-eating scoundrel."

"Cheers." We all clinked our glasses.

I touched my lips to the champagne then let 'em rip. The tears I'd saved up for too long gushed out of my eyes and rushed down my cheeks like a burst dam. I caught each tear with my champagne glass and drank no more.

Rosvita muttered something about hoping I wasn't having yet another nervous breakdown, because I definitely had some of the signs and symptoms. She started crying because I was crying. Becky got up and hugged me and blew her nose right by my ear.

"Is it . . ." Becky said, "is it the governor?" At my pained expression she buried her head in my curls.

"He'll come around, Jeanne, don't you worry, now, don't you worry."

But I would. I did. I worried.

Hours later, after Becky and Rosvita left, I cleaned up my deck, then settled in a chaise lounge with a cup of lemon tea in one hand and my cordless phone in the other. I could hear a breeze skipping through the tops of the trees. It was good to be home. The only problem I currently had was that my body had many locked up orgasms and my heart was scared to death that it would not see Jay again.

I left a message on Jay's answering machine before my nerves gave way and I collapsed into a shaking, quivering mass of fear. "Hello, Governor. This is your ex-communications director. I'm calling to get your opinion on a memo to see if it's phrased correctly. The memo says: 'To whom it may concern, the governor of the state of Oregon, Jay Kendall, is requested at the home of Jeanne Stewart as soon as possible. Please come for dinner and dessert.' "

I hoped.

Oh, how I hoped.

I went running in the late afternoon when the sun was on its way down to sleep. I thought about the endless hours of the campaign. I thought about my speech to the advertisers when I told them they were pointless, *pointless*! I thought about keeping Johnny and Ally Johnna in my heart, but not letting grief rule my life any longer. I thought about my mom and antique-shopping and coffee and her fabulous clothes and her rumbling, echoing laugh. I thought about the trial and Slick Dick. I thought about my new home and what kind of job I should get next.

And when I got to the place where I had tackled Jay, I stood completely still. I remembered the crash into Jay, the roll on the ground, my fear, telling him my problems, how he listened, and how he made love to me recently, right on that spot, our lips never leaving each other's. I thought about how he held me when I slept, how he felt when I hugged him, how I trusted him, loved him, and wanted to dance through life with him until we were both so old all we could do is hold hands in bed and watch the animal channel.

I ran on and on and the river flowed and flowed and I did not raise the water level with any more tears. Not one.

After an hour I limped back onto my porch and stretched out my aching legs. Running is good for the soul, me thinks, good for your soul. I wanted to race in and see if Jay had left a message, but I restrained myself. I heard one of the owls hoot.

"At least you're not running naked."

I darn near jumped out of my shorts as I whipped around toward that gravelly voice.

Right there, no kidding, right on my deck, was Jay Kendall. Beautiful, kind, funny, smart Jay Kendall, who had never held it against me for tackling him naked.

Jay and I didn't leave my house much for the next few days. When we did, I had a large diamond on the third finger of my left hand and a promise to marry him here, in Weltana, in one week.

The wedding was kept secret from the press.

We were married by the local pastor, a man who had been a friend and a fly-fishing partner with Jay for years. The wedding was right by the river, right where I'd tackled Jay. I had hoped for a warm winter day and we got one. I figured that my mother had had a talk with God and insisted, *insisted*, on the sun being there.

No one could ever say *no* to my mother, and that sun shone through a soft blue sky like spun gold. Soman and Becky built this incredible white wooden archway. Bradon and Olivia went to the florist and bought huge bouquets of roses to go next to the archway (it was off season for garden roses in Oregon), and Emmaline wrapped all the surrounding trees in white satin ribbons and huge gold bows.

Donovan sang three opera songs about lifelong love that made everyone tear up and Soman sang a song from the islands about passion and mangoes that made everyone laugh. Bradon played on a mini-piano, the notes floating across the river.

I wore a red dress. Freeing, happy red. It was silk with an Audrey Hepburn-type style to it. Around my neck was the gold dolphin necklace from my father, and in my hand was one of the crosses from my mother, and a huge bunch of hot house orchids wrapped in gold ribbon that Jay gave me. On my feet were the running shoes I had on when I tackled Jay. They didn't show, but I thought they were perfect. Even better than heels.

The fir trees rustled as Jay and I said our vows. I couldn't help a few tears slipping down my cheeks, and Jay's eyes were so filled, they looked like melted blue chocolate, but we made it through, his hands in mine.

After we were pronounced man and wife we shared this passion-blasted, I'm-With-You-Forever type of kiss and we hugged for so long, the minister laughed and stepped in to wrap his arms around us followed by Soman, Becky, Emmaline, Bradon, Olivia, Rosvita, the Lopezes, Donovan, Charlie and Deidre and the kids, and Linda, Margie, Louise with their matching glasses, and everyone else clapped and laughed.

Rosvita and Donovan had set out tables covered in crisp white tablecloths on my grass and catered the event. Underneath a huge tent hung with hundreds of strands of white lights and many space heaters, we had pancakes and omelets; the Lopezes brought vegetarian burritos and Zelda brought her pies.

It was, and always will be, the happiest moment of my entire life.

* * *

Roy sent Slick Dick his bill with his new rates reflected in the balance-owed section. On the thirtieth day, as court-ordered, his check arrived.

My mountain bike also arrived from Slick Dick. It was mangled. I packaged it back up and sent it to the judge.

The judge told Slick Dick to pay me triple the cost of the bike within fourteen days or he would jail him.

I got a nice big check!

In the memo area he wrote, "Bitch."

I laughed and donated the money to a nifty afterschool science class at my mother's school.

Emmaline flipped off the lights in the loft and lit four candles. We all took our seats in our own special beanbags: Becky in blue, Soman in yellow, Bradon in green, me in purple.

She blew one candle out. "That one is for Jeanne who ran naked along a riverbank to haul herself back to a new path of independence, of contentment and hope, a path away from her scorching anger."

She blew out a second candle. "That candle is for Bradon who planted roses with his wife, *finally*, and in the process saved what was most important to him—his marriage."

"Amen to that. And thank God it's winter and I'm done plantin' roses 'til spring." Bradon sighed. "But if I have to plant a rosebush every day for the rest of my life and wear a straw hat on my bald head to keep her, I'll do it."

Emmaline blew out the third candle. "That one is for Soman." She glared at him. "His mission was not fulfilled. His mission ended up being one of destruction. His mission damned us all to violence."

"I was a damned attractive woman, though. Damnnnnnnnnned attractive." Soman strung those words out nice and long. He cupped his chest like he had boobs.

"You were okay," Bradon said, pretending to think. "A little long in the tooth and the hair wasn't my style, but okay."

"I almost hit on you myself, Soman," I said. "I thought your buttocks looked tight. *Tight*."

"See, Em? There wasn't no failin' on my part," said Soman. "I was a woman. A woman who had to protect her virtue. The mission was accomplished and now I am on a new path of peace and love." He strung that word out, "love," real long, too, then leaned over and gave Becky a smooch.

"Please, Soman." Emmaline lifted up both arms, like wings again. A white butterfly getting ready to take off. "Becky, you are the last candle, the last person who must do something to take herself completely off and out of your path of anger. What are you going to do?"

Becky didn't say anything, but I could tell she was thinking.

"It must be something daring, or something out of your usual path. Something new. I told you to sing at a karaoke bar and you refused. Refused. I was very disappointed."

Becky still didn't say anything.

Emmaline flapped her arms about. "Something that will change the very core of your being, shake you from complacency, rip you from your anger; something that will destroy the old Becky and embrace the new."

The silence was almost alarming.

"What will you do, Becky?" Emmaline asked. "What will you do to put yourself on a completely new path of healthful, spiritual living and loving?"

"You were right, Emmaline," Becky said. "I'm going to sing."

"Good for you, dammit!" Emmaline yelled. "Good for you, dammit!"

"Whoa, lady, that's a great idea." Soman wrapped an arm around her. "My lady can do everything. She can cook. She does crafts better than anyone I've ever seen. She can paint. And now this! She can sing."

"Where are you going to sing?" I asked, my insides already quivering with anxiety for Becky.

Becky thought and thought. There was that long silence again.

"I'm going to sing in a karaoke bar here in town, like Emmaline told me to do, because that's what scares me beyond anything else I can think of."

I swallowed hard as my anxiety was replaced by stark, free-flowing fear. Becky, fragile Becky, was going to sing in a karaoke bar? Lost Becky who tried to send herself on an early trip to heaven only months ago? Scared Becky who cowered often and jumped when Emmaline yelled? Unstable Becky who had slunk along on the dark and dangerous perimeter of life for years was going to sing? In a karaoke bar?

We all thought about it for a while. Bradon and I locked eyes. He looked as worried as me.

"All right," Emmaline said. "But this time, Soman, you're not going as a woman."

For three weeks we practiced in Emmaline's loft. Soman banged on the drums; Olivia shook the tambourine; Bradon tickled the keyboard; and Becky sang. Emmaline had surprised us all weeks ago and showed us she knew how to play a mean guitar.

I played the violin. I was rusty at first, but for the first time in twelve years I could think of Johnny playing the guitar and me playing the violin, and not break into a thousand pieces. I had missed my violin. I had missed music.

Bradon, who was a friend of the owner of the cool bar downtown we were going to, had found out when the next open karaoke night was and here we were. The bar was crammed with people, crammed with tables, crammed with empty bottles and glasses. It was not crammed with cigarette smoke. True to Oregon form, there was no smoking allowed. Consequently, I did not feel like I was living on the inside of a cigar.

The walls were made of brick and the ceiling, fifteen feet high with exposed wood beams, was painted black. Candles on table-tops provided most of the light.

And there I sat, at a table, with the other groupies, clutching Jay's hand, every limb in my body shaking with fear.

You would have thought *I* was going to be up at that bar singing my heart out.

But it wasn't me.

It was Becky.

Fragile, thin, pretty blond Becky whose flashbacks took her to ugly, chilling places.

Currently, Becky was outside leaning against the wall vomiting, Soman rubbing her back.

I was sitting with Jay, Emmaline, Bradon, Olivia, and their two twenty-one-year-old twin sons who were not, *not*, allowed to drink yet, according to Bradon. Rosvita, who was wearing her white gloves and a ring of flowers on her head, and Donovan, looking dapper and stylish in a silk shirt and well-pressed pants, sat with us, too.

"Becky must fulfill her mission here tonight," Emmaline said. She raised her glass to her lips. She looked pale. "This is her last step, the step she needs to take to get her off of her path of self-destruction. It is something she must do; it is part of the requirements. If she doesn't do it, I will flunk her and she will have to retake anger management." She took another giant gulp of wine and tipped the bottle again. "Don't any of you talk her out of it."

"I won't," Bradon said. "But I don't think throwing up on stage is going to be popular with the other guests."

I nodded. "Good point."

"Becky. Will. Not. Throw. Up," Emmaline said, tossing back yet another gulp of wine. "She. Will. Not."

Jay squeezed my hand. I leaned over and kissed him on the cheek.

Married life had suited us a little too well. While I was in Chicago enduring my trial that I had banned him from, he was able to catch up on postelection work. My brother later told me that he put in eighteen-hour days the entire time I was gone. Jay told me later he had to or he thought he'd lose his mind worrying about me.

After the wedding, we went to the San Juan Islands for our honeymoon and rented a house with a view of the ocean, the islands, and a few migrating whales. It was, we were later told, the least rainy December the islanders had ever seen.

In that green paradise, I told Jay I was relieved that I had not driven my Bronco into the ocean months ago. He hugged me close and sighed and I knew he felt the same. We spent much of the time in bed, but with our (very little) free time we hiked, we sailed, we sat by the ocean and threw rocks, and talked. For hours and hours we talked. It was as if we'd been waiting for each other for a lifetime, so we could talk.

We also had barbeques and brunches and candlelit dinners and food went down my throat smoother now, somehow, and everything tasted, well, how can I explain it? The food tasted like life. Like sun rays and diamond dewdrops and birdsongs and watermelon and lilies and bubblegum and dawn and the aurora borealis, all mixed together.

When we came home we hid out at my house, and his, in Weltana avoiding talking to the press, who had been informed of our marriage after we left for the islands. This was our first venture out together. If not for Becky, I would have been happy to be alone with Jay, exploring the river, visiting with the owls. This bliss would all end, though, and soon. We would be moving to Mahonia Hall in Salem, a Tudor style mansion built in 1924. It came complete with a ballroom, a wine cellar that I would fill with root beer, and a ghost who likes to wear dressing gowns. ME. Living in the governor's house. Go figure.

"I love you, Jay," I whispered to him.

He kissed me full on the lips. "I love you, too, baby."

Everything happened real speedily after that. Soman was beside us, his arm around Becky's waist, and we all stood up. A huge tremor zoomed through me like a miniearthquake and I hugged Becky. I saw stark, living, thriving terror in her eyes.

"Here we go," Soman said, his eyes popping with fear. "My

lady's gonna kick some ass tonight. Some singing ass." His voice cracked.

Seconds later we were up on that stage. Spotlights right on us, microphone in Becky's hand.

Soman hugged Becky, and started up the beat on the drums.

Emmaline plucked the guitar strings.

I hit the bow of the violin.

Bradon's fingers danced across the keyboard.

Olivia shook that tambourine.

And Becky stared. Stock. Still. Stared.

So we all stopped.

She turned around and Soman blew her a kiss. I saw raw panic in his eyes.

I saw raw panic in hers. Donovan stood and sang the first few words, smiling in encouragement.

Soman started the beat again on the drums.

Emmaline plucked the guitar strings.

I hit the bow of the violin.

Bradon's fingers once more danced across the keyboard.

Olivia shook that tambourine.

And Becky stared. Stock. Still. Stared.

Dear God, I thought. Donovan sang again, coming closer to the stage.

So what to do? I went up to her, my violin at the ready. "Run like a bird, Becky, run like a bird."

She knew what I meant.

"Sing your guts out."

"I should, shouldn't I?" she asked, her voice weak.

"Yeah, honey, you should. For you. For your future. For the way you've gotten over your past. Sing your guts out."

I saw a flash in her eyes, a flash of courage, a flash of determination, a flash of triumph, maybe, and she faced the audience and smiled. A sweet and fresh smile, like dewdrops and daffodils and vanilla ice cream.

So I nodded to Soman and he drummed. Emmaline plucked. I

hit the bow. Bradon's fingers danced. Olivia shook. But this time Becky opened up her mouth and I swear the voice of the lead singer of God's choir came right on out.

We had practiced, the group of us, but Becky didn't have even half the power during those practice sessions that she had that night.

She darn near blew that smoke-free bar away. It got real quiet, people stopped talking and laughing and listened, like in the movies.

When the song finished Soman rolled his eyes to the ceiling, as though thanking God. Bradon and Olivia stared at each other, eyes wide, Emmaline, for once, couldn't move. The audience was absolutely silent, which would have been alarming to me had I still been able to think at that point, relief flooding my body like vodka filling a shot glass.

Becky was not a good singer. She was a brilliant singer. Absolutely brilliant.

She put the microphone back in the stand and started walking off the stage, her head held higher than it ever had been held.

I followed her, my violin at my side, trancelike. Bradon and Olivia and Emmaline and Soman followed right behind me.

And that's when the applause started, tentative at first, as if everyone was realizing that glorious song was over, and they woke up and started whoo-eeing and banging their hands on the tables and when I turned around again I'll be darned if everyone in that bar, including the dapper Donovan, and sexy Jay, wasn't on their feet.

We did two more songs, Becky and the gang and I, up on the stage of that dark bar and each time we got standing ovations. They were both songs that we'd practiced together before finally settling on the one for Becky. As an encore, we simply played the first song and, if possible, Becky belted it out even better than before, but this time she was smiling and she yelled at the audience, "Everyone, sing it! Sing it! Sing your guts out! *Sing your guts out!*"

So everyone in the bar ran up to the foot of that stage and they sang their guts out. I couldn't help it. Midway through the song, I felt myself getting all choked up.

When the song ended, I kissed my violin.

CHAPTER 28

A week later, after Jay left for Boston for a national governors' meeting, I got a phone call from Charlie. His anguish hit me right in the heart as he rattled out his problem.

"I'll go and get them," I told Charlie over the phone.

"What?"

Must he sound so shocked? "I said, I'll go and get them and bring them back here. They're off for a school holiday, aren't they?"

"Yes, but . . ." I could visualize him pulling on that curly lock on his forehead. Deidre was at the hospital and she was mere hours away from an appendectomy. The doctors were concerned her appendix had already burst. He was with her. A neighbor was with the kids.

"Would you do that, Jeanne?" I heard the hope in his voice, the relief.

Must he sound so relieved? Was I that bad of an aunt? Guilt heaped itself on my head so heavy it felt like a piano had landed on my cranium. Yes, I was a bad aunt. But that's gonna change, I told myself. That's gonna change. "I'm coming right now."

And I did.

And that's how I came to have four kids at my house in Weltana for three days.

Jay was out of town so I tackled it all by myself.

It would have been less exhausting for me to run four marathons with an elf strapped to my back than to take care of the kids, but the run to the finish was the sweetest thing I've done in a long, long time.

When Charlie arrived at my house to pick up the kids days later, they all hid from their father.

Which was okay with Charlie because he wanted to sit down and relax by the river and have the turkey and avocado sandwich I'd made him. When the children could see he was staying for a while, they emerged from their hiding places and gave their father a hug.

The kids' visit had been a combination of a circus in pandemonium/a human disaster/mildly controlled hysteria/and exhaustion (on my part). When the kids first arrived, we sat around and studied each other as one might do with a colony of peaceful extraterrestrials sporting antennae and multiarms.

I did not have a clear and sparkling idea of what to do with four children for days on end. Shortly, though, Jeanne Marie and Theo had a fight and started hitting each other with pillows, and Tommy shot his dart gun at both of them. Julie Anne got into my purse, stripped down naked except for her tutu, and used my makeup to decorate her stomach.

I got everybody settled when I told them we were going to have an ice cream trough big enough for pigs. I filled a whole bowl with three types of ice cream, and dumped chocolate sauce and butterscotch and tons of whipped cream on it. They gaped at me in awe for two seconds, then dug in.

That joy lasted about fifteen minutes and things got dicey again. I couldn't blame them. They didn't know me, I didn't know them, and this predicament was clearly my fault.

I felt lower than a beetle's balls when Jeanne Marie asked, her spoon still swirling in the trough's bowl, "How come you've never come to see us? My friend Meredith has an aunt and she's there all the time. How come you're not?" (Jeanne Marie even looks like me. It's truly startling.)

And Tommy chimed in, chocolate all over his face, "Don't you love us? Don't you like us?"

Theo helpfully added, "Mom said you do love us, but you've been busy and sometimes you've been sad, too, and couldn't come. What were you sad about? Don't feel too bad 'cause you always send us the best gifts. I loved that giant shark jaw you sent me last year for my birthday. I took it to show-and-share at school and put it on my head. Plus I liked the ant farm. I still have all the ants." He whispered, "But don't tell Mommy and Daddy I said that 'cause it'll hurt their feelings. About you giving the best gifts."

I silently thanked Deidre. I did not deserve her running interference for my inexcusable neglect, but I sure appreciated it. "I do love you. I have always loved you."

"Really?" Jeanne Marie asked. "How do we know that?"

"Yeah," Tommy said. "You don't see us, you don't call us, and you expect us to believe that you love us?"

Well, I was stumped. How could I prove it? I had a small flash of wisdom. "Come on upstairs with me."

We all trooped upstairs and I opened the door to my closet and hauled out my scrapbooks. There was one photograph book for each kid that I had made with the photos that Deidre and Charlie had sent me by mail and e-mail and one photograph book of the whole family.

I had carefully worked on these scrapbooks, though much of it was done after midnight with a scotch on the rocks in my hands. It was my only "arty" outlet. Each page had a photograph or two, the cutesy stuff . . . the cutouts and paper decorations, the titles—"Jeanne Marie's first day of kindergarten . . . Julie Anne's first tooth . . . Tommy at his second birthday party . . . Theo at Cub Scouts."

At first the kids all looked shocked, but they made a beeline for their own scrapbook, laughing and talking, and when they were done, they all switched, then poured over the family scrap-book together.

They loved 'em.

They knew I loved them.

Even though many times during the visit I thought we were all out of control, like a freak science experiment gone wild, and I had no clue how to handle so many different personalities and ranges of extreme emotion, it was a splendid time.

And that was the most important thing of all.

When Charlie stood up to leave three hours later, the kids all scattered and hid again until he yelled at them to come out right away or he'd take all their electronic devices.

"I not leave I not leave I not leave," Julie Anne chanted. For good measure she jumped up and down nine times, one per word. She was naked except for her tutu and frog hat with the dangling tongue. I had learned from a couple of colorful temper tantrums that this action meant she was going to stand her ground.

"Why can't we stay for another few days, Daddy?" Theo said. "Auntie Jeanne won't mind and you can let Mom rest for a while more. You said you're not working right now, so you two can have a vacation."

Theo and I had talked about traveling a lot. We looked through a few travel magazines and planned an imaginary trip to Brazil for ten days, detailing all the stops we'd make. We drew a geographical map of Brazil with colored pencils and starred all the cities and villages we would visit. We copied photos off the Internet and glued them to the map.

"Auntie Jeanne can take us back in a couple of weeks. We like it here," said Tommy. I blinked rapidly at that one. Tommy had pressed about why I had not been in their life more because I was "so much fun for an old person." I decided on the truth, and told him that I had lost Johnny and Ally Johnna, and that interacting with kids was hard for me, but that I was getting better at it.

"So your heart got all cracked up, but it's not so broken now?" he asked.

"Something like that," I told him, "something like that. Want to go outside and look for snakes?" He did, and out we went, snake-hunting.

"We played in the river; we cooked pancakes with Donovan and Rosvita; we did crafts with Becky and Soman." Tommy said. "I caught a snake. We want to stay. Please, Dad?"

"I not leave," Julie Anne said again. Jump. Jump. Jump. Julie Anne had liked me, but I had not liked her temper tantrums. After I put her in time-out, she got out her crayons and drew a picture of a princess with a lizard head. She told me the lizard headed princess was me. I told her she was talented. We spent time drawing lizards together in tuxedos, ball gowns, ratty jeans, and rock star outfits.

"And Jeanne reads to us every night and she makes all the characters have different voices," said Jeanne Marie.

"Rosvita knows all about diseases and germs," said Theo. "I learned about Martin's disease which is periosteoarthritis of the foot and the signs of sodium imbalance which can cause bad cardiovascular problems."

My brother nodded, his eyes widening.

I giggled nervously, shrugging my shoulders at Charlie, as if I didn't have the slightest clue about what Theo meant by such a silly comment.

"I not leave! I not leave!" yelled Julie Anne, her red face all screwed up tight. I knew what was coming next, but her dad was here and I would let him handle the ensuing temper tantrum. "I eat pancakes with Rosie!"

We had met Rosvita at The Opera Man's Café. She had blushed every time Donovan came to our table. I didn't have much time to stare as I was handling four children, but I didn't miss that blush. Donovan looked at her gently, so endearingly gently, and brought her breakfast with a flourish, bowing low, as usual. She blushed again, a camellia in her hair bobbing up and down.

His opera song as he headed back to the kitchen was about love found, love to last for a lifetime.

"We don't want to leave yet," said Jeanne Marie. "Please, Dad. We want to make another mural with Soman and Becky and Auntie Jeanne's so rad."

But in the end, the kids lost, Charlie said they had to go. "Thanks, Jeanne Beanie," he said.

All the kids cried. I cried. I promised to come and see them soon.

And, this time, I meant it.

After, of course, I recovered from my weekend by sleeping fourteen hours straight through.

I called Deidre when the kids left, right before my marathon nap.

"You're still alive?" she asked.

"Still with the living. The kids are fine; we had a great time."

"Good. I won't have to ground them for weeks on end. Thanks so much for having them, Jeanne. I don't know what I would have done without you. Let me take you out to lunch."

Lunch. With Deidre.

"Anywhere, anytime, no kids," she said. "In fact, let's go to lunch and a spa."

A spa. With Deidre.

"We'll get this macadamia nut and chocolate body treatment I heard about. I've never had a body treatment. I need to feel like a woman again after all this. So how about it? Want to have macadamia nuts and chocolate bits spread out all over your body?"

Macadamia nuts. And chocolate. With Deidre.

"I can't think of anything better," I told her. "And if we get hungry, we'll eat our body treatments."

* * *

I went over to visit Therese one rainy, gray afternoon, when the wind was whipping through the trees. I called ahead, and when she saw me coming up the path, she ran to meet me, enveloping me in a huge hug. She was wearing a purple t-shirt and purple pants and smelled like chocolate chip cookies.

She threw an arm around me and ushered me in. "Come, come, come, Jeanne, I'm so happy to have you in my home."

The kids were in school and Ricardo was out working on another house.

I was not surprised with how lovely their rental home looked. Therese had gotten permission from the owner to paint and the whole interior was yellow with a couple of walls painted this pretty orangish color. It looked like the sun was setting in her home.

She had been to a number of garage sales and had bought pretty pictures and plants, and had used her sewing skills to make flowered slipcovers for some old pieces of furniture.

We spoke Spanish, of course, for most of the time, but halfway through the conversation, when we were sitting at her kitchen table, she insisted we speak English so she could get better.

"How is Alessandra?"

"She better. *Mucho* better. She in school. She want play basketball. Sports for girls. I don't know, but I say okay. Ricardo say she American girl, must be American. Play basketball." Therese clapped. "I proud of her. I proud of Roberto and Rudy, too. I proud of you."

"You're proud of me? Why?"

"Because, Señorita Jeanne, you save my family. You saved me."

I bent my head. Therese and I had never talked about the details of Dan's murder, and Roberto's involvement. The less said the better, that type of thing.

"Therese, I have to tell you, initially I thought Rosvita had killed Dan. That's what she led me to believe."

"That Rosvita, I love her." Upset at the memory, Therese put both hands over her mouth and didn't speak until she got herself under control. "Roberto went to Señor Fakue's house; he so, so mad at him for rape Alessandra that day. So mad. He hit Señor Fakue. Two time, he tell me, but Fakue, he grab gun and point it at my Roberto. Señor Fakue scream. He yell. Says, 'I kill you if you no leave. You no have job here.' Roberto, he runned home and tell me. Ricardo, he want to go to Señor Fakue's house and kill him for what he did Alessandra, but my boys hold him on ground. No, Ricardo, no, we tell him. Ricardo, he cried; he so mad and sad. We leave farm. We work for you. We hate him. Ricardo and Roberto and Rudy, they angry, angry like you, Señorita. You go to angry school, right?"

I nodded. Angry school. That was me.

"But that when I knew, Jeanne. I knew."

My head suddenly started to pound. "You knew what, Therese?"

"I knew I have to kill that Dan man."

Air was gone. There was no air in that house. "You knew *you* had to kill him?"

"Yes, I know, so I do it." She pounded a fist on the table.

"What?" I could suddenly hardly breathe. *"What? You killed Dan?"*

"Yes, me. You no know that?" She looked completely baffled. "I thought you know. I scared, so scared that Ricardo or Rudy or Roberto kill Señor Fakue or he kill my boys with that gun. My mens got mad and mad more and mad more. He hurt our Alessandra and pain get worse for us, no better. We go to clinic for Alessandra . . ." she put her hands on her mouth, stifled a sob. "That bad man. Give Alessandra disease, a sickness. I know my boys and Ricardo, they so mad now and I scare they kill Señor Fakue right away. They go jail. I can't have. My boys no go jail. No go jail."

Not again. I felt light-headed. It was another secret. Out and flying around and about. "Rosvita told me that Roberto did it and she told Roberto she would take the blame if it came to that."

"Our Rosvita, she is saint, but she confuse." Therese shook her head. "Roberto not kill Señor Fakue. I go to Señor Fakue house at night. I sneak through tree, I open door, I bring my gun, I shoot him. I shoot him for hurt Alessandra and the disease and I shoot him so my boys and Ricardo not shoot him, they so angry, and I not see my mens again, but for jail."

Pound, pound, pound. My poor head. "I don't understand, Therese."

"So confuse. So confuse. I tell my boys and Ricardo I shoot Señor Fakue and Roberto, naughty boy, he sneak over and see Señor Fakue dead and he go Rosvita. Help us, he say. Help us. Señor Fakue, he shot in head. He tell her we scared of jail, do we go to Mexico quick-quick? We no know what to do with body. She help us bring body your other house. She good lady." Therese's face gentled. "Her Spanish not too good. We no understand it. I no think she understand us but we love that Rosvita. Good lady."

Yes, there was a teeny-tiny communication problem.

I thought my head was going to explode. I held it in my hands.

"You see?" Therese went to her kitchen and put her hand through a huge bag of oats. "See the gun? That I use." She pulled out a gun, pushed some oats off of it. "From my . . . how you say?— from Grandpa. He taught me good shot in Mexico. No more Señor Fakue. Señor Fakue not hurt no girls again."

I pressed my palms to my temples before my head split in two.

Women have so many darn secrets.

"You more want coffee, Señorita Jeanne?"

EPILOGUE

It is not easy being the governor's wife. I was asked to come up with my own "platform." You know, *something*, some issue, some problem in Oregon that I could address during my husband's tenure.

I suggested these ideas to my team, my team consisting of Ramon, Riley, and Camellia, with appearances from Charlie:

Naked streaking along any river should be legal twice a year. Once during the holidays when in-laws invade. Once during tax season. It's so freeing, I argued. And it relieves stress. Their laughter indicated they were not taking me seriously.

Second idea: Once a month we have a statewide Glitter Day. Everyone must wear some sort of glitter on their body or on their heads. Like a glittery crown or glittery paint or a sparkling tiara or something. Those darn people laughed again.

My third suggestion was Bike Day. Twice a month, the first and third Tuesdays, all cars had to stay home and no one could ride on anything but a bike in downtown Salem. As I ride my mountain bike all over Salem and people wave at me all the time, I thought it was another outstanding idea.

That idea worked. On those Tuesdays all downtown streets are closed to traffic and everybody who wants to can ride their bikes without fear of getting flattened by cars. It's wildly popular and Jay and I *always* participate.

Next I said that it should be a statewide law that no one has to work on their birthday. Riley looked at his watch, said that was a fabulous idea, hummed the birthday song, and strolled on out.

It took us a few days, but I finally decided my platform should be literacy.

I figured I could go into a bunch of schools and read books to the kids and do all the voices of all the characters. After all, my nieces and nephews said I'm good at that. So I tried it, and I must say that I am a huge hit in the public school system and have been invited back again and again. One little boy told me, in all seriousness, "You're the best wolf ever." I thanked him.

Another little girl said, "I love your shoes." I told her a woman should always pay attention to her shoes because hip-hoppin' shoes are a sign of a woman living life with a capital L. (The newspaper printed that quote.)

On another note, Soman and Becky can hardly think anymore, they're so in love. Soman still works as an electrician in Portland and Becky works for Zelda making pies and cakes. Becky has a little house outside of Weltana and Soman is there often. Those two paint and do crafts together. Next week, a gallery in town is showing their work for a month and Becky's entire family is coming up for the week to see it. (This is their fifth visit and they are lovely people.) I have already bought three of Soman's and Becky's bright, happy paintings.

Soman told me he will be proposing on Thanksgiving when Becky's family is back again. "A man has to handle this man to man," he told me, referring to Becky's father, his shoulders back proudly. "So I'll ask her father's permission to marry her." He took a deep breath, running his hands over his braids and looking nervous. "But of course I'm asking Becky's momma first, to make sure she's cool with it."

Rosvita and Donovan are dating. He comes over in the evenings and they sing opera together and dance, because that's what Donovan has taught Rosvita to enjoy. And they read germ books because that's what Rosvita has taught Donovan to enjoy. It does seem like the perfect match: Opera and diphtheria.

Deidre and I had our macadamia nut and chocolate body treatment. I have never had food spread on me. I didn't eat it, though, and neither did Deidre, because it's mixed with hot oil and that would not have been tasty.

Deidre and I are also taking a cooking class in downtown Portland once every other week and we go to dinner. Sometimes she'll bring a really nice friend or two. It's the funniest thing because I actually look forward to these evenings. I haven't had girlfriends in forever. We call them "Cookin' with Gal Pal Nights."

I now find chatting about little things—gardening and arts and crafts and cooking—to be soothing. I used to think chat was stupid and shallow. But I get it now. Chatting is simply a break from life and from stress. When one is wading through the black tar of hellacious things going on in life, chat is pure and it's sweet. It helps one roll over the hard times in life, or roll with, whichever one must do at the time.

I see Charlie and the kids all the time, too. The kids think the governor's mansion is, in the words of Theo, "spooky and dark." Jeanne Marie said, "It looks like skeletons live here with a vampire." They're right. I can't say that out loud or it would make Jay look bad, but it's the truth. They prefer to visit me and Jay in Weltana for long weekends.

Each time, Theo and I draw a new map of some far-off country and plan a trip. We also do math. Every time I miss a problem he says to me reassuringly, "Math takes time, Aunt Jeanne. Don't push it."

Tommy and I take long nature/adventure walks, searching for snakes and owls and birds. We bring our binoculars. And we throw and kick balls at each other. He says I am the fastest old lady he knows.

Julie Anne has tempter tantrums still, but when she's done, we've learned that we both like to cook brownies. Chocolate brownies with chocolate chips are our specialty. She always wears her yellow tutu trimmed in black and her green frog hat with the dangling tongue.

Jeanne Marie has taught me how to write depressing poetry and I have taught Jeanne Marie how to play the violin. I'm practicing it myself about three times a week.

Dan the Migrant Devil's brother, I learned, is an executive with the World Health Organization. I suggested that he transform Dan's farm into a co-op of sorts. From Mongolia, where he was working, Sean told me, "Now you're talking. I'm all over it!" Dan and Sean were about as different as rat poison and cupcakes.

The migrant workers now work the land and earn a (solid) percentage of what they make on the farm. Several of the families live in the big house with permission from Sean, two are in a newly built guest home, and new guest quarters are being built for the other families.

They invited the public to Apple Month with a hay maze, petting zoo, and wagon rides in September; in October they sold pumpkins and made a huge corn maze; and in December they sold Christmas trees and delicious burritos.

Ricardo Lopez continues to help people remodel their homes. Therese is sewing pillows with bright fabrics and ruffles that are sold quite rapidly at a gift shop in town and a high-end crafts store in Portland. The boys are going to school, as is Alessandra. Alessandra looks better every day. She spends a lot of time with Rosvita and often comes to my house by the river to talk, or to help me with the garden, or to watch the river roll by. I believe, I truly do, that Alessandra will overcome this part of her life, as will the other Lopezes. They'll never forget it, but they'll overcome it.

She is still playing basketball.

They are applying for citizenship and are here legally.

On a bright, bright, bright note, I am remarkably, miraculously, wonderfully pregnant. We have not one baby, but two. It was a glorious day when the little home pregnancy kit said I was pregnant, even more glorious when my doctor said I was enormous for where I was in my pregnancy and discovered two little sweethearts, who we eventually found are both male. Jay was so happy in that doctor's office he bent his head and cried. I cried, too.

Although I am overjoyed about the babies, I will have to admit to these terrible and graphic flashbacks of the car accident that killed Johnny and Ally Johnna. Periodically, I have succumbed to my mind-numbing fears of losing the twins to another accident, and I sit and shake. I will also have to admit to nightmares where I have woken up screaming and swimming in sweat, but I work on beating back those icy fears every day—and in the arms of Jay every night.

Plus, I don't get in a car very often anymore.

Call me greedy, but I have already decided that when the twins are eighteen months old, I am going to try to get pregnant again.

Jay is thinking we should have four kids.

I am secretly thinking that we should have six kids, but I have kept this little secret from him.

Something tells me, though, that this secret, when it all comes to light, will bring him endless joy and a full life and a full house. Not to mention a truckload of grandkids.

And that's the best kind of secret of all.

THE LAST TIME I WAS ME

Cathy Lamb

ABOUT THIS GUIDE

The suggested questions are intended to enhance
your group's reading of Cathy Lamb's
The Last Time I Was Me

DISCUSSION QUESTIONS

1. Jeanne Stewart says, "To assume that a woman, any woman, is *completely* innocent is to be completely naïve." Is she right?

2. What was your first impression of Jeanne? Do you like her? Is she a feminist or a traditionalist at heart? Early in the book she said her goal was to be a full-time mother with many children. Would she have found that role fulfilling?

3. Jeanne says that most women have secrets, "Pretty big ones, if I do say so myself." What secrets did people have in this book? Is it true that most women have secrets? Do you have secrets? Do people tell you their secrets?

4. Which character did you relate to in anger management class? What personal growth, if any, did you see in Bradon, Becky, Soman, Jeanne, and Emmaline? Was there a session that you would have liked to take part in? Was there any point in your life where you think an anger management class of this sort would have been helpful to you?

5. Soman says that he has a "sluggin' problem." He also dresses like a woman to relax, gets in bar fights, and falls in love with Becky, an ex-addict. Where do you see Soman in five years? Ten? Will he and Becky still be together?

6. Bradon King says, "Every year more black kids drop out of school. Every year no one cares. I think the schools are glad to see 'em go. But then what happens to them? They're teenagers, Jeanne. Kids. And their future is, at the moment, zero. Why doesn't anyone care? Because the kids are black? You can damn well bet that if a bunch of rich, white sixteen-

year-old girls all started dropping out of school and selling drugs on the corner that people would be screaming their heads off and demanding change. And change would happen." Is that true? How would you describe Bradon?

7. After painting herself in anger management class Becky says, "I'm changing . . . Sometimes I feel small, sometimes I feel big. But I'm seeing color in my life for the first time and all I used to see was black." Why do you think the author put a struggling, ex-drug addict in the book? How is she like Jeanne? How is she different? Will she stay off drugs? Can you relate to the blackness Becky experienced?

8. Is Jeanne a heavy drinker or is she an alcoholic? Do you sympathize with her or do you think she should have gotten a grip on herself years ago and stopped drinking? Why is she able to quit drinking by the end of the book? Is her transformation realistic?

9. Jeanne becomes very close to the Lopez family and is, herself, one quarter Hispanic. She clearly sympathizes with their plight and the plight of the migrant workers. What does this tell you about her personally? Where would she stand on the current immigration debate?

10. Did the Migrant Devil deserve his punishment? What did his murder, and the covering up of the crime, tell you about the Lopezes, Rosvita, and Jeanne? Do you admire Rosvita who, in order to protect the Lopezes, was willing to go to trial over the Migrant Devil's murder? Or, do you think she was being colossally stupid? Do you think the Migrant Devil's death will stay a secret?

11. This book deals with Jeanne's drinking problems, her nervous breakdown, a murder, a rape, migrant workers living

in appalling conditions, women being abused by the Migrant Devil, a bar fight, drug addiction, an assault by Jeanne against Slick Dick, a courtroom trial, and grief. Yet there also were many humorous moments. Is it a correct reflection of life? How has the author interlaced humor and tragedy?

12. Jeanne says, "All women, feminist or not, have a right to take action against condoms that are worn by cheating men." Do you believe this? What does the peanut oil and condom incident tell you about Jeanne? Why do men cheat? Why do women cheat?

13. Jeanne assaulted Slick Dick. She admitted it. The jury found her not guilty. Do you think the jury made the right decision? Would you have found her not guilty? Was the verdict realistic?

14. Jeanne assaulted her ex-boyfriend with a condom and peanut oil knowing he had a slight allergy to peanut oil. She helped to bury the body of a man whom she thought her friend had shot. She actively participated in a bar fight. She committed perjury at her trial when she said she only put in two drops of peanut oil per condom. Is she a criminal?

15. Are Jeanne and Jay a good match for each other? What does she love about him and what does he love about her? Do you think that Jeanne will be a popular governor's wife? Do you think she'll like the role or balk at the constraints and the responsibilities?

16. If Jeanne came to dinner at your house, what five pieces of advice would she give you about your life?